FAMILY
Fireworks

A NOVEL

Sandra

SANDRA ELIZABETH REDMOND

author HOUSE®

AuthorHouse™
1663 Liberty Drive
Bloomington, IN 47403
www.authorhouse.com
Phone: 1 (800) 839-8640

Published by AuthorHouse 03/23/2018

ISBN: 978-1-5462-3549-1 (sc)
ISBN: 978-1-5462-3550-7 (hc)
ISBN: 978-1-5462-3548-4 (e)

Library of Congress Control Number: 2018903767

Print information available on the last page.

This book is printed on acid-free paper.

CONTENTS

⊘NE

Family Fireworks is the story of a family facing a move. The McFaddens must leave Jessie's house in Minneapolis to follow Dana, the husband and father, to his new job out west. Each member of the family must decide whether to go or not; they have lived with Jessie most of their lives and so face the problem of what will happen to their mother and grandmother. Each member of the family has a reason to go, and a reason to stay, but most of these reasons are secret. Only Jessie's difficult oldest daughter Bernice can care for Jessie in her home. But will she? And how much does independent Jessie know about the move?

The family plans a picnic together on the Fourth of the July. They believe they can work their individual ways to a joint decision, but since they are an opinionated, often quarrelsome bunch, neither the decision nor the all day picnic turn out to be easy. A number of unexpected events and people complicate yet also help shape the conclusion.

In a fireworks display, do individual sparks choose where they will fall?

The day just new – the sounds of birds like strings of colored lights, a celebration in the trees – while a boy walked down the re-born streets. A long-legged jaunty boy, hands in shorts' pockets. He'd walked a girl home; his body proclaimed it. No one seemed to see him; the windows in all the big old frame houses were unblinking. Everybody was asleep; these houses, like bodies, anchored dreamers.

The boy walked up the driveway of one three-story dignity, a house with chipped white paint and friendly trees. He went around to the back and let himself in by taking off a loose screen and falling through the open window.

Inside the air was close and still, a collective family sigh. This house was like a ship, full of sleeping passengers. The last time it would be that quiet all day. Eddie nodded with pleasure and went to the back porch, to an icebox that guarded the back door and an earthenware sauerkraut jar between its squat spread legs. He took out a full bottle of milk and swigged half its contents down, then examined the remainder with delight. Half a bottle of milk! Straight from the bottle! And no one knew. Replacing it, he shut the door of the icebox and looked at his watch. Two hours before he dared practice. Well he wasn't in the mood to go to sleep that was for sure. He went to the walnut sideboard in the dining room and took out his model kit. Returning to the kitchen he sat down at the table by the window. In the rising morning light, he began to glue together the Flying Dutchman, a six mast sailing ship. It was intricate work and he breathed softly with the pleasure of his own creation.

Two

In the house next door, Mr. Miller entered his kitchen. He rose early – about five. Might as well – couldn't sleep once the sun was up. And Mrs. Miller had had a troublesome night. He poured himself some water from the jug in the icebox.

Mr. Miller didn't mind changing the sheets. Gave him something to do that made his wife feel better. Not much did anymore. He looked out the side window at the Fallsworth back yard. The door to Amsden's trailer was open a crack. Someone had been in there last night and hadn't shut it properly. One of those kids likely. Maybe he should tell somebody.

Mr. Miller shook his head. No use. Ever since his neighbor Amsden Fallsworth had dropped dead opening his garage door, nobody over there paid much attention to doing things the way Amsden liked them done.

Sad, Mr. Miller thought, a sad world. Amsden kept that trailer neat as a pin. He and Jessie had driven to Florida in it every winter for years. And that Ford of theirs – brand new when he died. Now that teenage boy was driving it. Still it comes to us all, he thought as he turned away and walked to the back window and looked out at his garden. The peas had come in thick. Couldn't eat them all. He'd give some to his daughter next time she came over. And the carrots – they needed thinning. Lord how he hated doing that – women's work. Maybe I should move us out of this neighborhood, all this work he thought for the hundredth time.

Mr. Miller opened the back door and the noise of the birds hit him in the eye – a mob of sparrows was chattering away in the fir tree. Like they're making important plans he thought – all that noise – and he leaned forward with pleasure to watch some pecking at the ground near the tree. Yup – they were picking up seed and discussing what to do with the day. They fly around in gangs just like people, he thought, not for the first time. Part of the pleasure of being old for Mr. Miller, was thinking the same thoughts all over again like they were new. He caught sight of a blue jay.

Blue jays were his favorites. Some people said they were pests. Mrs. Miller used to say that and he'd say no they aren't, just loners, that you had to hand it to them – blue jays stayed out of trouble. They are trouble, Mrs. Miller would come right back at him. Now she didn't say much of anything. Except those little noises in the night like an old dog. Did she feel pain? He couldn't tell. Never mind, he thought. I'm still a blue jay – flying around staying out of trouble.

He walked out on the back landing that Mrs. Miller had called the back porch. She'd tried to make things sound important. Or she used to. His daughter said they should put her in a nursing home. Came right out and said it. Said taking care of her mother was going to kill him. Thinking that made Mr. Miller feel a little dizzy.

He took a deep breath. The rosebushes were half way down the long narrow yard; the red roses were small this year – too hot he reckoned – but they had a scent, some anyway. He'd planted them for his wife. She'd wanted white but he'd said no, white don't have a scent. We had some fine times jawing Mother and I – he thought – not arguments but giving out opinions. One thing they'd agreed on was that their grandson shouldn't go to war. Didn't make no difference – he'd joined up anyway. Well who listens to the old when you're young? I sure didn't he thought and patted the back wall of the house. Painter did a good job. House looked good.

He walked back inside, through to the hallway where the smell of old urine was strongest and listened at the foot of the stairs. She was sleeping. Good. He'd have some time to himself.

Everything about the Miller house was white – walls, shutters, fence, even the back shed where Mr. Miller kept his gardening tools. Inside the house the rooms were as clean as a hospital; though the smell of Clorox was fighting a losing battle. White doilies lay across the backs of the three big gray chairs in the living room; white cloths covered all nine pieces of dark mahogany dining room furniture. Both

Millers had snow-white hair, and an old white cat named Snowball that slept on their bed.

In the kitchen Mr. Miller moved around making himself some breakfast. At eighty-two, he didn't move too fast. He made some tea to take up to the Missis along with toast. Sixty years they'd been together. Hardly a real spat except when that postman got too friendly. Long time ago but Mr. Miller hadn't forgotten.

Good idea – making plans for the day, he said to himself, standing at the stove stirring up the gummy goop he liked best – oatmeal mixed with cream of wheat and a few specks of corn flakes. Dishing it up, he sat down at the gray table against the kitchen wall and looked at the clock – 5:30. The open trailer door next door still worried him but if he did call over there they wouldn't be up. Young people except for old Jessie.

Now there was a good-looking woman in her time.

Pop. Pop. Pop. Bang. Bang. From the yard behind his came the crackle and snap of firecrackers. Fourth of July. The noise made him think of his grandson – Lord how that boy had loved fireworks. And next thing you knew he was marching off to war – still just a kid. Shipped over to die for a bunch of people he'd never heard of, who wouldn't thank him. Mr. Miller didn't trust the British any more than the French, didn't trust anybody far off that asked American kids to die for them.

Mr. Miller had been over there the first time. You didn't forget.

He thought about calling his daughter. She'd offered to take them for a ride last week and he hadn't been up to it, but heck today was the Fourth of July. She'd want to talk about her boy. Well, I put the flag out for him, he thought. All the neighbors did too.

Pop, pop, pop, pop. Snap, pop. More crackers. Not as many as twenty years ago. The neighborhood was getting old just like he was. Mr. Miller liked the sound of firecrackers, the way the cordite smell hung in the air; as a boy he'd thrown down strings of them, backing away so the crackers twisted and snapped at his feet like snakes. We made some excitement on the Fourth in my day he thought.

He put away the tea and took out the coffee can. By golly he was going to boil up some coffee. Celebrate. Then he'd wash the sheets; hang them out. Maybe even thin a few carrots before it got too hot.

$\mathcal{T}$HREE

In the mustard yellow bungalow on the other side of the Fallsworth house, Mrs. Blunt rolled over in her big soft bed and groaned. She heard the firecrackers spluttering and crackling outside. An ugly noise. No way she was going to get up. Into her mind came that man she'd dated forty years ago who'd blown off two of his fingers lighting firecrackers. What a dope. Where'd she meet him? She couldn't remember. He had hairy ears, she remembered that, and smelled of kerosene. Sometimes all she could remember of people was their smell.

Whoosh, bang, crackle, whoosh, whoosh. She opened her eyes. Roman candles whooshing up in the back yard behind hers. Waste of money in the daytime. Weren't they supposed to be illegal? Must be that new bunch. Renters. English she'd heard. Made no sense. Like the Chinese family with the twin girls a couple of houses down. Dressed those girls like dolls. They owned the Chinese restaurant on the corner. Next to the bar. Next to her brother Ned's grocery store.

Mrs. Blunt leaned over to look at the clock and groaned – five thirty. Usually she slept till noon on Sunday morning. She settled back on the pillow. Wow she had some headache. That damn cheapskate Bert.

Mrs. Blunt turned over and waited for her head to follow her body. Then she struggled to sit up. Today was the Fourth of July. Her brother was coming by. Fourth of July – what could you expect but more noise? The room was dark, musty smelling. All the curtains were drawn; the blinds pulled down. Mrs. Blunt didn't bother to look out the bedroom windows anymore, not even at the Fallsworth house just across the driveway. A bunch of kids running around over there now, and no Jessie at the window waving at her to come over for coffee. Jessie and Amsden – they'd been okay. They'd signed the pledge when they were both sixteen and they hadn't understood her special problems but so what? Who knew anything about anyone anymore?

Mrs. Blunt yawned and stretched out her arms; she shook her hands a little so the circulation came back. Yes – Amsden and Jessie, they were kind – sweet even. No – wait a minute – Jessie wasn't what'd you'd call sweet. And Amsden wasn't a man for many words. Come to think of it, he was cranky most of the time. That plump second daughter Rose Corrine – she'd married early – that good looking Irishman – but since the war they'd lived with her parents next door. The oldest girl – Lily Bernice – she was a right bitch – smelled of some kind of oily cream she put on her hair – she moved away.

Mrs. Blunt took a whiff of her own armpits. She liked the smell of sweat. Especially sweat on men. Stop thinking that, she reminded herself, that will only make you feel sad. But then she looked at her arms. The sadness didn't go away. Mrs. Blunt's arms were wrinkled and fat now. And she was already too warm. Her headache wasn't getting any better either. Maybe I'll get up, she thought, Ned's coming over.

She lay back. She thought better in bed than anywhere else. Those other two girls – the younger ones – she couldn't remember their names. One baby had died. The other one- some kind of scandal. She went up north during the war. They never talked about her. Tears of self-pity came into Mrs. Blunt's eyes. That girl had been forgotten. Like she was. More tears. She wiped them off with the edge of the sheet. Thought – So what? Who cares anyhow? Why the heck think about some dumb neighborhood girls? Nobody thinks about me. Her head was pounding away. Her back ached too. She groaned and flopped on her side. Mrs. Blunt had a soft unhealthy fat body acquired over years of bending her elbow to lift the glass of whiskey she preferred to everything else. That morning, however, Mrs. Blunt thought how she'd kept up one standard. No cheap whiskey – and no cheapskates either. That asshole Bert. Never again. Unless he brings something better than a four dollar bottle expecting ten dollar fun. Fun. Hah.

Mrs. Blunt sat up. Whiskey was a dangerous thought that time of day. Better get out of bed. Do the dishes. Clean up the place. Her brother would like that. Ned was bringing over groceries from the store. He said she wasn't eating right and that's why she was developing a cough.

Just as Mrs. Blunt thought that she coughed – a deep ragged sound that came up from her belly and burned through her chest. Funny she thought, I don't smoke and I get a cough, and cheap bastards like Bert smoke like chimneys and sit around with their cheap whiskies, and they're fit as fiddles. She thought about a drink. No – not yet. She owed Ned that. He cares about me, she thought, even if he does rag at me. Thank god for Ned. He's all I've got. I could make him lunch.

There isn't any food in the house. That cheap bastard ate it all.

Ned's bringing food, you ninny, she reminded herself, he's bringing lunch.

Her round alarm clock said six o'clock. Mrs. Blunt got up, waddled on swollen feet into the bathroom and washed her face. From the bathroom window, she saw in the Fallsworth driveway five magpies standing around a crow. She turned away, touched Jimmy's face. She had a photograph of her two baby brothers next to the bathroom mirror and she liked to touch Jimmy's face every morning. They were so cute sitting in the bathtub. Jimmy had his arm around Ned. Jimmy was laughing. Mrs. Blunt eyes filled with tears again. What did he go do such a stupid thing? Fly some beat up plane over China – to help some ugly Chinese people who didn't give a damn about him? Why Jimmy? she asked his baby face. Why'd you do such a dumb thing? But she knew her brother had loved flying; and that he'd had some wildness in him that she and Ned didn't have. He'd looked for places to fly his brains out.

She wandered into the kitchen, shuddered at the stack of bottles and dirty dishes, the overpowering smell of stale beer and garbage. She put the big plaid apron over her nightgown. Crack. Pop. Snap. Whoosh. Crack Crack. Firecrackers were stuttering away outside from every direction. She put the stained old coffee pot on the gas fire which sputtered in complaint. This kitchen is dirty, Mrs. Blunt thought, but vaguely like it belonged to someone else.

Meanwhile, out on the driveway, the crow – a black medium sized young female on her best behavior – looked in a blasé way just past the black and white magpies surrounding her. That made the gang of five suspicious. As the neighborhood bird police, they knew a thing or two about crows. Crows were only nonchalant when they had their own reasons. Was she snooping around their neighborhood pretending not to be the spy she so obviously was? The crow didn't move and neither did the five magpies.

$\mathcal{F}$OUR

Across the street, in the three-story blond brick apartment house, Myrna Henderson saw the cluster of birds paused in the driveway of the big house opposite. She'd been looking out the window while she combed her long brown hair, hair that reached to her ankles and took all day to wash and dry but which Joe had liked. She kept it long to remember him. Sometimes he'd combed it. She'd taken the two stars out of the window years ago, but they hung inside on the wall. Her hair still wet and smelling of baby shampoo, she sat on her bed, and combed it and thought how Joe would have liked seeing those magpies, and those brown squirrels chasing each other up and down the tall elms, and especially that old rust colored neighborhood tom-cat prowling his way home on the sidewalk below her. A cat pretending he couldn't see six big birds staring each other down.

Joe's last letter – Myrna was reading all the letters again – spoke of how there were no animals, no birds, and how all the men struggled against the endless dreary sky. 'Sometimes I dream of Minneapolis in the summer.' he'd written. 'Remember how we bicycled to the lakes at night, how the full moon shone in the water? You looked so beautiful swimming at night. I liked the feel of your body in the water.'

All this was in his last letter – before he'd died. Reading it was both pain and bliss. He'd never seen his daughter. Myrna had written to him but by then Joe was in prison camp. He'd died there, the exact date Myrna didn't know, nor did she know the place, nor the time. Myrna knew nothing but that her husband was dead, dead now for years – how many four? But when she read his letters, love jumped into her, all the old feelings for him came alive and swept through her, and made her cry.

She stood up. Ran the comb through her long brave brown hair. Looked out. The crow hadn't moved; neither had the magpies. Then a string of firecrackers went off, nearby, making a loud splattering noise like hot grease in a frying pan, and all five magpies shifted and shook their wings. The crow took a small step sideways. But none of them backed further away from confrontation.

Myrna put down Joe's letter and leaned forward at the window to watch the birds, and then saw the tall boy walking down the street. He walks like my brother, she thought. Still sometimes she thought she saw her husband or her brother on the street or at the window of a streetcar. Her brother was still listed as missing in action, but she and her father knew he was dead. His ship had vanished in the Atlantic. He'd written only two letters to her father; Leo wasn't a letter writer, only an eighteen year old kid who'd joined the coast guard. Why'd he done that, the war almost over?

She sat back down, took out another letter. She read them on the Fourth of July because Joe had died for his country and she was proud of him. Myrna couldn't imagine what a soldier's life was like, but she knew that Joe was a hero, and that she would remember him all her life as young and strong and beautiful.

The magpies stood in a circle staring at the crow spy until at last, with an air of indifference she flew slowly away. The magpies marched off in several directions.

What was that all about? Eddie McFadden thought walking up the Fallsworth driveway. He'd just caught the finale of the bird showdown because he'd been up all night necking with Carol Prentice. Eddie walked round them. What did he care about bird politics? He was engrossed in a new found sense of lust. The birds didn't move.

Eddie was tall and lean and wore black rimmed glasses and blue shorts; this morning he wasn't wearing a shirt. Nor did he care to explain to anyone, even if they'd dared ask – where his shirt was. He went to the back window of the Fallsworth house, took off the screen, and slipped inside.

Upstairs, in the house like a ship, Eddie's family, the Fallsworth and McFadden clan, were still asleep, were a collective breath drawing in fresh morning air from fearless open windows. In and out, in and out, old and young, they were drifting mariners drawing in all their newborn world had to offer – the sweet hope of flowers, frivolity of butterflies, persistence of insects, tenderness of green leaves. Yet in their sleep rose each person's private world – dreams that held out old, forgotten, should have been forgiven, shriven and shaven, stamped out and swirled away thoughts and memories, all too often thick with emotion.

I didn't know all that, Violet Marie, the lost sister thought looking in on all that went on that morning. I didn't know what it all meant, what its value was. I left too early, too angry. She knew by then caught in that far away place, thinking about her past, forced to remember and at last understand what she couldn't before. How much pain will there be? she'd asked, How much unbearable regret if I go back?

"You won't know until you encounter the others at 31 West 35th Street," they'd told her. "You'll see your mother Jessie; your sisters, Lily Bernice and Rose Corinne, your brother in law, Dana, and your nephew, Eddie and niece, Helen; also a few neighbors."

"Please no dogs," Violet Marie had asked, knowing that finding them would break her heart. She'd loved dogs all her life. In the old Minneapolis neighborhood, dogs were sometimes the only blurs of moving life – stretching in the heat, or researching a cat, but strictly for amusement. Oddly she remembered best too the subtle shift of insects on the ground, their movement like objects at the corner of an eye. And the layer after layer of green branches above her that made the sky seem the same mysterious promise as an underwater world gazed at from a glass bottomed boat. Unfortunately Violet Marie's memory couldn't make her family magic. Her family was all too human, as far back as she could remember they were all too human.

Now, on that Fourth of July in 1948, with a sweet new morning advancing, the sun found Violet Marie standing outside looking around, found all the upstairs sleepers, but as the sun mounted past their windows, climbed into a blissful blue high heaven, and finally lost itself in the branches of the guardian trees; heat rose too; warm air flowed through the old screens of the ship house with as much surety as it parted the lilac bushes and stinging nettles. Violet Marie faded away while inside the house, each person was warmed; only later would they be brought to a boil. Unable to anticipate this fate, they slept on. Only Eddie stood beside the pantry cupboard eating the last of the rhubarb pie.

The phone rang – a loud, shrill, horrible sound. Eddie looked at the clock – 6:30. He threw down the pie plate, bounded up the four stairs from the kitchen onto the landing that led upstairs, ran down the four stairs on the other side that were the shortest way into the living room, and reached for the phone on its third ring.

A girl breathed into the phone.

"Carol?"

"I'll be there."

"Here?" Eddie stiffened. He wiped rhubarb from his lips. "Now?"

"Tonight. At the park. I'll find you."

"Great," He looked out the window above the telephone stand. The magpies were gone. He noticed for the first time the cracks in the cement driveway. "That's great."

"Eddie, you're adorable. You're like Frank Sinatra. You sing like him."

Eddie leaned against the wall and repressed semi-cynical remarks,

"Yeah, I try. But mostly I play piano."

"Oh Eddie, I can't sleep. I keep thinking how wonderful you are."

"Yeah," He swallowed a yawn. "So see you tonight. If you don't find me, I'll find you."

"Where?"

"You got any ideas?'

"Is your family going? Can I ride with you?"

Eddie suppressed a shudder. "No. Car's full."

"My brother said he'd drive me."

"Norbett!"

"My parents are visiting some relatives. But I can stay as long as I like. He promised me."

"Norbett's going to be there?"

Carol's voice shrank to a whisper, "I have to go with somebody."

"Norbett will be hanging around?"

"My brother doesn't care what I do. Just tell me where I can find you."

Eddie still thought of his family. "The baseball diamond – we could meet there."

"O.K. But when?"

"After the fireworks start – when it's dark."

"Oh, Eddie, I can hardly wait to see you."

"Yeah. Me too Carol." Eddie let a yawn escape. "Now I gotta sleep for awhile."

"Sweet dreams," she whispered. Click. Eddie put down the phone.

I'll get a key made and oil the back door hinges so nobody hears me when I stay out all night, he thought as he took off his sneakers and padded quietly up the stairs. Eddie's plans for the future now included Carol, and maybe some other girls.

On the second floor of the house, the air was heavy and warm. He went into a bathroom that reeked of cologne. Aunt Bernice, Eddie thought, the smell made him sick. But then Eddie didn't like Aunt Bernice, and he didn't like the reason she had come down that weekend – to discuss what to do with Grandma. Like she was an old car or something. He took off his glasses, washed his face with blackhead removal cream he'd hidden at the back of the cupboard, then brushed his teeth. Went back to thinking about Carol. I'm going to be good at it, he marveled, I'm going to know how to do it.

He crossed to his room, undressed, slid onto the double bed he'd dug out of the garage. He'd rescued it because it was big, and because Aunt Violet's name was scratched into the headboard. Nobody in the family talked about her except his Dad who said she'd probably been a spy for the British.

He traced her name with one finger and thought how Carol had acted like she had done it before. I'll bet she hasn't, he thought. She said it hurt. Just proves she's a virgin. So was he but he wasn't going to tell her that.

Outside, the air was warming, the fireworks were dying away. They'd been put on hold until that night, when in further celebration, a great massed cloud of fire and sparkle would rise up into a dark sky like newborn stars going home. Eddie lay in bed; and, still fixed upon his own sweet truth, traced the Violet Marie carved into the headboard one more time. It seemed a talisman.

Before I leave Minneapolis I'll sneak Carol into this bed, he vowed. It was an impossibly daring idea – the kind he liked.

. . . .

$\mathscr{F}$IVE

*Fireworks artists like all artists dream their creation
first, but where do their dreams come from?*

I n the room at the top of the stairs, in the house like a ship, two
drifting mariners – one old and one young – lay sleeping. They
were breathing in droplets of new and memories of old – in and out,
in and out – not just persistence of insects, frivolity of butterflies, and
sweet hope of flowers, in and out, in and out, but past and future lives
too. Such sleep is deep but by seven-thirty the sun had advanced into
heat; and the young girl on the cot under the window, seized by light's
urgency, opened her eyes. Immediately she closed them again, not
wanting to wake but the light said she must so she sat up and looked
out the window at an empty street. Helen, daughter of the house, was
never short of ideas that improved ordinary life, however.

If I run away I'll leave a note like one of those stories where the
girl is desperately unhappy and cuts off her hair and pretends to be
a boy. It's aggravating the way I've packed my bags a couple of times
and then something comes up and I have to unpack them again. The
girls in the stories never wear glasses and they get into all sorts of
interesting adventures – like serving as cabin boys with rude seamen
as their only companions. A lot of them learn to use the sword so
they're expert and they fight alongside some guy they fall in love with
only he doesn't notice. Apparently men don't notice things a lot of the
time. The nobleman doesn't even know she's a girl until one day her
hair falls down – long hair falls down sooner or later.

Thinking that, Helen touched her own hair, which was short and
stood up in spiky driblets. Hair might be a problem, she decided. And

I'll have to practice sword fighting with Eddie again. But when we use the barbecue skewers he doesn't fight fair.

He pokes the wrong places. Helen touched her breasts, which had begun to balloon out in an unpleasant way. How could she disguise such big knobs under a rude seaman's shirt?

The young and sensitive girl named Helen vehemently kicked the light sheet down to the end of the cot, which then skittered in protest on the hardwood floor. Why are there so many problems to solve when it's already hot? she thought. She hated sleeping in her Grandma Jessie's room. All night with my face against her grubby curtains, this sensitive girl thought.

'Take 'em down, wash 'em, nobody's stopping you,' had been her brutal mother's only helpful comment. Just because Helen had made a simple remark about how bad it was for people to breathe in dust all night.

Helen avoided touching the rotten sheet she'd put her foot through in the middle of the night. Of course her mother arranged it so she got all the rotten ones. She lay back down and closed her eyes so that more ideas came.

One thing was clear the girl was able to run away to sea and do all those things because she was tall and extraordinarily brave. Sooner or later she saved the guy's life and he was grateful. There was this scene where she had to be disrobed while unconscious. She has malaria or a saber wound or something and some ancient guy like a doctor loosens her shirt, then straightens up, wise old face filled with astonishment. 'My lord, young Mathew is a woman.'

The nobleman – who is very good looking – fails to his knees and takes the small white hand in his. He's never noticed before just how dainty that little hand is. Up to then she's been doing a lot of dirty work.

'A woman! Yet single-handed she saved my life.' Because someone's tried to poison this guy or blow his brains out – they were always doing things like that in the early days.

Fireworks snapped and popped outside. Helen knelt on her cot and looked out the window. Across the street two boys her age were chasing a ginger cat up the street, throwing strings of firecrackers after it. The cat was moving pretty fast.

Boys are so brutal, Helen thought. Maybe I won't run away. People don't run away much anymore anyway. I don't personally know anyone who has. Though if I had some decent sheets I could knot them together and climb out Grandma's window. They do that at boarding schools. Girls in boarding schools acts like scamps and break all the rules. Too bad my family refuses to send me to a boarding school.

The cat was out of sight. The two boys paused outside the apartment house across the way. A woman had stuck her head out and was telling them to stop doing what they were doing. At least that's what it looked like she was doing. The two boys walked away.

She flopped back down, and the cot skittered in complaint again. Even with the window open, I'm breathing in dust, she thought. Those curtains smell like the school closets where the teachers keep their shoes. She thought of the weird pair of lime green shoes the English teacher wore – obscene green her friends called them. They didn't match any of the poor woman's drab clothes.

'Drab' was a great word.

Helen was reading a page a day in the dictionary. She searched for a new vocabulary word to describe her own condition. "I am demoralized, and distracted," she thought. Demonized is a great word but it doesn't fit my current circumstances.

Downstairs Helen's brother Eddie, older by three years and unwilling to sleep his life away, had gone back downstairs, picked up his half-finished ship's model, put it back for safe keeping in the sideboard, and gone into the living room. He was sitting at the upright piano in the corner, his music open, looking at his watch, and waiting. Five minutes passed. He smiled – eight o'clock.

Scales. Played over and over; then, after a pause, more scales this time double speed. Later, when he was properly warmed up, he planned to run through 'Flight of the Bumble Bee.'

Upstairs, irritated beyond redemption by this noise, and knowing she was still breathing in deadly dust, Helen flopped on her side, away from the curtains.

Is that ever hateful! Eddie just wants Daddy to notice. Eddie will do anything for attention. He has a way of doing scales so it sounds like the piano itself is grateful to him. She tried not to listen to the opening bars of 'Flight of the Bumble Bee.' He believes in torture. When he took medieval history at school Eddie did a paper on medieval instruments of torture and he probably included the piano.

She closed her eyes. Such thinking exhausted her, especially because she kept realizing how miserable it was going to be riding around all day with a drab and demoralizing family, how her own plans for exciting events had been completely destroyed by a selfish mother. The movie would be gone next week. She'd planned to go to the Tivoli, a seedy theatre where hard looking blondes in the ticket booth did their nails while they sold tickets, and which had been forbidden to her by uncaring parents.

Carol's brother, Norbett had seen the movie and he said it was really something. In one scene a bunch of slave girls were standing around in metal bras looking humble and then – well, according to Norbett – there was a rebellion in the ancient city and they did things you had to see to believe.

She wanted to see, and believe.

"I'm sorry dear." Her mother had a sickening way of saying sorry. If you didn't know her you'd think she was sincere. "Aunt Bernice is coming up for the Fourth of July weekend. We've got a lot to discuss. We need you here."

"Discuss, discuss. We're always discussing something. Nobody listens to me anyway."

"Go next weekend. What theatre is it?"

"It'll be gone by then."

"It's important we do the right thing for Grandma. She's very frail now."

Helen opened her eyes and looked for the first time at the old woman lying in the narrow bed beside her cot. Grandma Jessie lay on her back, hands folded on her chest, mouth wide open. Is she breathing? the sensitive teenage girl thought. She propped herself up on one elbow to get a better look.

It's horrible to sleep in the same room with someone that old. She looks a thousand years old. And I hate the way her teeth smile in that glass of water. Her bed isn't mussed – like she hasn't moved all night. Actually she looks a little dead.

Helen lay back down. She felt a little spasm of horror. People died in bed all the time. Mr. Hanson did. Mother said Mrs. Hanson woke up in the middle of the night and reached over to touch him and he was cool to the touch.

Ugh. The sensitive teenage girl tried to think pleasanter thoughts. I wouldn't mind a metal bra but I wonder what it feels like in the winter.

Daddy said Grandma could go anytime. He told me that once.

What do you wear with a metal bra? Probably those big see through trousers.

Grandpa just fell over and he was dead

Helen straightened up and looked over once again at the old woman in the bed against the wall. Grandma's still not moving.

She lay back down again. What should I do? Tell someone? Wait a few more minutes? I can't hear her breathing. What if she's dead?

Dropping to her knees beside the huge four poster the beautiful young girl sobbed uncontrollably, "Grandmother, oh dearest grandmother." She kissed the still white hand in a paroxysm of grief.

'Paroxysm' is a great word but I wish I could spell it.

Across the room two union officers cleared their throats and shifted their feet. They had those jockey caps with straps under their chins and now they took them off as a mark of their respect. The captain who was very good looking strode across the room and grasped the young girl's creamy white shoulders. He gently lifted her to her feet.

"Courage, Miss Loretta," he whispered. "You have friends here."

"You Yankees broke my grandmother's heart – taking our land, changing our noble way of life." The clear sweet southern type voice broke. Miss Loretta wore a hoop gown with little puffy sleeves – probably lime green. "How can I call you friends?"

Dejectedly the captain let his hands fall, "This damnable war."

Waves of piano music floated up through the house; sailed into every room, roused other dreamers one by one. In the big bedroom at the end of the hall upstairs, Dana McFadden, Helen and Eddie's father, got out of the double bed and glanced warily out the window. Dana was tall and naked, his body tested and strong. That morning Dana was worried. After a year working in Denver, his real home, his real family were right there before him now – to be encountered. That morning, coming home seemed to him both a curse and a blessing and the piano music, a warning.

Throwing on a pair of shorts, he headed down the hall for the stairs. Last night, after his long train trip from Denver, he'd dumped his duffel bag in the kitchen and claimed the downstairs bathroom. He felt safe there. It was big and old fashioned; most of the plumbing was as old as the house, but his father-in-law had built shelves where everything could be put in a proper, well hidden place. And the door had a real lock.

Dana didn't look in on Eddie in the living room, but by then, his son was playing with his eyes closed. 'This is the Army Mister Jones, No Private Rooms or Telephones' filled the living room with high energy.

Upstairs, Helen got out of bed. 'Demonized' might be the right word after all."

$\mathscr{S}$IX

Why do some sparks fall a long way while others wink out half way?

Why are some brilliant and others faint?

How many colors can they be, yet how many colors do they become?

Downstairs, Eddie was playing March of the Slavs (or was it Slaves?). In the bedroom at the end of the hall, Dana's wife, Helen's brutal mother yawned, stretched, and got up. Wearing nothing at all, her body sweetly plump, Rose Corinne wobbled over to the chest of drawers and without looking in the mirror brushed her frizzy hair just enough to calm it. I'm so glad Dana is home, she thought, but he does seem awfully tired. Maybe I should talk to Bernice alone at first. Too bad she and Mother never really got along. I'll have to be careful what I say.

Rose Corinne went to the closet and took down a pink and white short duster housecoat. She heard the piano crashing away below. Goodness Eddie is certainly practicing this morning. He'll miss that piano. Maybe in Denver he'll join a band.

He has so much talent.

Her sister, Lily Bernice, a large blonde woman, lay in the room next door. She was wide-awake and looking at a poster of a grizzly bear on the back of the closet door. What an odd thing in a girl's room, Lily Bernice thought. You wonder her parents allow it. Is the girl normal? She couldn't avoid the March of the Slavs. My God, that piano is loud. The boy has no talent.

The last of the fireworks were snapping away outside. The window was open, but it didn't let in any breeze. Not that there is any, Bernice thought, No breeze off the lake down here. It will be a damn hot day. She remembered the summers here – the bed too small, the room too small. Violet and I were poked in here while Rose Corinne had a nice big room all to herself, thought Bernice, and into her mind came the vision of her new sweet luxury apartment in Duluth, her last Sunday there eating doughnuts in bed and listening to violin concertos on the radio.

Still half asleep, Rose Corinne turned around when her husband came back into the room. She hung her duster back up again. Fireworks crackled outside. Dana went to the window to look out. Two kids across the street were throwing down strings of crackers, but a young woman from an apartment house shooed them away. Rose Corinne watched Dana go over to the bureau, take out a tee-shirt from the drawer, and put on his watch. My goodness he's in a hurry this morning, she thought. He gathered up his pocket change. How much money did he bring with him? Rose Corinne wondered, Enough to get us there on the train? Shall I tell him about my unexpected windfall?

No, she thought, not yet.

"Come over here," she said and sat down on the bed. She was still naked. She patted the bed beside her. Dana sat down, his body tense. She never eats candy, he thought, maybe chocolate that's all; why that peppermint smell?

"Darling, I've missed you." Rose Corinne leaned against him. "You must be tired. Are you serious about going back next week? It's not much time." She touched his cheek with one warm moist palm "Why not take it easy for a day or two. I'll look after you."

Lily Bernice, middle-aged with tinted blonde hair, treated with respect by all her office staff, was reduced to faint moans as more excerpts from great operas billowed up from below. She was not the last of the dreaming mariners to be tossed from the seas of sleep, but one of the more reluctant ones. However, she was sprawled across a narrow bed and Bernice was large – Wagnerian she'd heard someone say about her once. This remark and what she then read about the influence of Wagner on Adolf Hitler had motivated her to listen to opera for a short while, but she'd thought it excessively overwrought and generally messy. That morning, as her nephew rolled into March of the Toreadors from Carmen – one of her mother's favorites – Bernice couldn't help herself. She groaned aloud, and let self-pity seep out of her many pores.

Oh why have I come? We could have talked on the phone. Next it will be. "I'm called Little Buttercup." Her mother Jessie had played, and sung, that one too.

Like most big women, Bernice could dribble self- pity on herself for hours. How she hated this girl's room which she had been forced to occupy for the weekend. It was excessively overwrought and generally messy. Full of things Bernice disliked most – loveable little stuffed animals, ruffles, Bobbsie Twins on a Raft books, and love comics.

Dana got up, went to the closet, and knelt down to scrabble amongst the shoes there for his rubber boots. "I've got ten days – lucky to get that. I don't want you to face the move alone." He turned to look at her. "I want you with me. And I want your mother to go too." There's something going on, his wife thought, His voice sounds funny. She went over and leaned on him as she took down her pink duster, but when he stood up he moved away. She put the duster on, buttoned it. "I'm frying two chickens for the picnic. Have you had fried chicken as good as mine in Denver?"

Boots in hand, Dana looked at her, face expressionless. He was poised to flee.

"People feel sorry for a lonely man" Rose Corinne's voice turned sharp: "They cook meals for lonely husbands more than they do for wives."

Bernice rose from her prison bed. Went to her night case, took out her brush. Don't play games, she said to herself, brushing her hair with heavy-handed strokes. You've come down from Duluth to sort out Mother. That's what's important. But then she gave an involuntary shiver, like a car trying to start, as the thought came that there was another reason too – one she didn't want to think about.

She put down the brush. Her body felt sweaty. Shall I try to get to the bathroom before the rest of the mob? she asked herself. I could use a bath. She eyed the grizzly again and with sudden determination put on the new turquoise silk Japanese dressing gown over her old cotton nightgown – not that anyone here would notice it was silk, or ever know it was a present from a man. My secret life – that thought came now with a bitter taste. Never mind, concentrate on staying sane this weekend. She'd taken to speaking sternly to herself ever since she'd moved to Duluth and taken the job as an office manager.

She padded down the hall to the bathroom before anyone else could wedge themselves in there and not come out for hours.

She tried the door.

Drat. Somebody's in there. But at that exact moment her niece Helen stepped out and, shooting a grimace of displeasure in her aunt's direction, stalked back into the room she was sharing with Jessie, and shut the door.

.Bernice felt a twinge of guilt; after all she had taken the girl's room. She decided against a bath, instead hurriedly washed her face and brushed her teeth. She surveyed the disarray of towels, the mess of toothbrushes and globs of toothpaste, the overwhelming signs of subhuman occupation in the upstairs bathroom, and wished once again that she were home, home where two clean towels hung geometrically perfect, straight lines that soothed – oh yes, her little bathroom with its gleaming tile and scent of White Shoulders. This bathroom smelled of Dettol and blackhead cream. Oh dear, she thought, how soon can I leave? Do I really have to stay until Tuesday? Still I don't look bad, she thought looking into the mirror, pleased in spite of herself with how well her perm had turned out. I can't let them get me down. I'll just have to keep my spirits up. That's what her girlfriends had said. 'Bernice, you just have to keep your spirits up. Going home is no fun for anyone.'

The third sister, the beautiful but long dead Violet Marie was not at home there either – she was barely there at all. Not much of the ghost sister could be seen but she would see everything. She looked in on the middle-aged woman with the blonde tinted hair sprawled across the single bed in the smallest bedroom, once Violet's bedroom too, saw her sister moaning because she hated opera music so much. Violet Marie also knew that Lily Bernice hated messy piles of teenage possessions hiding even more distressing under layers of clutter. That was the way the room had been when they'd shared it!

Violet Marie was wicked enough to laugh when she saw how the first strains of Gilbert and Sullivan's "I'm called Little Buttercup" rolling up from the piano below, caused her sister's lips to quiver. Her sister had been so much fun to tease!

Violet Marie was pulled up sharply by Those In The Know who were guiding her." Get busy." they said," Do what you came to do."

Talk about macabre! Rigor mortis – that's what it's called when dead people stiffen up. Helen was up and still eyeing Jessie.

Grandma looks pretty stiff, – like she hasn't moved all night. Oh great, Eddie's playing a funeral march. Of course he always plays that just before he quits practicing.

She moved to the side of Jessie's bed.

Grandma looks like a witch. She has funny eyebrows and her cheeks are sucked in like a tent that's fallen in. She looks dead actually.

Helen knelt down and put her head on the old woman's chest. She listened for a heartbeat. Nothing. She smells of Noxzema but Grandma always smells of that stuff. Helen's chin touched the old woman's hand. Icy cold! She leapt up. Dead. Her Grandma was dead!

No picnic today.

She did not know how beautiful she looked there in the doorway of the doomed southern mansion, long hair cascading down her back, brown eyes full of tears. The dainty white hand on the captain's arm trembled. She's a delicate flower of the south, the union captain thought, his heart in his throat.

Good thing he wasn't wearing that hat with a strap under his chin!

Helen hated it when thoughts like that came. She walked over to the mirror and made a face. Hi Cutie, she smirked and then made several other faces: angry, snobby, silly, moronic, sexy. She tried several versions of sexy, pulling down one shoulder of her nightgown until one small breast emerged. Watching her, Violet Marie felt exhilarated. More were coming – more memories; it wasn't so bad visiting the others – they were everyday humans just like she had been – the same dumb thoughts, same brave tormenting stupid emotions.

Brave woman, Bernice thought to herself, Bernice you are a brave woman. Lily Bernice liked to talk to the mirror, to tell her weakling Lily self that together they could overcome all fears, override all silly notions. You are brave, mature, sophisticated, she informed her reflection. Bernice couldn't tell herself she was beautiful like her sister

Violet Marie had been, or even plump and pretty like Rose Corinne. No, she knew she was too square, too big, too Brunhilda. Bernice understood that vision to be a large blonde Amazon warrior wearing a helmet with horns. But she knew now only too well that men could love her, had loved her – especially Sam.

The phone rang. She froze.

It rang and rang and rang. Then it stopped.

Oh Sam, she thought, as a gust of emotion went through her, weakening both her knees and her bowels, oh Sam, Sam, Sam, will I see you again? Did you call me just now? Was it you, you, you? I don't dare answer the phone here.

"Do you think I should talk to Bernice first thing this morning?"

Dana, head down, was down once again pawing through his possession in the closet. What is he looking for now? Corky thought,

"Do you want to talk to her? Today? She'll only be here a day or two." He stood up, looked at his watch. It was almost nine o'clock. Outside cars muttered by.

"Corky I want to wash the car."

"Who called this morning?' she asked.

"Called?" Dana stood up, held his socks and boots close to his chest.

"This morning -.somebody telephoned early this morning."

"Don't know. Make some coffee. Give your sister a chance to wake up before you say too much."

Dana moved toward the door.

"And last night. Somebody telephoned late last night." Corky waved a hand around. "The phone rang last night. You were the only one up. It rang twice. You must have answered it."

"A wrong number." Then he was out of the room, thinking as he went down the stairs. Am I gonna survive the day? Man, I'm in trouble.

He heard the phone ring. Nope, he thought, and headed outside.

At the piano, Eddie, turning pages to decide what to play next, didn't answer the phone either.

The phone rang and rang and then stopped.

Next door, Ned walked up the stairs to his sister's house. The smell came out and grabbed him. She's sure no housekeeper he thought. Clothes, papers, garbage were stacked up on the porch. He'd tried to put boarders in but the kind of men – somehow it was always men, that moved in on his sister weren't the kind to pay rent. Ned sighed. She'd never change; it would be all downhill – there was nothing he could do. Something had happened to his sister when Jimmy died. And when that damn husband of hers had come back from Germany and beaten the shit out of her. Still she was his sister and he'd do his best for her. The house was in his name now. She'd always have a home.

He shoved open the front door – the lock was broken – padded back to the kitchen where Mrs. Blunt, sleeves rolled up, was doing dishes. Ned's spirits rose. She didn't look too bad. He put down the sacks of groceries on the counter and watched her unpack them. She was like a kid, like it was Christmas instead of the Fourth of July. She began to plan what to do with the chicken.

"Naw." he said." "Cook it tomorrow. I'll take you out to eat today."

He opened the bottle of rye. Good thing he had a business. Business kept your mind straight. You didn't grieve too much – not like his missis always talking about their kid blinded in one eye. At least he could give the kid a job in the store. The kid was already chasing women around now. That's about all some of them did learn in the army.

Ned caught a glimpse of a black rabbit as it bounced through his sister's tall grass. The grass was waist high, everything overgrown. How was she going to get that mess sorted out? He wasn't going to do it that was for damn sure – maybe he could hire someone to clean it up. Her lawnmower was sitting in the middle of the back yard, rusted out.

Ned poured Mrs. Blunt a shot glass of whiskey and put it down on the counter. As soon as you finish the dishes, he said, and she smiled at him. She doesn't look too bad he thought again – her hair tied back like that reminds me of when she was a kid.

Grass was too tall for a lawnmower anyway. Need a blow-torch or something.

For the first time in days, Mrs. Blunt was happy. She finished washing the dishes while he told her his news.

$\mathcal{S}$EVEN

While this family lay sleeping, breathing in droplets of the morning, all the clamor of the outside world, the important events of 1948 in the U.S of A. – the Berlin airlift, the London Olympics, The California commie conspiracy, the death of Mahatma Gandhi, the birth of Israel, the victory of Joe Louis over Jersey Joe Walcott, the invention of Scrabble, the presidential race between Harry Truman and Thomas Dewey, even a polio epidemic in the city of Minneapolis – all these were nothing to the sleepers, breathing in and out, in and out. Such events did not exist in the private dream worlds they drifted through. When they woke, knowledge came only in dribs and drabs as they submitted themselves to it. And why would you do that when your own world was so interesting?

There was a way you could tell if somebody was dead. The sensitive teenage girl got up and went over to the chest of drawers, put on her glasses, opened the top drawer, and took the little chipped mirror from Jessie's black handbag. She went over to sit on the bed beside her grandmother. Jessie didn't move. Helen could feel the bones of the old woman's hip as she held the mirror against Jessie's lips. You were supposed to see a cloud on the mirror; then you knew the person was breathing. She waited. Nothing happened. No blur on the mirror, no kiss of life. At that exact moment, Eddie played the Death March again. Helen heard the phone ringing but she didn't care.

In Jessie's dream, Violet Marie was bending over her.

"Well then, Mama."

"Oh Violet, I am glad to see you. Will you be staying long?"

"I'm dead, Mama."

"That's too bad. Do your sisters know?"

"One does."

"Does your father?"

"He's dead too."

"Still he should be told. I thought you might have seen him."

By now in the dream they were sitting together at a small table drinking tea.

"Violet Marie, do you know now?"

"Yes."

"Oh I am glad. Does your father know?"

"Of course."

"He never spoke of it."

"Well you know Father."

"Oh I do miss you, Violet? You've been away such a long time. Why don't you visit us?"

"That's why I'm here, Mama."

Then Violet Marie was gone.

Neither of them heard the phone ringing.

"Please, Miss Loretta, let us help you. You need money to buy food."

The Union Captain looked like Carol's brother Norbett – the same dark hair – also tall. Not like those boring blond short Confederates.

"No. You must not tempt me." The beautiful southern belle turned away; she wished to be alone, to look one last time at that dear figure on the bed, silent in death.

Helen was still in her cotton pajamas sitting on the side of her cot. Maybe I will cry she thought. Fall on my bed sobbing. Though if I got dressed and went downstairs I could break the news to everybody. I'd stand in the doorway and speak in a calm voice.

"Death visited our little room last night." They would be shocked and speechless. The whole family would stop what they were doing and stand faces white, listening to me for a change." I'm very much afraid there will be no family picnic today." I'd say that for sure. Helen got up, pulled on white shorts and a white peasant blouse. She looked at the old woman on the bed. We will have to put her teeth in – she'll look a lot better dead that way. Yes definitely when they lay her out they will have to put her teeth back in. I hope Mother doesn't expect me to do that.

I might even make it to the movie. After all I was the one who found her. I could easily be in shock. Helen stood by the door. This house is ominously quiet. The clocks have probably stopped. I don't really feel like crying but I guess it will take a little time. Death is so sudden.

She went over and put the mirror back in Jessie's black purse.

The beautiful southern belle paused to look back at the huge four poster bed, at the small still form in it. There was a sweet smile on the wrinkled old face – mostly because its teeth were in. The pale white aristocratic hand on the door handle trembled; the Union Captain took a hesitant step forward. So did Helen when she saw Jessie's face. Oh great, Grandma's lips are moving. She's not dead."

Jessie opened her eyes. "You got your own bed," she said. She pushed back the covers and struggled to sit up.

"I wasn't in your bed, Grandma."

She can't even die in an interesting way, the sensitive teenage girl thought as she marched out of the room. I think I'll take a bath.

Bernice crawled back onto her narrow bed. The house was wondrously silent. She pushed up the pillows and looked into the mean little eyes of the grizzly bear. Ha to you, she thought. For a brief moment she caught a whiff of perfume, strong and unstable, the kind Violet Marie used to wear. Never mind, she thought, Sam bought me perfume too, lots of it.

Jealousy is a primitive emotion – Sam would say that. Jealousy is a primitive emotion and we are all too civilized for it. For awhile he made me feel civilized all right, she thought and she remembered how whenever Sam visited he brought her a box of chocolates. She got up, took out the box of Trinity chocolates from her suitcase, and carried it back to bed.

I'll get up when I smell coffee, she thought.

Next door Ned looked out of his sister's window and saw Dana walking around the kitchen across the way. I'll ask that guy next door if his kid wants to clean up this yard, Ned thought. A kid will want the money. And I can keep an eye on him. A kid won't move in on my sister.

Dana didn't see Ned looking over at him. He was thinking of Mattie, his Denver landlady. If she'd gone out more she wouldn't have started inviting him up. Nothing would have happened. Nothing much did. But when he stopped going upstairs for cups of tea, she turned angry. She was lonely, was always upstairs; it had been a near thing. She was an attractive woman. She'd told him he couldn't bring his wife and family there. Dana thought strolling around the back yard, a world of trees and back gardens familiar to him. They were the patterns in his life, reminding him he was in Minneapolis, back in the big old house that had been his second home for many years. He felt calmer, thought, I'll take them all back with me, find some other place to live, make Denver work for them too.

He walked over to the garage. The door was pulled down tight. Good, he thought. Maybe we could drive it back. Dana loved that car of Amsden's. It was a sanctimonious blue. It made him think of his father-in-law, a fine and righteous man that had welcomed him into the family.

When Dana thought of Mattie he thought of her modest brick house in Denver. Built in the thirties, full of quiet corners and shadowy spaces, it suited his landlady, or she it, both retiring, both gentle and imbued with elegance. In Denver he'd return from work at night to his basement apartment, but also to the sounds of a woman moving around in the rooms above him. As he lay on his bed, he heard her soft footsteps, heard the opening and closing of cupboard doors, the nudge of pans on the stove, the delicate clink of the second hand china she used every day. After a day spent with men and missing his family, he would try to resist the sense of childhood those sounds created in him. But her cooking defeated him – the buttery warm smells of cheese melting, cookies baking, meat and potatoes frying. He took to drifting upstairs around suppertime, sitting at the kitchen table watching Mattie prepare her supper.

She smiled when he came up. Showed him bottles of whiskey her husband had left. He never took a drink. But when she made a pot of tea, he accepted a cup. She was lonely; her husband, still overseas, seemed in no hurry to come home. And after six months in Denver, Dana didn't like his work at the manufacturing plant for machines that made ammunition. The war was over but they were still making bullets. He was lonely too. He began to do small repairs around

Mattie's house. She began to invite him to supper. Soon it seemed natural, easy to spend every evening together. Too damn easy.

.Dana looked up at the tall dignified old house – white with dark green trim, and at the back three stories of gray wooden stairs that led to an attic apartment rented to nurses, and a second story one where Amsden and Jessie had lived their last years together. This house was their domestic world, he thought, and what a beautiful world it was – full of love and commitment. Not like my family. Dana, his mother, sister had struggled to survive in a series of rented houses full of confusion, pain and desperation because of his father's drinking.

Dana looked at his watch – 9:00 – that phone call this morning – she'd called him last night. But not to say goodbye. It was a mistake talking to her, he thought. He went over, opened the garage door and looked at Amsden's blue 47 Ford. You beautiful baby, Dana thought, I could kiss you, and learning forward he planted his lips on the right windshield. You don't need washing, do you? But I want to do it anyway. He got into the driver's seat, backed out onto the driveway, and as he got out of the car, saw old Mrs. Miller standing on their back porch staring at him. The fireworks had stopped. What was she doing out there? Then Mr. Miller came out and led her back inside.

I'll talk to Mattie again only when I'm in Denver with the family, Dana thought. I've been a fool. I know that. He wanted everything back the way it had been before he'd gone to Denver. This big sweet ship of a house rescued me, he thought, looking around the yard again. Marrying Rose Corinne and living here was the best thing that has ever happened to me. I'm not risking that.

"What's it like?" Eddie emerged from the house, strolled over hands in pockets.

"What?" Dana was bent down, scrubbing hub caps with a brush attached to the hose.

"Colorado."

"O.K."

"Better than here?"

His father stood up, braced his legs, stared at Eddie as though there'd been a sting in his words. "In some ways."

Eddie came closer, bent over to examine a fender. The scratch was so minor only he knew it was there. The silence went on and finally he looked up.

Dana was still standing looking at him, water rushing out of the hose across his feet, unheeded. "Why do you ask?"

"I don't think I'm going."

"What do you mean?"

"I'm not going to Denver." The words sounded more resentful than Eddie intended. "I'm old enough to go off on my own."

"Yes." His father bent down again to scrub at the undercarriage of the car. "Yes you are."

"I have other plans."

"That's all right." Dana's softer tone hung in the air.

Around them the morning gardens dozed in Sunday splendor. Warmth and life unfurled as they must, without human interference. The spasm of fireworks seemed finished; only bees and flowers busied themselves, the hollyhocks and morning glories displaying their usual flamboyant fuss. Not many people were moving yet: on the Fourth of July only afternoon picnics and night fireworks displays were required of anyone.

"What are you're thinking of doing? Going off somewhere?"

"Maybe."

"You got any money?"

"Not really. Not enough anyway."

"You talked to anybody about this?"

"No."

"Well don't. Not yet."

"What do you think, Dad?" Eddie walked closer, the floodgates unleashed. "I could go to Texas. Get a job on the rigs. Or join the air force. Not wait for the draft."

"The air force," His father's voice was full of concern mixed with scorn. Military service was a dangerous topic. Dana had been turned down for flat feet and because he had a family to support, but also, or so he suspected, because he and his parents were born in Ireland. Dana had spent the war years in "war-related industries." Not a heroic role for a proud man during the biggest war of all time.

"You don't want to go on to college?"

"No."

"High school?"

"I hated every minute of it." Words, feelings were boiling up in Eddie.

His father looked at him and smiled. "Is that so?"

"The teachers talk to us like we're a bunch of dumb kids."

"Well aren't you?"

Eddie looked over at his father. He felt his throat unclench.

"Not as dumb as they think."

"Finish high school."

"I have."

Dana was genuinely surprised. "I thought you had another year."

They stared over the top of the car at each other. Dana had left home at sixteen, had finished high school at night.

"Do me a favor. Don't talk about this today. We've got enough on our plate."

"Why is she here?"

"She?"

"Aunt Bernice."

Dana walked over and turned off the water. Inside the house, the phone was ringing again. The back screen door of the Miller house opened, and Mr. Miller, elderly and precise, re-emerged to squint over at them.

"Why shouldn't she be here?" Dana spoke mildly. "It's her home too." He gave the hose to Eddie. "You finish up here."

Dana walked to the back door and went inside. Eddie turned the water back on and worked on the car, knowing that his father would notice what he did, that he would be pleased. Eddie didn't see the black rabbit. Only Mr. and Mrs. Miller, familiar with the renegade, saw it bouncing through the Fallsworth's back garden. They were surprised nobody did anything about it. That black rabbit was eating the last of Jessie's flowers.

$\mathcal{E}$IGHT

Beyond the old white house the world warmed – July sun, July heat. Yet it was still early, just 9 o'clock. Still cool in the shadow of things. The green of the lawn and trees, the effortless blue sky, all said paradise, paradise, paradise. Birds, attentive to housekeeping, suggested improvements now and then. The black rabbit thumped through the yards – Old Miller's enemy, a rabbit with stiff aggressive ears like black telephone receivers, a rabbit who'd weathered the years, who'd wandered the back gardens of the Minneapolis neighborhood gathering information and vegetables. Sometimes he tantalized the neighborhood dogs, but none stirred that morning; it was too early, too hot to pursue an attack dog reputation. Except for the occasional car there was no noise. No one mowed a lawn to satisfy a conscience, no children scattered through underbrush in search of devilment, even the cars moved slowly, quietly. Perhaps serenity had flowed through the night, had waited through the noisy early hours until Sunday tranquillity was at last victorious over fireworks confusion.

Or was it the calm before a storm?

Eddie didn't see the rabbit, but he did spot Aunt Bernice peering out the window. He thought she was looking down at him. His aunt had opened the trailer door last night at a highly inconvenient time. Carol hadn't noticed and he certainly wasn't going to tell her, but now that he thought about it, Aunt Bernice deserved to be taught a lesson – the one known as 'snoopers never prosper.'

Half asleep, staggering to the window to get a breath of fresh air, Bernice was shocked to see a black rabbit. She wasn't looking at Eddie washing her father's car. Someone was always washing her father's car. Even she in days past had washed her father's car. No, it was that amazing black rabbit hopping unabashed through the gardens, a huge well fed fellow. She'd seen nothing like that in Duluth.

Is it someone's pet? Bernice thought, If it is no one around here would admit to it. She watched the rabbit munch remnants of flowers from her mother's garden, watched him flap and bounce back and forth through Mrs. Blunt's wilderness, dance back into Jessie's potato plants, and bounce down and around Mr. Miller's ambitious still a victory garden spread. Bernice was dumbfounded – impressed too – by his boldness, ability to live off the land, and by the fact that no one else appeared to notice the marauder.

Mr. Miller watched that damn rabbit bouncing through his carrots for a third time. The black bastard had been terrorizing the neighborhood for six years. He took down the slingshot from the hook on the wall, selected a stone from the dish on top of the shelf by the back door, opened the door, and slammed one, then a second stone at the rabbit. The second was a direct hit. The rabbit shot up into the air and bounded away. Mr. Miller went inside. By golly they were going out. He'd call his daughter Carol and tell her so.

About ten o'clock, Myrna Henderson's sister-in-law called, "I know you're thinking about Joe. I am too. You come over and have lunch with us." Myrna put away the letters, put up her hair and put on lipstick. Her daughter came in and hugged her.

"I got a shock last night." Bernice said, watching the coffee arrive in her cup. Corky was so clumsy in the morning.

"Oh?" Please go away, Rose Corinne was thinking. She liked to be by herself in the kitchen for the first half-hour in the morning. "What from?"

"Eddie."

"Oh?" Please, please don't tell me anything. Rose Corinne liked to read the newspaper gently, starting with the entertainment section. She never listened to world news until noon.

"He was in the trailer last night. At three a.m."

"Oh?" Corky's voice rose a little. Now she wanted to know. Everything.

"What was he doing out there?"

"He was with some girl." Bernice face was mulish. "A very young girl."

Her sister's mouth formed a round oh but no sound emerged.

"They were in bed. I caught him in bed with a girl. I got a shock you can believe me. Opened the door and there they were naked as jaybirds. He was on top."

"Never mind the details." Corky snapped, reaching for her coffee. She'd forgotten to take the pot off the fire; she could hear it boiling hard, and now she rose and took it to one side. That gave her a chance to turn her back on her sister.

"I thought you'd want to know," Bernice said sulkily. "I haven't a clue who the girl was."

"I'll speak to him, Bernice." Corky turned around and her face was secure.

Pleasant-looking. Noncommittal. Inside of course she was exploding with rage.

How dare Eddie! They had enough problems without getting some girl pregnant. She just hoped he had the sense to use some form of protection. She'd have to speak to Dana. Maybe he could talk to Eddie. She went to the icebox and yanked out two chickens. Threw them into the sink. Probably that Carol – the little wretch had been over night and day the last two weeks. A veritable whirlwind of questions, statements, ultimatums, and warnings stormed through Corky. None of which showed. She sat down and picked up her paper.

Bernice was irritated by this air of indifference." Maybe you ought to warn him."

"I'll talk to him, Bernice." Corky looked up and managed a kindly voice. "Thank you so much for telling me."

Now Bernice exploded inside. She'd gone through that hell last night of finding some little squirt doing it with a poor innocent young girl, a squirt that was her own nephew and her sister didn't care enough to get upset. Well she'd say something to him then. These young fellows had to be stopped somehow; they were always getting some poor little girl in trouble.

Bernice rose. Majestically she stood to her full height, face serene too. "I think I'll take my coffee upstairs. I have a letter to write."

"We'll be going in about an hour or so." Her sister said icily.

"Thanks. For making the coffee." Bernice's voice was equally icy.

"No problem" Corky said to her newspaper. Bernice sailed out of the room.

Bam Smash Crash — the inner worlds were fireworks of fury and warning.

Eddie pulled out his summer white trousers and a new blue and white shirt. It might have been Carol calling this morning. With luck she'd get to the park. Maybe they'd have a chance again. To fuck. He didn't dare use the word with anyone, especially not Carol, but he liked thinking it. Fuck. Maybe they could disappear into the bushes somewhere. He went downstairs and outside again. He still didn't feel tired.

Dana came out of the downstairs bathroom and headed out the back door. He said nothing only gave a weak smile to Corky who watched him in silence from the kitchen.

It was kitchen in which nothing hung on the walls. What was going on anyway? she thought, all these men running around pleasing themselves and nobody else.

Dana felt his back prickling. He walked up the driveway to the front yard and was surprised to see the Saturday paper lying near the front stairs — they must have been too busy meeting his train to notice last night. He sat down and broke the paper open but he couldn't concentrate. He still couldn't get Mattie out of his mind. She had no children, no friends, and few resources.

Does she have the will to leave her husband, to get out of that punishing isolation? he wondered. Probably not. Mattie reminds me of my mother.

Dana's mother had never been able to break with his father. Despite patterns of abuse, years of neglect and drunken sprees, his father had always convinced his mother to take him back; Dana and his sister couldn't understand why she yielded. They'd both left home early. His sister Jean had stopped speaking to their father when their mother died of heart failure at fifty but Dana couldn't quite bring himself to do that.

His father had no one left but Dana and an old drinking buddy. He and his buddy survived together in a rented room in St. Paul. Sometimes his father sobered up and contacted Dana. I'll have to call before we leave, Dana thought, but he was glad Denver was far away. He wouldn't have to visit his dad or expect visits.

Honor your Father and Mother – he'd come to think of that as a joke.

He tried to read the paper. War somewhere. Always war. And he was helping them make bullets.

Jessie was sitting up facing the day. And herself. She set both feet on the floor and lurched herself up, then wrenched a stiff body over to the chest of drawers. She looked in the mirror. When she was younger she'd made a point of not looking before nine a.m. Can't bear the sight of me too early, she'd say to her friends, might have a heart attack. Her friends would laugh. You always looked good Jessie, your hair with that natural wave. Now she looked first thing. Was she still there? Sometimes the strength of a dream upon her, she'd see herself young again, slipped into one of those selves she promised herself she'd never stop being. She picked up the hairbrush.

There's not much hair to brush, Jessie thought– so thin now, straight as a board, and white. I'm old all right. But not wise. At least not so you'd notice. In fact folks act like I'm asleep. Asleep, awake – they are coming together; sometimes I can't tell them apart. Was that Violet or that silly girl I saw this morning? Being old was more betwixt and between then I expected. Like living in an apartment where nothing works. Going downhill and the landlord gone out forever.

She put down the brush. That's enough of that kind of thinking and that's enough of looking at me, she thought, the worst part of the day's over. She turned away, went to the closet, and struggled out of her old white nightgown. She took down a frayed camisole from the closet. It was Sunday somehow she knew that.

I have some praying to do she thought. What'd Amsden go on talking about wrestling for when it was Sunday?

The dreams of Amsden were getting stronger and stronger. Last night they were watching wrestling. They used to do that together after he bought the television. They'd had some good fights about watching it too. Yes she remembered now – in her dream they'd been watching one of those wrestling matches – a bunch of men in leopard skins and stars and bars.

Staggering a little Jessie stepped into the long drawers she wore summer or winter. It didn't seem to matter anymore whether it was hot or cold outside. Whatever she wore was just right. You get too excited watching wrestling, Amsden, she thought. You believe in the villains. You believe Evil walks around in big fat men wearing skimpy pants. Never made sense to me. I think Evil smiles a lot, looks pretty and talks smooth. A fat man isn't going to tempt anybody much.

Jessie took down a shocking pink suit from the junior department from the closet – her Sunday suit. She was going to church. She had some praying to do. Jessie hadn't heard the fireworks. Nor did she know it was the Fourth of July. Jessie didn't care much about that sort of fuss anymore. But she did care about Sunday.

Jessie liked Sunday and she had reason not to like the Fourth of July.

Bernice pushed the pillow against the wall and looked into the yes you eyes of the grizzly bear. Hello sweetheart, she smirked, how'd I do down there? Sipping her coffee she practiced her refusal.

I'm sorry but I have too many responsibilities. Mother can't live with me in Duluth and I can't come here. She'll have to go with you to Denver or into a home.

Then her sister would say – No, not a nursing home. Oh no, please Bernice. You can get a transfer – you told me that.

Did I?

It was going to be delicious. She would be cool and efficient. She would be her real self for once.

Wearing gold lame and valuable jewels, the dragon lady slithered into the hall of mirrors. The men there looked frightened. She was so beautiful, so sinister. She smiled and held out her cigarette in a diamond holder; instantly men sprang forward to light it.

Helen picked up a toothbrush and smoked decadently with it. I am the Dragon Lady she murmured in a throaty voice. Most of the men blanched. But one, taller and handsomer than the others – somewhat like Norbett – walked over to her.

Rattle, rattle, rattle, a polite little questioning sound. Aunt Bernice, Helen decided. Anybody else would have knocked or said something but Aunt Bernice was funny. She didn't like people to know she frequented such places.

Helen leaned forward and thrust out her chin. Another spot – they were like holes you leaked through. Opening the mirror cabinet she took out the beauty grains, removed her glasses, and sprinkling grains into her hand, mixed them with a little water. Like a magic potion she thought.

The man stared at her spellbound. Those beautiful eyes, that face, that hair, he moaned, you are magic. Kiss me you fool, the beautiful but evil woman drawled. You're driving me wild, he sighed. She laughed wickedly and then slowly agonizingly kissed the mirror leaving a smear. He cried out in pain. At least tell me your name!

I really am driving him wild, the dragon lady thought with satisfaction.

Rattle, rattle, the door knob chattered. This time with an added poignant shove like someone couldn't believe the door was still locked. The sensitive teenage girl turned on the cold water and rinsed her face and hands with great splashing sounds. The door knob noise stopped. Aunt Bernice is too polite to nag, she thought.

Helen wiped her face on her mother's private face towel and thought about the difference between the words 'provocative' and 'provoking.'

Definitions of Fireworks:
   a pyrotechnic display
   an explosive device for producing a striking display of light as
   part of a celebration
   a display of violent temper or fierce activity

NINE

In movies they showed the woman's face looking stunned when she was kissed.

But what did the man look like? Helen pulled one sleeve down so some flesh showed.

Flesh was a great word.

The doorknob rattled.

Opening the cabinet, the sensitive teenage girl scooped out a handful of her brutal mother's special honey-scented face cream. Humming a little, the girl sat down on the toilet cover and rubbed cream into her feet.

Knock Knock Knock.

Another poignant shove of the door knob, then silence.

Helen rose, reached into the cabinet, and took out her mother's nail polish. Clear of course, Mother is too mundane to buy anything else, she thought.

She painted the toes of one foot. Carol wore nail polish. Eddie said Carol had sexy feet. Helen leaned forward to admire her handiwork. She thought, my foot doesn't look sexier. The polish smells like car wax.

KNOCK KNOCK KNOCK

Somebody out there is getting pretty desperate.

She flushed the toilet several times as a warning to the desperate person and started on a second row of toes.

The visiting dead person, Violet Marie, watched her niece applying nail polish and laughed. She'd played around in this taj mahal of a bathroom just like her niece. Her father had redone it to please Jessie, filling it with mirrors so that it became a place of self-education -and self-seduction. Even the ceiling had a mirror because Jessie had complained she couldn't see the back of her head. Why that should be important had remained unclear to Violet, but as a girl she'd found examining herself in the upstairs bathroom a heady experience – right side of head, left side of head, top of head, right back of head, left back of head. You thought differently about yourself when you saw the top of your own head. And all those side views – well a new sense of self was required.

Or selves because each mirror, like a splinter of broken glass, reflected a different self.

All the women used the upstairs bathroom.

Watching her niece prance and pose, Violet remembered how difficult it was to come out of that bathroom – or to get anyone else out of it. But self-seduction was not for Violet Marie any more. There was no face to look at, no toenails to paint – though she was still connected to life, still part of her family, and with them for this one day. To be dead was to hear everything; Violet found that could be quite awful or quite wonderful.

She was there to tell herself the truth about her own life. You could become different selves in the real world too – or so you thought. Violet had been in many ways a run of the mill sinner, seducing Dana while he was dating Rose Corinne, trying the same mean trick with Lily Bernice. Violet Marie had not been particularly nice, nor violently bad, but she'd been too sure of what she was doing while she was doing it. Now she had to go over all her decisions with the proverbial fine-tooth comb.

Eddie stood by the car debating. He hated waxing a car. Dana was fussy, would point out some place Eddie had missed. But a connection was still there with his dad, so he ambled into the empty garage, found an old chamois cloth at the back, and rubbed wax into the front and sides of the Ford. The sun on his back felt good.

He was looking forward to the picnic now. If only I could talk to somebody about last night – about what it was like and what I should do next. But another guy his age might understand. But he might try to move in on Carol too.

He took a break, glanced into the windows of the closed garage. One of the two garages held the car; the other side was never opened, its doors permanently locked. Inside he could see the jumble of old furniture piled higher than the small windows. As a kid, he'd been afraid to look in that garage because the furniture appeared alive, to be screaming for help, pounding on the glass, trying to get out. Like those pictures of people in newsreels – Help, help, we're suffocating, gassed, shot, buried alive. Those newsreels had seemed to have nothing to do with Minneapolis, but still, even as a child, he knew they were real people, suffering somewhere and what happened to them mattered. But that morning Eddie thought, The war's over. That's just old furniture piled against dirty windows, and he went back to rubbing the car until it shone.

Rattle Rattle Rattle.

I wish they'd stop bothering me, thought the sensitive teenage girl. She gazed into the mirror. Yes, you are a warrior queen. Your people (that includes the apes) must be free. She flushed the toilet again, and ran water into the sink.

The beautiful jungle savage struggled against her captors. In a few moments they would force her to enter the arena, there to undergo the supreme test – war to the death. She was not afraid. They would strike off her chains, open the iron gates, expose her to the huge crowd. What was she wearing? Probably not much. Helen took off her clothes.

The front screen door opened behind Dana.

"Do you want some coffee?"

He turned around to look at Corky. "Great."

She came back a few minutes later with a mug. Her face was grim.

He tried to smile. "Looks like a great day for a picnic."

"They're a lot of work."

"You want some help?"

She stood behind him, paused as though thinking. He wished she'd go away.

She's looming over me again, he thought, Corky has a way of doing that. As if any moment, she might fall over and crush me. She isn't a big woman, not like her sister, but sometimes she seems bigger than me. He didn't like thinking that.

"I'll come in and help you. Soon as I drink this coffee."

Still she paused, tight-lipped, silent. Dana's stomach tightened.

"Eddie's up to trouble," Corky said.

"What'd you mean – up to trouble?"

"Some girl. Bernice caught him."

"You're kidding." Dana smiled to himself. No wonder the kid wanted to talk.

Corky looked down, shifted irritably. The sun had found them on the steps.

"I am not. Last night she caught him in the trailer. Probably with that Carol, Helen's friend. The girl's been over here night and day."

That surprised Dana. "Wasn't it locked?"

"We were in there – Helen and I – going through some stuff of Mother's. We must have forgotten." Corky paused. What's he smiling for? Doesn't he think this is important? She looked up the street. This is my street, she thought. I grew up here.

Dana stood up, coffee cup in hand. He knew Corky and thought, I should try to get her to talk. But her anger may have something to do with me.

"I can't believe we are just going to pick up and leave. I can't believe it."

She shot one long full glance at him and went inside. He felt his body flush.

She knows, he thought. Damn it, she knows.

Eddie was sitting at the table by the window spooning in cereal when Corky came into the kitchen. She approached the chickens. Okay, time to cut you up and fry you. But first...

"What time did you come in last night, Eddie?"

"Don't nag, Mom."

Corky stopped dead in her tracks. "What do you mean by that?"

Eddie went on eating cereal and reading the back of the Rice Krispies box.

"What do you mean, don't nag? What's that supposed to mean?" Corky picked up the chickens, threw them down on the cutting board, took out the butcher knife. "How'd you get in the house?"

"The window."

"I suppose you thought you were smart coming in a window?"

"I am smart Mom."

"That's dangerous – leaving a window open. We could have had a robber."

"You're the one that left it unlocked."

"Me?"

"Somebody did. I'm too busy to run around unlocking windows."

He poured the last of the milk into his bowl, poured in more Rice Krispies.

Snap, Crackle, Pop.

"Busy! You're too busy!" Corky slammed the frying pan onto the stove. Poured in oil and turned on the gas. She hacked chicken into pieces and dipped them one by one in flour. I wish to heck Eddie would go out in the world and get some of that smart aleck knocked out of him, she thought. Both my kids think they know everything.

"You're not too busy to stay out all night. What were you doing anyway?"

"That's my business, Mom."

It was his calmness that enraged her. What did they teach kids at school anyway?

How to talk to your parents so they wanted to club you with a frying pan? She dropped pieces of floured chicken into the frying pan simmering with hot oil. A quick sizzle and they were committed.

Eddie rose and put his dishes in the sink. "When are we leaving?"

"I have no idea. And I don't care."

Corky ran water into the sink. Glared at her son. Why was she doing all this?

Who cares if I fry chicken or not? Why do it?

Except that Jessie had always cooked chickens, made a big picnic lunch on the Fourth of July and maybe this was the last time – today – the last Fourth of July picnic together. So I care, she thought. That's what it comes down to – I care.

"I washed the car for Dad." Eddie said "And waxed it."

"Well, are you going to tell me? What you were doing last night?"

"It's my business, Mom."

He strolled away. Corky went on turning chicken, removing

cooked pieces, flouring new ones, all the time thinking of the arrogance of men – all of them.

Do they think there's no one else in the world? I wish I'd shouted at Eddie – What you do is everybody's business. He thinks it's not his business to listen to his mother anymore; he thinks he doesn't need a family. We'll see about that.

When she was a young woman – before she married – Rose Corinne had traveled. She'd had a job as a tutor to an acting family. She'd seen other places and other people. The job hadn't lasted that long, but it had marked her, taught her there were lots of ways to live, to be. She'd liked being a stranger. But she'd liked having a home to come back to too. There was safety in that – having a place to come home to – a family.

I don't want to leave Minneapolis, she thought, I don't want to leave this house. Not while Mother's still alive.

Why do we have to go to Denver? Why can't Dana find a job here in Minneapolis or St. Paul?

It was shaping up to a fight she could see that.

Jessie opened the door and peeked out into the hall. She felt in danger somehow. There was an energy moving through some of these people that was dangerous. They speak and think with their motors running too fast, she thought. More and more she liked staying in her room, in her bed. Liked sleeping in. But that was dangerous too. Everything could be taken away from you if you slept too long and too well.

You have to keep moving – Amsden used to say that. Keep dressing up and making plans. You have to remind people you're alive. They have a tendency to forget.

She tried the door of the bathroom but it was locked – somebody in there. She skittered down the hall and into the bedroom she and Amsden had once shared.

It was empty – the sheets on the big bed thrown back. Rose's clothes were strewn about. She's a messy girl. Doesn't listen to me anymore.

Jessie sat down on the bed. Amsden would care about her having money.

She was glad for the dreams of Amsden. He was an anchor holding her to what she knew, who she was. Amsden always did that for me, she thought. Saying don't worry, sweetheart, I'm not leaving you. I love you. He always said that so she was sure of it. He was saying it in her dreams now.

She got up, went down the hall, tried the bathroom door again. Locked.

Lord sakes, they do spend time in there. Well, I'll go downstairs, she thought. Make a phone call. She started down, treading carefully in her purple knitted house slippers. She held on to the banister, took each step as it came to her to do so.

Up from the kitchen came the thick smell of fried chicken and she thought,

It is Sunday. I smell fried chicken. Rose is a good girl even if she is pigheaded.

KNOCK, KNOCK, KNOCK

Someone is obviously suffering untold agonies. The sensitive teenage girl turned on the bath so that water rushed out. She went and looked in the mirror. Yes, those were definitely breasts. The crowd roared as the beautiful young savage girl stood panting, triumphant, wearing only a leopard skin bikini, which showed every inch of her voluptuous body.

Voluptuous was a great word.

Violet Marie walked down the front steps of the old house, past her brother-in-law Dana, who was reading the newspaper and didn't look up, or even know she was there. She could feel the warm but still mild air. She looked up and down the street. The sidewalk was as she remembered it – a dizzying blur of white stretching out in all directions as far as she could see – a creamy relentless path leading on to forever. Over all arched the splendid trees, majesties that hid from view the sky, and all the intricacy of what really lay beyond. Cars were a distant threshing noise along Blazedale and Nicollet.

Avenue. An occasional car coming down 35th street stirred the neighborhood silence like a stone thrown into a pool. Mostly their street was empty air all morning, though by late afternoon, Violet knew the space around them would become heavy with heat, the neighborhood dogs would refuse to move, and impudent squirrels would retreat to the upper branches to carry on their quarrels. Or were they love affairs? Yes she thought with joy: This is Minneapolis in the summer. And on our street, each moment ticks forward just as it ought; each spark of life is a small sweet stab of truth.

Around her, Violet Marie could hear the tick tock sounds of summer, the staccato of braggart grasshoppers in the heat, the busybody buzz of hornets and flies and bees.

Violet knew that tonight, cicadas and crickets would send out their Morse code messages: we are here; we are alive; are you there? are you alive? – to the night, to the moon, to the stars.

A black Chevrolet pulled up in front of the Millers' house. Dana looked up, and saw, as Violet did, Mr. and Mrs. Miller emerge from their house, the old man helping his wife down the front steps. He wore brown pants and a bright blue shirt. He looks like a blue jay, Violet thought. Mrs. Miller wore a starched white dress. She looked around with vague eyes, yet Violet had the odd sensation that Mrs. Miller could see her. The two old people got into the car, were driven away by a middle-aged woman with a sharp nose.

Bambambambam

"I'm taking a bath." The sensitive teenage girl stood naked by the tub, waiting for her toenails to dry, but ready for her bath so she wasn't lying – exactly.

KNOCK KNOCK KNOCK

Holding the spear aloft, the jungle princess raised her eyes to the emperor's box. One bare foot (with nail polish) rested on the prostrate form of a woman who looked very much like Mother. The crowd hushed. They too looked to the emperor. He had blue eyes. Would it be life or death?

Jessie went into the kitchen where pieces of chicken were piled up, some cooked and some uncooked but floured and ready to go. The fire was turned off and the coffee pot was empty. Well, what's going on here? Jessie thought, and walked slowly, carefully back to the stairs. She was ready for church. She might as well go. But she was thinking about Amsden, or rather thinking at him like she often did. Never mind Rose, she thought, I'll go to church now. Get my purse. She started back up the stairs.

Why'd you love me so much, Amsden? You never took a step those last years without looking at me. If I were smiling, well fine, but if I frowned, heaven help us. It was a terrible burden. You weren't the sort of man who wanted to hear a whole lot of truth. You didn't even want to talk much. Well, I'm talking to you now and telling you some truth you may not want to hear. Cause I got a lifetime of words saved up. People with me these days are talking nonsense, so I plan on telling you everything – once I've prayed on it.

She went into her room, closed the door.

BAMBAMBAMBAMBAMBAMBAMBAMBAMBAMBAM

"Get out of there!" Corky raged.

Helen turned off the bath water, replaced the nail polish, screwed the top on the face cream, shut the mirror, straightened the towels and flushed the toilet again.

"I'm just about through."

"You bet your life you're through!"

The brutal mother was out of control again. The sensitive teenage girl brushed her teeth, paying special attention to the back molars. She replaced the toothbrush, put on her underwear, her shorts and peasant blouse. Only then did she open the door.

The brutal mother was right there, face splotchy with anger. Aunt Bernice swept past them both into the bathroom, looking embarrassed and locking the door behind her with a relieved click. Helen and Corky eyed each other with malevolent pleasure. "Next time I'll use my key." Corky said.

"I'm sure you will, Mother. Whatever you do is either provocative or provoking."

"What does that smart aleck remark mean?"

Helen elbowed past her mother. She opened the bedroom door to reveal Jessie sitting forlornly on the edge of her bed, researching the black handbag.

"Every cent is gone." she hissed.

"No one has any privacy in this house anymore." Helen flopped on the cot.

Corky leaned into the room. "You watch yourself, Miss Smarty Pants."

She didn't look at Jessie, who stood up and, holding the black handbag, staggered over to her daughter. "That girl had her hand in my purse."

"Do you mind Mother? We're trying to get ready to go." She turned back to her daughter. "You just mind your manners or you'll regret it." By then Jessie was staggering in a little circle, thin legs in wrinkled stockings, feet in purple bedroom booties. Corky didn't notice that her mother was wearing her shocking pink, go-to-church-on-Sunday suit. Her daughter's attire was a different kettle of fish. "Are you wearing those short shorts?"

"Of course."

"Today?"

"Yes."

"And that blouse?"

"Yes." Helen picked up a comb from the dresser and began to arrange her fuzzy head of hair; she pretended an air of great accomplishment. Oh Miss Lavender, your hair is ravishing today.

"It's not appropriate attire."

"It doesn't matter to me."

"It should."

"Well, it doesn't."

"I'd like one of you fine ladies," Jessie's voice cracked ominously "to tell me why I have no money in my purse."

Her daughter looked at Jessie for the first time. "You don't need any money, Mother."

"I need collection money."

"You are not going to church today, Mother."

"Is that so?" Jessie's face took on the look of a pencil that's been sharpened way too sharp. "Well somebody's taken all my money.

"Shut up about that money!" Corky roared. She stormed out the door and flounced down the stairs and into the kitchen.

Jessie sat back on her bed, still holding the handbag out in front of her, while Helen examined what could only be termed an extravagant hairstyle. Silence reigned.

Outside the birds were conferring in the trees. Their conference was a long one; they were discussing the magpies, which once again were harassing everyone. Sometimes they followed cats down the street, clacking with amusement. They'd guffaw when, dignity breached, the cats broke down and turned to notice their existence.

One big bold fellow specialized in tweaking the tails of dogs while they slept. So the birds chattered on and on about how something ought to be done. The sparrows liked meetings and the robins believed in community efforts, but somehow no one ever got the blue jays or woodpeckers to their gatherings. Humming birds? They never showed up unless honey was given out.

.

TEN

"Good morning dear." Bernice turned to greet her niece who was backing into the kitchen reading as she walked. Bernice's voice was bright. Somebody might as well be cheerful. The cheerful aunt was wearing a turquoise and white flowered dress and white pumps. "And how are you this fine morning?"

"Fill up one of those thermoses with milk." Corky commanded her daughter. She was at the stove poking at floured offerings in a heavy iron skillet and wincing resentfully from the hot fat. Corky had a bandana over her hair and wore an old blouse and skirt, and thought Bernice looked like she was going to afternoon tea at the Ritz.

"When I finish with this I'm going for a walk." Bernice announced in a high tea voice. "If there's time." She was standing at the counter near the sink wrapping cooked chicken legs in wax paper, handling each one as though it were an unclean object.

The air was filled with smoke, doom, and the smell of frying chicken.

Helen closed her book, wandered over to the icebox, opened it and peered inside. She pulled out an empty milk bottle and held it up.

"Mom."

"Drink apple juice."

Corky caught up the coffeepot and came over to the sink next to Bernice. She filled one of the two tall thermoses with fresh coffee. "We just have to live one day at a time, Bernice." She screwed the thermos cap on with quick vicious jerks of both hands.

Helen leaned over the open door of the icebox, an absentminded look on her face.

"Where's the apple juice?" She opened her book again. Corky

could see the title – 'Lives of the Great Queens.' The girl's a certifiable idiot, her mother thought.

"In the cupboard. And shut the icebox door. Bernice, I really don't think it would be that long."

"One day's too long." The cheerful aunt patted wax paper around a chicken breast putting it to rest forever.

The awesome odor of burnt sacrifice filled the kitchen. Corky rushed back to the stove and rescued several pieces in distress. Her mind was turning as dark as the chicken. Everything always her doing everything. She turned down the gas fire.

"What do you expect us to do then?"

"I have no idea. Isn't that what we're going to talk about today?"

"Well let's talk. Right now. It's up to you and me, Bernice."

"I get the impression your idea of agreement is for me to take charge of Mother."

Helen stopped pretending to read, closed her book and wandered over to the cupboard. She slid back the heavy gray door to the tall pantry cupboard at the back of the kitchen, a cupboard six feet high, eight feet long with shelves of canned goods, shelves of boxes of soaps and powders, shelves of old dishes, pots and pans, tools. Her father liked full shelves. Whenever he came home from a trip, no matter how long he'd been away, he'd arrange everything on the shelves. He liked the cans to be in alphabetical order.

He was doing that last night, Helen thought.

"You are so selfish, Bernice."

"I'm just realistic."

"Don't you think it's time you did your share? Or do you really want Mother to be put away. Like some old dog."

Bernice's mouth tightened. "Put away is a bit strong isn't it?" How typical, she thought, Corky manages to forget that she herself was always Mother's favorite. Bernice began to pack the wrapped chicken pieces into a narrow red tin box.

"That's for sandwiches." Corky said sharply.

"Well are you making any?"

"If and when I have time."

Corky poured the last of the orange juice into a small jam jar and sipped at it.

She wanted to run away, to scream, at least to lie down. Already the day stretched forward like an enormous treadmill.

Humming a little, Bernice picked up her cup and came over to pour herself some fresh coffee.

Not that that Corky had left her much. No sense getting upset this early in the day. She went back to the counter and continued arranging chicken in the red tin box. Corky was due for hysterics soon. Why bother with sandwiches?

"Mother, there isn't any apple juice."

"Oh for heaven's sakes, it's right there."

Corky joined her daughter at the letter A – applesauce, apricots, apple butter, a package of almonds, and that little jar of chocolate covered ants Eddie gave me for Christmas as a joke. I keep forgetting to throw the wretched things out.

"Eddie drinks it all. He takes everything. He drinks a whole can by himself."

"Don't be silly." Corky rummaged around in the odds and ends at the bottom of the cupboard – she threw everything there to be filed by Dana. No apple juice.

Her daughter plucked the can from J for juice. "Found it."

"You can make sandwiches, Helen." Corky walked back to the stove.

The sensitive teenage girl followed the brutal mother.

"Haven't you seen him? He drinks milk out of the bottle."

"Make sandwiches."

Mother lives in a funny little cocoon, Helen thought, 'Hear no evil, see no evil,' and the third one…whatever it is. She opened the apple juice, poured herself a glass, reopened her book, went back to the cupboard, grabbed a handful of stale gingersnaps, and began to read, eat cookies and drink apple juice standing up.

Tall, beautiful Eleanor attracted universal respect and attention.

Yes naturally. How satisfying to be a queen.

She lost most of her teeth by the time she was thirty.

Her teeth!

And to compensate she was never seen smiling.

Not even in bed? You could turn the lights off. That was definitely something she wouldn't like about being Eleanor of Aquitaine. But in those days it was probably a good thing to keep your mouth shut.

Fourteenth century France was a tumultuous place.

Tumultuous is a great word but what does it mean? She needed more apple juice.

"Will you get out of my way!" Corky slammed the heavy skillet off the burner. She added more pieces of floured chicken, began the long lament of sizzling fat. "Stop wandering around. Do something useful."

"Like what?"

"Make sandwiches." Bernice leaned over from her safe corner.

"Pour apple juice in that other thermos." Corky snapped.

"She's not some old dog, Rose Corinne. She's our mother. This is her house."

"Tell me something I don't know." Corky stepped back from the hot fat spitting out. She should put the lid on the skillet but she couldn't find it.

The telephone rang. The two women stopped what they were doing, looked at each other, and let it ring, once, twice, three times. "Aren't you going to answer it?" Bernice asked.

"I don't have to do everything do I?"

"I'll get it," Helen said. She put down her book and went around the long way into the living room. The phone had stopped ringing when she got there. Instead she encountered Jessie sideways on the couch talking into the receiver, long wrinkled fingers clutching the handle. She looked furtive.

"Must have been in the night," Jessie muttered.

"Who is it, Grandma?"

"Some I don't recognize."

Jessie caught sight of Helen and talked faster. "Somebody here. One of them."

"Give me the phone, Grandma."

Jessie winked up guiltily at her granddaughter and made helpless flaps with her free hand, but her teeth continued to click dramatic syllables out over the airwaves. "Is there something you folks can do?"

The sensitive teenage girl reached for the phone. "Get off the phone."

Jessie turned sideways and curled up. She pressed the receiver against her thin chest and went on whispering. "May not be able to talk much longer."

"Who are you talking to Grandma?"

"Yes, yes, somebody here. Some girl."

Jessie had an intense look on her face. She was at a command post on the front lines. She'd dialed the phone, hoping she got the numbers right and they'd phoned her right back as promised.

Helen reached for the phone again but Jessie curled still further away.

"Hang up Grandma."

Jessie was listening intently while someone, somewhere talked to her.

"GET OFF THE PHONE!"

Jessie jumped with shock. The invisible someone somewhere must have faltered too because she straightened up and her voice firmed.

"No, go on. I'm listening. It's all right."

Helen knelt on the sofa, leaned over and grabbed the phone. Without another word, Jessie yielded. Helen heard the dial tone. Jessie looked at her.

"And who are you to speak to me that way?"

"I'm Helen."

"Huh." Jessie sniffed. "And what's that supposed to mean?"

"I'm your granddaughter."

"I'm supposed to know you am I?"

"I slept in your room last night." Jessie stiffened. She remembered all right – the thief girl.

"I called the police. Told them you stole my money."

"It wasn't me that took your money. Talk to Mother."

"I suppose you're taking me someplace."

"We're going to the park, Grandma."

"And who is going to church? Anybody?"

"It's the fourth of July. We're not going to church."

"I am."

"No you're not. You can't. We're going to the park."

Jessie stiffened with outrage. Everything dangerous was closing in on her.

"And who are you to tell me what I can and cannot do?"

Jessie stood up. Nobody went to church anymore. Well she did. She scrunched out of the room, ignoring the thief girl.

Helen leaned back on the sofa. It was turning out to be a very tiresome day.

The beautiful movie star lay weeping exhausted by her tragic experiences. She was wearing a skin-tight red satin dress. Let me take you away, he murmured and ran long lips up and down her sleek arms, nibbling delicately on her pale aristocratic ears.

Helen thought about lips. Ernest Haycox was always writing about men with long lips. What exactly were long lips? They're obviously nobler than cruel lips or fat lips.

How many kinds of lips are there? She'd never noticed. Actually nobody else wrote about lips much. Rosebud lips. That sounds corny. Pinched lips – those are the kind the mathematics teacher has. Haggard lips. No eyes have to be haggard.

She lay on her back, hands behind her head, staring at the ceiling. She ought to have a bedroom as big as this room. She got the worst of everything.

How about pancake lips? Sausage lips, prickly lips? Soft velvety lips.

Your lips are so soft and velvety he said nippingly in her ear. He felt like a rabbit. The black rabbit liked to nip your fingers. She was feeding him carrots.

Sometimes she almost heard their voices in her ear, those handsome men that someday would chase her around, buy her diamonds, and wade through alligators to rescue her. She could hardly wait. Life's an adventure – both her parents had said that. 'Crimson Sails,' the book Carol loaned her said the best adventures women had were with men. That was scary – especially after her experience with Norbett.

She really should tell someone what had happened.

Sitting up she saw her father go into the kitchen and wash his hands at the sink. His face was calm, long lips set in a pleasant line. Daddy has long lips, she thought with pleasure. Turning she saw out the dining room window that Eddie was talking to a man at the back door of Mrs. Blunt's house.

"Yes," Eddie said to Ned, "Yes. I can do it. Next week."

Jessie went into her room to collect her hat. These people were all talking nonsense. She took down the hatbox with the bucking bronco on it, the one that Amsden had brought his Stetson back in. He'd been proud of that hat. She took her summer white straw hat out and put it on. When she looked in the mirror she saw her hair was brown and long, combed up over combs to give her thin face some body. She didn't need makeup–that color in her cheeks was her own. What would happen if one day you stopped tugging on sleeves and calling out instructions? Stopped opening doors and watching people's faces? It took some thinking about. It's all very well you telling me you love me, Amsden, but now you have to let me talk. Surely to goodness now that you're dead you can stand a few complications.

Dana brought his cup to the kitchen table by the window. He looked out at the back yard. In the driveway a newly waxed blue Ford gleamed in the morning sunlight as though under enchantment. At the bottom of the garden a tall hedge blocked the neighbor's yard, a green wall against the world.

Best not to mention the smell of burning, he thought.

He looked around the kitchen. This is home. No matter how far I go, where I stay, this place, the long windows looking out over the yard, all this is still my home. The first time I came into this room, back when I was courting Corky, I knew that.

Without speaking, Corky picked up the coffeepot from beside the stove and poured him the last of the coffee. Dana looks nice, she thought, in that old white dress shirt and long pants. I'd almost forgotten how handsome he is. He's too handsome almost, those blue eyes and black hair, that Irish smile.

Dana took a sip of coffee. "She's up the road. Your mother."

Corky whirled around at the stove. "Oh no!"

"Just two or three houses. I saw her from upstairs."

"Mother again." Corky said, "that's all we need."

"That happen often?" Bernice was wrapping chicken thighs with immaculate precision. They all three spoke in quiet voices, the sudden setting up of a private bubble that immediately commanded Helen's attention. She went to the doorway.

"Once and awhile." Corky said tersely. "Someone should go after her."

"Want a piece of chicken, Dana?" Bernice held up a chicken thigh not yet wrapped.

"No thanks."

Bernice wrapped up the thigh and put it into the red tin. She closed the lid. She washed her hands at the sink and reached for the tea-towel. Corky at once came and leaning down brought up another towel from under the sink.

"Use this one, will you dear?"

Bernice flushed, hesitated, wiped her hands on the towel, put it back under the sink, picked up a loaf of bread and some butter and began laying out slices of bread in a row like a deck of cards. Corky abandoned the remaining chicken and came over to sit across from Dana.

"Is she stirred up?" he asked, "Your mother?"

"Probably." Corky said.

"She doesn't know anything about anything anymore." Bernice scoffed.

She sliced cheddar cheese and laid out the slices symmetrically on the neat row of white bread slices she'd buttered. I like doing this, the cheerful aunt thought, then I can eat the sandwiches and not worry what's in them.

"Who knows what she knows, I don't." Corky was back at the stove and appeared to be addressing the pieces of chicken waiting in the frying pan.

What does she mean by that? thought Dana.

"Is it safe to let her go off on her own?" Bernice asked. She took out slices of bologna and placed one slice on each piece of bread.

I'm helping here, she thought. I'm too old to chase Mother.

I'm making too much chicken, Corky thought. I hope we eat it all. And why doesn't someone else chase Mother down? I'm too tired to even try.

Dana thought I want to be alone for at least a week. I need time to think. Why is it so difficult to find a time and a place to think?

"I suppose I could go." he said; but added "Any more coffee in the pot?"

"She's trying to get to church." Corky said in a tight voice.

Bernice took out a package of cigarettes from her dress pocket and leaned over to offer Dana one.

He shook his head sadly "I've quit."

"Really?" One of Bernice's rather bushy eyebrows went up. "How long?"

"Over a month now."

"Good for you. Brave. I couldn't." Bernice lit a cigarette and blew a thick cloud of smoke out. "Somebody told me about some people who never did find a place out in Denver. Six months they were looking." Bernice took an emphatic suck of cigarette. "They slept in their car half the time."

Helen couldn't help it. She had to come into the kitchen and find out what they were talking about.

"How far is the church?" Dana didn't move.

"Five or six blocks." Corky threw in tablespoon after tablespoon of coffee.

"She's an old woman. "Bernice said with conviction." I doubt she makes it."

Corky opened her mouth to argue and decided against it. Let his sister think that.

Dana looked over at his daughter, smiled that charming Irish smile. "Helen, you go after your grandmother. She's down the street."

"Why me? Why not Eddie?"

"Because you're here and he's not. Now go on. Quick."

"She's on her way to church." Corky said.

"I already know that."

"Well hurry up then. It's almost eleven."

"This is so stupid." The sensitive teenage girl muttered as she went out the backdoor. Dana watched her slow down and walk very slowly away from the house.

I wonder if it's worth going out there with her, he thought but knew that, just like Corky, he was tired. It was going to be a long day. And so instead, he sat, and thought, and drank coffee, ate a cheese and bologna sandwich, and watched the two women fight.

Eleven

Myrna Henderson and her daughter came out of the apartment house across the street, and got into an old black Buick driven by a somber faced young woman. The two women kissed and right away started talking about Joe. In the back seat, the little girl Suzette, who was given that name by Joe in a letter, looked out the window with great excitement. A ride in a car was a rare treat. They drove away, up Nicollet Avenue.

Helen walked the length of the Miller fence. The back yard was like a desert – sharp shadows cut by an unkind sun, ferocious heat beating down. She went to stand under the big elm in the center of the yard. What if there was no water? They lay in the shadow of the plane; the man was whimpering in pain. Be brave – the woman tried to smile through cracked lips – we are all paper cut-outs in the hands of fate. The man coughed up more blood. It was getting pretty messy.

Helen's friend Carol had seen the movie and said it was really something.

They both had that funny kind of riding pants on and were lying in the wreckage of their plane; they were still in shock when they were captured and the Arab guy chose the girl aviator for his harem. The servant types – eunuchs they called them – explained how she was supposed to act humble. She had to walk in with her head bowed and arms crossed over her breasts but the girl aviator refused. She went in head back, eyes blazing. The sheik was impressed. He could see she was different. For one thing she was tall. But the rich playboy was no help. He had a mustache and was a weakling.

At the bottom of the Miller yard six foot tall sunflowers turned their mocking yellow faces outward at her. I hate you, she thought, using mental telepathy to strike them dead. She'd read about it. But you had to train your mind to do it right or you might get into trouble.

She walked over to the small trailer. It had been parked near the house in the summer as long as she could remember. When Grandpa was alive he and Grandma had gone to Florida in it every winter.

She tried the door and found it open. It was supposed to be locked. She leaned into its dimness. It was a little house inside with chairs and a table and a sink, even a lamp and a bed; when she was little she and her friends were allowed to play house in it, but only very carefully. Even then it had smelled old and musty.

A small folded up piece of paper lay on the cracked linoleum floor by the door. Picking it up she worried it open. 'I must see you again.' The handwriting was dramatic; the ink, blue. 'Why haven't you called? I love you desperately.'

Desperately was underlined three times.

She slipped the paper into her pocket. She could be a spy like Mata Hari carrying important secret messages.

Oh, it's only a love letter, the spy said, airily, tossing her gorgeous mane of red-auburn tresses.

Tresses is a great word.

They would torture her of course.

She closed the trailer door, went around the house, started up the street.

"All I'm pointing out is that there's no guarantee that you will find a house and there's no guarantee Mother will like being there." Bernice was puffing out smoke with every long breath.

"It can't be that bad." Corky looked at her husband. He said nothing.

What's to say? he thought Bernice is right. It is rough. He'd been in Denver for six months and there weren't many houses to rent after the war.

"You could run out of money." Bernice continued.

"We've got money enough for six months." Corky came over to stand beside Dana. She touched his shoulder. But only if I decide to go, she thought.

"G.I's coming out drive the prices up. First thing they do is get married."

Bernice thought, do I have to tell them everything? Why doesn't Dana say this?

Dana patted his wife's hand. "Your mother Corky. I'd better take the car out."

Corky started, looked at the clock, Good god, quarter to eleven. "We'll never catch her. She's probably going inside right now."

"Maybe Helen stopped her."

"Somehow I doubt that." Bernice stubbing out her cigarette in a saucer so annoyed Corky she came over and snatched it away from her sister.

"What does it matter anyway?" Bernice said." Let her go to church."

"You have no idea what you're talking about, Bernice. She makes trouble."

"Oh? And you want me to take care of her? That's great. I never ever could handle mother you know that and now you're putting pressure on me to quit my job and stay here with her. That's a recipe for disaster."

Bernice marched out of the room.

"I did not tell her to quit her job. Did I Dana?"

Outside the long windows, the world had warmed. The sun was high, parting the trees with energy. Flowers had straightened, grown serious. Insects hummed, buzzed, established beachheads. It was full day on earth, life a nectar under a blue bowl sky.

Eddie came into the kitchen. "I've got a job," he said. "Next door – Mrs. Blunt's brother wants someone to clean up her yard. I said I'd do it."

"Take the car, Eddie."

"Why Dad?"

"Your Grandma's trying to get to church again," said his mother. "Oh Christ."

"Watch your language," Dana said sharply. "And do what your mother asks. Helen's already up the street looking for her."

"Wish me luck."

Eddie went out. Dana followed him, stood by the back door, watched Eddie assault the car with heavy hands and feet. His father went over to the driver's window.

"Watch how you drive this baby."

"Sure. What'd you think about the job?"

Dana waved a casual hand, "Sounds O.K. We'll talk about it later."

Eddie drove the car out of the driveway and onto 35th street with compassion until he got to the corner of Nicollet Avenue and 35th Street. Then despite the total lack of traffic on Nicollet, he gunned the Ford's motor and raced across it at high speed.

Back in the kitchen Dana went over, put his arms around his wife who was worrying the chicken again. She didn't turn around, but leaned against him so that both their bodies hollered: Yes yes, but then their minds said: No time, too complicated, I have to have the truth, and all these people around here will bother us. Dana stood back.

"I've got a motel lined up. That's something anyway."

"A motel for six months? What about your basement apartment? Could we live there?" There was a silence that went on.

Dana shifted further away from his wife, went to the back door.

"And I've got a couple of friends keeping an eye out for houses." He said in a stiff voice. "Houses come on the market and you've got to catch one right away."

"What friends?" Corky asked in an equally stiff voice. She put the remaining cooked chicken out on a plate. "If mother's in church, we won't get away until noon."

"Let's collect what we need." Dana said, "We need blankets. We may have to sit on the ground. Can your mother sit on the ground?"

"How will we pay for a motel for six months?" Corky didn't look at Dana.

Jessie was happy walking but her feet hurt. She was wearing her white Sunday shoes but they seemed too small. Looking up and down for traffic, she waited a long time at the curb on Nicollet Ave because there wasn't any.

Amsden there's so much I need to tell you so I can die in peace. I want to die shriven like medieval folks. Confessing my sins so I can go to heaven.

I don't know if you have time to forgive me but God does. And I'll forgive you in case they've shown you something up there you ought to regret."

"Is there an up?"

Jessie's spark was bright, as small and bright as a star.

Helen saw Jessie well ahead, a small figure hurrying along. She began to run.

But she was angry. Why was she out here conspicuously behaving in such a stupid way?

She thought, the thing that worries me most about my life is that all I know are boring women, women without any sense of adventure. I'm surrounded by mundane people, practically suffocated by them. How can I escape this awful fate? I want an interesting life. Like the dragon lady.

Then she remembered the note. She felt in the pocket of her red shorts – yes it was still there. She stopped walking, took the note out, read it again. Desperately sounded pretty desperate. It's probably for Eddie, she thought, girls call him up all the time now. Well it isn't mundane exactly, more like a mystery, a Nancy Drew mystery.

I won't tell Eddie I've got it anyway.

She looked up and saw Grandma crossing Nicollet Avenue.

The closer I get to death the less I want to know. It seems to me I ought to die empty of the hardship of knowledge.

I hate Nancy Drew.

Bernice came downstairs wearing not only the turquoise and white flowered dress and white pumps, but also a white beaded necklace and a large straw hat.

"I'll go for my walk now," she said.

"Fine." Corky was reading the newspaper. She was sitting on the front porch in one of the old rocking chairs.

Bernice went down the front steps and set out to walk around the block.

"I haven't done this in years," she marveled as she turned the corner onto Blazedale Avenue. It was a one way street designed to funnel rush hour traffic away from the city center and Bernice remembered the warnings of childhood – Don't go past Blazedale. Don't play near Blazedale. Don't ride your bike on Blazedale.

Blazedale has killer instincts, she thought with amusement, but in fact she'd rarely walked down the street, or driven on it, nor could she remember anyone choosing to do that. In fact its row of stern screened two story houses still looked indifferent to the fate of anyone who lingered, who didn't hurry somewhere else.

I never did like this neighborhood, Bernice thought with satisfaction. Despite the grandeur of the front porches, she thought the tightly trimmed trees and lack of gardens and flowers made the houses look like they'd just had their hair cut by an opinionated barber. She was enjoying her own crazy opinions when she saw someone she recognized. There, in a back yard, a fat man bending over. She stopped short, her breath caught. That's Clarence Taylor. A flash of anger shot through Bernice. A hot stabbing anger that made her eyes hurt.

The bastard. He's still alive the bastard.

TWELVE

Sitting on her front porch, reading the Saturday paper, Corky heard the R& B, the jazz, the boogie music coming from Mrs. Blunt's porch. Sometimes Mrs. Blunt played jazz records at night sitting on her porch alone, and Corky would creep out and listen because that music made Corky feel alive, made her remember Chicago and New York, her adventures as a tutor to those vaudeville children.

Nobody knew just how much Corky liked that music or that she'd visited some of the clubs on 52nd street in New York, and on the south side of Chicago, had drunk bootleg gin and listened to the black musicians.

Corky was afraid to tell her secrets. Once out they became someone else's property, became their story too but with a different judgement on the facts. Her kids kept asking her about her vaudeville year but she didn't want to tell them anything about it.

Next door, Ned sat with his sister on her porch. He'd brought a new record – 'Shortnin Bread.' They liked to sit together on the Fourth of July and think of Jimmy though they didn't talk about him. Jimmy had liked Rhythm and Blues and Jazz, all that country music so playing it on the Fourth of July was their way of remembering him.

'Put on the skillet, put on the lead, Mama's gonna make a little shortnin bread. That ain't all she gonna do, mama's gonna make a little coffee too.'

Mrs. Blunt sipped at her whiskey and tapped her toes. Thought how those fellows that made that music were lost angels. Jimmy had said that. Not fallen angels he said – though some of them fell – but lost, lost because they were dropped from heaven into a place that didn't love or respect them nearly enough, but being angels they gave of what they were anyway, gave to everybody their music, their joy and creation, their harmony and hope when people were a mess of anger, hate and hurt.

I need more whiskey or none at all, Mrs. Blunt thought, I'm thinking funny today.

"How's your wife?" she asked Ned.

"She won't talk to me. But the kid's coming along."

Jessie paused at the next corner while a car full of Sunday hats turned left.

"What do you think you're doing?"

Jessie looked around. She'd been followed.

"You're not supposed to cross Nicollet Avenue."

The thief girl. The one with the big ideas. Too much fat leg showing.

Helen took hold of Jessie's arm. Her grandma looked at her with hornet eyes and thought, that girl should comb that hair of hers. She looks like a fussed up hen.

The sensitive teenage girl tightened her hold. "You're not supposed to go to church," she said.

"Let go of me." The who-are-you-to-talk-to-me-that-way old lady yanked her arm away and marched across the next avenue, body jiggling lightly as though she were hanging on an invisible clothesline. The sensitive teenage girl ran to catch up – and grab her bony shoulders.

An elderly black Studebaker turned the corner and slowed to a crawl; the people in it turned around to goggle out the back window. Violence in the streets! On a Sunday morning! Was there something they should do?

Please God, the girl prayed, don't let Grandma act too dramatic. Jessie pulled herself away with conspicuous disdain and moved up the street as fast as she could. The Studebaker full of hats drove around the block and came along side the poor old lady under attack, the people inside were keeping an eye on what was going on out there.

Helen stopped and let Jessie walk away. Grandma has a funny way of walking on the edges of her feet, she thought, she looks like one of those fast moving water bugs on Lake Calhoun. Jessie crossed the next intersection. When she was safely a block away the Studebaker full of hats turned left and vanished.

Helen ran hard, caught up with her, this time stood in front of her on the sidewalk.

"You're supposed to come home."

Jessie walked around her. Drat girl.

"They said you should come home."

"Who said?"

Helen thought for a moment. Grandma had her known favorites. "Dana."

"Dana?" Jessie stopped.

"He sent me to get you."

"What for?"

"We're going for a ride. To Minnewana Park."

"Minnewana Park."

"Yes."

"We go there all the time."

"Yes." Helen looked around. They were standing on the sidewalk of a street she didn't know very well. Trees here were pinched, oddly shaped, various sizes. The houses were different too, mostly one story old houses, houses with fronts of pink concrete and back yards with mustard yellow garages.

"I'd like to go to Minnewana Park." Jessie said, squinting up at this tall busy-headed girl. Rose Corinne's daughter. She turned and looked up toward the church.

In that direction another street of low snoopy-looking houses stretched away into the distance. She let Helen take her arm and they walked together back to Nicollet Avenue.

"Who's going on this picnic?"

"Mother, Daddy, Eddie, me, Aunt Bernice."

"Lily Bernice?" Jessie snorted and life surged into her pinprick eyes.

Just as they reached Nicollet Avenue a streetcar appeared in the distance, moving up its track toward them with certainty, with a promise never ever to leave its tracks.

"I'm not going anywhere with Lily Bernice."

The sensitive teenage girl had some sympathy for this point of view.

"It is supposed to be a family picnic, Grandma."

The streetcar passed them, its domestic clatter at odds with an animal appearance, then it was gone, leaving Nicollet as wide as the Missouri again.

Still they stood side by side on the curb. The girl stared down at her grandma.

What a funny old face she has, everything about her squashed and eccentric looking. The old woman gazed up at the odd stalk of a beanpole girl.

Likely not a brain pod in her.

Behind them church bells rang out and Jessie's face darkened.

Myrna Henderson and her sister-in-law Gloria sat in Gloria's back garden, enjoying the daughter Joe never got to watch grow up play with Gloria's small dog, Butch. "I wish we had a garden." Myrna said. "Then Suzette could have a dog."

"Let's pray for a garden," said the sister-in-law who was religious.

This neighborhood hasn't changed much, Amsden. The faces have though. Everyone interesting is dead.

Here's where the garage burned down. Remember? A sharp anguish on the horizon – we all ran down from the church to watch the tongues of fire. They lost a Cadillac in that one. Made you start reading the Bible again. That was after Violet left.

By the way somebody's taken all my money. Nothing in my purse.

Those years when I was alone in Deep River with the girls and you were up here making money, I wrote you when I needed some but you didn't send much. Too busy making it. You were mean with money Amsden. Take any with you? Remember that bet we made who'd live the longest? You owe me fifty dollars.

Why did you tell me in that dream I had to get on or get off?

Living without you ain't that easy, Amsden.

Every day I'm putting on clothes and taking them off, putting on dresses and taking them off, as long as I live I've been doing that. Only some are packed away now, like all those shirts you died and left down in the basement – never out of the boxes most of them. My thoughts are like that now too. I take them out, look at them, sometimes wear one for awhile, then put them away again, but some have been in boxes down in the basement so long I hardly recognize them. Before I die I want to take them all out and look at every last one, then throw them away.

I want to die without clothes and without thoughts.

First I'm going to church though. I like that fine feeling you get after the hymn-singing. Goes to your head.

My I feel strong. My feet are warm and thoughts are bursting up in me.

And where was Violet Marie in all this? Like the black rabbit, she was wandering through the back gardens enjoying herself. Like almost all recently dead people she was more interested in re-acquainting herself with the world of trees, flowers, sun and sky, than she was in examining her own faults. She liked the sentinel trees, just as she had as a child; leaning back she looked up and through them and thought as she had as a child that it was like looking down into an underwater world from a glass bottomed boat, the depths full of mysterious promises. But so was hearing other peoples' thoughts – that was something new. And surprising.

Violet's spark was a sharp golden thistle.

THIRTEEN

At that moment Dana was sitting in the open garage out of the sun. A scattering of tools lay on a newspaper stretched out on the ground; three blankets hung out on the clothesline in the sun, and a green short wave radio sat on a box in front of him. He'd tuned into a station in Winnipeg; the song they were playing was 'Faraway Places.' When the faint music stopped and an announcer came on to give Canadian news, Dana thought – Forget Canada I wish I could. He twiddled the dials until he found another station with music. The reception's better he said to himself. The radio was his, one of his first purchases after he'd left university. He'd wanted to see the world then.

I probably never will now, he thought, but somehow he didn't mind, though he knew he still had the Irish wanderlust that had driven his dad out to the bars every night. Whenever he thought of Canada, Dana remembered the helpless anger he'd felt as a young boy watching his mother's face, the confusion that came when he saw her glance with tenderness at his big burly stupidly drunken dad breaking dishes and singing about love. What's love? he'd thought as a boy. Is love letting your family starve? His dad hadn't been a violent or cruel drunk only an irresponsible one. All Dana could remember of his boyhood was the cold, being hungry, selling newspapers on corners, dragging his dad out of bars. We were cold and hungry too often, he thought, without food or coal because Dad went to the bars before he got home with his paycheck. As a boy he was shamed by his dad and shamed too because his mother seemed powerless to change their life. She always took Dad back, Dana thought, she was so free with forgiveness.

Mattie has the same look as Mother when she talks about her husband.

He turned the swing music up. 'Once in Love with Amy, Always in Love with Amy.' I wouldn't mind taking Corky dancing he thought. We used to do that – go dancing. She's a good dancer. He couldn't imagine Mattie dancing. And I never saw my mother dance. But maybe she did when she was young and carefree. I hope so. Dad never took her out anywhere – too damn selfish. He never apologized either even when he lost a good job because of a binge. Is that why he did it? So he didn't have to work?

After his mother died Dana had made a few more attempts to help his father for her sake; he'd picked his dad up at the drunk tank, taken him to his room in St. Paul. Then one Fourth of July his dad had come over to 35th St. late at night. He was drunk and pounding a broken one-sided bass drum. Eddie and Helen had thought it funny, but Amsden and Jessie, teetotalers their entire lives, were shocked and Dana was furious.

He told his dad to stay away and he stopped sending him money.

I haven't seen him for a couple of years, Dana thought. His cousin had told him his dad still got drunk, still fell in the gutter. If I stay here I'll never get away from him.

It had been a shock to Dana – the Denver apartment. He almost didn't take it, he'd been so struck by its similarity to his past, a past he never talked about even with his own kids. The one big room held a table and chairs, a bed, two pictures of mountain scenes – one like the one in his mother's bedroom-, an old green sofa that made up into a bed like the one he'd slept on as a boy, – the davenport his mother had called it-, and an old desk where he stuffed letters from Corky and the kids. It too was one like he'd had as a boy.

Now Corky was hinting the whole family could stay there. Never!

There was a deep well of anger and shame in Dana. He knew that. One that had been with him a long time. By the age of sixteen he'd recognized the easy contempt other people showed his family; in Winnipeg they were just one more poor family dependent upon an Irish drunk. At last one cold March angry after helping his drunken father lying in the road in front of his own high school, he took his mother and sister away to St. Paul without leaving a forwarding address. His father didn't find them for nearly a year; friends kept a conspiracy of silence.

He'd made a few attempts to help his father after his mother died, he picked his dad up in the drunk tank and took him to his room in St. Paul. Then one Fourth of July his dad had come over to 35th St. late at night. He was drunk and pounding a broken one-sided bass drum. Eddie and Helen had thought it amusing, but Amsden and Jessie, teetotalers their entire lives, were shocked and Dana was furious. He told his dad to stay away and he stopped sending him money.

The sun was touching him, he could feel heat on his brow. He thought, the most important thing is I don't have a job here. Too many men are back from service in Minneapolis. There are more jobs in Denver. The weather's better too. The far away music on the short wave radio wove itself into the warm air as Dana sat listening, churned up inside. And what about Jessie? Will we have to leave Jessie in a nursing home? We can't do that. No, somehow we'll take her. That's one thing I'm certain of – I won't leave Jessie behind. The song floating out and into him now was 'You're Getting to Be a Habit With Me.' Mattie's slow smile – a smile like his mother's – so rare and delightful he'd tried to coax it out of her just as he had sought his mother's as a boy.

Coming up the sidewalk Bernice saw that Corky still sitting on the front porch reading. She slowed down. Shall I go around back? I'd just as soon avoid trouble. Dana's probably back there and he doesn't seem to be in the best of moods. Bernice liked her brother-in-law but she had to admit he was a moody man. Not like Sam. Sam was a talker, a laugher – one of the things she'd liked best about him was that he was cheerful or he had been.

Maybe he isn't right now, she thought. Last night – calling Sam – that was a mistake. I don't want him to know that I know. But right then- that morning- she wanted to talk to him because he was the one person she could tell that she'd seen Clarence Taylor still alive, still fat, still a bastard. I can't think of anybody else who would understand, she thought. She'd told Sam what Clarence Taylor had done to Violet Marie and Lily Bernice, two innocent little girls. Not innocent anymore, Bernice thought.

Violet Marie the dead sister who had heard all this didn't agree.

She'd joined her sisters on the front porch as she had so often as a child when alive. Then she'd felt like the bad little girl in a good little family but now that she was dead she felt very innocent indeed. You learn so much more once you're dead she thought. You learn you didn't have as much control over things and people as you thought, there being so much gauze between yourself and the truth, so little clarity and so much confusion. Why, thought Violet Marie, none of us half notice how beautiful the world is, how people's souls or lack of them can be seen in their eyes, how pure dogs were whatever their personalities, and the way life floats in the air all around people.

Meanwhile, Bernice decided, Certainly, I should go up the front steps and face Corky. What's the matter with me? We all want to do the right thing today. Putting mother in a nursing home is not appealing, but it's not impossible either and if Corky wants to discuss, well then let's discuss. A nursing home could be a temporary solution until they get settled out there. But she dithered on the front walk, stood looking up that long long street past Blazedale where their old school was. As a girl she'd liked walking to school. carrying school bags full of possessions. I should have gone in that direction this morning. Still, she thought, what I really want to do is to go upstairs, pack my bags and leave, even if there is only one bus to Duluth on Sunday.

It was a tempting idea.

But so is the fact that Sam's only a few miles away, she thought, if I came down and took care of Mother here I could see him. He could come over to the house. Mother goes to bed very early and wouldn't hear a thing. She wouldn't even notice.

It would work!

The very thought made her sick to her stomach. With excitement, with wanting, with fear of herself. Quit a good job? She might get another with her accounting experience, then again she might not. But to live at home, cheek to jowl with her mother!

Bernice started up the front walk. Corky didn't move, didn't even look up. Lucky little Rose Corinne and her charmed life, Bernice thought, She's ended up with everything hasn't she? Rocking in her easy chair. Then Bernice felt ashamed. Where is that nasty voice coming from? she wondered, ever since I found out about Violet's death that voice comes more and more.

She went up the front stairs, opened the screen door, stepped into the porch.

There was always the same smell of old papers and mold. Bernice detested that smell. Corky was sitting in a rocking chair tearing a strip out of the newspaper.

She looked up, "What was that baby's name, Bernice?"

Bernice sat down in the rocking chair beside her. "What baby?"

"The one born before me."

"Haven't a clue." Bernice took out her cigarettes.

They'd rocked these chairs right over as children, Bernice and Violet, frightening themselves silly, once even breaking open Bernice's head. But lucky little Rose Corinne never got hurt. Never got into trouble because she wouldn't think of rocking too hard in a rocking chair. Violet is the one who got into trouble. Sam claimed it was all Violet's fault. And most of the time you could believe Sam. He wasn't exactly a liar. O shut up, Bernice told herself, leave it alone. Sam didn't exactly tell the truth either.

Bethany Baptist was a humble church of red-orange brick. There were no stained glass windows to sanctify it, no towering spires to alert passersby. It lacked lush green lawns and official looking parking lots and had never succumbed to a playground. One wooden sign, planted slightly askew and dangerously close to the sidewalk, detailed the sermon of the week and various church officials. Several small commemorative plaques were inserted rather like gold fillings into the bricks around the front doors.

Over the years in keeping with its neighborhood, Bethany had become more eccentric looking. Several building campaigns had been abandoned in mid-stream and the church still sustained their makeshift constructions. Scaffolding pressing up against the building in several places looked designed to keep the church from moving in an unguarded moment toward either heavenly reparation and hallelujah repairs, or decay and final judgment.

That brilliant morning, by then advancing toward high noon, an immaculate blue 47 Ford sat in the no parking zone directly in front of the church. The motor was idling, its sound raspy and ill-tempered; the young man behind the wheel wasn't smiling either. Though he didn't appear to notice the old woman staggering past the car, nor the desperate looking young person following her, he did look over when the two engaged in hand-to-hand combat.

I wonder if I should honk, Eddie thought, watching Jessie beat off the teenage girl twice her size. He resisted this awful thought since church service had already started; he knew that from the stout sounds of the first hymn coming from within. He also recognized the yattering sound of the dialogue between the two combatants nearby – though it was brief. Eddie watched Jessie walk up the front walk, clearly intending to pry open one of Bethany Baptist's heavy front doors. He saw his sister follow her grandmother, saw her spread a red shorts and white peasant blouse clad body across those doors to secure the entrance. Jessie retreated down the sidewalk and stood hands on hips, glaring at her granddaughter. Helen stayed spread-eagled just in case.

All those people inside praying for peace while these two goofs are doing that, Eddie marveled, slumping down behind the wheel to avoid detection. He reached over to turn on the radio and therefore missed the moment when Jessie fell down. But when he straightened and saw her lying crumpled before her beloved church, a sad little misshapen heap, he knew he was in trouble. If Grandma were hurt, he'd catch some of the blame. He turned off the radio that by that time had clamped onto a sermon somewhere.

He leaned out and thumped on the side of the Ford. Helen looked over. She waved and then bent down to help Jessie up on her feet. After she brushed off the back of the old woman's shocking pink Sunday suit from the pre-teen department, Helen came over to Eddie. He scowled, "What ARE you doing?"

"She won't cooperate."

"What'd you do, push her over?"

"I didn't touch her."

From inside came the roar of a hymn of battle, all organ throttles out.

Eddie roared the Ford's motor in response and leaned over to open the door on the passenger side. "Get in."

"I can't leave her here."

"Did I say you should? Go get her. I'm supposed to drive you home."

"She won't come."

"Get her over here."

There was a grand swelling of organ sound, Eddie and Helen looked over at the same time and saw Bethany Baptist's great heavy doors had been opened. Perhaps by God, but certainly by Jessie who disappeared inside.

Helen heard birds singing in the apple tree beside the church. They sound happy, she thought. I wish I had a stone I could throw at them.

FOURTEEN

Mr. and Mrs. Miller were riding around with their daughter Karin Mr. Miller suggested they visit his parents' grave. His daughter agreed; there was no grave for her warrior son, his body had never been found, and they sometimes did that on the Fourth of July. Mrs. Miller stayed in the car while Mr. Miller and his daughter threaded their way around gravestones and trees and dead flowers in vases. The graveyard seemed to Mr. Miller an orderly place.

Then Mr. Miller stumbled going over rough ground and fell and was surprised for he was usually steady on his feet and he lay there a moment and a wave of bad feeling swept over him and he thought, does this mean I'm going soon? Is that what falling down in a graveyard means? Karin his daughter who had no sense of humor came over and said, Get up Dad you can't lie around in a cemetery; the dead don't like it.

When they got back to the car, Mrs. Miller was gone.

As they walked around looking for her, he saw a different kind of order: the uneven ground that had caused him to fall and the busyness of the high clouds; saw graves sinking into the earth, tree roots savaging gravestones, rabbits and ground squirrels prying out secrets with their holes, a wind rising and blowing blossoms apart, and crows and magpies and robins and owls spreading their wings on journeys having nothing to do with yesterday, only with NOW.

They found Mrs. Miller, or Mother as Mr. Miller called her, sitting on a gravestone looking lost. She also looked large and untidy and somewhat insane.

She got up when they told her to although she didn't know who they were just then.

She is lost, Mrs. Miller thought, I have lost her. Maybe my daughter's right.

Bernice took off her big straw hat. She was still thinking about Violet. How in school she'd been so boy crazy she'd shocked the rest of the kids. Even the way she moved – like something abandoned lay inside her. She scared most of the boys right out of their pants. Bernice chuckled to herself as she watched Corky tearing up last night's paper. Then she thought, well really I haven't even had a chance to look at that paper.

"So you don't remember, Bernice?" Corky asked.

"A silly idea – giving us flower names – Rose Corinne, Violet Marie, Lily Bernice and …yes I've forgotten the dead baby's name too."

"Do you think Mother remembers?"

"I doubt it. Why do you want to know?"

"Oh just something in the paper." Corky shoved the piece into her apron pocket. She got up to go into the house but then stopped and hovered in front of Bernice which forced her sister who hated looking up at anyone to stand up too.

"I'd say you two are in trouble – this wild jaunt to Denver," Bernice said.

"We'll find a place."

"I've moved five times. Believe me – a motel is a motel is a motel."

"I think you said that."

Church and palm fans whiffing the air. The rich smell of the bouquet of flowers on the table in the vestry. Oh Jessie did love those first moments standing at the back of the church. She loved to be late, to stagger down the aisle to the front rows under the eyes of the minister standing tall in the pulpit above them all, past the row after row of good seeking ever more good, some smelling of light perfumes and shaving soap and hair oil and even tobacco. If she came in late everyone would know she was there, still alive, and present and accountable before God in a public place.

Hallelujah!

Jessie walked down the aisle. She and Amsden had been married in this church. Oh it had changed, but it was the same too. She stopped by the third pew on the right hand side. That was their pew, their family and this morning only a stout couple in black sat there, and glancing over saw her, and almost frightened looking, slid sideways so she had a small narrow spot right by the aisle. Jessie gave a little sigh of satisfaction.

I'm here. Thank you God. Hallelujah.

Music began rumbling out and the choir rose. The smell of the flowers on the table below them rose too – gladiolas and roses and chrysanthemums and daisies were their own anthem. Then the voice of the preacher thundered out like a crack opening in a wall. And everybody around Jessie began dozing off. But not Jessie. A little hum of pleasure rose up in her.

There isn't anything like church to settle a body down more, she thought, I'm glad I'm here. The church looks fine. Everything bright and joyful. Everyone dressed in white and pink and yellow. Pretty dresses. I had so many.

You bought me pretty dresses, Amsden, you wanted me to wear them.

Then Jessie remembered her dream. When you said for me get on or get off, Amsden, I said not yet. Said got to finish what I started. And you looked at me – that half-crabby sweetheart way of yours and said, What's so important you have to finish?

I don't think I know yet. Dreams and real life are mixing together now.

I suspect it's this long conversation with you, my dearest old husband. And with something to do with the family. Have you forgiven Violet?

Outside Bethany Baptist, a brother and sister sat in a beautiful blue 47 Ford pursuing cooperation.

"Go get her I said." Eddie revved the Ford's motor viciously. "If she finds a place to plunk down in there we've had it."

"Go inside?"

"Yes." Eddie leaned over and opened Helen's door again.

"I can't."

"Yes you can."

"I'm afraid."

"Get in there before she sits down." Eddie's voice was hoarse.

"I can't go in there and drag her out."

"Say she's having an attack."

"Of what?" Helen got out but then leaned back into the car. "Go with me, Eddie."

"No."

"People will look at me."

"So?" He gunned the mother again. "O.K, I'm leaving you here." He reached over, slammed the passenger door and started to pull slowly away from the curb.

Helen jumped back. "NO EDDIE!"

"You're wasting time."

"It's not fair, Eddie. Why is it always me?"

"Get away from the car." Eddie gunned the Ford so hard its beautiful blue fenders trembled.

"What if she falls down again?"

"You've got five minutes."

As a family the McFaddens hadn't gone to Bethany Baptist. It was Grandpa and Grandma Fallsworth's church. Dana's Irish birthright had taken the McFaddens into the Presbyterian fold, and a downtown church, Westminster, a large edifice with imposing exterior and seriously dark interior. At Westminster a phalanx of elders, big men in funeral black, had occasion to march down the aisle together, and the choir hung so precariously over the congregation the pores of sopranos could be seen responding to their high notes.

Eddie and Helen, however, had several times as children attended the Bethany Baptist Summer Bible School. Eddie recalled this experience chiefly for the memory of emerging unscathed into the bright heat of a late summer afternoon. He recalled whole summer days at Bible School were spent marching round and round a large bare room singing B.I.B.L.E., YES! That's the BOOK for ME! under the suspicious eyes of an unidentified male person while a woman pianist toiled and sweated in the close air of a corner. One day Eddie refused to go. And so adamant was he that Helen was released as well. But their recall remained as vivid as those of prisoners of war after interrogation.

On Mrs. Blunt's front porch, both she (her name was Greta but she didn't like to use it because it sounded German), and her brother Ned were half asleep in their chairs. Mrs. Blunt's porch chairs were big tattered and comfy – old living room chairs. The piles of smelly papers were gone; Ned had taken them to the back of the yard. Let the kid next door throw them out, he thought, maybe I'll pile up some other junk and pay him to take them away. He was content in that hour, almost happy because he and Greta were together in a good way. For the first time in a long time he wasn't in a hurry to go home.

Lily Bernice lit a cigarette, blew out the first smoke as though kissing each molecule goodbye. "You're serious, you are really serious about me taking care of mother."

Her older sister, sweet little Rose Corinne, touched her big younger sister's tight right fist. "We could rent this house and Mother go up with you to Duluth, or you could stay here for a month or two."

"And what about my job?"

"I have some money and so does she; you wouldn't lose financially."

I'll bet Bernice couldn't help thinking, when did you and Dana ever have any spare change? "Very neat, very tidy. I see. You have it all worked out."

"It would only be until we sorted ourselves in Denver."

"Do you remember how hard I worked to find my apartment in Duluth? How long it took?" Bernice tried to speak calmly but her voice was going up. "I looked forever for that place."

"Well what about there? In Duluth. Could you manage Mother there?"

"It's small. It's very very small my apartment. And I'm gone all day."

A vision of Bernice's sweet little luxury apartment was now hanging in her mind.

"Not even for a month or two?"

"No." Bernice's voice became a knife slicing up certainties. "Absolutely not."

"Why not?"

Now they were standing facing each other: Miss Big and Mrs. Small, Bernice refused to look at her sister, instead was staring straight ahead. Corky tried to look up into her eyes but Bernice took another suck of smoke and blew it up and away from Corky who stepped back as though assaulted.

"I guess I can't talk to you, Bernice."

"No, maybe not."

And with that Corky stamped into the house, up and down the

small flight of stairs which led both upstairs and into the kitchen, a route she never followed unless furiously angry, which she was. Bernice followed her and started up the stairs.

"Please don't smoke upstairs, Bernice." Corky called out.

Bernice went down the stairs again, out on the porch and threw the cigarette into the grass. How does she know? Bernice thought. The she thought, maybe I'll sit here for a few minutes and finish it. So she went outside picked up the still burning cigarette, sat in the rocking chair that Corky had sat in, picked up the paper she'd been reading and tried to figure out what the article her sister had torn out of the paper was about. It was from the obituary pages but that didn't necessarily mean it was one because they carried wedding, anniversary, and every other kind of personal information too. She looked at her watch. Noon. I'm hungry, she thought. Maybe I should eat some chicken. Or a sandwich. I'll wait until Corky is out of the way and sneak some food up to my room.

As the sun advanced higher and higher, the porch had grown darker and darker. Sitting forward in her chair, searching through the paper, Bernice was the first one to see the black and white police car with the bulbous light on top pull up in front of the house and stop. A policeman got out, straightened his gun belt with an easy gesture, took his hat out of the back seat and put it on. He strolled in a leisurely way up the driveway and as he passed the porch she recognized Hank Hakkenson. He knew Sam. At one point they'd walked a beat together. She stood up but he didn't see her.

Maybe it's something to do with Sam, Bernice thought.

Helen opened the front doors of the church. Please God, she prayed, don't let her act too dramatic. Inside the church the air was full of Fairest Lord Jesus and a sea of hats. She almost turned and ran out. Then up the central aisle she saw Jessie moving on the arm of a distinguished gentleman usher, a man with white hair and the lean nervous head of an elderly greyhound. He smiled with relief when Helen came forward to take Jessie's arm. The last time Grandma had gotten inside Bethany Baptist she'd fainted in the aisle on her way out.

Jessie didn't like long sermons. Clearly this gentleman usher remembered her spectacular fall in front of the pulpit during a sermon on taking responsibility for personal salvation. The minister had called Helen's mother first thing Monday morning.

Reminds me of coming up the aisle with you, Amsden, after our wedding. Jessie thought. Worried to death. Wondered if you were the right man. Did you wonder too?

In the back yard, Dana was still listening to the radio, still churned up inside because he didn't know what to do about going to Denver when a police officer came around the corner of the house. At the same time, Corky came out of the house carrying a box. She feigned astonishment. "Why Harold Hakkenson, how are you?"

Dana stood up, walked over and took the carton away from her. He put it down on the ground, and stood arms akimbo while the other two talked.

Violet Marie heard it all because now that she was on the other side of the mountain she knew everything her family and neighbors were thinking and feeling especially when they talked about her. Which isn't often enough, she thought. I wish I could give these people some advice. Like how right after I died I sobered up. It was like there was no such thing as alcohol. That it hadn't existed except in my mind.

There were rules however. The rules were dead people could only be seen and heard in dreams, though they could stir themselves into thoughts occasionally using a great deal of energy. Once in a very very blue moon they could manifest themselves.

Those were the rules. Violet Marie, however, was a rule breaker from way back.

FIFTEEN

"Where are we going?"

"Get some gas." Eddie stripped the gears turning the corner onto the one way avenue downtown. Helen didn't even know its name. Jessie sat in the back, directly behind her. She was staring out the window as though everything out there mattered.

"I want to talk to you Skip." Eddie said.

"Don't call me Skip."

"We're going to have to get her."

"Who?"

"Jeez you're dumb." He flamed a look at his sister who leaned out the window to catch some air. It was getting hot.

Why is he so mad all of a sudden? She turned on her own thoughts the way she'd learned to do in the hospital. Melinda now walks alone in a cruel world. Doomed to loneliness by an inhuman brother, she endures much suffering for the sake of a handsome lover. But she has many exciting adventures as she roams free until she finds her tall lover again "I have found you my darling," the beautiful girl with raven hair tresses cried.

"We will have a few stolen hours of bliss in this secret place," he crooned into her shell like ear. "You have risked everything to be with me."

"Actually I have," she murmured into his big ear.

Oh Lord, Norbett has big ears. Why does my mind do that? Helen frequently worried that her mind was out of control.

Eddie gunned the motor and turned up Nicollet. "I want you to help me."

"Do what?"

"I told you fix – Aunt Bernice."

"Why?"

"Shut up."

"She's not that bad." Helen said this only to annoy Eddie not because she believed in what she was saying.

"What do you know anyway?"

The contempt in his voice hurt her feelings. She leaned out the window but this time a bug flew in her eye and she gave up.

Melinda and ...the handsome guy walked and talked together by the sea, rode horseback through the forest (she had a white horse), and together the two lovers created a beauty beyond imagination. And Melinda never ever saw her family again.

Except her dad.

The inhuman brother was destroyed by a....

Eddie rammed the Ford into a Texaco station, the one where he worked on weekdays. Helen thought the station looks unwashed and unloved, though not because it's Sunday morning; it always looks that way. Semi-depraved.

Depraved is a great word and I know what it means.

Squealing up against the pumps, Eddie shut off the motor and sat drumming his fingers on the window edge until a plump boy with a squashed alarmed face emerged from the station. He blanched when he saw Eddie but ambled over.

"Fill it up?" he said.

"Yeah. And call me sir."

Holding the nozzle as a protective device, the fat attendant approached the rear of the car and began filling the tank. The heady promise of gasoline floated in upon them. Eddie opened his door, got out and walked over to the station and went inside. Helen and Jessie sat in meditative silence. A moment later Eddie stuck his head out of the empty station.

"You been to Clancy's?" he called out.

Helen sat up straighter. Clancy's was the local pool hall, a place forbidden to Eddie as semi-depraved.

The chubby boy nodded. "Yeah."

"Get any you know whats?"

"Yeah."

"Give me a couple."

"Nope."

"You'll never use them. You haven't a hope."

Chubby screwed the cap on the gas tank, closed it up, returned the nozzle to the pump and ambled over to Eddie. "I live on hope my friend."

"I could make it worth your while."

"Try me."

They disappeared into the station. Helen and Jessie returned to their meditations.

Jessie had her head back against the car seat. Her eyes were closed. But she wasn't asleep. *Glad I got to church today. Though don't remember the sermon. Someone rushed me out. Folks are always trying to spare me suffering. Church ain't suffering. And they take me places I care nothing about.*

Like this one -this is an ugly place we're sitting in. Too much cement. And these young folks. Talking nonsense all the time. Those two boys are a funny pair. Couple of goofs. What are we doing here – all this cement?

Helen sat looking straight ahead. She was worrying about hoopskirts again. Melinda might be forced into wearing one. In those days anything could happen. What kind of underpants would show when you sat down? And that Great Grandmother that Grandma had told her about who was crippled for life because of a hoopskirt. They sounded dangerous. And did Jefferson Davis wear a hoopskirt when he tried to escape from the Yankees? She'd asked a teacher at school when they'd studied the Civil War but the teacher said, "Your questions aren't wanted, Helen." Grandpa Fallsworth had told her about Jefferson Davis. He'd been full of historical information about the Civil War because both his and Grandma's Fathers had fought in it, but on different sides.

Think a lot about Florida these days. How green it was, how full of life. Florida gave me joyfulness after all those years into our together, Amsden. Remember the long slow drive down there? Leaving the white heartache of winter and slowly warming, growing together as we drove -Tennessee and the Carolinas, driving into Atlanta and Tallahassee? Like stations of the cross the cities were, and then the green hope of Florida, the tangled nature of it, green and neon, and the old trailer park beside the orange groves. Every morning we breathed in life and the scent of oranges. Amsden I loved you more than I can ever say, and I love you now, just as much.

They all wanted me to marry you – my Pa, Stepma, sisters – they thought I was too flighty and you were a steady man. But I wasn't so sure. I'd had my secret heartaches and felt there was in me something that others wanted to batten down – some fancifulness. But Florida was fanciful. Those years we went down there every winter – those were the happiest years of my life. Not afraid of dying now cause Heaven may be quite a bit like Florida. But I can't imagine either one without you there too. Can you tell me, Amsden, have you forgiven Violet? If you have than you can forgive me.

Eddie came out of the station carrying a battered khaki army duffel bag. He stuffed something into his pants pocket, came over, opened the trunk of the Ford, threw the duffel bag inside, opened the door on the driver's side and got in. A wave of sweat odor aggravated the hot air in the car.

"What'd you put in your pocket," asked the sensitive teenage girl.

"Wouldn't you like to know." replied the sweating semi-depraved brother. He started the car and then leaned over and punched his sister's arm. "What's gray and green and comes in cans?" He chortled in an unpleasant manner. "Cream of toad soup."

"Why are you bringing a duffel bag?" asked the determined-to-be-snoopy snoopy sister. But she received no reply because Eddie was watching two girls trudge across the broken concrete of the dispirited Texaco station. Both were short and skinny, one had big buffed up hair. Both wore very white very short shorts. Eddie and the plump attendant who had come out of the station to fill the gas tank of a battered Reo truck watched them attentively. The black Reo's gas tank overflowed and a gush of gasoline surged round the truck parked perilously close to the beautiful blue 47 Ford.

"Hey moron." Eddie called attention to the flawed performance of an everyday activity. The chubby attendant threw a hasty glance at Eddie, then slapped the nozzle back into the pump and screwed the cap back on the Reo. He went the window of the truck and spoke to the unshaven driver who was so busy trying on sunglasses he didn't noticed the gasoline pond. Helen leaned out to see what happened next.

"How does gasoline explode?" she asked. "Do you have to throw a lighted match into it?"

"Don't know, don't care." Eddie said and waited for the chubby attendant to approach the car. "Got a match handy?" Eddie chortled.

"Buck fifty you owe me," Chubby said glancing nervously over at the Reo. The driver was still manhandling his sun glasses.

Eddie waved a lordly hand. "Put it on my bill."

"You have to sign for gas."

"I already did."

"I'm gonna check and you owe me a buck fifty."

Chubby retreated to the station. They waited. The car was hot.

"She's going to give me a lecture on VD."

"Aunt Bernice?"

"Who do you think? Bad enough Mom and her respecting womanhood speech."

Horrified admiration shot through Helen as she looked at Eddie. His voice was a growl. He looked rough-edged. Even his black framed glasses looked vicious. She didn't exactly know what VD was, but it was definitely semi-depraved.

Chubby re-emerged and snail-paced his way over to the car. He looked anything but vicious. Eddie drew out a wrinkled dollar bill and waved it back and forth in Chubby's face.

"Wish me luck, my friend." Eddie said and drove away but slowly so he could drive by the two girls and bang wildly on the side of the car. "Yoo-hoo, I'm coming to get you." The girls exploded into giggles and began to run, stumbling pigeon-toed into awkwardness because of their high heel pumps.

"Our car smells like gasoline." Helen said looking back at the gasoline pond. The Reo truck was flashing away too. Nothing exciting appeared to be happening. Too bad she thought, I've never seen gasoline on fire.

On the sidewalk, the two girls in very short shorts were threading their way through a group dressed for church – mothers in pretty summer dresses and white gloves, fathers in white shirts and dress pants, sweet little boys in white shirts and bow ties, moppet girls in black patent-leather mary-janes and little white hats. All these church goers walked with their hands dangling down so as not to touch anything, even their new shoes wouldn't squeak.

In the back seat of the beautiful blue Ford Jessie opened her eyes and sat up.

"What's going on?"

"Nothing Grandma." Eddie said. "Skip, you do what I tell you to do today."

"On a picnic?"

"The perfect opportunity. Are you listening Toad? Skip the Toad?"

"I don't want to Eddie, please don't make me do anything." She was whining, she could her own voice. How could she ever be Eleanor of Aquitaine if she whined? Oh well, Helen thought, no teeth. I don't want to be her anyway. She probably wasn't very tall. Eleanor Roosevelt is tall but she's built like Aunt Bernice.

"Did I hear my sermon?" Grandma asked in a semi- feeble voice. It was too dangerous a question to answer and they didn't.

The Blue Bomb roared onto Blazedale Avenue.

It must have been church you were driving me to, Amsden. You never did like me to walk though I didn't mind. You said it wasn't proper but I think you wanted to show off your car. In that dream – what did you say? – You got to get on or get off. Yes you were driving the Ford, the old black one and we were on our way to church and you. said, Jessie you've got to make up your mind, and you stopped the car and you opened the door and I got out.

Violet never saw this fancy new blue one we're driving around in today. Have you seen her at all? Talked to her at all?

Fancy getting so excited about buying this car you dropped down with a heart attack right there on the sales floor. Course you said the 47 Ford had everything you ever wanted in a car.

We were too proud then – riding high. A body shouldn't be too proud. That's inviting trouble.

"I'm not going, Skip" Eddie was staring at the wheel in front of him.

"Don't call me Skip." Helen said. "On the picnic?"

"To Colorado. With the family. I'm going to Texas. To work on the oil rigs."

He glanced at his sister. Can I trust her? he thought. "Don't tell Mom. Dad knows but nobody else. First I'm gonna help out with Grandma."

Helen wanted to ask, what do you mean 'help out?' but by then they were turning into their driveway way too fast barely missing a pious white Chrysler moving at ten miles an hour. They arrived just in time to see police interrogating their parents.

Hank Hakkenson officer on duty was a medium sized man with a medium look about him. He wore the summer uniform but had taken off his hat. He looked hot. He looked patient. He looked at Corky and smiled a lot.

"Rose, your mother called again. Apparently you have some suspicious characters around here." Both Corky and the officer shot brief flicks of glances at Dana whose mouth tightened in response.

"Thanks so much for coming yourself, Harold." Corky said.

"Hank. No trouble, Rose, a pleasure, always a pleasure."

Every time Officer Hakkenson said Rose, Dana's face tightened up just that little bit more. They were all three standing in a circle discussing what to do about Jessie when she herself rolled up in the back of the Ford with the two young people in the front seat. Corky dusted her hands, wiped them on her apron, went to help her mother out of the car.

Officer Hakkenson took out a notebook, put on his hat.

"I have to write another report, Rose."

"I know Harold. And I am sorry. We're a little upset these days. I don't remember. Have you met my husband, Dana?"

The two men managed a stiff handshake.

"Upset? Sorry to hear that." The policeman's voice was smooth. He took off his hat again and put it under his arm. There was a shiny cast to his bald spot.

"We're moving." Dana said firmly. "Out west. Hank, we're busy packing up."

"I'm sorry to hear that." Officer Hakkenson turned to Corky with a look of surprise on his face. "You didn't tell me that Rose." His tone was reproachful.

"We're only making up our minds just now." Corky said. Jessie wandered by her on her way into the house. Helen stood beside her mother listening. Eddie went into the garage.

"Well I'm not surprised with that good luck you've had, Rose." Officer Hakkenson said. He was writing in his notebook. "Folks come into a bit of money and they want to do something with it."

Shut your big mouth, Corky thought, with vehemence and hastened to fill up the silence. "We're worrying about what to do about my mother. I may stay with her."

Corky said this so firmly that both Eddie and Dana looked over at her. "I just might stay on with her until things work out." She looked at Dana with a challenging stare. Hakkenson's face curved upward into a medium sized smile. He had a Christ-like smile no doubt about it.

"Whatever's best. We'll miss you Rose. Well I'll be on my way then." He put his hat back on, closed his notebook, adjusted his gun holster and belt, and turned to Dana.

"I went to school with Rose. She was the prettiest girl there and you never forget a pretty girl, do you?"

"How many years ago?" Dana asked, moving closer to this saintly policeman.

In his boyhood he hadn't trusted policeman much.

"Too many." Corky said, walking over to her husband. She turned to Hank Hakkenson. "Well thanks Harold. We'll keep an eye on mother."

She noticed Bernice was looking out from the doorway. Officer Hakkenson noticed her too. "Your sister's home."

"Yes."

"Moved back did she?"

"She's just here this weekend. We're going out to Minnewana Park for the day."

"Mind if I speak to her?" Officer Hakkenson's voice was smooth.

What on earth for? Corky thought but she went over and leaned into the doorway and said, "Bernice can you come out here?" though she could clearly see Bernice lurking at the back of the kitchen.

"I'll meet him out front." Bernice said in a quiet voice.

Without another word Dana went into the garage to talk to Eddie and so missed the sight of Officer Hakkenson walking up the driveway away from a surprised Corky.

Helen saw the look on her mother's face. "What's wrong Mother?"

"Nothing."

"What did he mean people having luck?"

"That's just something people say." Corky went into the house.

SIXTEEN

Violet Marie thought of the upstairs bathroom, and a great gust of joy filled her. How real, specific, and glorious it now seemed. And the opera music her father had loved. The closet full of her mother's canned fruit. The clothes hanging in the dark basement, still waiting for them. How odd she thought, that I remember such everyday things. I never liked to stay home when I was a girl, now I'd like to be here forever. Never mind, said Those Who Knew a Lot More Than Violet Ever Would. Everything you were then and are now is love. Wow, thought Violet, I like these folk.

She remembered how on cold winter mornings she and Lily Bernice would wake to their father's opera singers, tired scratched records because her father had played them almost to death. Lily Bernice hated those morning concerts, but Violet hadn't thought much about music one way or other. Music was music wasn't it? Now she knew better.

She was looking at the old bathtub with its claw feet and great sloping back. As a child she'd stood up in it to examine all those extra selves in the mirrors high above her, had bent down to watch the last of her bath water swirl down into the dark nervous drain. That only a faint silky gleam of it remained below had worried her.

Other times she'd stood in the bath water, and opened the cabinet doors above the tub, had gone through the little bottles and boxes, nibbling on this and anointing herself with that. Everything had smelled so odd and fine, each taste distinct.

Like people, she'd thought then, like all the funny people she saw, but she wasn't able to tell her parents that, or even Lily Bernice because her sister was so often engaged in a horror of something or a fear, or a notion. Notions were the worst Violet remembered because Lily Bernice's notions usually meant Violet Marie washed dishes or carried a suitcase. More memories came. Violet became exhilarated by them. No, it wasn't so bad, coming back, visiting the family, not at all. It was in that bathtub she'd discovered there were parts of her body unknown and different, that touching those parts awoke a mysterious sweetness that could sing so deliciously to the rest of her.

Those Who Were There to Guide This Lost Soul had to drag Violet away. She was having too much fun. The upstairs bathroom had that effect – even on the dead.

At the back of the open garage Eddie poked around in the tools. The lawn mower was old but he thought it would work. He wanted to go next door and start on Mrs. Blunt's yard door right away but there was not enough time. Not today anyway, he thought, but tomorrow. Today I could go around the neighborhood and drum up some more yard work. If I make enough money, I can make some real plans.

Eddie had pulled the lawnmower out and was looking at it when Dana came back into the garage.

"Did you put some gas in the car?"

"Yeah."

"What's this yeah business?" Dana sat down at his radio, started dusting it off.

"Yes I got some gas – at the station. You owe me five dollars."

"I owe you? Who's been driving it?" Dana turned on the radio. "I dug out my old radio. Got Canada this morning, Eddie." Then Dana thought – does he care about that? Why'd I even mention it? He was awkward with his son. Dana felt he hardly knew him after a year away. And they were different, very different.

"Dad. I'll need the lawnmower for Mrs. Blunt's yard. Her brother promised me dollar an hour. I could make some real money."

That was something Dana didn't understand about Eddie – his drive for money, for privacy, a willful drive for selfhood and independence that Dana had never known. Dana had thought the needs of others were as important as his own, but Eddie, it seemed to Dana, put himself first too much. And before he'd left for Denver, he and Eddie had exchanged blows at the front door, because Eddie had disobeyed him, had snuck out of the house without his permission.

"What do you want money for?" Dana was twirling radio dials.

Eddie wished he could say 'to pay for rubbers,' but he didn't. He was cautious around his dad. His dad was different somehow, a stranger now.

"Dad I'm serious."

"That's a jungle next door, Eddie. Grandpa's old mower won't cut grass like that. You'll have to use a scythe. Cut it down by hand first."

"Maybe there's some kind of bigger mower I could use. I could rent one."

"It's too small a yard. And where are you going to get money to rent something? You don't want to start out spending money."

Dana continued to try out stations – sermon, church music, sermon, Fourth of July, big band music, Sousa marches, jazz. Well jazz would do. He didn't know the artist but he sure could play the piano. Eddie rolled the lawn mower out a few more inches, leaned over to look at it.

Dana listened to the jazz piano. Damn he was starting to like that modern music. "Who's that playing?"

"Cornbread? Wynton Kelly. He's real young. I could take the lawn mower over there and try it for ten minutes."

"You'll break the machine. I told you. You'll have to cut grass like that by hand. Old man Miller next door has a scythe. Pull some weeds for him and he'll loan it to you."

Eddie made a face. "I hate pulling weeds."

"Don't we all," Dana turned off the radio. "Let's go. Where's your mother?"

But Eddie ignored him, wandered further to the back and was poking around pulling out small garden tools when Corky came in.

"I can't talk to her. She's impossible Dana."

"Bernice."

"Yes. You go ahead. Find us a house then I'll come with the kids in September."

"I want you to go with me, Corky. Next Saturday."

"I'm not asking any favors from her. She's impossible. She hates Mother."

And what about your father? Have you thought about him? Don't you want to visit him? Aren't you worried about leaving him?"

"Corky listen. I want you to go to Denver with me now. We need to find a place to live. It's not that easy out there, the town's booming."

Tears welled up in Corky's eyes. "I can't leave Mother. I can't. Bernice wants to put her in a nursing home."

"I know. And we won't. And I'll go see my dad. I want to be sure he's sober though." Dana came over pulled his wife close, held her. She put her head on his chest.

"You've got that apartment. We could stay there."

"No."

After a careful moment, they pulled themselves away, stood a little apart.

Behind them Eddie knelt and concentrated on scrabbling around in the tools.

Officer Harold (Hank) Hakkenson and Lily Bernice Fallsworth were standing close together too; she was on the steps by the front porch, Hank just below her. They spoke in quiet voices.

"It's not doing him any favors, Lily Bernice – your calls. He's been suspended."

"What for?"

"Corruption. They're monitoring his calls. He's under investigation."

"I can't believe it."

"Nobody can." He put his hat on. "Hey. I best be on my way. Fourth of July is a holiday for everybody but us. See you again I hope." He walked down the sidewalk, turned, waved a hand. "You're looking good, Lily Bernice."

Bernice wanted to call after him, Say hello to Sam but she didn't. She just waved.

And thought – what a nice man. She went back inside the porch and sat down on the bench beside the door, and lit a cigarette. Just in time to see her niece arrive. Helen plunked herself down on the swing at the other end of the porch and stared at her. She's a funny girl, thought Bernice, but she was determined to be friendly.

"Are you looking forward to doing some things with your friends this summer?"

Bernice asked in a determined-to-be-friendly voice.

"I have no friends." was the hollow voiced reply.

"No friends?"

"None."

A silence fell marred only by the squeaking of the porch swing.

Eddie went next door to the Millers' house and rang their bell but there was nobody home. He went over to Mrs. Blunt's house and without asking her permission opened the back gate and went into her yard. The grass was tall and coarse. There were a few daisies struggling along the back fence and wild looking bushes shielded her house from the neighbors behind. It's a real mess, Eddie thought, a lot of work, but Mrs. Blunt's brother said he'd pay me by the hour. He looked over the lawnmower rusted out and broken at the back fence, scratching his hands and arms and legs on the raspberry bushes running wild there. Her lawnmower was junk. But he liked the fact that that the yard was his task, his responsibility, and that he would be paid for taking charge of it.

"Are you quite sure you haven't got a single friend?" Bernice asked "Wasn't there a girl around here yesterday?"

"Not one, Aunt Bernice. Not a single friend." Helen stood up. All the swinging was making her sick to her stomach.

"Where is everyone?" Bernice asked.

"Busy," her niece said sternly.

"When are we going?"

"I have no idea. No one makes any plans around here. This is a very inefficient family, Aunt Bernice."

Silence fell once more on the shadowy front porch.

There was a small window at the back of the kitchen above the old blue long table where the family sat for breakfast. The table was covered with picnic food and as Corky packed it up she looked out at the sad tattered backyard of poor Mrs. Blunt.

Poor Mrs. Blunt, her parents had called their neighbor, pity making them patient. No husband, no sons. Gossip had it that a husband was somewhere in Australia, but poor Mrs. Blunt didn't always live alone. Sometimes there were men, men who came and went over the years.

The garden had grown wilder and wilder as the years passed. Birds loved it and Corky loved to watch them in it. The neglected apple tree, the stubborn buckthorn and locust, every bush and flower running riotously free soon crowded out any order and any plant except the grass. But the trees and bushes were full of robins and blackbirds, bluebirds and sparrows, thrushes and wrens, blue jays and humming birds. Squirrels came and went in twos and threes, the infamous black rabbit called nearly every day.

Packing up the food, Corky thought how charming Mrs. Blunt's yard looked that morning. I usually think it sad, but this summer, today it looks inviting, she thought. And I may never see that garden again.

I think I should try to experience as soon as possible the sex act. I believe it is my destiny. Though I do not know if I am capable of attracting the opposite sex. Carol is. That is obvious. Surely I ought to be able to. She's not as smart as I am.

I do not think those illegal activities with Norbett count as experience, but what choice do I have living with such a mundane family?

Huddled over the remains of a bleak fire, the famous woman sculptor played with a big ball of wet clay. If only there were someone she could throw it at. Her beauty (she was tall) and intelligence (enormous) went totally unappreciated by a group of savages masquerading as a family unit. Sweeping aside several great works of art she had just created, she let out a loud sobbing cry of despair. All the works of art fell to the floor with a crash followed by the great woman sculptor.

To think that bastard Clarence Taylor is still roaming around. Mother made us take those music lessons. Her children had to be musical, thought Bernice. I was only fifteen when I started on that clarinet. What did I know?

She hadn't been a good student and she didn't remember why she'd picked the clarinet except that she could play in the band. Clarence Taylor was the band teacher – young then, a big heavily muscled man with coarse features. Violet had taken lessons from him too. Somehow Rose Corinne escaped, Bernice thought. Was she already at college? No, she sang in the school choir and at church. Over the years, Bernice had told herself the story of her own bravery in the face of depravity, but never to anyone else, so every word was securely locked into place.

At first I didn't do anything when he touched me but one day when he brushed my breasts several times and then the inside of my thigh I went home and told Mother I was not taking any more clarinet lessons and was quitting the school band. Mother was furious, and said oh yes I was, but I remained very calm and very firm. No more lessons. She still wouldn't listen but when I smashed the clarinet against the garage door then she paid attention. She listened all right when I did that!

Bernice lit another cigarette to celebrate her past courage.

She thought of Violet, two years younger, who had continued her flute lessons, and as the weeks went by began to play small determined sounds. Violet began to look determined too, and alert. Bernice thought then how Violet didn't quit the lessons for over a year. Every week she went down the street to Clarence Taylor's house, sometimes the lessons ran on so long Mother questioned her, but Violet only smiled. She enjoyed those lessons, Bernice had once opined with a sense of disapproval. but now, sitting on the porch that Fourth of July Sunday in 1948, she thought with a certain amount of surprise, and guilt. I got used to her going there alone, down to his house. Maybe something bad happened to her too. I never did tell Mother about him. Maybe I should have said something, maybe that would have changed her life.

I don't think I have a very clear idea what sex is about and peeking in windows with Norbett is not helping. I wonder if Aunt Bernice has ever had Sex.

Helen came over and sat closer to her aunt.

"I have one friend, Aunt Bernice. Carol. She's a year older than me."

"I saw her. A little blonde girl. She was with your brother last night. They were in the trailer. I don't think they were behaving properly."

"Oh." Helen stood up, hesitated, went back to sit on the porch swing.

"They are going to get in trouble behaving the way they were behaving."

"Oh really? How interesting." Helen tried to sound totally bored and uninterested. Inside she was smash, crash, fireworks. So was

Bernice, who gathered up her pack of cigarettes and marched out, highly offended by that snip of a girl not caring in the least about her friend. Bernice swept up the stairs and into her humble room where she kept box of Trinity chocolates which she immediately took out of her suitcase, and opened and began to pluck chocolates from; she then found her small bottle of Bristol Cream Sherry, poured some into a water glass, dug out the bus schedule to Duluth, sat on the bed, and cried, a little. I am so lonely here, she thought, in the midst of this, my own family.

I am lonely. Then suddenly, oddly, she thought again of her younger sister Violet Marie – thought how maybe Violet had felt that way too. But moving on to Rose Corinne, she remembered how her older sister always seemed to have a good looking guy hanging around to protect her. Rose she decided was never lonely.

Sherry and sympathy rarely go together, Violet thought watching all this.

"Were you on the phone?" By then Corky was upstairs too, changing into a pretty yellow dress. Dana was lying down on the bed watching her.

Jesus I'm tired he thought. And we haven't left the house yet.

"I thought I heard you make a phone call." Corky said.

"Let's get going"

"Who'd you call?"

"Tom Shannon."

"Your cousin? You wanted to stay away from him because he was too political."

"I do. He is. But he sees my dad."

"Tom called here a couple of times while you were away."

"Eddie told me."

"I wouldn't let him come over."

"You did right." Dana got up off the bed. "Dad's in the hospital."

Corky spun around. "Dana, no, what happened?"

"He smashed his head. Fell in the gutter. I said I'd go over Monday and see him but only when he's sober. Are you ready?"

"Yes. The food's packed. It's downstairs on the kitchen table."

"You did a great job on it this morning."

Corky came over and touched his chest. "I'm sorry about your dad."

"Are you surprised? My dad's my dad."

Dana didn't know how bitter his voice sounded.

"I'd like twenty minutes to myself before we leave." Corky said as they went down the stairs together. "I've been rushing around all morning. After all it is Sunday."

"O.K." Dana said. "I'll make a couple more phone calls."

Outside the day was advancing as it must. Heat rose and with it flies and bees and butterflies, hornets and ladybugs, grasshoppers and beetles, quite the usual assortment of creepy crawly and flittering fluttering insect life, while all through the trees, birds made a fearsome noise, a chattering fireworks of sound, but cheerful.

I want to be a heroine. It is perfectly possible I could discover a country in Africa. Though as I read through Great Women n History there weren't many women explorers.

I have absolutely no intention of being a nurse.

Carol and Eddie? Is that why she came over all the time? She said she was my friend. Liar Liar pants on fire.

A shadow fell across the screen the sensitive teenage girl. She looked up to see Officer Hakkenson standing outside. His genteel face looked uneasy.

"I need to talk to your aunt."

SEVENTEEN

On their way home from the cemetery, Mr. Miller's daughter Karin swung by a nursing home she knew about. She stopped the car in front and said, "Let's take a stroll inside, Dad." She looked at him with those deep brown eyes of hers and he knew he had to listen. Her hair was gray now and she was a good woman, not soft hearted, but kind in her own way. She'd worked as a WPA administrator during the depression years, and a USO coordinator throughout the war, but the Government was replacing her with returning war veterans. Her husband had worked himself to death at an early age.

"Come on Dad," Karin said again and opened the door of that beat up Chev that had served her so many years but she didn't baby enough. He looked around at Mrs. Miller who sat in the back seat bolt upright and silent.

Karen got out. "She'll be o.k. for a few minutes, Dad. I'll lock the car."

They went inside. Karin spoke to a fat woman in the small front office; then she and her father went up and down the halls peering into rooms where the very old and mostly senile lay in beds or were strapped up in chairs. Most of them were thin and pale and had their mouths open, but what Mr. Miller noticed was their silences. There were a lot of silences in that place. There was the big wide silence of the whole nursing home with its squeaky carts and occasional voices that met you as you came in the door along with the urine and medicinal smells. But there were silences in each and every room too. When you went into a room, sometimes you found a silence so sweet, a soundlessness so intense, you didn't want to leave. In other rooms there was a cotton batten wall of silence that made you almost stop breathing. Worst of all were those dry rooms full of tight faces and silences that were prickly, or angry, or murderously alive, silences so terrible you wanted out of there fast.

Walking back out to the Karin's old Chev, Mr. Miller felt full of wonder. He thought, Human beings don't just make noises, they make silences too. And that's where the Missis is now, deep down in her own silence, a place where I can't follow her, or even help her out, because I don't know what happens in there when your body is still alive. Maybe it's part of God's plan, maybe not.

They were driving down Nicollet Ave toward Mr. Miller's house because Mr. Miller wanted to make lunch for Karin when his daughter finally said, "Mom belongs in a place like that now, Dad. If you want to stay in your house, you need help with her. If you have an accident or a stroke or something, I'd have to put you both in there. And I want you to stay in your house as long as you can, you know that."

Mr. Miller knew that. He thought. I'm still a blue jay and I want to go on making lots of noise. Of course he didn't say that to his daughter, he only said, "I'll give it some real thought, Karin, and I thank you."

Behind them, Mrs. Miller sat enthroned in silence. And with his new attunement, Mr. Miller realized she wasn't the least bit lonely in there.

Upstairs in the Fallsworth house, Jessie lay on the white cotton picnic clothes her daughter Rose Corinne had laid out for her on her bed. Jessie was deep in her silences which were full of conversations with her husband.

Yes I met with Billy Black, Amsden. You know that now.

We went to the park for the day. Took a boat out to the island, sat and talked and yes even kissed, but that was all. He asked for my forgiveness – he was going to war and he wanted a clean conscience and he asked about our child and I showed him a picture of her. He wanted to meet her and I said no – that she didn't know and she would never know because she loved her father – you – too much and that you had been good to her beyond all reckoning, which you were Amsden. But I never told you about that day, and then Billy Black was killed over there in France, and why would I say anything bad about him then? But meeting him, yes kissing and feeling some love for him again, helped me to forgive all that had happened to me. That had made me bitter against the town we'd grown up in, and the church that turned its face from me and I could settle into our life so much calmer inside, a kind of sweetness came into me that day, Amsden. So forgive me for not telling you; it was for the best.

Then Jessie sat up. Woke right up. She was supposed to be going somewhere. She touched her chest. Yes she was wearing her jewelry and her Sunday suit. They would probably come collect her any moment and she was ready. Be ready to go, Amsden had been saying to her just then, and she was.

He was a good looking man Corky had decided. He wore his hair long and pulled back like an Indian brave, but it curled as no Indian hair ever did. He was just plain male beautiful. And being innocent little Rose Corinne Fallsworth, she'd blurted that thought out on the very second day she knew him, that afternoon when they met for coffee on the street corner.

"I must say, you are one of the handsomest men I've ever set eyes on."

"Why thank you, Mam. I try to be." And he'd smiled a sudden sure smile.

But to Rose Corinne (for she wasn't Corky to anyone in her vaudeville tutoring days) he didn't look like a man who needed to smile. Too strong a man, she thought that day. They'd met standing side by side on a downtown New York Street looking in a department store window draped with Fourth of July flags.

"Those are kind words and you are obviously a kind lady."

"I try to be." Rose Corinne had laughed and then, when she saw the flash kindle in his eyes, she wished she hadn't said those words.

Now why does he come into my mind like that? Corky thought, those twenty years later. She was on that famous shadowy front porch only just vacated by other family members. She was resting and rocking and thinking about an important development in her personal past, which was an activity new to Corky and one precipitated some months before by a letter from a lawyer delivered by Harold Hakkenson. She was in her pretty yellow picnic dress, and she looked pretty that morning, but she was frowning with the effort of searching her memory so diligently.

Is it because I met him on the Fourth of July and today is the Fourth of July?

Or is it because his money is resting on my conscience, just hanging over me.

And me not knowing whether I should tell my husband that I have five thousand dollars in the bank that's a gift from another man?

Corky could ask such questions of herself, but rarely could she answer them. Instead she usually ran away hoping some answer would develop out of the woodwork or at least from another person's mouth. But she was all alone in this one – mystery money in the bank and should she tell her husband?

She patted down her hair – hair not unlike that man those twenty years ago, hair that was frizzy, fuzzy, never quite tame.

"Dana I'd like twenty minutes to myself. I've been rushing around all morning. I'd like to sit on the porch and rest."

She'd said that, mostly wanting space to think out what she would tell him but then he'd been so impatient to get back to his precious telephone, he was right away standing by the door ready to run. Why hadn't he said let's go, and make us get in the car and get going on this picnic? I told him the food was ready, she thought, but no, he was happy to stay. Off he went to his precious telephone. 'I'll be downstairs. I'll make some more phone calls.' That's what he'd said.

There's something going on, Corky thought. Out on that porch she was getting darker then the porch.

Of course beyond her lay a world much bigger than she or the house, the family, the city of Minneapolis, the government in Washington (currently then ablaze with a presidential campaign and all its hoopla, manoeuvring, and speechifying – nobody thought Truman would be re-elected with that Missouri twang and those bad suits, and a mother-in-law living with him permanently).

Another even bigger world lay beyond all that fuss with a sun that was high and blazing down, where thin clouds scooted by with suspicious speed and a few fat ones looked up to something in the northern sky. Heat was rising and with it came a new and mixed smell from that greater world – odors subtle yet available – water from nearby lakes, gasoline from moving cars, diesel and asphalt, smoke, fir trees, mown grass, crops in distant fields – everything and anything that couldn't be seen or acknowledged on 35th St, but were still there, part of the air they breathed in and out, in and out.

New sound was arriving too, driving out the life noises of early morning. –cars rushing along the two main boulevards that held 35th street between them like a string on two frames – Blazedale was at full tilt by 12:30 that Sunday, Fourth of July – churchgoers coming home, picnickers going out, people touching base with their families or just roaming around the city – a whirligig irritated buzz was Blazedale Ave.'s contribution, its reminder that people were rushing to get somewhere fast fast fast. Nicollet Ave, on the other hand, offered not just a constant traffic hum but the clattering, mumbling, clang of trolleys as well as people shouting out of cars at somebody on the street they hoped they knew. Nicollet Ave was untidy, full of odd stores, slightly dazed pedestrians, and the occasional important life event like a dog being rescued from certain death or a carload of soldiers whistling at a teenage girl. Dogs rarely died on Nicollet Avenue and teenage girls sometimes got picked up.

Were all those new smells and sounds from the outside world what caused this family to begin to drift, to hang in corners doing nothing, rather like fish in an aquarium going nowhere but looking brave about it? Were their inner selves as ready as their outer to meet the world at Minnewana Park, a big old hugely popular park that would soon be chuck full of people celebrating the Fourth of July? Everybody in the family by then seemed busy and secretive in their own private busyness. Just like the clouds.

Eddie rang three doorbells in search of yard work but nobody was home.

Eddie's spark was a great burst of red followed by a series of popping sounds.

Bernice sipped sherry and read a good mystery in her room, which was hot but at least private. Officer Hakkenson had suggested they meet at Minnewana Park. He said he'd try to get Sam there, or at least tell him to call her. He'd said "Sam mentioned your name as a collaborating witness but he didn't have your new address or phone number, didn't know even what city you were in. Do you want me to give him that information, Lily Bernice?"

She'd said no, right away and he'd flushed, "I'm kind a torn here, Lily Bernice. Sam's a good cop. But you're a fine lady. Don't want to step in somewhere and make a mess of things. And call me Hank. All my friends do." He'd flushed beet red. Well now what? she thought.

He might be there – Sam. But she didn't know whether she wanted to see him at all. When she'd asked Hank why Sam had been suspended, he'd said 'suspicious deaths.' That made a chill go down, and up, her spine. Bernice hoped her mystery book 'Details of a Bloody Hand' would be engrossing.

Helen was sitting in the living room, keeping an eye on her Daddy while he telephoned people, until he told her to go away and stop bothering him. He hadn't really noticed her since he'd come home and that made her sad because she admired her daddy more than anyone in the world, especially because he looked like a Roman Statesman.

She went upstairs to get the new diary he'd brought her from Denver.

Jessie opened her eyes when Helen came into the bedroom they shared. She was sitting on the edge of her bed. "I'm ready to go." Jessie said.

Helen didn't reply. She drew out her suitcase from under the cot and pawed through its contents, but couldn't find any shorts shorter than the ones she had on. She did extract a pair that would be tighter. Too tight – she didn't want her bottom to bulge out. She found the diary, which had a lock and key and PRIVATE written across it.

"You're supposed to change your clothes, Grandma." She said in passing.

"I'm ready to go." Jessie repeated, and Helen turning around saw she was still sitting staring into space. Let Mother deal with it, the sensitive teenage girl thought and grabbing her diary she went downstairs, out the back door, and sat on the gray steps that mounted up to the apartments, empty since Grandpa Fallsworth's death. With a deep sense of purpose, she undertook to report in the new diary horrible recent events.

Dear Diary, if I am not careful I shall remember. It is not a pleasant memory believe me and I may suffer permanent brain damage. I keep seeing Carol's brother Norbett turning from the window – the hair shooting straight up from his head. No Lie. The look on his face I shall always remember.

Total amazement.

Stupefaction? Great word, but it may not be exact enough.

Horror. Yes horror. I can say no more at this time. Even thinking about our experience together makes my skin crawl. Also I am deeply disturbed about Carol. I have learned today, Dear Diary, that she and my brother are consorting. I shall have to look that word up. Diary, I'm glad you're here. Since I have no friends now I have absolutely no one else to talk to.

I shall speak to Carol about her betrayal today. And I really ought to explain to her what a disgusting wretch her brother Norbett is so she will be utterly devastated. Unfortunately, thought, I have now decided that I do not want to go to prison.

I read Les Miserables five times and know that For Sure.

"Dad, Can I have the car for twenty minutes?"

"No." Dana was spreading blankets across the back seat of the car.

"Why not?"

"Because we're leaving."

"When? I want to see if I can get some more yard work."

"As soon as your mother has her little rest we're going."

His voice didn't sound quite right so Eddie turned and went back inside the house and into the empty kitchen. He opened the door of the icebox, stuck his thumb into the potato salad, pulled out a great glob which he ate, then stuck the thumb back into the potato salad again. He was sucking his thumb when Dana came in.

"What are you doing?"

"Eating. I'm starved."

"So am I." Dana sat down at the table. Eddie pulled out the potato salad and sat down beside him. Dana reached over and got two forks from the silverware drawer and gave one to Eddie. We used to do this, Eddie thought, Dad and I, only it was bread and milk at bedtime.

"Bread." Dana said. He reached over to the bread bin, pulled out a loaf, spread potato salad on several slices. It felt companionable, the two of them sitting side by side eating sandwiches. "I used to eat potato salad sandwiches with my Dad," Dana said. And then the sharp thrust of grief stabbed him – his dad, his dad, god knows what was happening to the old man at that very moment – nobody who cared with him with him – and Dana choked on his sandwich. Eddie thumped him on his back. "You o.k. Dad?"

Dana nodded, unable to speak. Story of my life, he thought – me unable to speak, only to feel. Just like my Dad.

"It's Grandpa, isn't it Dad?" And Dana nodded and then a great love for his son rushed through him like a healing wind.

EIGHTEEN

Corky sat on the front porch rocking in her favorite chair. The hum and swish of herself alone – everything ready, the lunch prepared. Now was the moment to settle herself.

She tried not to be angry at Bernice. She didn't like being full of hate, feeling depressed. But she didn't want to go on a picnic. Not today. Yes it was a beautiful morning, the Fourth of July. So what?

There, you see, I'm cranky again, she thought, because it's not just Bernice.

What is going on in Dana's mind?

He's hardly spoken to me except in platitudes, in husband and wife non-committals. Yes, no, I'll do it tomorrow. And his father – why doesn't he want to talk about his father?

And oh oh oh she thought with a kind of pain going right through her body, starting you know where and passing up through her heart and head, he hasn't touched me, coming in so late, the big bed filled with him, I barely felt him ease in beside me.

Not a touch, not even much of a goodnight kiss, more like what you'd give your mother.

That had never happened on other homecomings. Usually he'd crawled into her warmth, spooning her into him, his whole body cold with journeying, give me, give me hands. What was going on now that he was so quiet, so distant? It's hot, she thought, yes, we're not going to cuddle when it was so hot, but still – he's been away almost a year.

Rose Corinne was afraid. They'd lost the habit of wanting each other, lost the speaking of truths. He's departed from me, she thought. I can feel it.

She rocked in the chair, finding comfort in its smooth oak

curves – her Grandmother Stewart's chair. Would they take it, or leave it? There were so many old things here in this house, here in her childhood. How could she leave them, leave it?

Was it wise to burn the bridges of safety?

Well, still, she thought, taking a drink of coffee, still hot, yet bitter to the taste already. Still we have to go; there's no work here; Dana has a job out west and that's more than he has in Minneapolis.

But do I need to go? That small niggling thought began again. Why? Why go with this man when he's already gone from me? If it's too late for us, then what's out there for me? Anything but struggle and heartache? Perhaps there's a better future here, alone. I'm not the least bit afraid, she thought, I've been alone before.

Helen came up the driveway and bent down to collect the morning paper Dana had left on the front stoop. At the same time Jessie arrived in the front door of the house. She was swaying, her eyes closed, face white. She looked like she was trying to recall something important but was likely to fall over first.

"Take Grandma back upstairs will you Skip? She needs to lie down."

"Don't call me Skip, Mother."

"I'm sorry, dear, I'm trying to remember. And give me the paper. You can take the comics."

"Thank you, Your Majesty."

"Oh by the way, did she get to church?"

"Yes."

"Did she get inside?"

"Yes."

"Damn."

"They brought her right out though. She didn't even get to sit down."

"They'll call on Monday. They always do. Thanks dear. Take the comics."

Helen stomped up the steps, smashed open the screen door, dropped all the paper in her mother's lap, and gathered up her grandma. How easily I become everyone's servant girl she thought with high indignation.

High indignation was one of her favorite moods.

A mood fortunately available to her when Eddie caught her coming down the stairs after helping Grandma onto her bed.

"Do me a favor, Skip."

"My name is Helen Miranda." Eddie ignored the inevitable new middle name.

"Get Norbett off my back at the picnic."

"Norbett! Who invited him?" She sat halfway down the stairs, the light was dim there. What did Eddie know?

"Carol. Her brother's a twerp."

"He is more than that."

"Maybe we could maroon him. On Duck Island. Stake him down for the ducks to nibble to death. Or better yet whistle in some vultures."

"Mom said Carol couldn't go. How come she's going all of a sudden?"

"I invited her." Eddie was now leaning down looking right into her face and he wasn't smiling. "You got a problem with that kiddo?" Helen hated his James Cagney imitation. "Only I didn't invite Norbett. Carol says he's going anyway – he's playing baseball – the guy can't pitch believe me – so she can get a ride with him. But I have some plans for Carol and I don't want him hanging around. That's where you come in, Sweetheart. He's in your class isn't he?"

"Not exactly." Gym class yes, Literature no.

Norbett has seen my naked legs in gym class, Helen realized. What a horrible thought especially since together they'd now seen more parts of a human body than legs.

"Concentrate kid. Are you listening to me?"

"Barely."

"Do me this favor will you? Lure Norbett away so I can be alone with Carol."

His sister's eyes widened. Carol was supposed to be her friend. They hadn't told her. They hadn't told her anything. There was a curious sense of loss.

"And don't tell Mother Carol will be at the park. Keep your mouth shut for a change and I'll make it worth your while."

"How? What can you give me that I'd even want?"

"I'll teach you to drive."

It was a stunning unexpectedly stupendous idea. Immediately

Helen saw herself behind the wheel of a large limousine, or even a convertible. She'd wear a long silk scarf, but not as long as the one that woman was wearing who got strangled when it caught in the wheels of her car.

"Are you concentrating?" Eddie snarled. "I can't see your face it's so dark up here. Why are we stopped here anyway?"

"You are supposed to put both hands on the wheel. I saw how you were driving back from church, one handed." She tried for a high moral tone but failed, somehow with Eddie, high moral tones crashed and burned. "So I'm not sure you should be teaching anyone else how to drive." He started down the stairs. She stood up and followed him "However I accept. I will try to at least talk to Norbett while you and Carol do awful things in the bushes."

"We are not going into the bushes." But she could see by the smirk on Eddie's face that was exactly what he was planning on doing. "Just keep quiet about her coming and about me teaching you how to drive. We have to wait until Dad's not around."

Out on the porch Corky opened the newspaper. Around her life pushed itself forward against time and through space and making noises doing that – cars scattering silences, doors opening and closing. Here a slice of ringing telephones, there a spatter of radio. The murmuring of human voice pressing against voice, occasional precise important pursuits of cats by dogs, search and destroy missions by insects. Birds chirping. Lawnmowers racketing. Bells on bicycles and horns of cars. The surprise of music.

Corky read the news. Unimportant important news. Then she turned to the obituary column and stiffened with shock.

Dead. Newell. He was dead. James Newell died after a long illness. She was shivering. Alert. The whole day seemed aimed at this moment. This knowledge. Survived by five children. Three wives. A memorial fund to be established by his students. James was dead – after a long illness. He'd had enough time though and enough…sentiment…to arrange through the police that some money came to her.

No, no Corky thought, it was more than sentiment, it was a kind of love.

Then a rush of memory filled her mind and heart.

"Beautiful. You're beautiful too."

When Corky had turned away from the jewelry store window, she'd looked right into his dark eyes. He was about forty, twenty years older than she, but he didn't look fatherly. He had broad lips curved into a smile, but the majestic face of an Indian, those stern truthful eyes.

Rose Corinne didn't know in those days that she was beautiful. That day she'd been wearing a white dress – a little pleated suit with a short brown and gold bolero jacket. She wore her thick black hair long then; it was so curly it refused to do anything but frame her pretty face. Her complexion was nearly olive, smooth and unblemished and her eyes were almond shaped and deep brown. Seductive eyes, her many boyfriends had told her, eyes you could swim in which never penetrated but instead pulled that other, that stranger, into them. Her lips though not full had a pleasing smiling shape. Her whole face warmed upward, sang truths of belief and innocence.

"Do you like beautiful things?"

At once she turned away. He was trying to buy her something. To buy her. She walked away from the allure of the window.

"I do. Especially beautiful women too."

She sucked in her breath with shock. Now he was walking beside her! He was trying to pick her up! She looked the other way – into the array of shop windows.

The New York neighborhood was one of small old stores, brownstone houses, people sitting on the stoops watching the world go by. Beside her the street was like a familiar river streaming with cars. It was a hot hot Saturday afternoon in New York and she knew no one in the city. The vaudeville family she was travelling with were visiting friends for the Fourth of July long weekend.

"I'm sorry. I didn't mean to frighten you. You're a respectable person. So am I." He had a marvelous voice, resonant and deep. She turned to look at him and saw that he was still smiling. He did have a friendly face, she thought. He wore a light blue summer suit without a tie; there was a fine bead of sweat under the shock of his black curly hair. "I noticed you because you have hair just like mine. It's a bitch isn't it?"

She couldn't help smiling back. As they walked he came closer to her and she didn't move away.

"Have you ever had a permanent?"

"No."

"I did once. To straighten mine. I looked peculiar, like something sad had happened to me and I wasn't going to recover."

She smiled again. Unconsciously her steps slowed. She was now no longer fleeing this stranger but matching his pace. It was an odd conversation to have with a man, she thought, about hair.

"Maybe we have negro blood in us. What do you think?"

Shocked she speeded up again. There was something too bold, too unpredictable about this man.

"Just joking Italians have curly hair. That's what I am – Italian."

His skin was olive like her own. They were in some curious ways alike, she thought, and once again her pace slowed. She turned to take a shy sideways peek at him. He was walking proudly, throwing out his body with its full smoothly muscled chest. He had muscular legs, short arms, a prizefighter's body. She noticed how people parted in front of them; together they'd become formidable but it was because of the man, his prizefighter walk made people hesitate to push their way through.

"Hot today, huh? July in New York's a stinker."

"It's hot in Minneapolis too."

"That's where you're from?"

"Yes. At least I was. What about you?" It was so comfortable talking to him. Shy small town Rose Corinne found it easy to talk to this man.

"I'm a visitor too. I'm from California. I teach at UCLA."

"You're a professor?" That scared her right there.

"Anthropology. I study people. That's why I'm talking to you. You're under study right now, Miss Beautiful from Minneapolis, so be careful. I might find out something about you, you wouldn't want me to know. Do research that would bare your..."

She stopped so precipitously two women behind her walked up her heels, and muttering irritably moved around her. "I've got to go," she said. She'd come to a trolley stop and she knew she ought to break away. This wasn't the kind of man she could take home to meet Jessie and Amsden.

"…soul. We all have one, don't you agree?"

"It was nice to meet you." she said primly.

"Do you really have to go?" His face looked so sad, she felt guilty.
"Yes."

"Could we have some coffee first?" he said, simply looking straight at her.

"I don't know anybody in this town. Not a soul. My wife's just left me. I have work to do in Italy after the holiday and we were supposed to go together but she's fallen in love with somebody else."

"I've got to be some place at five." she'd lied, fearing him, fearing the loneliness she could feel in him, and knowing it rested in herself too. She'd been on the road for three months, with strangers all that time, and somehow he created in her from the first the feeling that she knew him already. And how could that be? How could she know so soon the heart of a stranger? An attractive man who wanted her to pay attention to him? She wanted only Dana in her life by then, anyone else would be confusion.

Dana was the handsomest man she'd ever dated. Tall, black hair, green eyes, he'd created in her from the first a proud sweep of emotion, a passion so strong that for the first time in her life, pretty little Rose Corinne Buttersworth was frequently afraid, afraid she'd lose such a brooding, bright, handsome man. That summer he'd gone to work in Montana to test his grief over the death of his mother, and his love for her. He wanted to earn enough money for their wedding in December. That's what he'd promised her and she'd been looking at wedding rings in the jewelry shop window. She was sure of Dana, surer than of herself. He was a serious man. Since his mother had died a year ago, he was bound to her alone; each week he wrote long delicious letters of promises and hope. Still it was odd being so alone all the time, wandering around strange city streets on a Saturday afternoon, nothing to do but look in store windows and no money to buy anything.

"What about tomorrow?" James had said. She'd asked his name but hadn't given hers. They stood on the corner, the sun still hot, around them people flowed, all going somewhere, intent on whatever lay downstream.

"I'm not sure. Usually I'm tutoring my children on Sunday."

But when she saw the droop of his mouth, the light imperceptible sag of his shoulders (And how did she see all that and he a stranger?), she relented.

"I'll meet you tomorrow afternoon. But there's not much open on a Sunday is there?"

"In New York? Sure there is. I'll buy you lunch or supper. The museums are open. We could walk in the park."

"That's okay," she said hastily, anxious now because he was moving too fast, making assumptions when all she was doing was being friendly.

"You like Italian food? There a restaurant up the street from my hotel."

"Just coffee." She said firmly, trying to mean it. She was a pretty woman and she'd had enough experience to know he was closing in for a date, for a cup of coffee at his place at the end of the evening. Let's meet right here."

"On this corner? Or by the jewelry store window?" He looked at her, something deep and smiling in his eyes. He was experienced too. She'd felt a little flutter of fear again. He wanted her, she could tell, and he was an attractive man. But all she needed was Dana. Her father was buying her a pearl necklace and earrings for a wedding present.

On the shadowy front porch, Corky read the obituary slowly and carefully. A memorial service to be held Monday afternoon in the University Chapel. Surrender to a long illness. A visiting professor. He'd been teaching right here in Minnesota when he died and she hadn't known. Five children. She read their names, one by one. She'd never meet them now. Not one. The thought filled her with an inexplicable sadness. Nothing said about his wives. Not in the paper. Oh James she thought, I don't want you to be gone, that bright light extinguished.

Eddie came out the back door. Dana was sitting on the orange crate in front of the garage, the radio beside him. He was sorting through Amsden's old toolbox.

"There's some beautiful old tools in here, Eddie. Real classics." He stood up and yawned, stretched. "What'd you decide about the yard next door?"

"You got a phone call Dad."

Dana brought his arms down abruptly. "Man or woman."

"Your cousin."

"Tom? Tom Shannon?

"Yes."

"Is he on the line now?"

"No. I told him you were busy."

Dana slammed down the lid of the tool box. "Stick this in the back of the car will you, Eddie? Did he leave a number?"

"He's at home. I think it was about Grandpa MacFadden. He said it was important."

"I'll call him. Where's your mother?"

"Front porch I think. Can I use the car for a few minutes, Dad?"

"No. I said we're about to leave."

Dana closed the toolbox and carried it into the deep calm of the garage.

Eddie stood for a moment rocking on his heels, hands in his pockets, then strolled over to the orange crate and claimed it.

He turned the dials of the radio, heard sermons, news, music, most of it faint.

Dana came out.

"I thought you wanted me to put the tools in the car."

"I thought better of it."

"I can get Texas on this radio but not Colorado."

"What do you mean by that?" Dana's hands clenched at his sides which his son didn't notice, only the tone of his voice caused him to look up.

"Nothing."

Dana walked into the house. Eddie shut the radio off and stood up. He was awfully tempted to get in the car and drive it around anyway. His own personal set of keys were in his pocket. Nobody knew he'd had them made at the garage.

Upstairs, Jessie lay on her bed resting. She'd closed her eyes as soon as she'd lain down, too tired even to take off her jacket. Have I been to church? I think so. Oh it's delicious to lie floating, knowing I've been somewhere and done something already today. That's a good day now.

The room was warm, heated air swam around her but she didn't notice. More and more heat and cold were outside her, penetrating only when she paid attention.

I've been to church. That nuisance girl was there too. What was I thinking about just now? Something sweet smelling. Oh yes, the lilacs, the knowing of lilacs, the lilacs down the lane. Walking to the school, smelling lilacs, yes oh yes.

NINETEEN

The icebox door yawned wide as Eddie stared with gloom at its collection of half empty condiment jars. There wasn't much potato salad left, or much of anything of interest in there.

"We're out of milk, Mom."

"Shut the icebox door." Corky was mopping down the counter. All those breadcrumbs would bring in ants.

"Is something burning in here? Or someone?"

She turned around with the fury of whiplash. "What you say that for?"

Eddie pretended not to notice, took out a jar of olives, extracted the last three with his fingers, threw them in his mouth, and put the jar down on the floor beside the icebox.

"Might as well finish these, right Mom?" He munched on olives as he walked over to her. "Aunt Bernice sure works her way through the milk."

"Oh grow up." Corky threw the breadcrumbs into the trash under the sink.

"You want me taller?"

He touched her shoulder. "Hey, cheer up Mom. You want these out to the car?" He motioned to the boxes.

"Ask your father – if he isn't on the phone again." Eddie noticed the tone of voice, and touched her shoulder again. Gee she's short, he thought, not for the first time that summer. He'd grown two inches in the last five months.

"You know there's trouble with Grandpa MacFadden?" he said in a low voice. Then Corky's temper cooled. Of course, yes, there was that weighing on her husband – she had to remember that.

"Yes, I do know that. But your dad would go over to St. Paul if it were serious."

Eddie picked up a box. "Maybe Aunt Bernice gets up in the night and drinks milk."

"Well you ought to know. You're the one that's wandering around to all hours. And I mean it about the window, Eddie. And about getting that girl in trouble. There's a lot of things young men don't think about but mothers do."

"Yeah yeah, I know what you mean Mom. I heard you." He went down the back steps pushed the door open with the box. "I don't want to go to Denver either."

"Roaming around all night. Doing God knows what. I won't have it, Eddie."

He came back inside, walked through the kitchen. Corky was rinsing dishcloths, hanging up tea-towels. She liked to leave the kitchen tidy hanging up. "You'd better move out if you want to alley cat around. What time did you come home last night?"

"I didn't Mom. I'm still out there." Eddie called from the living room. He was dialing Carol but the phone rang on and on with no answer. They've probably left already if Norbett's playing ball, he decided. Norbett can't pitch. He should be playing outfield.

"You little smart aleck," Corky thought, but she relaxed. Eddie was her favorite human being, mostly because he acted from quick sharp bursts of anger, or equally from deep wells of affection. She wanted to tell him about his dad, to let out all her feelings of hurt and betrayal but you couldn't do that – not to your kids.

Eddie came into the kitchen picked up another box.

"When do we get to eat this stuff?"

"What's so important you had to make a phone call?"

"I'm arranging to watch a baseball game." He went out, Dana came in.

"Did you tell Eddie he could open the cookies?"

"Never mind. We're all hungry."

"Where is everybody anyway? Are you ready to go?"

"Are you?"

"Still trying to get Tom Shannon." Dana said and went through to the living room. Corky looks tired he thought. And sad. He knew he was hurting her, neglecting what was important to them, and maybe driving something between them that could never be retrieved. Yet he couldn't say anything, because he didn't know what to say.

Now more and more when Jessie dozed off she fell back into dreams that held her rather than she holding them. And because she had been a good woman her dreams were beautiful, even the days, months, hours that were difficult, painful, sordid or despairing, when she returned to them in dreams she saw that even in those times her small life had been encased in a world as beautiful, as tender, as sure, as the world she experienced when happy.

That morning eighty year old Jessie lay on her bed, resting on the summer clothes laid out for a picnic by her daughter, and as she fell asleep, a powerful dream rose up into and around her, and the voice in the dream was the voice Jessie had not had time to hear much in her long life. It was the voice of her soul reminding her of memories that had been buried long and deep by Jessie. Now they come into her consciousness but as related by her soul, parts of her life now appeared as a beautiful fairy tale.

At the same time Helen, sitting outside and writing in a new diary with PRIVATE written on it, was unwrapping a new self, a persona, one that made her less self-dramatizing and more powerful than she expected, a self that soul mixed itself into so she might grow up strong.

Dana had told his landlady Mattie that he was bringing his family back to Denver, that he was giving notice he wouldn't be living in her basement apartment any more. Now when he told Corky he wasn't going back there it would be the truth, but his knees still felt weak. Mattie's voice had been so quiet, so sad. He'd hurt her. But hadn't he made her happy too? And quite suddenly like a piece of puzzle put into place, he thought, my dad made my mother happy sometimes too.

He called his cousin Tom, two, three times, but there was still no answer so he had no way of knowing how his dad was doing. He hadn't thought to get the name of the hospital. Maybe he's in the drunk tank again, but no this time it sounded more serious. Dad's seventy now. Christ, I didn't remember his birthday this year.

Harold (Hank) Hakkenson drove to the park. He hadn't known

Corky's younger sister at school, but now he thought what a fine looking woman she was. Very fit.

He hoped he hadn't told her Sam was accused of complicity with murder. It might not be true. Hank hoped it wasn't true.

Those Who Are In The Know asked Violet, Do you remember the man who asked you for love – physical love – as his life was inching toward death? Was that right or wrong? Violet said, I don't know, I don't like questions like that. I did it, but I don't know if he died happy. Does anyone die happy? As soon as she said that she knew it was a stupid question.

Dana put away the radio. If there was one thing he didn't want to hear at that moment it was Irish songs. His dad on his way to getting drunk would sing Irish songs.

As Bernice read her mystery Details of the Bloody Hand, part of her thought. I'm going to fix that bastard up the street once and for all. It was a thought she didn't really pay attention to but the seed was planted.

Myrna Henderson sat in Joe's sister's back garden watching Suzette play with the little dog named Butch. Butch liked to lick Suzette's face and the little girl laughed so merrily that Myrna's eyes filled with tears. She thought, Oh if Joe could only see her now, how happy he would be. Why did he have to be the one to give up his life and others didn't? The unfairness of that stirred in her a familiar hot anger at other people who were lucky and happy and enjoying their little daughters laughing, but just at that moment Gloria came out of her little house with a tray of ham and cheese sandwiches and glasses of lemonade. She set down the tray on the old wooden table beside their chairs, sat down and said, "I have something to tell you Myrna. I've met someone. He's still in service, stationed in Germany. On his next furlough we're going to be married and I want you to be my maid of honor."

Right away Myrna felt ashamed of her anger because she was happy for Gloria.

"Are you going to Germany with him?"

"Probably." Gloria said, "And I can't take Butch so I hope you find a house with a back yard so you can take the dog. Butch loves

Suzette," and they both looked at the child that Joe never got to see grow up, play with a little dog that loved her. The two women talked about a wedding that Joe wouldn't be at either. But was he there that afternoon, might he be at the wedding because he was in their minds and hearts?

"Why don't you rent a house?" her sister-in-law said. "My landlord's moving his daughter into this one, or you could have it. She's got two kids."

"They're impossible to find." Myrna said, "No one even advertises them."

Dana came back through the kitchen. Corky was standing up, nibbling on cheese and crackers. She said. "If we go to Denver, I suppose I should go through those things of Violet's and throw most of them out.

"Violet? There still stuff of hers in the house?"

"Oh a few things, photographs, her year book. I think her flute's around here."

"A flute? Violet played the flute?" Talking about Violet made Dana nervous.

Violet now saw that one of her parents' chief virtues had been that they hadn't needed her, hadn't needed any of their daughters who had thus been free to follow their own life designs, their own fates – good or bad, or somewhere in between. How many people are really really bad? she asked Those Who Are As Close to All Knowing As Ordinary Mortals Are Ever Going To Meet but they only replied – Define Bad.

"Hello"

"You have betrayed me."

"Skip!"

"Your friendship meant everything to me and I'm crushed to learn that you are a complete liar."

"Skip."

"I never want to speak to you again, Carol. And your brother is much more dangerous than you realize."

"Norbett?"

"You probably don't know just how perverted he is."

"What are you talking about?"

"Please don't come to this house ever again. And leave my brother alone."

"Did Eddie tell you to say that?"

"He thinks very highly of you, Carol and I don't want to disillusion him."

"About what? Listen Skip this is true love in case you don't know. We are desperately in love."

"You may think that but you are deluded Carol, you and Eddie are just good friends."

"Oh; yeah. How do you know?"

"He's my brother."

"We don't need your permission. You're an idiot."

"There are other fish in the sea. I hope you know that."

"What does that mean?"

"Eddie is very attractive to other women.'

"Like who?"

"Never mind. I don't want you to commit suicide or something."

"I can do anything I want with your brother. He's madly in love with me. So are a few other people but I happen to like him best. You little snot."

It was Carol at her most obnoxious. Her voice had a tight sing song sheen to it. Helen imagined her face, sharp-lipped and narrow-eyed like a fox.

"Carol, you are not Queen of the world."

A bitter tinkling laugh – a la Duchess of Windsor.

"Of course not. Don't be such a child. You little snot."

"Is your brother there? Norbett?"

The Duchess of Windsor voice vanished. "Why do you want to know?"

"I wish to speak to him."

"Forget it."

"It is he that should know my wrath."

Another tinkling laugh. The telephone felt slippery in Helen's hand. Fury surged up from her toes right through to her head and ears.

"Eddie and I may have a few surprises for you, darling. Try not to be too angry, little one." Carol's voice had departed from the high breathless plane to a deeper Marlene Dietrich rumble. "And stay away from Norbett."

She hung up.

Helen held the receiver for a moment then dialed Carol's number. Carol answered.

Helen spoke rapidly clipping her words, radio announcer fashion. "It is extremely rude to hang up on people, but then you are a rude person aren't you, Carol?"

Carol slammed down the phone again. Helen dialed again, Carol answered again.

"Everybody at school despises you, Skip. They think you're a stuck up little snot."

"You probably don't realize that Eddie will soon be leaving for Texas."

"Who says?"

"He did. So don't make too many plans. There may be another woman involved."

"You're just jealous because I'm blond."

"Nazis are always blond."

Clunk, a simultaneous hanging up. Helen stalked down the hall pausing briefly beside her own bedroom door, which was shut.

"Time to go, Aunt Bernice."

Immediately a great rustling of papers and boxes went up behind the closed door.

Helen sulked into Jessie's room. Grandma was still laid out on her bed, mouth open, eyes closed. Probably not dead though, the sensitive teenage girl thought.

She marched down the stairs, out onto the porch and sat down on the swing. Swinging with one foot on the floor, she imagined herself rolling huge boulders down on Carol from a high desert bluff.

TWENTY

E ach day when I drove my carriage to the school, I carried Billy's handkerchief next to my heart. He'd given it to me that evening as we walked down the lane. I'd started to cry. I was so homesick. Passing through a lane full of lilacs, their scent reminded me of home. I thought of my sisters, my mother and father.

Billy did have a kind heart, and he tried to comfort me, and that's when it began.

I was afraid right from that evening. It's hard to remember fear though. The memories I do have are the slow spread of darkness around us, the gold rim of the setting sun, the soothing touch of his hand on mine, and yes, the sweet, sweet smell of lilacs. Oh it does sound like a cheap novel, Amsden, one you'd never read.

After that year, I couldn't read one either. But sometimes our lives turn straight into that cheap novel.

Helen hesitated in the doorway. "Mother says to come down and get in the car, Grandma."

Oh yes, the smell of lilacs, and the deep sweet whisper of Billy Black saying my name. 'Jessie, Jessie.'

"Grandma. Wake up."

Then as Helen felt in the pocket of her shorts, she touched the piece of paper she'd picked off the floor of the trailer and she forgot about Grandma. She took it out and read it again.

I love you desperately. Was that Carol's handwriting? She wasn't sure. Still it was valuable. Revenge is sweet – heh heh heh – thought the sensitive teenage girl as she tromped down the stairs.

"Mother, she won't get up."

"Take these thermoses out to the car and be careful where you put them."

Corky thrust the two big thermoses into Helen's arms. Just then Dana came in. He took them away from his daughter.

"Get in the car," he said to her. "Just sit there and don't move."

"She can help." Corky protested. "And where's Eddie?"

"Out there in the car. Trying to convince me to let him drive. Did you tell him he could run an errand?"

"No." Corky said.

"Collect your mother. At the rate we're going we'll never get away."

Corky sighed. She sat down at the kitchen table.

"Do you think I should make her change her clothes? She's wearing a wool suit."

Dana shoved the two thermoses in the last of the milk carton boxes.

"Let her do what she pleases."

"Mind that thermos." Corky said.

He started down the back stairs.

"Do you miss folks in Denver?"

Something inside him shifted wildly. His head whipped round. Corky was looking at him with over bright eyes. "Why do you ask?"

"You've been so down in the mouth since you got back."

"It's a big step, moving."

"But you're keeping this new job?"

"I don't know."

"What do you mean you don't know?" Corky's voice went up. "Isn't that why you came back? Why we invited Bernice down this weekend? I thought we'd decided."

Dana came back up into the kitchen, and set the box with the thermos down by the sink. "It's a big decision, Corky."

"You're not making sense to me."

"Maybe I'm not making sense to myself."

"Is it your dad? I thought you'd decided you couldn't help him."

"I can't. He won't change. That's not it."

"There's somebody else isn't there?" Dana's head jerked back as though he'd been slapped, and seeing this Corky plowed on. "It's complicated isn't it? Taking us all back there when she's there?"

Dana hesitated but it seemed impossible to lie. He sat down beside his wife.

"Yes."

"Yes what?"

"It's complicated going back."

"There is someone else?" Corky stood up. Her voice widened, deepened, took on a tone of alarm. She'd been hoping and praying.

Dana saw her surprise. He tried to back away.

"Why do you think there's someone else?"

"All those phone calls. From your landlady. It's her isn't it? Was that her last night? Somebody called you last night. And this morning. Oh Dana how could you?"

What she couldn't say was how he hadn't taken her in his arms, that he hadn't made love to her, though those were the thoughts in her heart.

The kitchen still smelled of fried chicken, of coffee and toast, of burnt jam and spilled milk. Smelled too, faintly, of dirty dishrags and sauerkraut, old wax and wet paper bags, the inside of rubber boots and garbage not taken out. It smelled of family life, past and future. The kitchen seemed real; their words did not.

"Tell me the truth, Dana."

He knew. Knew the moment was there in that kitchen, its outcome like an abyss opening during an earthquake. What he didn't know was how to lie.

"I do care about somebody besides you. But I love you."

"Oh Dana." His wife's face was flushed, her eyes challenged him. Hurt and anger sparked out of her like an electric current.

"It's not either or. This person, this woman, needs someone to care about her."

"So do I." burst out of Corky. "Oh brother, so do I."

"I love you, Corky. I always have."

"Be quiet. Don't you dare say anything like that."

"This other person needed love." Dana said working through the words. "And I was lonely. But I've said goodbye."

Corky stood still, there in her kitchen. What can I say? she thought, her mind a blank. But her feelings weren't; her feelings were rough and ready and about to explode if she weren't careful.

"I want you to understand why it happened." Dana said his voice dry and matter of fact. "But to know also that it's over, it's finished."

"Are we going on this picnic?" Corky said in a rough voice. "Better take the boxes out. I'll get Mother."

Dana couldn't move, not then. He thought, I can't take another step away from this moment, and this woman. I have loved her for a very long time.

He managed a few more quiet words. "That person in Denver – she'd just lost a child. She has a bad husband."

Then words exploded out of Corky, "So do I, so do I. I'll get Mother."

"I was away from home a long time."

"I told you this would happen! I told you when you went!" Corky's voice rose to a near shriek. She stood in the center of that kitchen like stone, face white, breath coming fast. Oh she wanted to strike him. It was true. All her fears were true. He had left her.

"I'll take this out to the car." Dana stood up, awkwardly took the box of thermos from the counter by the sink. "I won't run away, I promise."

"Yes you will, yes you will. You're always running away." Her voice was like breaking glass. An awful feeling surprising and sharp swept through Dana then. Without a word he turned and walked out of the kitchen. Down the back stairs, out into the yard. He went over to the car, balanced the box on the front fender and opened the trunk of the beautiful blue Ford. For a moment he leaned over, his breath coming in short gasps as though he'd been struck in the chest.

She'd said those very words. I heard my mother saying those same words.

Christ, how could I be at this moment in my life when I hear my own wife saying them? How has it come to this? Dana looked up at the summer sky, so milky blue. He had to shade his eyes against the sun.

Eddie and Helen sitting in the back seat quarreling were too busy to notice him.

How could they know then that Dana's spark was a great stalk of silver rising up into the sky, then falling into slivers of silver tinged with blue, a spark not easily seen under a hot summer sun.

He'd stood as a child and watched his dad and mother exchange words of anger and recrimination, his dad swaying from the leftovers of some massive hangover; his mother, in his mind's eye invariably in the kitchen stirring soup. We ate so goddamned much soup, he thought. Potato peeling broth a few times when the old man had spent his whole pay check. And now I'm supposed to hang over him in a hospital bed?

Dana's hands were trembling. He was alone with all this. His son and daughter yammering away in the back of the car about some nonsense of their own, his wife in the house in a rage, and here he was awash with guilt, and anger, and love.

I hated the old man when I was a child, Dana thought. Do I still hate him? I wished he would go away, would never come back to hurt us, to wound my mother.

Well my wish may come true now but I may lose more than my dad.

Dana put the carton with the thermos in the back of the car. All I have to do is get in this car and drive away. Kick the kids out, and take off. He wanted to do that. That was what was so terrible to him. That was what his father had done. Over and over. God help me, Dana prayed, I won't do it, I'll never do that. Not to anyone I love.

On the second floor in the big old house like a ship, Jessie was deep in her dream, sailing through a beautiful summer in Iowa. The town of Prescott rested on green fields as far as the eye could see; from a distance it appeared on the horizon like a ship becalmed on a sea of emerald green, one where no storm could penetrate.

Remember how folks used to take turns boarding the schoolteacher, Amsden?

It was more than two months before I stayed with the Blacks. Driving up my heart was beating hard. I hadn't seen Billy since that night with the lilacs. I was confused and afraid, yet stirred by the thought of him. When I drove up no one came out of the house Nelly, up to the manger inside that barn and tied her up, loosening her traces, not yet to greet me. It was a big house, and at the back there was a stable. I pulled my mare, ready to believe I would spend the night there.

Remember the calm of a stable, Amsden? The smell so strong and sure – oh a truth all of its own. Standing in its quiet, I told myself to be cautious, to act proper, but then I heard the quick sound of footsteps, felt suddenly arms embracing me. I jumped and turned around; Billy Black bent close to greet me, and to kiss me again.

Corky hurried into the bedroom, "Get up Mother, we're going." Jessie didn't stir. "Did you hear me, Mother? Get up and change your clothes."

When Dana went back inside, the kitchen was empty. He went into the living room and tried Tom Shannon again. This time his cousin answered and told him that his dad had slipped into a coma and things didn't look so good, but he wasn't dying yet. They agreed to meet at the park, so Dana could give Tom the money to pay for a hospital room. Dana didn't want his father in a charity ward.

I'm not going to tell Corky yet, Dana thought. Let's get this picnic over and her mother sorted out, let Corky cool down, then I'll go over to St. Paul and see if there is anything else I can do. He said a prayer then, something he didn't do often enough. He prayed for his dad and he prayed for his marriage.

Bernice hastily jammed one more chocolate into her mouth, scattered chocolate papers into the wastebasket, and shut the Trinity box. She stuffed it into her suitcase which she'd partially repacked just in case she found the courage to leave early. Sitting down again she poured herself one last shot glass of sherry, then tucked the bottle in the overnight case on the bed beside her. She took out a spare pack of cigarettes and put that into her purse. There, she thought, I'm prepared for this nightmare journey into the psyche of my family and friends. As she sipped the sherry, she congratulated herself on splurging on Bristol Cream this time; it was so deliciously sweet when she finished, she stuck out her tongue and licked the inside of the shot glass. Yum yum. She tucked away the glass and rose. Her time of torture had come.

Oh how I do hate a family picnic, she thought going down the hall. She pretended not to see Corky yanking clothes off Jessie.

That evening Billy led me into that house. It was a high fashion house like one you'd see in Minneapolis or St. Paul, the large rooms were full of dark furniture. The evening was dying down, daylight slowly separating itself from the land, leaving only a sky painted with light, then even that illusion faded into darkness. Remember the darkness in the countryside in those years, Amsden? It came down like a heavy cloth thrown over the whole world. The serving woman announced her departure after spreading out a supper in the dining room for me. We went on talking and talking while the house seemed to draw in and steady itself around us. Oh we had so much to say! We were young. Billy rose once or twice to go to the mahogany sideboard against the wall, to pour rhubarb wine into fine crystal glasses. I felt so elegant and grown up.

"Mother sometimes you make me so cross." Corky pushed Jessie into a sitting position and pulled her legs to the edge of the bed.

Jessie blinked drowsily. "What's wrong?"

"We're all waiting for you. We're going out."

"Oh for land's sakes. I don't want to go somewhere now."

"Yes you do."

"I've got things to do."

"Don't be ridiculous."

"Who's going?"

"Everybody."

"Will Violet be there?"

"Don't start on that. Here let me help you."

Dana backed the Ford down the driveway and stopped beside the front porch. Eddie and Helen got out. Dana looked at his watch. Almost one o'clock.

Outside the sun was now in full command. Directly overhead, blazing hot, it brooked no interference, demanded total allegiance. In houses up and down the street small children were screaming in play and rage. Cars of strangers threshed nosily along 35th Street. Lawnmowers whirred nearby. A few houses away, a dog barked feebly and seemingly without cause but with persistence.

The Fallsworth front porch however was in shadow. On it sat two women in rocking chairs, side by side.

"Well Mother."

"Well Lily."

"Looking forward to the day?"

"No." Jessie turned her head to observe her daughter beside her. "Are you?"

"Of course. I haven't been in that old park in years." Bernice said

"What park?"

"Minnewana."

"Where they found Violet?"

"They didn't find her there."

"Oh yes they did."

"Don't start that Mother, please."

Bernice thought of the sherry upstairs; depression was setting in.

She could feel the sharp tang of the liquor in her mouth, her body warming, warming, heat rising into her head. When she'd left Sam, she'd left drinking too so it was a moral lapse, an error of judgment to bring that sherry. Still that moment on the porch, she was enjoying it, and the sense of passion it brought into her. She wanted to challenge her mother, to accuse her of hypocrisy – oh yes Bernice remembered very well that time when Father was up in the Twin Cities. I was old enough to understand something more than lemonade and tea biscuits was going on when Mr. Black came to call, she thought. Oh yes, you have your little secrets don't you Mother? But so do I.

A car pulled up across the street and two young women got out. A little girl and a dog waited in the back seat. Myrna Henderson and her sister-in-law Gloria hurried into the apartment to get some bathing suits because they planned on taking Suzette and Butch to Lake Calhoun for the rest of the day.

"We're going to Minnewana?" Jessie asked.

"Yes."

"Today?"

"Yes."

"Good." Jessie rocked in her chair, setting up a sly wobble.

Bernice stared across at Myrna's parked car. The little white dog Butch was now barking at a carload of boys in baseball caps who'd driven their ancient Pontiac alongside. The boys barked back at Butch until he grew hysterical with fury. The little girl Suzette sat in the back with her hands folded, pretending nothing was happening. Butch barked and barked. Finally the boys in baseball caps stopped barking, and with a rusty roar of pseudo power the Pontiac drove away. Just then Myrna and Gloria came out of the apartment house arm and arm, and they too drove away.

Dana sat down in the shade of the front steps to watch this neighborhood drama. He took off his fedora hat, the only one he had. It was hot. Eddie and Helen wandered up and down the driveway arguing about who'd left the trailer door open.

"Stay close you two." Dana reminded them.

Oh is it really over? Bernice was crying out in her heart to the heavens. Is this all there will be now? Am I now too old for passion? Will no man ever look at me again? I want to want. I've had a secret life. Oh God, you know that. You know me. And Bernice started to pray that Sunday on the shadowy front porch. Oh God make my life a fulsome thing. Make my life a burning! Please, please God. Depression was there all right. Liquor only made it worse. If I can't have Sam then I can have this – myself warming myself up into caring about life, threatening dark thoughts with extinction.

I need to find something to talk about with others around me, she thought.

"Why did Father buy that car, Mother?"

"What car?"

"That car." Bernice pointed.

"Is that his car?"

Corky emerged from the house. "Phone call for you Bernice."

Bernice stiffened. "For me?"

"A man."

Bernice's face went white. She rose and sailed inside.

TWENTY-ONE

Outside and beyond the car, it was a wonderful day – the kind that instructs playfulness, invites song. Recent rains had washed the air; the sun sparkled. Everything was sharply defined. The day itself, in fact, was advancing as it ought – east to west, night through day to night again. Time not really anything except a river moving through eternity. Only men and women were counting minutes.

Maybe Sam will be there, Bernice thought staring out at the road ahead. Minneapolis has changed in the year I've been away. Has Sam changed too? Maybe it's been a mistake breaking it off. I didn't expect to be so lonely. Is he angry at my calls? Being Sam he wouldn't say. How much trouble is he in? Whatever he's accused of – he's probably guilty. I wonder how he looks. Has he lost any weight? Does Officer Hakkenson approve of our meeting? He seems a decent man. Thinking all this gave Bernice the shivers. She was afraid, of what she didn't know.

Why are we always driving a carload of women around? Dana rubbed the steering wheel with the palms of his hands. It was already boiling hot inside the car; he was sticky and irritated. Surrounded by women. Goddamned women with their problems. He felt an overwhelming sense of loss, a homesickness for the workshop at Benny's Manufacturing, the silence of men working, intent skilled work on bridles, harnesses, belt buckles and saddle ornaments. On his first job in Denver, most of the men had been older than Dana – steady quiet men, some handicapped, most of them satisfied they were doing something with their lives. Maybe if Dad had had a skill like that he wouldn't have taken to drink, Dana thought. Will he ever call me again in that quavering voice saying, 'I'm square son, come see me' – as though I were the parent, a parent with endless patience, and he the child.

Dana had told Tom he'd meet him by the baseball field. He'd brought all the money he had that morning to give to his cousin for the hospital and he planned to go on Monday to St. Paul. I'll visit Dad and check his bank account to see if there's any money left in it. Not likely he thought. I'll have to tell him I'm going back to my job in Denver – if Dad can hear me that is. Dana wasn't too sure what 'in a coma' meant.

He was driving down Blazedale Ave, part of Sunday traffic speeding along. Everyone was moving out of the city, escaping its heat. The family knew the route but it was hot in the car, the kind of hot that makes people scream or fall asleep. Or start a fight.

Amsden, what it's like in heaven for women – if there is a heaven that is? Because what's a woman supposed to expect when there are no breasts on any of the Holy Trinity? Where's a woman supposed to put herself – as a servant of the Lord – the Lord being male? I'm old enough that I think about such things and I worry about who decides what a sin is. I hope it isn't you.

"I checked the back door." Dana said.

"St. Dana." Corky's sarcastic voice. Bernice turned and looked at her.

"I hope I didn't hurt your feelings this morning, Corky."

"I don't want to talk right now, Bernice."

"Did I hear a sermon today?" Grandma's voice was precise.

"I don't know." Corky said. And I don't care she thought.

"I don't like missing my sermon."

"Oh be quiet mother, you and your sermons." Bernice snapped. Squashed between Dana and Jessie, she was forced to look ahead, at the road. "You've caused enough trouble today."

"Smart are you, Lily Bernice." Jessie's voice cracked like a whip. "Real smart."

She looked up with tight little eyes at the daughter beside her in the front seat. "All the time smart. Night and day smart."

"Yes I am, Mother. As a matter of fact I am smart."

"Dana," Corky looked for help, but her husband just stared out at the road; driver of a car concentrating on the road was a safe position to take with his family, he'd decided. Plus he was debating routes to the park. Maybe I should turn over onto Nicollet Avenue. Blazedale's faster but there isn't as much to see. Dana had forgotten how noisy and troublesome a family could be, how much they needed distraction.

"I'm hungry," Eddie said.

Bernice glanced at him. "You ate a good breakfast, my lad."

Helen was sitting in the back seat between her mother and her brother and so felt Eddie beside her tense up. He slid forward so that he could speak into Aunt Bernice's ear.

"I'm not your lad."

Bernice turned right around and looked at him with big pink-tinged eyes.

"A fact for which I'm grateful."

"You ever thought you don't know everything? That ever occur to you?"

He's angry. Helen saw it in his face. He's angry a lot, she thought.

"I know as much as you, my lad, as much if not more."

"No you don't. You just think you do."

"Let's not quarrel." Corky said. She looked out the window with a face as stern as one carved in marble. "I have a headache."

Bernice looked over at her. "I do appreciate you giving me the front seat Corky, you know how carsick I get." But what she thought was – I have no guilt about it either.

"You don't know anything about Grandma." Eddie said.

"She happens to be my mother." Bernice's mouth was sharp, her nose pink now.

"So?"

"So I know something about my own mother."

"No you don't." Eddie slid back. "Because you don't love her."

"That's enough," Dana said. "That's just about enough, Eddie."

They rode in silence for the next half an hour. Up and down the rolling hills outside the city. The tickle and pickle hills Helen and Eddie used to call them as children, giggling going up and down them. Now there was only glum silence. No laughing, no joy allowed inside the car that day, anyway. But they all indulged in thought, much to Violet's enjoyment because she was along for the ride too.

Violet was learning how to move around in thought land. That's what she called it anyway. Because although she could barely see the people – the gauze between the eternal or immortal, and the mortal was substantial, and sound didn't travel all that well when you didn't have eardrums – thoughts, oh thoughts came through beautifully, and sometimes yours went back, but she was finding that she thought differently on the eternal side of the gauze. Oh yes, you were careful what you thought once you were dead. Because there was no privacy, not that you needed any though you still yearned now and then for a secret or two. And how long would that last? Only the Folks Standing Around Telling Her What she Could Do and Not Do knew, or maybe they didn't. Anyway Violet Marie was beginning to see on that Fourth of July 1948 (dates were slipping rapidly away) that her family were interesting thinkers even if they weren't that exciting as doers. She sympathized especially with her niece Helen and was determined to guide her a little out of those banal romances she seemed trapped in. Too many love comics as Jessie would say. But Jessie! Well wasn't her mother a surprise!

Eddie jabbed Helen in the ribs. "Hey Skip, what's gray and green and comes in cans?" he chortled. The sensitive suffering Servant Girl leaned away from him.

Alone, all those years alone, then someone would find her. Tall, beautiful, she would draw this man to her. He would be tall too, would make love to her passionately in a far-off place, and she would risk everything to be with him. Against all odds they would live the life of Wild Gypsies. They would know Bliss. And would die together, locked in each other's arms.

"Anyone mind if I smoke?" Nobody bothered to reply. Bernice lit the cigarette.

"I've forgotten how far Minnewana Park is from the city. It's quite a drive isn't it?"

Dana turned up a side street to get to Nicollet Ave.

"What a lovely day," Bernice continued to smoke while she talked, which meant she puffed out little steamers of smoke. "Lovely, lovely day. But hot."

"It's always hot in July." Helen said.

"Of course." Bernice turned again this time to look at her niece. "Is your friend going to be at the park?"

"I have no friends, Aunt Bernice."

"Carol. Her name's Carol, isn't it Eddie?"

Eddie flamed a look at Bernice, Helen stared grimly at Aunt Bernice who didn't mind; she was the kind of person who liked to poke sticks into cages.

"Did I hear my sermon today?" Jessie asked. This time she looked at Dana. He reached over, turned on the radio, found a sermon instantly, one about a man who prayed to God for help with a job and got a Studebaker. The family listened in silence for some minutes but when the subject turned to Hell and Damnation, Dana shut off the radio. "We should take Mother's purse away." Bernice said. Jessie looked sideways up at her, like a small dog examining a mastiff. "She does nothing but worry about it."

"Did I turn that stove off?" Jessie spoke in a soft voice to nobody in particular.

"Now let's see -we were trying to think of the name of that baby that died." Bernice said to Dana. He shook his head and kept his eyes on the road.

"What baby?" This time it was Helen who slid forward.

"We had a baby sister who died at birth. We never saw her. Did we Corky?"

"You have fat thighs Skip." Eddie poked Helen in the leg. "Anybody told you that?" The viciousness of this remark brought tears to the Wild Gypsy's eyes.

"Mother"

"Eddie." Corky said in a dead voice. She leaned her head against the back window hoping to fall asleep. "Eddie. Please." He looked out his window.

Helen thought. I am in the middle of the back seat as usual. Between Her Majesty the Queen and the Dark Prince.

"I thought her name was Pansy." Dana said.

"Well done, Dana." Bernice said in a charming voice. "You're right. Pansy. But she had a middle name like the rest of us. What was her middle name? Rose Corinne, Lily Bernice, Violet Marie, and Pansy…"

Rose Corinne's head was bouncing against the back window. If only I could sleep through all this, she thought, but she couldn't help listening. How can Dana remember such things and I can't? She reached out and poked her mother in the back. Jessie turned around in slow motion.

"What was Pansy's middle name, Mother?"

"What Pansy?"

"Your Pansy."

"I don't know what you're talking about." Jessie turned back to her window.

Bernice stirred irritably, "What's the point of talking to her?"

"She had black hair, Mother. Remember?" Corky wasn't going to give up.

"Black hair?" That intrigued Helen. The Servant Girl's hair was blah brown.

"I believe I turned that stove on." Jessie told the window in a small ominous voice. "Sure as anything."

"It started with a D I think," speculated Bernice in a determined voice. "Dorothy? Doreen? Darlene?"

She held out her pack of cigarettes to Dana. This time he took one and stuck it in his ear. Corky slid forward and tapped him on the shoulder.

"Dana you promised me."

"Traffic's picking up," he said." Let's hope they're not all not going to Minnewana Park."

"Your shorts are too short." Eddie poked Helen in the leg again.

The Servant Girl leaned away from the Dark Prince and toward Her Majesty.

"Stop it, Eddie." Corky said wearily.

"The baby that died." Bernice plowed on. "I never saw her. Did you Corky?"

"No." And shut up about it, Corky thought.

From the backseat Helen could see Grandma staring intently

out the side window. Riding in the car she looked out that way, with a strange hunger as though she'd never seen such things before and might never again.

"Grandma knows." Helen ventured, but nobody seemed to hear her.

"What'd she die of?" Eddie asked.

"Apparently she cried and cried and then threw up. Then she died." Bernice took a long thoughtful drag of smoke. "Rose Corinne, Lily Bernice, Violet Marie and Pansy."

"Irene?" Dana said.

"Why don't you ask Grandma?" Helen suggested.

Bernice turned around to look at her niece. "I doubt she remembers."

She turned to Jessie beside her. "The BABY, MOTHER – THE ONE THAT DIED. WHAT WAS HER MIDDLE NAME?"

Jessie ignored her, instead looked out the window. They were down to gas stations and country stores, a few used car dealers, almost out of the city.

.Corky couldn't stand it any longer. Why should Dana have all the answers? She reached out and poked her mother in the back again. This time Jessie didn't turn around.

"Mother, what was Pansy's middle name?"

"Pansy?" Jessie turned her head to follow an interesting object on the sidewalk, then chose another to concentrate on.

Bernice stirred irritably, "What's the point of talking to her?"

"You don't suppose I'd do a thing like that?" Jessie asked the window. "An awful thing like that?"

"Something like a name just bothers the life out of me." Bernice said. "I have to work and work until I remember it."

"An awful thing like that?" Jessie's voice was louder. They could all hear her now. Corky slid forward. Touched her mother's shoulder. Spoke into her ear.

"What are you talking about Mother?"

"I was making some coffee."

"No you weren't mother." Bernice said. "I never ever saw you near that stove. Now stop it."

"An awful thing like that?" Jessie queried the window sadly.

Corky looked at her husband, "Was Mother on her own in the house, Dana?"

"How should I know?"

"You have to keep an eye on her every minute."

"I was on the phone." Dana knew instantly that was the wrong thing to say.

"Of course." Corky said sharply. She slid back.

"Rose, you don't suppose I left that stove on?" Jessie now turned haunted eyes on her daughter in the back seat. Dana took the cigarette from behind his ear and put it in his mouth. They all heard the click of the cigarette lighter announcing itself.

"Dana." Corky said her lips pale as she watched him light the cigarette.

She forgot to put on lipstick, Helen thought. Mother is definitely developing a problem with her memory.

"I do believe I did." Jessie informed the window. "I did leave it on."

"You promised me, Dana." Corky's voice was dignified.

"Pay absolutely no attention." Bernice said, "Don't listen to her."

"You did promise Dana."

"What were we talking about? Oh yes, middle names. I've always been glad we were given sensible middle names. Thank the Lord for Bernice I used to say."

"I was in that kitchen making some coffee."

Silence. Helen waited. Nobody said anything so she did. "Mother. Grandma…"

"You did promise, Dana…"

"Seems to me I do the awfulest things sometimes."

"Mother."

"Lily. I never ever looked like a Lily."

"Witch."

"What?"

"Mother."

"Do you intend to break all your promises to me at the same time?"

Dana turned and looked at Corky. He has killer eyes, Corky thought. Just like Eddie. Like Father, like son. She put her hands in her lap and looked straight ahead.

"Hope they left some windows open."

"Mother."

"WHAT?"

"Grandma keeps saying she left the stove on."

"Well don't listen to her."

"I can't help it. She keeps saying it."

"Why?" Bernice gave out her best, loudest chuckle. "Why on earth would she turn on the stove? Ask yourself that."

"To make some coffee?"

"How do YOU know THAT?" Bernice chuckled again.

"She said so."

"She said." Bernice chuckled again.

Eddie hated the sound of her laugh. He was muttering something even Helen couldn't hear.

Corky leaned forward. "Were you in the kitchen?"

"Me?" Bernice recoiled surprised.

"I'm talking to Mother."

"Don't believe her. She's making it up."

"I hope I didn't do a thing like that." Jessie said, "I wanted some coffee."

"You had two cups." Corky said grimly "I made it. I gave it to you. You took it upstairs to your room and drank it."

"I did? Good. I wouldn't want to do a dangerous thing like leave a stove on." Corky slid back, let her head bounce against the half open window frame.

"Maybe I didn't." Jessie said in a weak drifty voice. She turned back to her friend the window. "Maybe I didn't do it after all."

"Mother, stop it." Bernice said. "Stop talking tripe."

Eddie was the first one to notice they'd turned around. He watched his dad go round a block, then turn back up Nicollet Ave. The wise Roman Statesman profile didn't change, the wise Roman Statesman said nothing. That they all noticed A silence fell upon the gathering. Wuffle wuffle wuffle went the tires on the blue Ford Amsden had bought just before he died.

Dana slipped into thinking about Mattie. She'd seemed almost biblical to him. She never exploded in anger, never broke down with grief, never failed to be patient. She appeared to experience life as a mild winter without much sun.

How does a person pass through life so quietly? Dana thought. She liked to read, sometimes she sewed. She'd invariably looked meticulously groomed, her face serene, voice soft. Around her had hung a faint ever present sadness, a vague distress yet one that seemed easily routed; she responded with a mild pleasure to small gifts and everyday conversations.

Naked she was as tranquil as dressed; she made love with the cool languor of night swimming. She'd seemed so manageable, so particular and clockwork in her personality. He'd felt surprise that such an elegant non- demanding woman even existed.

Now I can see why her husband might leave, he thought, without children, without a wife of energy, a man could drown in too much calm, in complete passivity. But for a time he'd found her comforting.

James Newell was my education, Corky thought looking out her window at Nicollet Avenue returning into spaces and small square boxes of stores, and odd homemade looking houses mixed in with big expensive ones. The edges of the city lacked definition, were ragged and disorganized looking. Maybe that's good, Corky thought, maybe being ragged and disorganized is good. I'd like to try being that way again. That's the way it was with James – everything unexpected, ragged and disorganized, yet something in me changed forever after those days with him. After being with James Newell, I knew who I was. Maybe it's a good thing I've remembered him, Corky thought leaning her head against the window as the opening up moods of the city swept by again. There's a piece of me that belongs to him. He taught me there was more to life than Mother and Father, more than my sisters and my boyfriends.

Amsden, where did you put the big bible? For years I thought you gave it to one of the girls but none of them said they knew a thing about it. I had all sorts of names and addresses written in it including that drat baby. What did you do with it? I thought maybe I'd have it buried with me. Do you think Violet had it? She was the oddest girl.

The train was pulling out, and she the famous wartime spy was on it. She'd escaped the assassins sent to eradicate her. With the help of two of her lovers she'd managed to find a ticket on this last train out of Paris. She was dressed in ugly working class clothes, dark drab coarse materials, but her beauty she could not disguise. It was her only weapon against the brutal nature of her fellow travelers. She looked around the car. A brutish lot sunk into their own sordid lives.

If Sam doesn't come I'm going to write out everything I know and send it to the police. That's the only way to really punish him, because Sam deserves punishment, not just for the way he treated Violet but the way he treated a lot of people. He's a liar. Charming, rugged, but a liar. I know that now. No wonder his wife doesn't care if he runs around. She probably decided to put with his lies for the sake of his children. But what if he's there? What do I do then? I wish I'd never called him. Or told Hank Hakkenson I'd be at the park picnic tables sometime this afternoon.

"Nobody light a match when we get there." Eddie had warmed to the possibilities. "The house may be full of gas. One match could send the whole thing up."

"What are you talking about?" Corky asked crossly.

"Maybe Grandma didn't have time to light the stove." Eddie was relentless. "Maybe she was interrupted right after she turned the gas on."

"She's playing a game." Bernice looked down at the meek little white head turned away from her and spoke with staccato clarity. "I know all about her little games."

"You never know." Eddie said. "There could be gas in the house now."

Helen liked that idea. She could see them returning, walking into a house reeking with gas. She alone would make it to the telephone and dial for help; everybody else would be knocked out. She'd gasp out the address. Can you get to a window and break it? the fireman would say in an urgent voice – there were some very good looking firemen just down the street. The police would come too. She'd crawl over the crumpled bodies of Mother and daddy and Aunt Bernice and Eddie – she could see herself accidentally stepping on Eddie's face as she reached the window. When the emergency squad broke in she would be at the open window taking great heaving breaths of clean night air, her hands dripping with blood, her half-naked breasts heaving and they'd say…

"Great, it's one thirty and we're back home again." Corky sat bolt upright. Dana turned into 35th street "Why do we go? Somebody tell me that. Why do we bother?"

Helen felt the piece of paper in her pocket.

"I found a note in the trailer." she said.

There was a silence.

"What kind of note?" asked Eddie.

"I'll never tell." said the world famous spy.

"Why did you tell us then?" her mother snapped.

"Because I want to find out who wrote it."

"Why don't you show it to us?" Aunt Bernice was smooth. "Pass it around so we can all look at it."

Tempted the world famous spy took the paper out, unfolded it then thought better of it. She put the note back in her pocket.

"Where did you say you found it?" asked Dana.

"In the trailer. On the floor."

"You've been going in there?"

"Everybody has, Daddy."

"What did it say?" Eddie's' I don't really care' voice.

"It was a mash note."

"Mash note?" Bernice's voice contained revulsion.

"Love stuff." Eddie said, "Mash notes are…"

"Never mind," Corky snarled.

"Look at them," Violet was disgusted. "They talked about this being their last picnic together and all they do is think about themselves. What's the matter with them? I'd like to give them all a wake up smack."

Whoosh.

Minnewana Park, Minneapolis, Minnesota, the USA, North America – they all disappeared and Violet was up, way up, in the gauze curtain reality looking down on earth. The earth was its usual beautiful blue earth self.

"Now, Violet," Those Who Were In The Know said. "You've got to smarten up. You're getting caught up on being alive, part of your family again, developing opinions, wanting to change things or them.

Stop it, Violet. You are here to do one thing and one thing only, and you've gone over and over with us how you will go about doing that."

They didn't raise their voices because they didn't have any but they certainly made it clear that they were impatient with Violet.

Did she care? Was she intimidated? Not really. Not very.

Next she was standing above the sky, or so she thought. Millions and billions and trillions of stars stretched out in every direction, some bright, some pulsating, they were of every color, shade and hue, a few so pale they almost weren't there at all.

"No, we are not above the stars," said Those Who Knew A Lot More than Violet, "This is a soul map and all those lights are soul sparks. We keep track of you that way."

"So many are so bright," Violet was surprised.

"Oh yes, oh yes. We all find our own way of signaling God. Very few lights go out. But of course very few are brilliant either. Now Violet, concentrate, this is what you have to remember::-Family warfare is over for the dead. It's all about spiritual development."

Violet hated the way those words came into her – so definite, so powerful – her own fading thoughts fading even more, and she helpless to mount rebuttals to their superior knowledge. She had hated superior brained people when she was alive – now they were her mentors! She could never again be a dumb little bunny with malicious thoughts and sensual preferences. Was eternity going to be one long boring university seminar?

Their thoughts came crowding in again, "You yourself organized this expedition Violet Marie Fallsworth. You begged and begged us to do this. Now get busy and do it."

Whoosh. Slap Blop.

The Keepers of the Soul Map had dropped her down through the gauze into Minneapolis, Minnesota, U.S.A. – just outside Minnewana Park.

"Doesn't that look like Violet?" Corky said, pointing out a short stocky dark haired woman with an odd face, or rather a face with an odd expression on it. She was trudging along, head down, totally overdressed for a picnic, but heading for the entrance to the park.

"And that looks like my jacket, the one she kept borrowing and never returning," Bernice said with surprise.

"By gum," thought Violet, "if I'm doing this, I'm doing it with some pizzazz."

Violet had tested a lot of boundaries when she was alive, she'd known how far she could go, at least until that fateful afternoon when she'd gone too far. But now she didn't know how much free will she had as a dead person.

Well she'd soon find out.

TWENTY-TWO

From a distance Minnewana Park was a pastoral scene, a landscape of summer with all its generous greens: oaks, elms and maples enlarged by long individual lives; grassy lawns well defined by paths and roadways; gardens random and formal; also a baseball diamond, football playing fields, horseshoe rings, shuffleboard courts, rugged clumps of bushes and slender strips of woods; carefully tended hillsides; a gray-blue lake with two gray-green islands and graceful yielding shoreline; a small lively amusement park; scattered concession stands in bright colors; and a cluster of secluded redwood picnic tables.

High above the park the cloudless sky was a blue bowl, the golden sun a guardian researching its own creation. July heat had made everything flower, and there were flowers everywhere, everywhere that the tides of people would permit, for the citizens who crowded Minnewana Park on this Fourth of July Sunday were blossoming too. They were spreading blankets on the ground, taking off confinement of cars and houses, revealing themselves in shirtsleeves and sundresses, shorts and bathing suits. They scattered themselves across the landscape, walked the paths, played ball or shuffleboard, swam, watched ball games, strolled through gardens, followed the shoreline, fed ducks, rowed or paddled across water, ventured up hillsides and into bushes and woods.

On closer inspection more could be seen, and heard. Each patch of possession, each gathering of people, each just arriving car contained its own world, its own drama.

"That baby had no hair. Bald as an egg." Jessie reached out with wry wrinkled fingers and toyed with Bernice's hair. "Not like Lily. Lily had lots of hair."

Bernice stiffened. "Thank you Mother."

"Irene." Jessie said.

"Irene? Are you talking about Pansy, Mother? Pansy Irene?"

Bernice fluffed up her firm perm and manhandled the name of the baby as though it was a foreign word.

"Lily had lovely blond curls. Not like now." Jessie looked sideways up at her daughter. Bernice dropped her hand from her hair.

"My goodness it's hot," she said.

Dana kept his mouth shut and his eyes on the road. Helen sat forward; she could still see the fine dusting of ceiling plaster across his shoulders. He'd brushed most of it out of his hair. She wondered if she should tell anyone what had happened in the house.

Nobody else appeared to have noticed. Maybe she did have talent as an international spy. Pamela. That was the perfect name for a spy – Pamela Resolute.

They were approaching the park entrance.

"Christ!"

Dana swerved the car and then braked to a halt. A sheepish mutt looked over apologetically at them and then continued trotting across the road. A red open roadster behind them blared its horn. Dana drove on.

"Oh I wouldn't want us to hit a dog," cried Corky "Wouldn't that be awful? I'm glad you stopped Dana."

"I would. I'd like it." Eddie was sitting upright now.

"No you wouldn't Eddie."

"Yes I would. Go back, Dad. I'll see if I can get him with my door."

"Eddie."

"Ruff Ruff Ruff Ruff." Eddie stuck his head out his window and facing backwards barked out the window.

"Is that necessary?" Aunt Bernice said in a sophisticated aren't you rather an amusing-little-twerp voice, not bothering to turn around.

"Yes." Said Eddie. "Ruffruffruffruff" This time he kept his head inside the car and barked at Aunt Bernice who didn't notice.

"Stop it Eddie." Corky said. "You're giving me a headache."

Eddie reached over and patted her hand. "Oh the poor itty-bitty mumsie has a headache." Corky laughed out loud. "Because the brave little mumsie is going on a picnic with her rotten itty bitty little family."

"Stop it, you bad boy." But Corky was laughing hard now. She has a good laugh, Helen noticed with some surprise. She watched her mother push Eddie's hand away and then they started wrestling across her lap. When her mother laughed it was like a spring opening, bright water gushing up into sunlight.

Rose Corinne's spark was crystal, green, and rose – all three colors rushing up, overwhelming each other over and over.

They'd entered the park through a side road by then, and were driving slowly along it. The car windows were open and they could hear the sounds of people.

"Only one born with real red hair was me." Jessie didn't appear to be talking to anyone in particular, but once again was looking out her open window, breathing in park people sounds and smells. The road was a narrow winding passage into a whole world, one that Jessie remembered.

Minnewana was a big park, planned big and kept big. No city father ever dared nibble away at its edges, or change its internal certainties. Sprawling across acres of land, held itself together with a network of paved roads and gravel walking paths, Minnewana boasted a large lake where not only row boats and canoes could be rented and ducks and geese fed, but an island from which fireworks were dispatched on public holidays like the Fourth of July. Though a popular destination for aspiring lovers, on firework display occasions no boats were allowed to land on this island. In the narrow arm of the lake at the north end, a second little plot of land called Duck Island, was so unappealing few boaters landed there. Even ducks avoided it.

Despite Minnewana Park's appearance of order and planning, its many traditions, there remained something mysterious about it, something dark. Rumor had it an Indian burial ground had been bulldozed over to make room for the shuffleboard courts but no bones or arrow heads had ever emerged and so this remained a rumor. It must be remembered that there have always been landscapes that hold mysteries, no matter how overbuilt and well organized they can appear, below their surface – a fire of chaos smolders away. People who live on or near these landscapes usually know about these fires of chaos underground. If they're lucky, or smarter than most, they remain respectful. If they are stupid, or stubborn, or willful, if they pretend that outer order is all there is, or should be, sooner or later thin eager tendrils of chaos appear above ground, and then – well then everybody better look up, up past even the soul maps and their keepers, way way up to where chaos begins, and where the designer of its submission to order remains. Then this original Aegean stables will once again be given to human kind to clean since who else can face chaos so well, and accomplish the tasks of Hercules so intelligently, than a species both animal and spiritual, practical and sensual, passionate and calculating, brave and cowardly?

Minnewana's dark was not a bad dark, nor an evil one, only somewhat dark dark. Minnewana had unsolved murders, yes, but these were of the basic familiar sort- body dumped in ditch, bullet hole in head. But its mysteries were more unconventional.

Ammunition frequently worked its way to the surface.

Trees fell over suddenly.

Bushes developed strange diseases or wobbled around when there was no wind.

Rabbits appeared in winter white coats year round.

Flickering lights were seen on Duck Island and in fir trees.

Music came out of holes in the ground.

If Minnewana were an animal, it would be a big lurching one.

Families who went to the park every year believed the park never changed. This family had believed that too, but now they knew their day at Minnewana might be the last time they were together as a family, and so this changed how they looked at everything. Naturally they didn't discuss that fact, or any facts except the ones each was personally preoccupied with at the moment.

"Some of those places for old people aren't so bad," Bernice said. "I visited three in Duluth last week. Sensible people seem to run them."

"Is today Sunday?" asked Jessie.

"All day." Dana said.

Bernice stirred restlessly, "There're not all that bad is all I'm saying. I think at least we could discuss them as a temporary solution."

"What does that mean – discuss?" Jessie looked sideways at her middle daughter.

"What do you think it means Mother?" But Bernice didn't look over at Jessie.

Dana turned on the radio.

"I came to the garden alone. While the dew was still on the roses" A church service – Jessie leaned her head back and sighed with satisfaction. "…and the voice I hear as I tarry there, the son of God discloses. And he walks with me and he talks with me and he tells me…" Jessie closed her eyes and smiled blissfully; the rest of the family looked out at the park in silence. It had grown too hot to move, or even speak. There was no breeze left. For long peaceful moments the family drove along a narrow winding road listening to a sermon by a millionaire who swore it had been God who'd made the money. At a high point of self-congratulation, Dana switched off the radio.

"That's enough of that,"

"Look at everybody washing their cars." Corky marveled. All along the park road, people were sudsing down their cars with buckets of water collected from pumps and washrooms. This was a tribal activity, something everybody did, especially on the Fourth of July, though the city fathers had outlawed it long ago as dirty and inconsiderate.

"Are we there yet?" Jessie said. She didn't like being crammed against Lily Bernice. That girl is bossy, she thought. And cranky like her father. Amsden you were cranky, especially in the evenings when you'd say how bored you were. Nothing to do, you'd grumble and then you'd crank around and pick fights with the girls or me. Couldn't sit still for the radio, Not until the television Amsden – then you were happy – watching those fat men wrestling.

"Mother wake up and look at that little house." Rose Corinne pointed.

Jessie sat up, blinked. They were passing a bright pink hut with a fancy top.

"It looks like a strawberry ice cream cone." Helen said.

"It's a concession stand." Corky said.

"I could lick a cone like that." Eddie said.

"I know some people who have a house like that." Bernice had an ominous tinge to her voice. "That color and something like that on top."

Corky slid up to talk. "What do you mean, Bernice? Who lives there?"

"Women."

"Women? You mean…?"

"Yes," Bernice said, emphatically, "those kind of women."

"How do you know that?" Corky was shocked.

"I know things," Bernice said. "I get around more than you think."

"Your friend told you, didn't he?"

"Maybe." Bernice said, enjoying the attention her secret life was at last receiving.

"That policeman of yours?" Corky couldn't leave the subject alone.

"A cop?" Eddie was impressed. "How'd you meet him?"

"Never you mind. I wasn't arrested if that's what you're asking."

"I don't think you should talk about such things in front of the kids. I think you're a fool." Corky said in a muffled angry voice and slid back. I've had enough of this whole day, she thought, and now she'll start to smoke I suppose.

Bernice found her cigarettes in her purse and pulled them out.

"I know what you think," Bernice said in an equally angry voice "You've made it very clear to me." She snapped the purse shut, an authoritative sound. "Cigarette Dana?" She held the pack open, let a few cigarettes show to tempt him but he shook his head.

The park's crowded already he thought. So did Helen. She wasn't looking forward to a boring day with the masses. She leaned back, closed her eyes in resignation, and returned to Melinda, daughter of Lord Salisbury, who was being married against her will to an effete type. She'd read the story in one of Carol's love comics but she was changing the story to make it more interesting.

Smashing through the ancient church's rose stained glass windows (which was sort of a shame, but couldn't be helped) came a devilishly handsome buccaneer. "She is mine, this lovely damsel," he cried out in a Scottish type voice. The young bride rushed across the church to throw herself at…

"Everybody look for a parking place." Dana commanded. "Everybody."

Helen sat up again. Daddy is definitely the most interesting person in the family, she thought. She'd been watching him ever since last night when he'd arrived on the train. It was a whole year since she'd seen him. He was quiet and different somehow.

"I am looking, Dad "Eddie said, "But not for a place."

"What then?" his sister asked.

"Girls." Eddie said and laughed diabolically. "Girls. Hahahahah."

"That's enough, Eddie," Dana said. "Keep your eye open. We need a place that isn't too far from the road. Jessie can't walk too far."

"I can walk," Jessie said in a sudden forceful voice. "You bet your darn tooting."

Amsden and I walked in Florida every night. Every night up and down the road. We looked at the stars. We walked all over this park too."

The car fell silent. Unusual for Jessie to bring up Amsden – he'd been dead for two years, and after the first weeks, she'd closed her lips against any words about him.

If they talked of him, she listened but didn't say anything.

"You're thinking about Father, Mother."

Corky slid forward to put this question close to Jessie's ear.

"Yes," said Jessie. "Talking to him too."

"How different it looks." Bernice marveled.

"What?" Helen asked.

"The park. It looks so…overgrown. What happened to the Minnewana sign?"

"They're replacing it with a bigger one," Eddie said, "Something with pizzazz."

"Pizzazz." Bernice smiled at him and assumed her most sophisticated voice. "Pretty big vocabulary young man. You do learn things at school."

Eddie bit his lip, looked out his window, I have plans for you, Aunt Bernice.

I hate this park, Bernice searched her mind for the right word. Words didn't come as quickly when she'd had a few drinks, judgment, oh judgment came satisfyingly fast, but words to articulate that, they were clumsy and slow. I hate this park because it's so…middle class, she thought, mundane, all these families huddled around each other, keeping the central fire warm – the central fire? The scorn that was dripping from her mind into her heart suddenly flared up in a hot little flame of anger that caught her by surprise. She made herself look for a parking place.

"There's one." she cried, and Dana's eyes swung over to look.

"Too narrow." And he drove on.

How my mother loved this park, Dana thought as he drove, and it was such a long journey for her – the streetcar and then we walked a ways after that. She was a good scout, and she'd say how being outside the city made her think of Ireland, and its green. She said Minnesota was green, but Ireland was greener, and wetter, and more beautiful, but sadder too, full of pain and anguish. Minnesota wasn't full of all that she said – of those feelings- it was a big stalwart, hard working cruel land, sometimes harsh, but she liked it better than Canada where…. Oh stop it, Dana thought, running on and on. She's dead and gone and now my Dad will soon be too. But I miss her, he thought, and was swept by longing for his mother's kind brown eyes. She'd listened to him, always; she'd love listening to him – his hopes and dreams, his notions of the world. She'd been his best friend until the day she'd died.

Well what had he been for her? Not a husband; no, she'd clung to his dad no matter how weak and outrageous the old man had been; she'd been a friend to his dad too, and he felt the warmth of that.

He'd been a friend to his mother. Suddenly he knew that. Why had it taken so long for him to see that? He'd taken nothing away from his dad that his dad had ever wanted or even needed. His dad's best friend had been a bottle. Well it was over, over, he repeated that, and waited for a gush of feeling for his dad to come, but it didn't and then he knew shame. Twice today shame was riding him heavy.

"There's a place." Corky called out.

"Mom are you crazy?"

"It's right next to the road."

"It's too close to the latrine."

"It's too far from the baseball field."

They drove on.

I remember, Rose Corinne thought, how we'd come here, the whole college gang and sit on the lawn and we had nothing – none of us – poor as anything, the depression on but we'd all bring sandwiches and eat them and then laugh and talk and someone would usually get up and give a speech about something or we'd all sing, and all around us the park was as clean and new as if it had been created that very morning. But oh I was always looking for some boy, someone I fancied, or was talking to my girlfriends about one that hadn't been kind to me, or had flirted then gone off with someone else. This park must be haunted with the dreams of girls like me, ghosts in all the trees, silly little things we were, running around giggling together, I remember doing that. Oh we laughed so it wasn't all sadness and heavy emotions. I try to remember it that way, as though sadness has more dignity than laughter. Laughter's best, and why do I never laugh anymore?

Rose Corinne saw a parking spot but hesitated. Why should she help Dana just because he asked and then she watched as another car, a Ford like theirs but black make a sudden violent U-turn in the road and snatch the place in front of them.

"Bastard," Dana muttered.

Eddie slid forward. "I know that guy." But his father said nothing, just drove on and Eddie slid back. He didn't like being ignored.

It might be the last time I come here. I don't care. It's pretty dull. I've been here a hundred and fifty times and always the same times and with the same people. Get out, he thought to himself, get out before you turn into a jerk, a real jerk instead of half a one.

I remember coming here when I was a kid and I'd run around playing airplane and then grandpa would take me down to the lake with a sailboat and we'd run along the shore making the sailboat go. Talk about rinky-dink, and riding the merry go round and buying popcorn and candy apples and cotton candy – it was all run together in his mind, a visit to the park and it was always the same and he loved it. He didn't like that thought and pushed it away. No, I want more than a rinky-dink little park and cotton candy. I want much much more, but he couldn't think what – then he saw two gorgeous girls walking side by side – twins. Wow.

It was the perfect setting for a murder and Pamela could see the body under the trees. She'd been walking along, thinking about her future sculpture plans when she saw a foot sticking out from under one of the fir trees. It was not a bare foot but had on a bright pink/ no red stocking. Was red too scarlet womanish? Perhaps but perhaps she was a scarlet woman. Pamela (Pam for short) walked closer...yes, a human foot. She pushed back the heavy fir branches and saw the face of a strange black-haired woman, a woman with a white face, and a scarlet mouth, a slash of red across her lips, but a slash of red across her throat as well. Pamela Resolute was not afraid of death, she leaned forward.

Well Amsden, Jessie thought, here we are again. How many times have we come out here? From the earliest days. Well there weren't any of these modern buildings or anything but the island and the trees, and we rowed out to the island remember? They had those big row boats then and you rowed us out there and we sat on the island, and you proposed to me and you told me about your daughter, and I told you about mine and we looked at each other and we said, yes, we'll do it – we'll one out of two maimed people and we did, and you loved me and I loved you all through it and here I am out in this park and I'd like to go out to the island. Yes I would, and sit in that spot where we lay down together. Remember how daring it was? We were in the shade of the trees and we didn't do anything that we called wrong then, only lay together and imagined the future when we would lie in a bed together and be man and wife. Oh you might have gone further but I said, no, I've learned my lesson and I'll take no chances, and you never pushed me, never, and I grew to love you for that, you didn't make me feel I must yield or think I would, and in that you were different then Billy Black and you were my husband from that moment on. Yes, Jessie thought. I'm going to go to the island today. That's a promise. But I won't tell anyone just yet as they think I'm too old.

It was the face of a woman without a doubt, but with a past, Pamela Resolute thought, and she leaned down and touched the locket around the black-haired woman's neck. Helen decided a better detective name would be Cassandra Brown.

"There's one," Dana said, "Perfect," and he whipped over and pulled the car in to the side of the road. By some miracle there was an open spot, an envelope of space between a battered Ford truck and a Plymouth sedan.

"It is awfully close to the bathrooms." Corky said in a hollow voice. She recognized it as the same parking place they'd passed ten minute before.

Dana shut off the engine. They sat in the hot car looking out. Not only had Dana found a parking spot but one hundred yards away from an empty table. This was a verifiable miracle. The table was still empty because a few yards further on lurked two ominous green military style buildings under tall trees.

"Dana it's right next to the…Dana are you sure…?"

Dana opened his door and got out of the car. His shirt stuck to his body with sweat. "Eddie, take the car and drive around." He reached in and took his hat, a beat up panama straw fedora out from under the front seat and put it on. "You can drive around some more, or walk around for that matter but it's too darn hot. Come back and get me when you find something better. I'll just sit here."

The family in the car watched him stroll over to the picnic table and sit down. They'd forgotten how stubborn Dana McFadden could be. After a moment, the two back car doors opened spontaneously and Eddie, Helen and Corky all got out. They were hot and hungry and their clothes stuck to them too.

Bernice and Jessie held out a bit longer. They sat side by side, a true Mutt and Jeff looking out, but finally Bernice scrunched across to emerge from the driver's side.

Yes, Bernice said. Yes I really do hate this park. And she remembered why. With Sam that afternoon when they'd come out here and he'd insisted on taking them out to the island and he'd buried all his papers out there, all the records he'd kept, and he'd said, Only you and I know they are out here. They were in a tin box. I can't trust my wife, she's such a snoop and I'll lose track of them out in some wilderness, but this is a place everybody knows and nobody goes to. We'll put it here – the money too – the tine box had twenty thousand dollars in it that Sam had taken in tips from the hookers and the pimps, Twenty thousand dollars was a lot of money and he'd dumped her now and did he think that she wouldn't know or wouldn't remember or care? Well think again Sam dear. We're going out to that island and we're getting that money and we're splitting it. I could use some money. Why I could put Mother up in her own apartment in Duluth with some of that money. She stood by the car watching Eddie curse his long sleeve blue and white striped shirt. I must have been crazy, Eddie thought, no girl is worth it. He ripped off the shirt and threw it into the back seat.

Corky looked at him. "Put your shirt on Eddie. It's Sunday."

"Mom, it's the Fourth of July." But he put it back on unbuttoned.

Corky took command then of the picnic.

"Eddie you and Helen help me unpack the food. Dana we need the keys."

Dana held them out. Eddie collected them. He went over and opened the trunk of the Ford. All the terrible magical food of picnic was waiting for them there, waiting to be unpacked, to be eaten – pickles and fried chicken, plums and apples, tomatoes and cucumbers, cheese, potato salad and hard boiled eggs, brownies and angel food cake.

Looking at all the boxes and bags, Bernice thought, The thought of all that food makes me feel ill, I just need little bites of this and that, not a mountain of food.

"Do you want some help, Corky?" Bernice didn't move away from the car.

"Yes Bernice. Take the potato salad will you?"

"Not much left is there?

"Who was that on the telephone?"

Bernice had an odd look on her face. "A friend."

"It sounded like Sam."

"It was Sam."

"Oh Bernice, you can't. I won't let you. You took that job in Duluth to get away from him. How did he know you were in Minneapolis?"

"I haven't a clue." lied Bernice and walked past her sister with the potato salad.

Corky followed her, and as they went back and forth between the beautiful blue Ford and the scarred picnic table carrying food and blankets and a blue and white checked tablecloth, they spoke in tight little sister voices which nobody else heard.

"He's a married man, Bernice."

"That doesn't matter."

"It does matter. It sure as heck does."

"I don't want to talk about it. Do you mind? It's a sensitive topic you know that."

Lily Bernice huffed away from her sister Rose Corinne, sat down at the table and stared moodily at the potato salad.

Lily Bernice's spark was a great purple gush of fireworks tinged with lavender and a great burst of raw white in the center.

Corky wanted to slap Bernice's face. Instead she went over to the car where.

Jessie still sat in the front seat.

"Come on Mother, I'll give you a cup of coffee." Corky opened the passenger door, and Jessie half fell out.

"Mind my arm," Jessie said crossly as Corky grabbed and steadied her, but she let herself be led to the picnic table and the seat of honor next to Dana.

That was fate, Dana thought, back at the house. Some kind of punishment – I was about to answer that phone. He looked up at the sky. Sorry, God, forgive me. But damn it too, he thought then, it felt good. And it feels good sitting here in this old park, too, he looked around with great pleasure now, thinking, all this space around me, a freedom today, when I need it most. He'd made up his mind to say nothing about anything to anyone all day.

Then Jessie was led up to sit beside him.

"Keep an eye on Mother, will you dear?" Corky went to the end of the table to unpack the food. "What kind of sandwich do you want Dana?"

"Doesn't matter."

"Well you've got to say."

Then his daughter Helen came over and sat on the other side of her daddy. He looked happy. Calm. She touched the powder on his shoulders and The Roman Statesman looked at her and smiled "Better go help your mother."

She stood up. She was beginning to learn there were walls between seeing, knowing, and saying, and no matter how much she wanted to tell her family what she saw she couldn't. The family gods wouldn't let her. There was God and there were family gods. Had she really seen him raging that way? Was it going to be that way everywhere she went – you see, you know, but you don't say.

Helen's fireworks were a rush of all colors, small bright sparks of red, blue, yellow green, and purple.

TWENTY-THREE

"Well here we are," Bernice said, throwing the blue and white tablecloth over the scarred picnic table. She'd decided not to comment on the bird-shit splotches, only cover the evidence.

"Yes, here we are," Eddie strolled over with the cooler, "all safe and sound."

Finally, Corky thought, bustling around, opening up boxes and sacks at the far end of the table. I never thought we'd get here.

When they'd returned home to check the stove, had driven up Nicollet Ave, turned into 35th Street and pulled up in their driveway, she'd wanted to leap out and run up the street. Run run run as fast as she could, but she didn't. She sat with the rest of them and watched Dana shut off the ignition. In silence the whole family watched him get out of the car. His face was grim.

"I'll check the stove," Corky had said. She'd opened her door, started to get out.

"Sit still. Nobody move." Dana walked over to the house, went up the front stairs. He was stepping onto the porch when Corky leaned across Helen to shout.

"The front door – don't forget to shut that front door really well."

He didn't turn around or reply, just disappeared.

I'll bet inside the house is cool, Corky thought with longing. The air in the car was getting heavier and heavier.

"That door – half the time it doesn't catch properly," she explained to Bernice who nodded. Hot and irritated they waited in silence. Eddie slumped sideways, apparently asleep, though really he was thinking music. Songs he liked ran through his head. They helped pass the time. Music was comforting. Music made you feel right.

Eddie wanted to be a singer, to stand on a stage and belt out music so that people sat thrilled, as he was sometimes just listening to it.

Nobody in the family knew that, and he wasn't about to tell them.

Helen was thinking about what it would be like to be the beautiful daughter of an English Lord with the face of a wise Roman Statesman. She was sitting upright, squashed between Eddie and her mother, both of whom, she'd noticed, were sweating.

Jessie moved. She pulled on the handle of her door.

"What do you want Mother?" Corky asked.

"I need to go."

"Are you sure?"

"Of course I'm sure." Jessie sounded oppressed.

"Take her in, Helen, please."

And that's how it happened that Helen was inside, marshalling Jessie around when the biggest event of the day occurred. She was upstairs waiting while Grandma pottered in the bathroom when she heard from below.

"YOU'RE SHUT, GODDAMN YOU, YOU'RE SHUT"

This roar was followed by a thundering crash. The whole house seemed to wince. She went to stand at the top of the stairs. Was that Daddy down there? Behind her, unnoticed, Grandma came out of the bathroom and drifted into her bedroom.

"Daddy?" Brutalized silence hovered in the air. "What's wrong?" Her voice was the barest of croaks. She was frightened.

She'd seen him late last night, sitting alone in the living room in his favorite chair, hands dangling down, eyes blank. When she went over and touched his arm and said, "Goodnight, Daddy." he'd only smiled and patted her hand.

Helen didn't want anything to be wrong with her daddy ever.

She walked slowly down the stairs. A soft trickling sound was coming from the front of the house. She crept into the living room, the noise was almost liquid in its steadiness. When she reached the front hall she saw her daddy standing facing the outside door, his head and shoulders covered with a fine gray white powder. Powder lay all over the hall floor. Looking up she watched chunks of powder reluctantly depart from the ceiling. A large scar of exposed rough work had appeared.

"GODDAMN YOU TO HELL." The Wise Roman Statesman roared in the same demonic voice, a voice she'd never heard before. He slammed the door again. "ARE YOU SHUT?"

She looked up again. More plaster was dropping steadily down; most of the hall ceiling was gone. "ARE YOU? ARE YOU?"

Powder dribbled down from above in reply. She saw with both horror and fascination that her daddy now had totally white hair. The English Lord with the Wise Roman Statesman Face turned and stared straight at her, eyes bulging with fury. She shrank back, but he didn't seem to see her. Why is he so angry? Has he gone insane?

He turned once more to the door, and opened it. The ceiling gave a warning dribble of powder. She could stand it no longer. She fled. To the front window that looked out on the front porch; which she opened. She climbed out, shut it, ran down the front stairs, stood waiting by the car. Corky got out, Helen got in. Everyone looked at her. Even Eddie sat up.

"Well?" Corky asked, "Where's Grandma?"

Helen's mouth opened and closed. She didn't know what to say. She'd forgotten her grandma. A small child drifted up, an unappealing child with a runny nose.

"Kin I go with ya?" the child moved closer whining. His runny nose combined with a dirty face gave him a tattooed effect.

"Beat it pipsqueak or I'll eat you." Eddie said.

The child retreated a few feet, "I don't like you."

Just then Dana came out holding Jessie's hand. They walked slowly, carefully over to the car. She was carrying her handbag and wearing her Sunday white hat with the two prongs that held it high atop her head. Corky turned to Helen beside her.

"What on earth were you thinking to let Grandma bring her purse and hat?"

Dana helped Jessie into the front seat, then came around and got into the car and started the motor. His hair was no longer white, his shoulders were free of plaster. He said nothing about what had happened as he backed the car down the driveway and into the street.

"Was it on?" Bernice asked. "The famous stove?"

Dana didn't reply.

"I hate you," the child shouted after them.

"I'm coming back tomorrow to eat you up." Eddie growled out the window as they drove away. "Rarrrrrararararar!"

"I'm telling my mommy," the child howled after them.

"Was that necessary?" asked Corky.

"Yes." laughed Eddie.

As long as he could remember Eddie had wanted to get away from the smallness of the neighborhood, the tightness of the house, the mean spiritedness of school. He knew he wasn't in love with Carol. And he didn't think she was in love with him. They were in lust and it was great. Only Carol now wanted more of him then he wanted of her, he could feel that. She wanted him to stay around, stay in Minneapolis but he wanted his horizons to keep expanding, wanted to go farther and farther away from home, to meet more and different kinds of people. He wanted to make enough money to buy all the music records he needed, to take music lessons, to be trained so well he could sing anything, and even to act on stage. He had a good voice, he knew that, and deep. He was a baritone, but Mr. Finley, the choir director at the high school said he might make it as a bass. He still had maturation, Mr. Finlay said, and he'd said too that basses were in demand. They'd stood outside the classroom, the choir room at high school, it sloped upwards like a real theatre and was his favorite room, his favorite class. Frail old Mr. Finley clearly loved singing and music of every sort and had taught Eddie about the logic in music so that everything one did, had to do, would do, could do, fitted into that logic – or it didn't become music. Eddie liked that kind of logic, not the parsing of verbs, or the recitation of mathematical tables, or the lists of the kings of England. He liked logic that breathed through something else to create a world that was visual and tactile as well as oral. He felt touched by the past when he heard composers who had lived long ago and yet he could feel their hearts still beating, could enter their emotions, their intuitions and inspirations.

Eddie didn't talk about this. Why bother he thought, Nobody in the family cares. Except Grandma. Jessie had taught him his first notes and had played piano for him when he was little. Now she rarely touched it, except once in awhile she might drift over to strike a few notes, swirling out a brief display of melodies she knew by heart. Now the piano was his. Mother had said it would go to him but Grandma's piano was old and dark and didn't belong in the wide world, it was just a little old humble piano in the corner of Grandma's living room. It should stay there with her until she dies, he thought, and Grandma shouldn't be taken away from it.

"My it's hot in the park,"

Bernice, who still in her summer second best dress and white pumps, stood beside her older sister Rose, who was wearing the Carmen Miranda blouse and skirt she preferred for picnics and unpacking sandwiches from the tin box. Bernice took the covers off the deviled eggs, mushy potato salad, fried chicken and raw vegetables. Rose examined the sandwiches. The blue sky over Minnewana Park was open and free, only a few happy-go lucky clouds roaming high above them. The sun was slightly slanted.

"It's not too hot." Eddie closed in on Bernice who stood waiting for the sandwiches. "You can wear a hat." He took a coke out of the cooler. "Thanks for the cokes, Aunt Bernice."

"Whatever do you mean – wear a hat?' Bernice was confused. Eddie rarely came up this close to her anymore. I'm hungry, she thought, no breakfast, all that chocolate and sherry. I could get sick today if I don't eat soon.

She stood by her sister, awaiting the sandwiches and ignoring her nephew. "I'd like to get a tan but my skin's so fair I burn in a couple of minutes. You're lucky, Corky, with that olive skin. You never burn."

"Hmm," Corky was not listening, she was taking apart sandwiches. "Who buttered this bread? There's practically no butter on these sandwiches."

Helen took the bowl of fruit, the glasses, the melmac dishes and set them out on the blue and white checked tablecloth, then went to stand by her daddy again.

He's so calm. His face looks so wise. Did it happen – the ceiling coming down? It seems like a daydream.

She had so many, after the long stay in the hospital, daydreams came and went and she couldn't always remember when they stopped and started.

When they had driven back toward the park, down Blazedale Ave, then onto Nicollet Ave, she'd watched him move the wheel with slow grace, a magician practicing a spell. All the windows were open and a small sweet breeze found them and leaning forward to catch that breeze, she'd seen the particles of plaster like fine grains of dirty snow. And now standing beside him she saw on his shoulders and in his hair the powder was there. It had happened, yet nobody else seemed to notice.

Dana wanted to say I love you to his daughter, but it had been a year. She's grown up, he thought, she's taller than her mother; so much has happened with the kids while I've been away. I've missed a lot.

"It's not too hot to go canoeing." Eddie's voice was so smooth and agreeable, his mother, father, and sister all looked over at him. He was standing close to Bernice, hands in pockets, rocking back and forth. "Remember how you took us out canoeing, Aunt Bernice?"

Bernice took the plate of sandwiches, put it in the center of the blue and white checked tablecloth, and sat down opposite Jessie and Dana. Eddie was making her nervous. "That was years ago."

"It was fun." Eddie came over and sat down sideways on the bench beside her.

"Did we do it here? This canoeing?" She looked at him with confusion mixed with doubt. I wish he'd go away, she thought.

"You taught me how to paddle. You were really good at it."

Bernice looked at her sister. "Do you remember canoeing, Rose?" Her sister was slicing tomatoes and thinking, I cut myself really badly once slicing tomatoes. I'd better concentrate. "Not really."

"We learned to canoe at Girl Scout camp. Went out every day in canoes, didn't we Rose?"

"I don't remember." Corky didn't look up from the plate of raw vegetables.

"I'll tell you what, Aunt Bernice." Eddie moved closer. Bernice shifted uneasily. "I'll take you canoeing today. Pay for it and everything. Sort of a payback for those good times you gave me as a kid."

You're still a kid, Bernice thought, with some hostility.

"Today?"

"Yeah."

"You want to take me canoeing today?"

"That's what I said"

His face is so smooth and agreeable, Helen thought, What's he up to?

"It'll be fun," said Eddie.

"Now?"

"Nah. Later. When the sun's not so hot. And our food's digested. Right Mom?"

Corky cast one murky look over at him and went on unwrapping food. The hardboiled eggs can go with the raw vegetables she thought. She looked at the slices of tomato and cucumber. Darn it, I wish I had a third vegetable. I thought I prepared some carrots. Yes. They were in the icebox in ice water.

"Dana, I forgot the carrots."

"Not to worry." he said. He and Jessie sat in safety at the far end of the table.

Eddie put his arm around Bernice.

"This might be the last time we ever go, Aunt Bernice. Remember how much fun it was, Skip?" He forced his sister to look at him.

She stood up and drifted closer. "I don't answer to Skip."

"Kid, you don't look like a Helen," Eddie muttered, "Helen launched a thousand ships." Then Eddie thought, careful old man, don't blow the dialogue with Aunt Bernice. "Sorry, kid. I'll remember next time. You want to go canoeing with us?"

"We must have gone three times, once with Aunt Bernice. I had to paddle in front all the time."

"All right, then." Bernice leaned away from Eddie's arm." Fine, we'll go, the three of us." She thought, I hope I know what I'm doing.

"Let's meet at five." Eddie stood up. "When are we eating Mom? I'm hungry."

"Five thirty." Bernice said firmly, remembering the rendezvous with Sam. If he comes that is, she thought. If he does I'll cancel the canoe ride.

"Sit down then." Corky dumped plastic cups from home into the center of the blue and white checkered tablecloth. "Dana do you want a beer?"

"Sure. But put it in a coffee cup."

"Do we meet here?" Helen asked. She had her own plans for the afternoon.

"You know that park bench half way down the hill? We'll meet there."

"Which one? There's more than one, my child." Bernice had acquired her superior tone of voice again. Recalling her secret life did that to her.

"The one that's above the boat place. You meet us there too, kid."

"OK."

"It'll be fun."

"Thank you for thinking of it, Eddie." Bernice was gracious.

"No problem," Eddie began wandering around in circles nearby, "Believe me, I'm looking forward to it."

"Rose, look over there." She motioned across toward a grove of trees. "Look at that those people over there."

"Where?" Corky glanced up from desserts she was laying out. I like this part of a meal the best she thought – putting the food nicely on plates, making it look good.

"In the bushes –you'd think they'd remember it's Sunday."

They all examined two pairs of legs sprawled side by side under a bush some distance away.

"Definitely a guy and a girl." said Eddie.

Bernice stood up to get a better look, "They don't appear to be moving."

"Maybe they're dead," suggested Helen.

Corky went back to her desserts.

"Most likely they're kissing, or laughing," she said briskly, but really she was thinking. I remember laughing a lot in this park.

"You'd think they could find a better place," Bernice's voice was tart, "Better than lying under a bush in a public park."

Corky stomped over and plunked the desserts in the middle of the blue and white checked tablecloth. She was getting angry. I'd like to laugh a little once and awhile.

"It's a bit too public for my taste." Bernice was fingering the sandwiches, noticing how much butter Rose Corinne had slathered on them.

"Yeah, Aunt Bernice, there must be bugs and dog doo and all kinds of crap in those bushes." Eddie took another coke out of the cooler.

As Corky put spoons in potato salad, and on the cucumber and tomato salad platters, she thought how much she'd laughed with James Newell. Joking with Eddie had broken those memories open. She remembered laughing hard, lying in bed listening to James rattle on about something that had irritated him. He liked to sit at the table under the hotel window and drink wine and expound on the absurdities of the universe. Those days in New York were full of laughter, even their parting wasn't sad – not really – though the energy of irritation and reproach were there by then, to be drawn upon and yet somehow they weren't. Somewhere along the line, James must have taken a vow not to hold grudges and he kept to it no matter what.

And me? I didn't really care enough. That's the truth, she thought. It's a mystery why I did it. Corky knew then that she'd always been a string of pearls girl, a homebody. What was it that drew her away on such an adventure? Not love but other true feelings, some of them deep, some inexplicable. Compassion for him, the desire to sooth an angry man? Yes perhaps but if I'm honest, also because I wanted to be there in New York, there in a grand hotel, going to museums, to the theatre, thrilled for once that I was the fine lady I'd read about.

Yes, James was education. Little Rose Corinne had been overwhelmed. He was a professor then, not yet a wealthy man. Oh I was pretty stupid, pretty young and foolish, she thought. I learned fast enough when a man takes off his clothes and takes you to bed, there's no mind, no museums and art galleries, then it's the man in his being, what he is – you're down in the basement of his soul. And James was a meatpacker, a tradesman; James had big hands and his apron on when he made love.

She didn't tell her parents or her sisters. It had been an impulsive act accepting his 'please come with me tonight' after only a few friendly dinners. Making love with him hadn't been all that interesting. He'd used precautions; she was glad of that. I've got three kids already, he'd told her on the second day. She'd been shocked. Three kids! My first wife's bonkers, he'd said crudely when she learned the woman was in a mental institution. James had just separated from his second wife, a wealthy woman, and he spelled out with relish and in detail how physically unpleasant that wife was.

James was, sweet little Rose Corinne soon found out, pretty crude. And inarticulate about his true feelings. But everything else, well I guess I felt I was on some kind of educational tour. James could talk about everything there was in the world: Art, history, music, politics. He liked having a young woman with him. He said as much. Young women shut up and listen, he said, students too; they learn something. A wife – wives, I should say – he'd amended with a coarse grin, they don't want to listen. Wives want to talk. And what they want to talk about doesn't interest me.

Well that's pretty blunt, she'd thought, remembering her own parents' brief dialogues about taking out the garbage, or buying a car. Those conversations worked as a cement that glued them together.

"My wives all wanted to talk about how they felt. But I say how do they know? How are they so sure? A feeling doesn't stay still long enough to be identified. How in the hell do they know what they feel? Tell me, do you know?" he'd demanded once.

They were in the hotel room; he was sitting on the edge of the bed. He was wearing his necktie and shirt and was in the process of putting his pants back on. She'd sat up in bed, sheet draped over herself, listening; she hadn't known what to say. Her body was still stinging from the force of his lovemaking. She hadn't really liked it that much she'd already decided. Hadn't liked him that close, his face up tight against her own. She could feel his brain ticking even as he pumped himself into her. She hadn't liked noticing all that. She and Dana had tried a shy sweet time or two after they'd gotten engaged, just before he'd gone west. But they'd been afraid she'd get pregnant.

Dana and I were so innocent, Corky thought then looked over at Dana who sat smoking a cigarette. Bernice gives them to him, she thought with annoyance. He was looking around. It had been romantic with him. When they were courting whenever he could afford it – which hadn't been often – he'd brought her roses.

Corky took a cup of beer and a plate with sandwiches, and potato salad, bread and pickles, hard-boiled eggs over to Dana. She pretended not to see the cigarette.

He looked up and smiled. "Looks good. Thank you."

A little wave of tenderness for him surprised her. She went back to the food to make her mother a plate and thought then of the time she was walking through the rain with a bouquet of red roses from Dana. When was that? She couldn't remember. Only the smell of roses in the rain. She and Dana had gone to college together. She'd loved him right from the beginning, more than anyone else she'd ever known, more than her father or her mother. Dana had always been the one. There wasn't much to lovemaking without love. Being with James had taught her that.

She prepared a plate for Jessie and took it over to her. Jessie smiled up at her so she pretended she didn't see the white hat with the two prongs on it.

None of the family saw Mr. and Mrs. Miller driving by in their daughter's car. Karin had insisted they come out to the park. Mother might enjoy the fireworks, she'd said, and she'd packed up three lawn chairs and some blankets for them to huddle in if they got chilled. But they weren't having much luck finding a parking place. Mr. Miller was looking hard, but he was getting tired and Mrs. Miller was asleep in the back.

"I wonder if I dare lay out in the sun," Bernice said. She'd sat down again and was examining her legs. "I'd love to go back to work a bit brown. But I have to be so careful." She helped herself to two sandwiches and some potato salad.

"Eddie's taking off, Mother." Helen said.

They all saw Eddie loping across the grass toward the four legs under a bush.

"EDDIE."

Eddie walked back and grabbing another coke, sat down at the table.

Dana was not listening to his family. He was looking around, his mind still far away. I almost answered that phone, he thought, I thought it was her. Mattie might be stubborn that way. The first time she called she'd asked about the apartment, but the second and third time, it was I miss you. When will you be back?

What if we all go back and I'm tempted to start up with her again? How can I know? She cast quite a spell. I was like a drowning man. I started thinking I'd missed something, and maybe I had because those funny little cries she made, her elegance – I didn't mind learning I could please a woman like that. But now all I feel is guilt.

He picked up his fork, tried to eat. It's over. I know that. What I have to worry

About now is whether we have enough money to make the move at all? I have to help my dad. He might be in the hospital for awhile; I don't know yet. I don't know even if he'll make it this time. The Denver company might advance me a first month's salary but I'd hate to ask. Besides do I want to leave Minneapolis? I could hardly wait to get back here and to see Corky, see the kids and Jessie. I don't think Corky or the kids want to go. And Jessie? We can't take her. Not right away.

He put down his fork again, drank his beer, thought – job or no job I'm scared of it – that's what it comes down to – scared, not of the job in Denver, but of losing everything here that means something.

Dana looked around. This is my world, here – Minnewana Park.

All around him people sat at tables, or on the ground. Most had the magic food of picnic before them. Some leaned against tree trunks or sat in lawn chairs or on blankets brought from home. Children ran around playing games, the smallest laughing as they tumbled over. The sounds were the hum of everyone doing the same things, with something to do and everything to be that day. It was his family magnified a hundred times, a thousand times. It was the fourth of July. It came into his mind that this would never end, this picnic, this being together.

As a boy, as a young man, in his loneliness, Dana had drawn on that fact – that he was part of everybody, that in a crowd he could find all the energy of being he needed. He'd worked for the railroad and he'd liked going into the train stations to feel the swish and murmur and hum of people going to and from home, all of them alive and purposeful. That was something to hold on to – people doing things, energy spilling out, and everywhere picnics – people eating at counters, in cafes, on the street, in the trains, in the park.

Jessie watched three women walk slowly by the car, they were half on the road and forcing cars to weave around them. The central figure was a large elderly woman leaning on the other two. She limped slowly on water huge legs, each of her massive arms gingerly held by the slighter, younger companion at her side.

Must be somebody thinks they're Henry VIII, Jessie thought. Amsden would have gone over to talk to those folks. You liked talking to women, Amsden. Remember that time I got so jealous, you were clacking away with some woman and I lit into you but you said, Jessie darling, she had the most amazing goiter on the side of her neck.

The women walked at a slow steady pace past the car. Majestic, they barely deigned to glance at a family picnicking right next to the latrines. Then, for a moment, the woman with the fat legs stopped and stared at Jessie; she was a round moon wearing glasses, hair pulled back in an untidy bun, and Jessie knew her. It was Mrs. Miller, helped to the lady's room by her daughter, Karin, and a nice young woman who had come to the park with her sister-in-law, Gloria, and her daughter Danielle and who were sitting on the grass near the three lawn chairs that Karin had set out for her parents. Mr. Miller had stayed behind because he was tired and liked playing with their little white dog Butch.

The majestic threesome swept on and into the latrine.

Well there's somebody that knows, Jessie thought. She looked around at the people sitting and standing nearby. None of these folks know a thing about being old, Amsden. You have to be old to know old. But I never felt stronger. I'm like an old nut – shrunken and rattling around in my shell. I'm as tight and dense and firm and solid as I could wish and if you planted me I wouldn't grow, but the rain wouldn't wash me away either and nothing and nobody can break me with their teeth now. An old nut. And until I lose this shell I'll stay around.

The food laid out, Helen sat down again and looked around. This park is ugly, she thought. Across the worn grass a couple were quarrelling with their two small children. Trash was scattered everywhere: cigarette butts, candy wrappers, paper bags. She felt gratified by all the litter. And by the trail of ants working its way up the side of the table.

The table was dirty too. Just because you cover bird droppings with a tablecloth doesn't mean you can forget they're there. Or the stink of pickle juice because Eddie broke the jar opening it with a knife. Most of the food looks hateful, especially the deviled eggs. They are bizarre in broad daylight.

"Mom, I think this thermos leaking."

An ugly park all right. The whole day will be rotten. My whole life is wasted by these useless family events. And mother in her Carmen Miranda outfit.

Behind Corky Eddie circled the table at an ever-widening distance.

"You're not going away, Eddie, until we finish eating." Corky didn't need to look at her son to know what he was doing. She unscrewed the thermos and peered in. She shook it. A sloshing sound. She looked at Helen. "What did you do to this?"

"Nothing."

"You are the clumsiest girl."

"I didn't do anything. I just carried it."

"It's our only coffee."

Jessie stumbled over the grass in her knit slippers. "Is that my coffee?"

"Just a minute, Mother," Corky took out a clean tea towel and began to pour coffee through it from the broken thermos into a plastic cup.

"Are you crazy, Rose?" Bernice said watching her.

"No. Desperate."

"You're giving that to Mother?"

"I'll drink the first cup."

Eddie moved closer, even Dana looked over; they all watched her drink the coffee. Nothing happened. She strained another cup for Jessie who sat down and stirred in three teaspoons of sugar.

"Coffee Bernice?"

"No. Thank you."

Helen took out a coke for herself. Corky and Jessie drank their coffee. Dana sat with his beer. Eddie circled. Bernice took covers off dishes of food and rearranged the serving spoons. This was family temporarily at peace. The food waited. Flies will be settling on us soon it seemed to say, though the ants attacked first.

"I shall certainly have tea." Bernice announced, brushing away the first daring ants. "The other thermos has tea in it doesn't it?"

Dana picked up his fork and ate slowly, enjoying the food Corky had prepared. Around him the land itself seemed to hum with energy, sounds magnified – people talking in their busyness, birds racketing in every tree, and small radios blared out inconsequences – news, pop songs, ball games. Near their people, dogs lazed about miserable in the heat but happy to be there. Squirrels bustled everywhere, tails bobbling with secret affairs having to do with picnics too. The sun splintered into glare on a hundred automobiles, trash barrels overflowed, and yet there was space, space between and around people, between their picnics and those of others, space like breath and people liked that, even as they waited, waited for the fireworks that night. If there were music here, he thought, music that the people couldn't hear, it would be deep and harmonious.

TWENTY-FOUR

B ernice sitting at the table smoking had been waiting for this moment. "The cake's in honor of father. It's his birthday next week."

Jessie smiled then. Sitting quietly, sipping her coffee, the spoon still in her cup, she liked having cake for Amsden. She was watching people go by. This place is crammed with people she thought. It's hot, too. The sun beats down on everybody alike.

You used to say that, Amsden. Used to be people sat in the shade of a tree, or under awnings or by their cars, or even umbrellas they brought. Here they're flung out like meat to be sun-dried. How many times have we come out here, Amsden? Well there weren't any of these modern buildings or anything but the island and the trees. We rowed out to the island remember? They had those big row boats then and you rowed us out there and we sat on the island and you proposed to me and you told me about your daughter and I told you about my problems and we looked at each other and we said yes we'll do it. We'll make one family out of two maimed people and we did, and you loved me, and I loved you through all these years.

Jessie took another small sip of coffee and watched two small women helping an enormous fat one walk toward the latrine. Don't they know gluttony is a sin? Jessie thought.

Yes Amsden, I'm out here in our park. I want to go out to the island. Yes I would and sit in that spot where we lay down together. Remember how daring it was then? We were in the shade of the tree and we didn't do anything that we called wrong then, only lay together and imagined a future when we would lie in a bed together and be man and wife. Two strong people again.

"Yes" said Jessie out loud. "I'll go. That's a promise."

"What Mother?" Corky was putting food into boxes and bags. Helen stood beside her not helping. "The mayonnaise is runny. I think I'll throw it out. And the potato salad – nobody ate much of it."

"Not with thumb marks in it."

"Nonsense."

It might be the last time I come here, Eddie thought, wandering in and out of bushes and trees. I don't care. It's dull, I've been here a hundred and fifty times, always the same times and with the same people. Eddie had been tied to his family with the strongest of bonds but now he knew it was time to break them. Get out, he said to himself, not for the first time in the last weeks, get out before you turn into a jerk, a real jerk, instead of half of one. He pulled at a tree branch until it broke leaving a raw edge. Strictly illegal, breaking things off trees and bushes in Minnewana Park. Eddie hoped somebody would notice. Nobody did. He remembered how when he was a kid they came here and he ran around playing airplane and his dad took him down to the lake and they ran along the shore pulling a little sailboat.

Talk about rinky-dink, he thought, and riding the merry go round and buying popcorn and candy apples and cotton candy and it was all run together in his mind, a visit to the park, and it was always the same and he loved it. He didn't like that thought and pushed it away. No. I want more than a rinky-dink little park and cotton candy. I want much much more, but he couldn't think more about that because he saw two gorgeous girls walking side by side – twins. Wow. I think I'll follow them.

It was the perfect setting for a murder and Helen could almost see the body under the trees. She'd been walking along, thinking about her future as a sculptor, but she hadn't found a sculptor name yet, when she saw a foot sticking out from under one of the fur trees. It was not a bare foot but had a bright red stocking on it. Perhaps this was a scarlet woman.

Maybe I could be a detective.

Cassandra Brown, detective. That's a good sign when the name comes right away, Helen thought. She stopped to lean closer and look. Yes a human foot, she pushed back the heavy fir branches and saw a black-haired woman, a woman with a white, white face and a scarlet mouth, a slash of red across her lips, but a slash of red across her throat as well. Talk about realistic. Since Cassandra Brown, detective, was not afraid of death, she leaned forward. No it wasn't a foot, it was a grubby red sign. DANGER Somebody had ripped it up and thrown it in there. But the black-haired woman?

"Helen!"

Cassandra Brown, detective, stood up and turned to face her brother.

"What are you doing?"

"Nothing."

"I have to talk to you. Do you remember what you promised me?"

"No."

"This morning in the car."

"No.'

"You are helping me with Aunt Eileen."

"Why did you organize us to go canoeing with her.

"You will see. You will see."

"I don't want to go canoeing. I get blisters on my hands."

She looked under the trees again.- Cassandra Brown at work. Cassandra would be fearless, would lean down and touch a gold locket around the black-haired woman's neck. She'd touch the body which was barely cold. Something's going on here, Cassandra Brown thought.

"Well are you coming? Don't just stand there."

TWENTY-FIVE

alk about realistic, she thought. Since Cassandra Brown, detective, was not afraid of death, she leaned forward. No, it wasn't a foot; it was a grubby red sign. DANGER!. Somebody had ripped it up and thrown it in there. But the black-haired woman?

"Helen!"

Cassandra Brown, detective, stood up, turned to face her brother.

"What are you doing?"

"Nothing."

"I have to talk to you."

"I'm busy."

"Doing what? Peering into bushes? Do you remember what you promised me?"

"No"

"You are helping me with Aunt Bernice."

"I don't want to go canoeing. I get blisters on my hands."

She looked under the trees again – Cassandra Brown at work. Cassandra would be fearless, would lean down and touch a gold locket around the black-haired woman's neck. She'd touch a body that was barely cold. Something's going on here, Cassandra Brown thought Eddie was glaring at her. "Well are you coming? Don't just stand there. Explain to me why you aren't cooperating when it has to do with Grandma. Do you understand that? We are rescuing Grandma. Oh Forget it. You're too young. Too dumb." He stalked off.

"By going canoeing? I don't understand." Cassandra Brown took a step or two after him, then stopped. "Talk to me, Eddie."

Eddie went strolling on. By then, he was thinking about those twins. Blonde hair and freckled faces, medium height, slender;

they'd walked side by side like bookends. He'd seen them again in the distance walking along the road. I wonder what it's like – sex with twins. Would you need another man or could you handle two yourself? It was such an exciting idea Eddie fell over into a bush directly in front of him.

"What are you doing Eddie?" asked his sister.

"What does it look like?" He snarled.

Back at the table, the picnic leftovers were packed away.

"Corky said, "Want to go for a walk?"

"Too hot," Bernice said, "Besides what will we do about Mother?"

"We'll wait for the kids. To come back."

Bernice raised an eyebrow, "Do you think they'll come back any time soon?"

"Helen will. We'll eat your cake then."

"I'm certainly not hungry." Bernice lit a cigarette.

"I'm hungry." Jessie said.

"You just ate, Mother."

"For cake."

Violet was there at the picnic too, but not all that happy. Minnewana Park was changing everything. Violet had been angry in her life, angry, angry, angry, and she'd loved the feeling of it. Anger had given her the energy to leave home, to go to Alaska, to learn to drink, dance and enjoy herself. She'd become a business woman; she'd owned two fur coats, had dangled men on a string whenever she could. When the war came, she'd joined the service and served her country surrounded by men in uniform.

Why Violet had been so angry – well mostly now she couldn't remember why, only how luxurious and strong it had made her feel. But there was no room for love in the self that anger created, no room for beauty in a mansion built by anger. Now, seeing for the first time others choosing love over anger bothered Violet. She didn't like the way the day was going.

She said to 'Those Who Were Supposed to Know,' "I want to leave now while I still feel happy." They replied, "Violet Marie, you have just grown an inch maybe two. Don't you want to grow?" "No, she said, "Not if it means this pain. I'm not used to this particular pain. It feels like regret."

"Too bad. You have to stay and see the whole day through."

"Ahhhhhh," she moaned but 'Those who were with her' paid no attention.

Twenty-six

The center of the park held a bowl; Minnewana Lake was water in that bowl. When the fireworks were shot out into the air, people watched from the hillsides; they waited for fireworks sitting at tables, on lawn chairs, lying on blankets or cushions they'd brought with them. There were no other lights – no concession stands, no amusement rides, nothing but darkness and fireworks. During the day however people wandered up and down and all around doing whatever occurred to them to do. The hillsides were dotted with patches of bushes and trees planted to combat this onslaught of people: and so a walk down to the lake meant a walk down a hill and around bushes and trees. There were any number of paths that curved and meandered along the slopes. Eddie and Helen were following one when they came to a y-junction. Eddie stopped and pointed left.

"O.K., kid, beat it."

"I thought we were going for a walk."

"We are, but not together."

"That's not very nice."

"No. But I've got things to do."

"You're going to look for Carol, aren't you?"

"Goodbye. Remember the bench at five."

"Five-thirty."

"Five."

He started off then stopped, unbuttoned his blue and white shirt and rolled up the sleeves.

"And keep an eye out for Carol. With any luck she won't stay around to watch Norbett lose a baseball game."

"I wouldn't help you out of a paper bag."

"I wouldn't step into one."

She watched him go down the right hand path, then disappear through some trees. She was getting hotter and hotter and madder and madder. I ought to follow Eddie, spy on them. Find some way to torture them. In the distance the merry-go-round music was a mocking roar from a giant windpipe. She took a few steps down Eddie's path, hesitated, then halted. What's the point? There's nothing fair about brothers. Men especially; brothers get everything. I learned that from reading those opera librettos. The heroines usually die, and they die singing. That's a sickening way to go, screaming your head off.

She walked down the left-hand path, hands in short's pockets. Most of the records were Grandpa Fallsworth's, so how come Eddie ends up with them all? Probably he likes them because the girls don't have a chance. If I were in an opera, I sure wouldn't die like that. As she passed a cluster of trees she saw a fat liver and white spaniel squatting under them. He looked like a friendly old dowager.

"Hi fella."

He made deep grunting noises.

Ugh, how revolting! Dogs are supposed to on a leash. I should report him.

She hurried past but couldn't miss the spaniel standing over his steaming load with an air of satisfaction. "Your hair looks lovely, Bernice." Corky leaned forward to touch her sister's marcelled wave. "It's so short now." She used to have such lovely long hair.

"I've got a different girl." Bernice said. "The last one didn't give me what I wanted."

"You take a nice perm. And that's a beautiful color." Corky leaned back and touched her own frizzy hair, a natural brown. I don't see why my sister dyes her hair, it makes her look older.

"I've always wanted red hair." Thank goodness Rose isn't wearing that corny bandana anymore. She's put on weight. "But don't you miss your long hair?" I wish I had Lilly Bernice's nose, she has a beautiful nose -better than mine. "No." Bernice turned sideways, stroked her, handbag, fiddled with its clasp. I wonder if I dare take out a cigarette? "I can smell those bathrooms." Corky stirred restlessly. "It seems to get worse as the day goes by."

Bernice shrugged her shoulders. "Not much we can do."

The latrines were whiffs of dark and dismal urgencies arriving like spooks, not to be noticed or discussed, but there anyway.

Dana got up from the ground where he had been sleeping, hat over his face. He yawned and stretched. I'm getting some rest. That's what I needed. The heat was thick, his shirt stuck to his back. Yet their table was under the trees.

Around them the circles of people gatherings stretched as far as he could see. There weren't many people moving around, mostly they lay yielded to the sun, or sat back under shade, silent, content or not content depending on their circumstances, but present at Minnewana Park on the Fourth of July, celebrating themselves along with the country. The children, too, were slower in pace and nobler in behavior. There wasn't a single scream of rage by them, nor had there been for over an hour. It was too hot to rage, too hot to run around looking for trouble – never too hot to argue though.

"I'm going to check out the baseball game." said Dana.

"Aren't we going for a walk?" Corky protested. I want to talk to him, she thought, I need to know what's going on with that woman – and with his dad. He's hardly mentioned his dad. We haven't any privacy. That's what we need – a conversation in private.

"It's too hot." I don't want to get into any discussions, he thought. I made my decision. I gave her what she wanted. "I thought we were going to walk around the lake." We used to walk around the lake on the Fourth of July – holding hands, Corky thought sadly.

"You and Bernice and your mother go." Dana stretched again.

"I ain't going on no walk." Jessie said, "I'm resting."

"And I'm having a smoke." Bernice opened her purse.

Corky stood up, her face, her whole body a protest.

"We are going for a walk," she said in a definite voice. "I need to talk to you."

She came over and gave Dana a kiss on his cheek. "It's important."

Her husband appeared to reconsider. "Ok. But come get me in an hour or so. I'll be watching the game."

"Maybe Eddie will go over there."

"Believe me, we won't find Eddie at the game."

He strolled away, hands in pockets, Panama hat pushed back.

"He's still a handsome man," Bernice remarked. Corky pressed her lips together but didn't reply. She sat down again, closer to Bernice.

"What was that name Mother told us?"

They both looked at Jessie perched at the end of the bench. She didn't hear them.

"Irene?"

"Pansy Irene."

"Well we never knew her." Bernice said heavily, "And it doesn't really matter does it? First there were four, then three, now just two."

They looked at each other, really looked for the first time that day.

"Three little girls dressed in blue." Corky half sang the phrase.

"She did rather overload on blue didn't she?" Bernice snuck another glance at Jessie who was gazing out across the grass.

"It was her favorite color."

"Remember the blue taffeta dresses?"

"Violet looked so pretty in blue."

"Taffeta was a pain in the neck. You had to be so careful." "You slopped something down the front of yours first thing."

"She always filled the glasses too full." Then Bernice's voice changed. "It won't do, Rose." Bernice said breathing smoke from the last of her cigarette," Surely you can see it won't do." The air around them became heavier. Corky looked over at her mother who was still staring straight ahead though she'd slumped sideways, half asleep.

"Corky, do you really believe I can come down here and take charge of Mother? I can't handle her. You know that."

"Let's not talk about it now."

"Her little games. She drives me up the wall with her little games."

"I know what you mean, Bernice, but they aren't always games."

"I don't play games." Bernice said hotly, turning around to look straight into her sister's eyes. "I never have."

Her sister couldn't help thinking, what bullshit.

Helen followed the path to where it met the lake. When she reached the lake, which was a bright blue under the midday sun, she nearly trod on a fat duck. It scrabbled angrily away from her. Several others waddled up from the lakeshore and quibbled at her. They're so spoiled, thought Magda Melody, non-tragic opera singer. Everybody feeds them. They are so fat. Fat is so ugly. What would a duck world be like? A duck universe? Nothing but water and beach, popcorn and other ducks. Nothing complicated that's for sure. Probably smelly. For the water's edge had the bite of duck and geese and rotting plants. There were: popcorn boxes scattered along the grass edge, and paper bags with remnants of bread in them. One duck had his head deep in one while his mate watched.

She walked slowly, hands still in pockets. It was almost too hot to breathe.

Magda Melody would sing about – what would she sing about? She'd have a glorious voice that's for sure. And wear low cut peasant blouses. Melody might be too sad-sackie a last name. Magda Momentous? No, that makes her sound huge.

Magda Motivated.

Stop it.

"On your left."

A boy's voice. He dinged his bell. She turned and saw Norbett on a bicycle.

Coming up the path behind her. Hastily she turned her back and walked briskly, pretending she hadn't seen him. He bicycled past, shot a glance back at her, then recognizing her, ran off the path and, bumping over the beach out of control, rode straight into the lake. Ducks flapped and scrabbled with indignation. She stopped, curious. Had he hurt himself? At school Norbett had a high accident rate, often falling into or off something, or else he was being punched in the stomach. Once he'd been high jumping in gym class and missed the mat entirely; they had to take him to the hospital on that one.

She stood and watched him. He sat up, the bicycle spread-eagled in the water beneath him. It was very shallow. He looked at her; he appeared unharmed. Too bad, she thought, otherwise I could rush over and succor him.

I wish I knew how to spell that word. It's kind of tricky.

"You're not supposed to see me." Water was dripping from his nose. Norbett wore glasses like she did and someone had trapped him in a barbershop and given him a severe brush cut. He took off the glasses and looked at them. "They didn't break."

He stood up, still dripping and yanked his bike out of the water. His clothes look like they'd been designed for a person two feet shorter, Helen thought. And he's too thin to wear shorts, his legs look like a stork's.

She didn't have a chance to say anything; he was wading in toward her.

"I mean it, don't tell anyone you saw me."

"Why not?"

"Because no one knows I'm over here."

"Why are you over here, Norbett?"

"Just don't tell anybody you saw me, OK?"

"You're looking very military with that haircut."

"Forget it." He got on the bike and still dripping water, rode away.

"If you're spying on my brother, forget it." She shouted after him. "He's a monster. He'll destroy you. Especially if I tell him what happened." He didn't reply or look back, just disappeared around the corner. He didn't even mention the horror night. But I haven't forgotten, Norbett. I never forget nights of agony.

She'd been taking care of those truly disgusting Klein children who lived next door to Carol's house. When Norbett came over she didn't think anything about it since he lived next door, but when he wanted to come inside she'd said no. After Mrs. Klein came home though and she'd started walking back to her own house, there was Norbett strolling along beside her. Naturally she thought he liked her, so when he said, "want to go for a walk with me?' she'd said yes.

Walking along the path in the park she thought, I guess I was unusually nervous walking home in the dark that night. I was up half the night reading horror comics. You get nervous speed reading forty horror comics. Personally I think the Kleins should censor their children's reading material.

I guess I thought it was safer walking with Norbett, that he'd be some kind of protection. Definitely what our English teacher calls a false premise.

She stopped to look at two geese fighting over some moldy bread.

So there we are walking along and suddenly Norbett says, hey come here, and he ducks into some strange bushes. Naturally I followed him.

The next thing I knew we were crouched down between houses, a narrow place thick with bushes. We were looking straight up into a lighted window and a man was standing there in his undershirt and no pants. Then he was walking around with NO P ANTS ON." Then a blonde woman came in walking around talking and she was TAKING OFF ALL HER CLOTHES. And the man –well, out came his you know like a great bullet twanging out. The funny thing was the woman didn't appear to notice, but Norbett sure did. He looked around at me with a kind of frozen surprise and I stared back equally horrified. Like what were we doing there in the bushes, was what we were both probably thinking. Norbett got me into that situation. Yes indeed. I should tell someone.

Though it was kind of interesting.

"Get down," Norbett hissed at me and I did. We crouched, our faces almost into the dirt -which smelled like dog shit or something kind of dead. We didn't know what else to do because if we moved, the man might hear us. What if he came out and caught us?

He'd do something to us – that's what we were thinking. Or I was anyway. I have kind instincts for survival. I could probably make it in the Yukon.

She watched the victorious goose waddle away with three fourths of the bread, the other goose gobbled the remainder down as fast as it could. The very worst part, she thought, was seeing that woman. Because of course even crouched down with my face right against the smelly dirt. I couldn't help looking up and seeing that she was full of fat and lines and freckles; she had more skin than anyone I've ever seen, including Mother. And she had a fat white face with mean eyes. And then that great solid bullet well he brought it over toward her; it was bonged out into space. That's when we figured out the window was open. Because not only could we see everything, we heard everything too.

"I gotta go out tomorrow," the woman said in a fat kind of voice, and she took off the last bit of her clothes, her bra. She was NA.KED! "I need some money."

"OK" the man said and then he lay down on the bed and she came over and lay on top of him. And at that exact moment Norbett fell over into the bushes – what on earth was he doing? I'll never know. One of the branches whacked against the window. Norbett was face down in a bush and he didn't see the woman get off the man and come over to the window and look out, but I did. Her eyes were extremely mean. But since Norbett didn't see her, he picked himself out of the bush and stood up. The woman's extremely mean eyes narrowed down to even more extremely mean eyes and she shouted something and I had to run. Behind me I heard Norbett running too. He was sobbing,

"Holy Jesus, Holy Jesus."

Helen walked along the path looking out at the people in canoes and paddle boats. They look like they're having fun she thought, maybe paddling a canoe would be fun too. She thought too that Norbett was not the least bit religious so he shouldn't have been swearing. Carol had told her Norbett was probably an atheist and would go to hell. I hope I never see him again, Helen thought, even if he is tall and pretty good looking.

She decided to get an ice cream cone. That would help her forget the Night of Agony. She took the trail to the concession stands. Ahead she saw the first aid station, a small building with a Red Cross painted over the door. The door was open. She'd never seen inside and so curious, stopped when she reached it and looked in. The building was small and dark with rough wooden floors. There was a desk and chair by the door and a long wooden counter under the window. A nurse, white shoes squeaking, was moving frantically back and forth to the counter which was covered with jars of cotton and ointments. On a stool in the center of the room sat a heavyset man with dark curly hair and angry eyes. He winced as the nurse wiped a bloody cut on his forehead. Whenever she turned away the blood welled back. Fascinated, Helen took a step or two closer and stood just inside the door. The nurse saw her.

"Wait outside please," she snapped, jabbing at the cut, the blood deepening in color. Wincing, the man rose slightly as though to get to his feet.

"The goddamned bitch. Jesus Christ, I should have knocked her block off."

"Sit still please." The nurse held his head and pressed a large square of gauze down on the cut. She had a stern set face like a bulldog, her square cap was set over white hair, her white dress, shoes and stockings made her body look heavy and masculine. She clumped across to the counter, shoes rubbing against the floor. Then click clank, jars were opened and closed, while the heavy lungs of the nurse made a breathing sound that filled the room. "This cut may require stitches."

"Jesus Christ."

Helen wanted to go in, to be part of the drama. She should have read more Sue Barton, Student Nurse books. "Excuse me, have you the time?"

The man looked over at her, eyebrows deepening into his eyes, "Who the hell are you?"

"You'll have to wait your turn." The nurse strode across the room and reached out to shut the door, from her stiff whiteness came a knifelike smell, a smell like hate.

Helen stood outside the First Aid Building door. Her feelings were hurt. She opened the door. "I only wanted an aspirin," she said and then hastily shut the door again. Two teenaged boys waiting outside looked at her, one said something to the other and they both snickered. She walked away. They stared after her.

"Hey," one called out. They came up behind her. She'd already learned there were good encounters with boys and there were the other kind. This one didn't look too promising. "Hey, hey you in the shorts."

Grimly she marched on, toward the ice cream concession. I'll get an ice cream and then go back. They caught up with her, then walked beside her.

"Where are you going, good looking?" He had a narrow face with pimples and deep set smallish green eyes. He was her height, the same age maybe, with long wispy blond hair like a baby's. He didn't look too clean. "What's up?"

"Nothing."

"Want to go for a walk?"

Oh my, Helen thought, they are all over the place. "No. Thanks."

The other boy, taller, more muscled, several years older, had dark hair and a lean bored-looking face. He slapped his friend's shoulder. "That's not the way to talk to girls."

He turned to Helen. "He doesn't know how to talk to girls." He returned to his friend.

"Let's go, I gotta get to work." They walked away. In a few minutes they were out of sight.

TWENTY-SEVEN

In many ways the Minnewana baseball diamond suggested a place of crucifixion. This was partly to the high mesh fence that stretched behind the six seat high bleachers. These bleachers formed a y behind home base and gave a good view of the game but many spectators chose to stand some distance away – behind the fence. This allowed them a special perspective – one through wire. They were not more protected from wild balls because when women softball teams played, balls went everywhere.

Some spectators, in particular the daring young males, shinnied hand over hand up the mesh fences to hang suspended in spread-eagled glory. Though dangerous, this position allowed them to watch the game from a high viewpoint, and achieving these precarious and painful positions had become a form of spectator sport. The activity did seem to depend on whether women's softball was being played or not, and there may have existed a mysterious relationship between male mesh hangers and female softball players in short shorts. No one had fallen from the fence heights in known memory but those impaled at the top looked so uncomfortable, more sedate observers in the bleachers were driven to turning around and looking up every now and then just in case one did.

The other reason that the Minnewana baseball diamond suggested a scene of pain and desolation was the fact that women's softball was played there. When the women's softball teams yielded to the men's baseball teams in mid-afternoon, more than gender and size of ball in play were altered – something both heavier and lighter came in with the men. They were given to standing around in calm clumps of mateyness muttering asides, bouncing about athletically, or exchanging cheerful banter with their opponents. Whether they were swinging two bats impatiently, or chewing gum in unison on the benches, the players on the men's teams looked very much alike.

Not so the women softball players. They exhibited flamboyantly different styles since they had to walk tightropes of extremes. Concealed in women's softball was a great hidden passion play that only the women understood perfectly. It was called Competence vs. Incompetence. A woman could either help lose a game while spending miserable hours looking hot, sweaty and stupid in front of a bleacher full of strangers – most of them men – then go home hand in hand with a man whose male athletic ability had been confirmed simply by sitting in those bleachers, or a woman could help win a game with a show of verve, athletic ability, globs of sweat, and exciting teamwork, then spend the rest of the evening sitting around drinking cokes with girlfriends. Many women met their Gesemene on a baseball diamond.

When Dana arrived, the stands were half full. It was hot and there was no shade except in the center section. Dust rose in the bare field whenever a player moved. The fence hangers were visibly drooping. The game had dragged on a long time; the Patton Panthers were playing the Carolina Warblers, and the score was 43 to 2. Dana knew at once which team had the 2 – the Warblers looked like they'd been out in the desert for a long time. He also noticed that their coach, a short enthusiastic young man with carrot red hair, was highly concerned with the throwing arms of two attractive infielders. They both needed constant body contact. The pitcher with the wonderful bouncy breasts also responded well to frequent hugs. The Warbler outfielders were all plump or very tall and were given to leaning over to rest with their hands on their knees, or squatting down with sullen looks of fatigue. The Warblers sported tight-fitting yellow jerseys: the infielders were in short shorts, the outfielders, baggy blue jeans. Periodically, in a spurt of communicative zeal, the Warblers squealed at each other. 'Throw the ball this way, Bobbi' or 'Way to go Peaches.' They all had names like that.

"Where are the Warblers from?" Dana asked the large man pressed against the fence next to him. "That's a church team." the man said grinding his teeth in what might have been a smile. "We ought to go to church don't ya think?"

Dana moved down the fence a few steps. This wasn't quite baseball as he thought of it, but he was new to softball. Afternoon heat seemed to rise all around him, the air was sticky and complete. Lower in the sky now, the sun grew large as it entered the heat haze. He looked around and saw his cousin, Tom Shannon, sitting in the stands. Dana hesitated. Tom was trouble. He decided to wait until the softball game was over.

The spectators in the stand were ragging the Warblers, calling out gamy remarks, or laughing with great rude guffaws at particularly clumsy attempts at catching the ball, or when the blonde pitcher on principle jumped out of the way if one came too close. The other team, the Patton Panthers were clearly divided as to whether to get out by striking out while at bat, or play on, grimly racking up another fifteen points but losing the crowd in the process.

Already the two waiting men's baseball teams stood together in massed impatience; players looked pointedly at their watches or swung bats to dispel their growing trapped energy. One or two talked to friends in the bleachers, outlining the serious problems created by sharing fields with women softball teams. Games running late was one problem but to some men the Panthers were another.

They represented the other extreme in women's softball. Their players wore green ball caps and professionally baggy green uniforms and sported a union logo. All were wiry women with short hair, none had an ounce of fat extra. If a Panther was large, it was with muscle. Very few bothered with makeup and many chewed gum with big masculine chomps. They jogged on and off the field in a mass, stood about in a tense clump while their coach, an older woman who looked like all the rest only shorter, delivered crisp words of advice. None of the Panthers had big breasts.

Watching all this Dana finally relaxed. He'd made his decision. They wouldn't go. The money would go to his dad. They'd stay with Jessie in the big old house. But it would be a struggle. He'd have to look for work right away. Call the new company and tell them to find somebody else. The dangers of tomorrow made the warm slow baseball afternoon seem almost seductive. I'm glad I'm here, he thought with surprise. I'm glad I have the money to help my dad. He climbed up into the: stands and sat down beside his cousin Tom Shannon.

"Hello Tom, long time no see."

Tom looked at him. "Hello, hello, I didn't expect to see you today."

It was an out and out lie, but then Tom was a liar most of the time. He was a man of medium height, with pale reddish hair and freckles. He looked a sport man, casual until you came close and saw his eyes, a water empty blue. He was pale too in his face and had a nervous mouth. He smelled of cheap soap.

"How's your family, Tom?"

"The same, the same. The wife's not been well these years. And did you ever get my note?"

"What note?"

"Well, well, you didn't then. I don't think your wife likes me, Dana."

It's Tom all right, Dana thought, stirring the pot as usual. But I'm here for one reason and one reason only, and I'll remember that. "My dad. Tom, how is he?"

"To tell you the truth, I don't know this morning. It was such a guffle getting here, Dana. My wife was sick as a dog in the night, she's having another and it isn't going well, so I didn't call the hospital, but it's ten to one your poor old dad is still in a coma."

"What does that mean?"

"He's breathing all right, but he can't speak. And no one knows whether he can hear or not. Oh his heart's beating away, sound as a drum, or so they said, but they don't know these doctors. What do they know, the bastards? Lying bastards those doctors, and rich as lords from our poor aches and pains." Tom leaned forward to take a sip out of a thermos; a whiff of whiskey hit Dana's nose. He noticed a bandage on Tom's forehead.

Has he been drinking all day? Dana thought. "I'll come over to St. Paul tomorrow. I need the name of the hospital and my dad's room number."

"Sure sure, I have it in my pocket." But Tom didn't reach into his pocket, instead he took another sip of the thermos. "Are you still not a drinking man, Dana?"

"No."

"You wouldn't want to come down to Duffys tomorrow, see some of the lads?"

Dana paused. Now here's trouble, he thought, there's always trouble with Tom. I've got to walk carefully through the thicket of Tom's speeches. And I'll hold off speaking of the money I brought for my dad to give him to be on the safe side.

"No. Sorry Tom. We're busy. We were thinking of moving west, though I don't know if we can afford to go now."

"With your father ill and all that."

"Yes. Well if you give me the hospital and room number I'll be on my way. I promised my wife we would go for a walk before the fireworks."

"Did she tell you about the note?"

"I said she didn't."

"Did that boy of yours tell you I telephoned?"

"Yes he did, Tom. Tom what did you send me a note about?" The minute he asked that, Dana wished he hadn't. Get up and go, he thought to himself. The less you know the better.

"We wanted to borrow your car, Dana. Just for a day or two."

"I wouldn't have loaned it. It's belongs to my wife,"

"Yes, yes, It's you that's married well we all know' that."

Tom's voice was truculent now. Sure sign he was drinking. Oh I know all the signs, Dana thought.

"Well I phoned because we have need of it again. This week. Your car."

"No."

"We'll pay you. Found money as they say."

Dana let the silence ride. The two men watched the game, muttering now and then some neutral remark. Whenever Tom shifted in his seat, which he did often, a strong smell of old sweat rose up through the overlay of soap and whiskey. The softball game was ending. One by one Panthers tapped out weak little pop flies which the Warbler catcher, a stern looking little girl in glasses, neatly caught.

She's the best player on the team, Dana thought, though proximity to the stands may have driven her to it. The Warblers staggered in while the Panthers gathered in a neat circle and emitted a hearty insincere cheer. The male players began running crisply out on the field. They wore white uniforms with varied colored socks and looked overheated already.

Tom Shannon rose. He walked down the bleacher stairs and went over to the small concession stand behind the wire fence. He bought a coke and a ginger ale and brought them back to his wat.

He gave the coke to Dana. "Here you are, Dana. In memory of when we were boys together." No, thought Dana, we were never boys together. But he didn't say this. Just sipped his coke and watched Tom pour ginger ale into his thermos.

"How long has it been since you've seen your father, Dana?"

"A couple of years."

"It seems he's dying now."

"I'll find out tomorrow."

The two men went on looking at the field where the Brake Heavens Braves were throwing around the ball, while the Ashton Electric Tigers swung bats and chewed gum. The sun was beating down on them.

"You're a hard man in some ways, Dana McFadden."

"You think so do you?"

Dana let the anger rise up. He didn't want to sit in the heat and discuss his father. Not with Tom Shannon. He stirred restlessly. "It's hot."

"Too hot." Tom agreed. "That sun's no friend today, that's for sure. Makes me wish I were back in Ireland." Dana stood up, coke in hand.

"I think I'll find some shade, Tom. Just tell me the name of the hospital. I can find his room when I get there."

Tom at last turned and looked up into Dana's face. "We'd pay you well and nothing said."

"I won't do anything for the cause. You ought to know that by now,"

"Did I say it was for them?"

"I don't have to guess."

"Who said it was for the greatest cause in Christendom? Who said that?"

"I want you to stop calling my wife when I'm not there."

"We could show you facts that would make you weep."

"I know it all."

"Do you?"

The game had begun. The bleachers were evenly divided. There were loud cheers when an Ashton Tiger batter made it to second base on a long drive into center field.

"My wife doesn't know what you're up to."

"And what are we up to? Sit down Dana. Have you got the money for me to take to the hospital?"

"I'll take it myself tomorrow. Is he at General Hospital?"

"No. Saint Anthony's on the third floor. All right, all right, don't be getting cross with me Dana. There's no harm in talking is there?"

"I don't want to know what you're up to, Torn." Dana sat down. Drank down the rest of his coke.

"He was a brave man your father. Over in France, all that."

They watched in silence while the Aston Electric Tigers went down and the Brake Heaven Braves came in to bat.

"You were gone a long time this time, Dana. Have you found work here?"

Well there's the question, Dana thought. And what could he answer? "I don't know."

Tom shifted in his seat, forced a long canny look on his cousin. "I can get you a job pushing papers if that's what's needed, to get you through the next little while. I know a job starting next week, if you're hard up these days."

Well there it was – what I wanted to hear and didn't want to hear and all at the same time, thought Dana. Take something from Tom Shannon? He's a dangerous man to be in debt to. But can I afford to be so proud? With no money in a few weeks if they didn't go back? He'd tried before in the Twin Cities.

He said nothing, pretended an interest in the game which was playing itself out with calm equanimity, the two teams were nearly indistinguishable.

"Sean Dugan's back." Tom said not looking at Dana.

"Sean Dugan's a bastard."

"He works here, at the park."

"At Minnewana?" This time it was Dana that turned and forced a look out of his cousin.

"Where?"

"Be careful or you'll bump into him. Your father owed him money, didn't he?" "It's nothing to do with me."

"In fact he owed quite a few of us money."

"I said, it's nothing to do with me."

"Well then, well then, not worth talking about is it? Is it?" Tom upended the thermos, taking a long time with his last swallow.

Peculiar how, talking to Tom, it all crone back, Dana thought, all the old neighborhood, the sweaty smell of the men, the stale beer, the huffy cigarette air in the small taverns, the streets with their old urine, and fresh vomit. Searching out his dad amidst the clutter and noise of the back rooms of taverns where these men met, where they downed their drinks and talked with hoarse smoke-roughened voices.

When I'm with someone like Tom, my past won't disappear, won't become the gentle old slanted house on Maple Street in Winnipeg, or the snug bungalow on Grant Ave in St. Paul, places in memory where my mother resides, no with these men my past becomes something darker, meaner, more intense. It must be true – that you can't escape the past, can't erase it. I tried he thought. I cut the ribbons, even forgot to look for my dad that last time his roommate called me.

My dad's going to die. I feel that in my bones. He's too sick from alcohol to live, his mind too fuddled to quit. The last time I saw him in the sanatorium – they told me he was drinking himself to death.

He remembered that visit, walking across the broken sidewalk, up the side stairs; it was an old rhummy sort of place; his dad had chosen it because he knew some of the men there and his roommate was already there on the cure. The roommate, a bit older than his dad was a man in his seventies so broken by drink, so starved and shattered looking, his own dad looked healthy in comparison. But they were cheating already, splitting a hidden bottle of cheap bourbon whiskey; the roommate even boldly offered Dana some. They hadn't made sense, either of them. When he'd tried to talk – by then his mother was dead and his sister long refusing to ever speak of or to her father again -he hadn't much to tell the old man except news of his own family. Usually his dad had been interested to hear of Eddie and Skip, and about Corky and Jessie and Amsden.

They were all kind to him, Dana, thought, when all was said and one; they didn't let their lifelong abstinence from alcohol cause them to refuse his dad hospitality.

But that visit his dad seemed unable to concentrate on the simplest facts, and at last, impatient, Dana had risen to go. He'd asked his dad to stay, to really give the dryout a try – Dana was paying for it after all – but a week or less, his dad had broken out and gone on another massive binge.

He'd called his son a month later, but he was drunk and Dana had laid the phone down without saying a word. Now he wondered – should I have gone on trying? It's easy to think that, say that, when you aren't there trying to deal with this person determined to kill himself slowly, by inches, to erase personality first before anything else. After all, its personality that makes a person isn't it? Isn't it?

Dana had thought that too many times. He got up to go.

"I'll take care of my dad's bill tomorrow, Tom. Thanks for meeting me."

Tom looked at him; his eyes were reddened now; his face flushed.

"No problem, no problem. Good luck to you, Cousin."

Dana walked away from the game where the Aston Tigers had taken the lead 3-1. I don't know, he thought, don't know what my dad's done, been up to, if anything. I doubt he's done anything except sponge money from anyone who would give it to him these last years. Still his dad had been close to those friends of Tom's in the past. The bully boys Dana still called them in his mind. What his dad owed Sean Dugan might have endangered him. Sean Dugan was a dangerous man.

The morning's alarms – the concern about the move, about what to do about Jessie, Corky's anger when she learned about Mattie, the lack of money, and what job he might find when he turned down the one in Denver all began shifting around his mind the moment he walked away from the baseball diamond. His dad, their shared past, the fact of his dad's coming death filled him then too, with guilt and yes even sorrow. And what he wanted then, there beside him was his wife, his darling Rose Corinne. She would comfort him. Dana went to find her.

TWENTY-EIGHT

A s the path neared the amusement comer of the park, it left the lake and followed the road instead. When Eddie reached this section of the path he slowed down and began looking for Carol Rydarski's car among the many parked along the curb. It was a Woodie Wagon and usually he couldn't miss it. But the traffic on the park road was heavy; cars cruised slowly almost bumper to bumper along two narrow lanes. In this portion of the park it was hard to remember it was a park.

Up ahead Eddie saw three girls his own age approaching on the same side of the road. Two were those twins with the long ash blonde hair. They were tanned and smooth looking, as though they'd spent the summer in warm lake water. He imagined them with no clothes on and the thought so excited him he had to swallow hard and look at the girl in the middle. It was Molly Ashford. Her strong eternally happy plump face brought him back to earth. Molly Ashford was one of those persons that enraged him.

They'd become enemies or rather he'd grown to dislike her because of the year book. He started out his senior year as co-editor but in November gotten embroiled in a fight with two of the teachers and they'd replaced him with a girl everyone liked – Molly. As far as he was concerned she didn't know anything. She had terrible taste in poetry for one thing; she liked poems about fluffy kittens. But Molly did know how to talk to teachers so they thought she was responsible. He'd never be able to do that.

Words wouldn't come out right anymore. Either they stuck in his throat like lumps of soft bread dough or came out angry, even when he wasn't, retorts like sharpened sticks that conveyed nothing of what he felt, only concealed the thoughts and emotions boiling inside him.

"Hi, Eddie, still mad at me?"

"You're not my favorite person, Molly."

"I hear Carol Rydarski is."

Eddie made a face at her. What the teachers don't know, he thought, is she's always slicing at people, always ready to hand you your brains in a paper bag. Still those two gorgeous blondes are standing on each side of her, with those curved half asleep mouths of theirs. Twins. Are they smiling at me or simply dreamy from some mysterious event, like they just had sex?

He decided it would pay him to be kind to Molly Ashford.

"Still you did a great job on the year book, Molly."

She looked blank for a moment, then she smiled her moon smile.

"These are my cousins, Edith and Emily Brown. They're visiting from California. They're here for a couple of weeks." Molly acts like she's organizing a Girl Scout expedition, or laying out the high school yearbook all squeaky keen and intelligent. He swallowed hard, concentrated on the twins.

"Nice names," He made a point of shaking hands, which so surprised them they started to giggle. They giggled together, their soft brown eyes warming. They've noticed me, he thought exultantly. He felt inspired to call even more attention to himself.

"You haven't been here before?" He let his voice sound amazed.

"No." the twins murmured in soft mouse warm voices.

"Never in this park?"

They shook their heads.

"I run tours," he boasted. "Ladies, come with me. I am the greatest tour guide you ever saw. I'll even take you through the Tunnel of Love."

Molly's mouth fell open. Edith and Emily giggled, soft secure little noises like warm hands on a cool thigh. Eddie thought am I really ready? Ready for girls who look so beautiful, so willing and able? Girls I don't even know?

At that very moment he decided he was.

Even Molly smiled at him. Appeared to like him. Though he didn't like her. He had to remember that. She was someone everyone fell into liking. Everyone at school did. She'd been voted Miss Congeniality in the yearbook elections.

People walked by, couples, families, edging past them while they stood in the path oblivious, chatting about California, how it was different than Minnesota. Maybe I'll go to California instead of Texas. The proximity of Edith and Emily smiling their dreaming satin smiles convinced him of that. He kept looking at them. Their hair was long and tangled and sun bleached. They were dressed alike in white short shorts and short sleeved blouses. They had tiny waists and long smooth thighs. He thought he could tell the difference now. Emily had a gold chain around her neck and a pink belt, and Edith was wearing earrings and a green belt.

"There's no Tunnel of Love in Minnewana Park, Eddie. Where are you going anyway?" Molly's voice was friendly. "Are you staying for the fireworks?"

Eddie couldn't help noticing the turquoise and white playsuit Molly wore made her waist look smaller and her chubby little bottom curvaceous.

"Walking around. My family's all here. I'm walking around with nothing to do."

He felt a little dazed from the heat and the proximity of the three girls standing so close around him. Grandma being left behind, Aunt Bernice due to be tortured, his mom and dad locked in conflict, Carol – all faded way way to the back of his brain. They were standing in the path next to the road just where it curved down to the small purple and yellow amusement park. A stream of cars drove past, crowds of people meandered by; around them too flowed the mocking windpipe sound of the merry-go-round – In the Good Old Summertime. The amusement park held other rides, but only the merry-go-round threw out a lure.

"Is the roller coaster scary?" Emily asked.

"We were afraid to go."

"Nah. I've been on it at least twenty times."

"You were?" said Edith – or was it Emily?

Even Molly looked impressed. She had short curly dark hair and a perfectly round face. He thought, I can stand Molly with cousins like hers.

"I can take you." he suggested. "Doesn't bother me."

"Oh would you?" said Emily – or was it Edith?

One of Eddie's friends had taken him up five times in a row. It had cured him of any fear of a roller coaster though the fifth time he'd thrown up on his friend's jacket.

"Only if we buy root beer floats." Molly said.

"After the ride." He said firmly, remembering his friend's jacket. "Just in case one of you has a weak stomach."

"Oh. I do," breathed Edith or Emily, "I have a baby stomach."

Baby soft, Eddie thought looking into those warm ash brown eyes. Was it Emily or Edith? It didn't seem to matter.

Jessie, spoon still in her empty cup, was gazing out across the grass. Bernice and Rose Corinne sat beside each other not looking at each other. Finally they both glanced over to see if the other was looking. Rose Corinne gave a weak little smile.

"What kind of a car did you buy, Bernice?"

"One like that." Bernice pointed to a bright red Buick Convertible.

"You bought a convertible?"

"Not very practical for Duluth but I've always wanted one."

"What fun!" Rose Corinne's bright tone dwindled away in mid-air and they sat without speaking again. Bernice lit another cigarette and Corky shifted down the bench a nudge in case the smoke came her way.

Sometimes Bernice congratulated herself on how she managed awkward situations – the long affair with Sam her boss at the police station, her Minneapolis apartment in building full of gossips, and now a small office in Duluth with its jealous bitchy secretaries. Yet I've survived intact, she thought, and I got away from the scandal. Her new job was a good one, she had an executive position with control over her time and she'd bought a new wardrobe and a jazzy convertible. She'd managed everything pretty well – considering.

In the night though when she woke up alone in the dark, especially in the winter on cold isolated nights, she woke to different judgments. Then she saw clearly that she'd be alone forever. She'd had only that one affair, a long season of the heart. Before and after Sam there'd been no one. And he had turned out to be a bad man. She knew that now. Though he'd started out straight, Sam Benson ended up going wrong. And that was bad for a policeman. Her brain told her that, and her experiences. But she still thought of him, with tenderness, remembering the many small ways he'd made her happy over their years together.

I have everything now to make me happy, but love she thought. All the elements in my life I lacked when I worked for Sam yet I don't have the person anymore.

She'd disciplined herself not to care, but found she couldn't lose a need for passion. She realized that around the time she bought the car. The exercise of going to show rooms and finding the salesmen condescending, some close to abusive – they'd treated her with contempt until they realized she, a woman, really was buying a car – those were men who once would have flirted with her.

She had several good women friends – school teachers – one had traveled overseas to Hawaii and Guam during the war. Neither had married and both seemed melancholy, rueful that they hadn't quite managed to be normal because they had careers. Bernice didn't see that as a failure. So many men died in the war – there aren't that many to choose from. She'd always, oddly, without real confirmation from her family, thought of herself as a success, a family miracle. She'd managed to avoid the trap of marriage, the slavery of commitment to a man for life. She'd thought that way for years and years.

And yet, and yet, increasingly at night, alone in Duluth, she woke up to herself to her own solitariness, and to the inadequacy of that. To be this much alone with oneself is that wise? She had asked herself that sometimes and now she asked herself that again sitting on the picnic bench, that Fourth of July, close, but not close at all to her sister and mother.

When she found out about Sam, about Violet's death, that knowledge stood between not only her and her family, all other human beings too. How could she say anything to anyone? Her friends? Could she confess to any of them or to the new acquaintances she'd acquired in Duluth?

She thought, I will carry that knowledge alone until the end of my life. And I can't come back to Minneapolis because it's beginning to haunt me.

In Duluth she'd begun to go to church, to search for answers. But something resisted in her, resisted a permanent, passionate relationship with religion. It seemed God could nourish her but that didn't end her loneliness. She tried to read. But at night, after a long day at the office she found she could only read mysteries, only unravel fictional plots, lightweight dilemmas, could only face imaginary death. And even so, sometimes suddenly she would look up from her book, swept out of it by the question overwhelming her – Is this all?

Is it? Is it? The question came again right there on the picnic bench. Abruptly Bernice rose from the park bench, caught Rose Corinne's eye. "I think I'll stroll around."

"But we were all going to walk around together." Corky said. She believed in family doing things together, being together; she was a person who was rarely alone, because she wasn't happy that way.

"I'll come back." Bernice promised. "I won't go far. Just stretch my legs."

"I told the kids half an hour. They can look after Mother. They do it all the time. Helen at least will come back."

"OK"

Bernice walked along the road. She wove in and out of people beside their parked cars, in their cars, walking to and from their cars. None as nice as mine she thought. She believed in that instant like all those others that security lay in checking to be sure it was still there – your friend the automobile – ready to take you away.

BEEEEP BEEEEP

A car horn. Eddie and Emily and Edith and Molly all looked over at the roadside next to the path. Cars had been passing them all driving the regulation fifteen miles an hour. But one car was moving much much slower -a Woodie, sleek and large and very very new. Carol was behind the wheel. She was wearing white frame sunglasses and she wasn't smiling.

"EDDIE!' She waved one hand and swerved a little then put on the brakes. The car lurched to a stop. Eddie winced.

"Is that Carol?" Molly said. "Where'd she get the car? She's a terrible driver."

"EDDIE WHERE HAVE YOU BEEN?"

"It's a darling car." Edith-Emily murmured.

"I heard her parents grounded her when she backed into a tree. I heard it was the only tree in a parking lot."

Eddie edged away from the girls and toward the Woodie. "See you later."

"No, roller coaster?"

"EDDIE!"

"I promised Carol I'd help her with her car."

Carol by this time had seen the girls. She stopped the car in a no parking spot, and leaned out to squint hard at the twins.

"MOLLY! HI!"

She couldn't place them. Her face darkened. They were good looking.

BEEEP BEEEP

She was leaning on the horn. People looked over curious. She waved at Eddie, and reluctantly, he strolled the rest of the way over to her, but slowly, one casual hand in his pocket. Behind him, Molly said something to the twins and he heard their soft voices in reply.

"Where have you been?" Carol said in a sharp voice when he came up. "I've been looking all over for you."

He leaned in the passenger side window. "I thought we were meeting later."

"So I can see."

Carol's pouty little mouth opened and closed with gasps of indignation. "I've had ever so much trouble driving this car around. There are millions of people here."

"Can't you find a parking place?"

"No. Will you help me Eddie?"

"Move over." This isn't so bad, he thought. He came around opened the: driver's side door and slid in. Carol moved to the edge of the passenger door.

"Norbett just jumped out of the car. I've been driving around and around. I can't find anywhere to put it. It's so hot and horrible." She sounded like she was about to cry.

"Hey don't worry." He smiled at her. She does look cute, he thought, that frilly hair do. Then he looked over at the three girls on the path, Molly, Edith and Emily. He waved. "See you," he called, "Let's take a rain check."

They waved and walked on.

"Rain check?" Carol pounced. "Rain check on what? Who are those girls with Molly?"

"Her cousins. They offered to buy me a coke," he said recklessly. Carol's neat little rosebud mouth tightened but then she leaned back and let her fabulous profile declare itself to the world, also to Eddie. He started the Woodie, thrilled to be driving it, looked over at her, and was thrilled to know she was jealous. That she wanted him. I remember exactly what that fabulous profile looks like in the moonlight, and what that whole clever little body of yours feels like in the dark, he thought.

It was interesting information, a whole new dimension on these maddening creatures, girls. It was a sweet new secret life he'd come into.

TWENTY-NINE

Walking along the path, Helen didn't see Mrs. Blunt, who lived next door, or Mr. and Mrs. Miller who lived on the other side of her grandma's house. She walked right past Myrna Henderson and her daughter Suzette and sister-in-law, Gloria. She didn't say hello because she didn't know them. Besides she was too busy thinking how mean the nurse at the Red Cross station was.

I hate 'Sue Barton, Student Nurse' books, she thought, as she walked down the path beside the lake. I will never ever be a nurse. Helen had spent eight weeks in a hospital isolation ward with scarlet fever when she was seven years old. She'd lain in bed for hours and hours, days and days, weeks and weeks with nothing to do and no one to talk to except strangers in white clothes whose shoes had squeaked even in the pitch black night. No wonder I don't like white shoes, she thought walking a little faster. The nurses were mean in the hospital too. They took away my food if I didn't eat it right away, one even took the ribbon off my potted plant and gave it to that bad girl who screamed all night. That was my ribbon, Helen's sense of injustice was building. That potted plant was all I had, in the isolation ward. We weren't allowed toys or books from home. Helen grew angry thinking about that ribbon taken away without her permission, about how there were no phones, no radios, no visitors from home, how her roommates came and went while she'd stayed on. In hospital she'd learned how powerful a word "No" was. If she thought about her mother or father, or Eddie and Grandpa and Grandma, or even the house on 35th street, she started to cry so she didn't let herself think about them. Instead she made up stories that made her feel better – adventure, handsome lovers, faraway places stories, girls who were extraordinarily brave stories. In hospital she'd learned an imagination could make the difference between lonely and not lonely, scared and not scared.

I could have helped her, Violet cried out, hearing all this. I know about isolation. I understand about imagination.

You weren't there, Violet, and you didn't care enough about your family to find out about them. You didn't call or write, said Those Who Know More Than You Do.

"Oh shut up!' Violet cried. Even after death she was bolder than she ought to be.

That afternoon Greta Blunt felt the emptiness of her neighborhood, everyone gone. She got it into her head she wanted to see the fireworks at Minnewana Park. Nobody answered at her brother, Ned's house, so she called up an old friend, a man she knew would be sober because he'd joined AA the year before. She hadn't seen him since. He said yes he wouldn't mind looking at the fireworks and yes he'd take her out to the park but only if she didn't bring along any booze. Not long afterwards, he drove up in a dusty green Ford pickup. When he came to the door, Greta was waiting for him on the front porch eating crackers and cheese. She got up to greet him.

"A car," she said, "Mike, you're getting to be a swell."

"Cause I'm sober, my wee darling," Mike said. He was tall and broad and Irish looking." I've got the odd bit of change in my jeans for a change. Are you ready to go?"

"This minute?" Mrs. Blunt was doubtful by then, ready to change her mind about going so far from home. It had been years since she'd been so adventurous.

"The motor's running."

"Shall I bring some cheese and crackers?"

"Great."

And so off they went to Minnewana Park to see the fireworks, the car windows all down to catch the breeze while they chatted away about all that had happened to them since they'd last met.

"I almost got married," Mike said, "but it didn't work out."

Greta was happy to hear that. She liked him. He was always such a gentleman, she thought. But when she saw the crowds of people at Minnewana Park, she was sorry they'd come. She stayed in Mike's green pickup until he made her get out, then complained about sitting on the grass until he brought out two stools. Greta didn't like being around successful people, people with families and friends like the ones in the park. An old sing-song chant she'd fallen into years before when her husband left her started up deep in her brain – I'm a failure, a failure, – the words came over and over, so familiar she didn't pay much attention to them until she said them out loud. "I'm a failure."

"No, you're not," Mike was pouring coffee from a big thermos into two grotty-looking mugs." You're just a person like everybody else."

'Just a person,' fell deep into her brain then, 'a person, like everybody else.'

Greta watched Mike's tobacco stained fingers unwrap a pouch of tobacco and tap flakes into white cigarette paper. He rolled the paper around the tobacco and licked the ends to close the cigarette. He looked at her.

"Wanted a drink today. Soon as I saw you, Greta. Cause we had some damn good times together getting drunk. Think we can sober?" He shielded his hand as he lit the cigarette. "I'm dry now. Plan to stick to it. Cause it wasn't easy – someone like me that's not all that bright."

"Hey you're my friend," she said, looking hard at him for the first time since they'd come to the park. "I'm no star turn neither."

"What's a star turn?" he asked.

Not far from them Mr. Miller and Mrs. Miller were sitting in their daughter Karin's lawn chairs thoroughly enjoying themselves. Mrs. Miller was feeding birds, throwing out crusts of bread and crumbs to a mob of noisy sparrows. Mr. Miller was sitting watching her. He felt tired, but happy. He watched people go by too. My word we're a strange species he couldn't help thinking, so many sizes and shapes and colors, such odd ways of behaving. He especially liked seeing the small white dog play with a little girl nearby. Suddenly the little white dog ran over and gave a leap and there he was, in Mr. Miller's lap, looking up at him with quite a doggy smile. Beside him Mrs. Miller watched this with a vague smile while the birds flew away in disgust.

Their daughter Karin looked up from her mystery book, and said, "That dog likes you Dad. You aren't feeding him I hope."

She's such a worrier – Karin, poor girl, thought Mr. Miller and he leaned forward and gave the little dog a kiss. Because at that exact moment he understood that he was lucky enough not to have a worry in the world.

Gloria called Butch back, scolded him for bothering that nice old man sitting in the lawn chair. She gave the little dog some water while she went on telling her sister-in-law that Myra simply had to get out of that dinky little apartment.

"Before I leave, I'll help you look for a house in your neighborhood," promised Gloria. Then Myrna confessed to her sister-in-law that she was jealous of her. They began to laugh and cry together over how different life could be, while Myrna's daughter Suzette read Little Lulu comic books, the only ones she was allowed to buy. They were all three stretched out on blankets on the grass. Myrna thought how good the grass smelled. From where they were, they couldn't hear the music from the merry-go-round – In the Good Old Summertime – but Gloria had promised to take Suzette for a ride on it before the fireworks started.

All around them moved tides of people, back and forth, carrying ice creams, popcorn, cokes, balls, hats, picnic baskets. A few were leaving, but more were coming, so many gathering, gathering for the fireworks, for the evening, for the chance to sit on a hillside all together watching Fourth of July fireworks.

THIRTY

B ernice walked as rapidly as she could. She'd told Sam she'd be at the picnic area sometime after four. All the tables will be full by now, she thought, but it doesn't matter, I'll find him. Her breath was coming in short gasps; she was frightened and excited horrified almost – that she was seeing him again after all that had happened. She was determined to tell him what she thought and felt about Violet and yet he was a strong man, a violent man, she knew that only too well. As she approached the picnic area she could hear the merry-go-round music – In the Good Old Summertime – grinding away, growing louder with every step she took.

She hesitated at the arched entrance to the picnic grounds. High bushes and wooden lattice works surrounded each picnic table. Every picnic table was in use – families or young couples unpacking food or eating it. Some bushes were in blossom with small pink flowers, and their scent turned the air friendly and sweet. So many people enjoying themselves. Minnewana Park has always been that way she thought, a good place for a picnic, for a romance. How many romances are going on here right now?

She walked through looking in at each one to see if Sam was there, sitting with his arms folded waiting for her. What if he's brought his wife and kids she thought, and stopped, struck by the horror of that idea.

I never ever wanted to meet them. I didn't even want him to come over to my apartment – that was his idea. I liked the way it started – in the office.

She'd been thrilled by his quick passionate kisses when she entered with papers to be signed, the series of breathless random embraces in hallways when nobody was around, even the blunt immediate sex in the office on the floor – once against Sam's desk. She'd liked the feeling that she herself never lost control, it was Sam forcing her, pushing her over some edge of rationality because of his need, not hers. She could laugh when afterwards he struggled with words, when he tried to tell her how important she was.

"I know," she'd reply in the new deep confident voice that came with their surrender to each other after months of indecision and turmoil. "I know because you've just risked everything."

He'd looked startled, his round plump face like a little boy's. They'd been lying on the floor beside the wall. Outside the drawn venetian blinds, the Minneapolis streets were dark with a long evening of April rain. He'd looked a little frightened too, she remembered later with satisfaction, knowing she had the keys to his family. By betraying his marriage, he'd placed them in her hands but that was a power she never cared to flex, not in the six years of their affair because she didn't desire what he so clearly did: a stable home life and children. She'd seen the drudgery her mother had bogged down in.

When she'd learned of Jessie teaching before marriage, how she'd owned her own horse and carriage, had traveled all over the countryside teaching music, Bernice thought: Does love and marriage mean you give up everything that's important to you? Yet she'd adored her father – her nature was like his – silent, independent in habit, austere in mood.

Father and I spent hours together without saying much, she thought, with us silence was a kind of tenderness.

She'd never had that with Sam. Impatient with the dangers of encountering others at the office, he'd hounded her for something more comfortable, yet remained too cheap to pay for hotel rooms. Giving him a key to her apartment had been a mistake, Bernice realized later, for she found she didn't want her own way of life endangered, didn't want her neighbors in The Maxwell Arms, the small apartment block where she lived, to see a police detective coming in and out of her apartment late at night. She knew her neighbors would talk, would watch for him, then gossip together. But Sam had insisted, threatened to call it quits. Finally she'd agreed but only after wresting from him the promise that he would come over late, and out of uniform. For several years he'd kept that promise, had slept in her arms until five, then gone directly to the station. He'd told his wife he was on night duty, once or twice told her he had meetings out of town so they could enjoy a weekend together. But Bernice never liked any of it: the tension of hearing his key in the door, of wondering if neighbors heard his heavy step, baritone voice.

He'd come in tired, would complain, as he probably did to his wife, how hungry he was or that there was nothing fit to drink in her apartment. Sam was fifty pounds overweight, a consumer of fancy cakes, rich pies, ham sandwiches at midnight – all of which she paid for. He liked to keep liquor in her apartment, but was fussy about the brand of scotch he drank, so she bought what he liked. But women in The Maxwell Arms noticed those bottles in the garbage cans outside. If the gossip became too open, Bernice knew she'd be asked to leave. That had happened to others in the apartment building branded 'scarlet women.'

As Bernice went from table to table she came upon a middle-aged couple holding hands over hot dogs and coffee. When she peeked in on them, they dropped hands, shifted guiltily, were clearly unable to pretend a marriage in a simple afternoon at the park. She and Sam had done the same thing – come to Minnewana Park, to see each other in daylight. Sam had looked older, more ordinary. Probably so did I she thought then, moving on. But our love warmed in the sun – just sitting together at a picnic bench, drinking cokes and talking helped keep us together. They hadn't kissed or touched, too afraid someone who knew them would walk by.

Bernice turned around, walked out of the picnic area, and started back to the family table. Well it was over. He wasn't there, he wasn't going to be there. It had been a stupid place to meet anyway. His wife never did find out, that was one good thing about it. In a few minutes she saw their family table, Jessie sat near Rose Corinne who was rearranging a last box of food.

Rose Corinne had found out. Her sister was been helping her clean her apartment when she moved out, when she'd found a stupid Japanese kimono that Sam had given Bernice in a rare fit of extravagance. Then some books he'd left behind – westerns and hunting stories – not the kind Bernice read. To her surprise, her sister said in a quiet voice, "I'm glad for you Bernice, glad you're not alone." And in the first years she'd been glad too; the affair with Sam had given her a sense of completion. Afterwards, for a time, she'd regretted the loss of the heavy footsteps, the sly key inserted in her lock, the whole sense of drama these brought, but she swept the regret away, told herself he would never divorce, never be more than a shadow in her life, was an angry and violent man.

Yet as she approached her sister and mother, Bernice suddenly thought, with fierce surprise: Is it really over? Is Sam gone forever? There was still in her a need to resist that fact.

She came up to the table and sat down between her sister and mother.

"That was fast." Rose Corinne said. She patted the last of the boxes she'd been wrestling with.

"It's so crowded. You can hardly move."

"Where did you go?"

"Not far. It's too hot."

Heat was spreading like water – thick and consuming. The sun, lower in the sky, was a yellow diamond dazzle. Some sat limply half asleep or reading. Others forced themselves to move around, to resist rest; they played slow ball games or ran errands, got root beer floats, popcorn and ice cream from the concessions stands, opened coolers of iced tea and fruit juice and coke. Little kids ate popsicles, their mouths like rainbows; fathers sipped beer and whiskey from coffee cups. Only over rare and unlucky few did bathroom smells hover in the air like buzzards.

"It smells pretty awful here." Bernice opened her purse and took out a cigarette.

"I barely notice it anymore," Corky said as airily as she could manage. She straightened. "Look Bernice, doesn't that woman look like Violet?"

Meanwhile Helen had reached the boat concession. The first thing she saw' was one of the obnoxious boys she met earlier. He was taking tickets. She decided not to go closer, but instead stood watching the boats go out. There was a long line of people waiting because, though the paddleboats and canoes were old and shabby, going out in them on Lake Minnewana was something you did on the Fourth of July. That's not the reason Eddie want to go canoeing, Helen thought however, he's planning something diabolical. Why is he so mean to Aunt Bernice? We'll probably end up taking grandma with us. I can't imagine leaving her behind.

She noticed a clock on the side of the boat concession hut. It was just after four o'clock. I have to start back, she thought. It's already a gruesome day, it can't get much worse. Then she saw the short obnoxious boy smirking at her. She moved away.

The tall handsome man would walk past. He'd stop and stare. She'd be looking with boredom at the crowded beach. She hardly noticed. People often stared at the tall sophisticated fashion model, whose name was Melissa Monroe. "You don't remember?" the man would say, voice trembling with emotion. She'd glance at him, lifting one perfectly manicured eyebrow to indicate the slightness of her interest. She was so often approached by these handsome strangers. "Do I know you?" she drawled in a cool amused voice. I saw you once long ago, the stranger swallowed hard (he was very good looking) "I've never forgotten you." He laughed then, a shaky shabby little laugh.

What exactly is a shabby laugh?

The fashion model, Melissa Monroe, walked away, cool, distant, pure.

'Pure' is such a beautiful word, Helen thought, walking along the path swerving to avoid duck droppings and popcorn boxes; it even looks clean. So does 'clean.'

There 'was a spot on the path where it left the' lake and wound up the hill; along it were clumps of trees and bushes, a thick screening of growth which seemed to say o.k., people, here at least you aren't winning. Their picnic table was just over the hill. Ahead on the path she saw a middle-aged man in a wheel chair parked next to the iron park bench – the bench Eddie had said was where they would meet to go canoeing. It was a vantage point; Duck Island could be viewed in the distance through a break in the trees.

She left the path to cut straight up the hill and so walked past the man. He had a calm satisfied look like Mr. Miller, their next door neighbor, though this man's hair was black and shiny, his eyes and nose and mouth pushed together by the fat of his cheeks.

"Nice day," he said as she came abreast of him. He was fat, and close up his face looked wide and silvery and flat. He was smoking a cigar. She slowed down, Have I seen him before? she thought.

"Sit down, take the load off your feet."

Not knowing quite why, she perched on the edge of the bench farthest from him.

He's a cripple, she told herself. I wonder what it's like to be a cripple.

"Lot a people in the park today. Lotta kids like you." His voice was thin and high, a voice that didn't fit his bulk. She watched how he moved his hands together, the cigar between two fingers, the tip wet.

"You got any boyfriends?"

"No." That's a funny question to ask, she thought. And she didn't like the look he had when he asked it. His mouth had fallen open slightly and now he pressed these fingers into each other; press, relax, press, relax. She found herself watching them. I should get up and walk on, she thought, but didn't move, instead looked around. People passed on the path below and beside them, but no one came straight up toward them, no one sat under a bench beneath the trees either, trees that were gloomy firs. Their scent was strong, an abrasive alien smell. Mean trees she'd always thought of them because nothing would grow beneath them, that ground was rough, in some places damp.

Above all it was quiet.

"You're kidding. Good-looking girl like you?"

There's something about cripples in the bible, she thought, you were supposed to be nice to them. They couldn't help having gimpy legs. This man looked awfully strong" Though. He had enormous legs and thick muscular arms. Above a thin beard, his mouth was a slash with no lips, like a fish.

Still she didn't get up. There was something eerie and familiar about this man and this place, like she'd dreamed it.

"No boyfriends – a girl like you?"

She felt a twinge of self-importance. He leaned forward and wheeled himself closer, an odor of cloves wavered between them.

"I mean it, she looks like Violet." said Bernice.

"She sure does." Corky had straightened with surprise. They both watched the woman plod past. She had her head down and was holding a clutch purse in one hand, a large black dress clutch purse at odds with her brief white and red summer attire.

"Funny how Violet had black hair. Like the baby. Two brunettes and two with black hair."

"Poor Violet – an accident like that. I don't think they've told us everything that happened up there in Alaska. It wasn't fair making her serve in the war."

"What's fair?" Bernice's voice was subdued. "Tell me what's fair."

Corky stood up. "I'm thirsty. Want a drink of water?"

Bernice looked at her a moment. She didn't move. "What do you want me to do, Rose? Do you really want me to come back to the Twin Cities? To take care of Mother for a while?"

"I'm tired of thinking about it, Bernice. Tired of talking about it. Everything seems up in the air right now. All I know is you and Mother have never really gotten along and you don't seem to be doing too well today. You have no patience with her."

There, thought Corky I've told her the truth. While Bernice thought, I think she's saying I needn't come down. Good. That's o.k. with me.

Jessie looked over at them, her eyes deep wells.

"My feet are asleep."

"Get up and walk around, Mother," Corky said. She rose, and poured some water from the jug they'd brought. "You want some water, Mother?" She held up her cup.

"They're so cold."

"Walk around the table."

"How can her feet be cold when it's ninety degrees out?" Bernice said in a low voice. "Sometimes Mother doesn't make sense."

She looked at her watch. Twenty minutes after four. Was Sam there now? Would he come looking for her? I'm safer out in a canoe. Good thing Eddie suggested it. But tempted, Bernice tried out a whole different idea with her sister.

"If I came back, I could sort out some things with Sam."

Rose Corinne didn't say anything. She watched Jessie walking around the table.

"Sam and I have a lot to say to each other." Bernice puffed out smoke.

Rose Corinne turned to tug at her sister's arm.

"Nothing. You have nothing to say to each other. It's over, Bernice. Leave it alone. Leave him alone. He's a married man."

"That didn't used to bother you."

"Well it does now. And besides I don't think he was good for you."

Or Violet, Bernice couldn't help thinking. She opened her mouth to tell her sister everything. At that exact moment Jessie halted in front of them.

"My feet are asleep," Jessie said in a firm voice.

"Walk around some more, Mother." Bernice looked up at her small fierce mother.

"Where?"

"Around the table." Bernice puffed out more smoke.

"Nonsense."

Rose Corinne stood up. "Mother, you need to rest. Why don't you lie down in the back of the car?"

"It's hot in that car," said Bernice.

"We'll leave the door open."

Bernice stamped her cigarette butt into the grass. She watched Rose Corinne walk Jessie, stiff and half asleep to the car. How can I ever be that patient with Mother? she thought. Or that kind? Rose is a better daughter than I.

The thought made her sad.

Jessie sank down on the rear seat. Rose Corinne opened the windows on the driver's side so she'd get a cross breeze. Not that there is any, she thought. She touched her mother's chest. "Are you okay there, Mother?"

"Yes. Yes I am tired. This feels good." Jessie closed her eyes.

Meanwhile Helen still hadn't moved. She didn't quite know why. Frightened? Hardly, she thought. This is the bench where I'm supposed to meet Eddie. Where is he anyway? And there was in her by then a certain amount of curiosity.

"You got a great body on you." The fat man's lips curved into a secret kind of smile. He wheeled his wheelchair a little closer.

Helen stood up. She'd been brought up on stories of cripples – her Aunt Jenny, Daddy's sister, had lived in a wheel chair until the day she died. I shouldn't be rude to a cripple in a wheelchair she thought. But just because he's a cripple doesn't mean he can be icky. She edged away.

"No boyfriend – how you gonna find out what pussy means?"

He was still smiling. She didn't know what he was talking about but she knew something was wrong with him. She looked around. Funny how there's nobody here. And look how wet the ground is under those trees. Sodden cartons and newspapers everywhere. They must have been watering the trees or something.

She looked down at the man in the wheelchair. He met her eyes and his smile started to close in, to draw up like an accordion, pushing itself into a small straight mouth. "You've got a hairy bit on you, little girl." He leaned a little sideways, head bent. His smile expanded. The clove smell rushed at her as he wheeled his chair forward. Get away from here, stupid, she told herself. I don't have to talk to him just because he's a cripple. My family, our table, safety is just up the hill.

She walked quickly away.

You dare not invade my privacy, the beautiful young girl stood in the doorway of a humble cottage, her long blonde extremely curly hair cascading down to her waist. She was five feet tall and had a nineteen inch waistline. The young and extraordinarily handsome nobleman -he was wearing white tights -smiled a dimpled smile and leaned forward to touch the glistening tears on her fair cheeks.

At the top of the hill, a family was playing ball, the mother stood waiting apprehensively for a small boy to pitch the ball. She held the bat well away from her body, legs stiff. The other children jumped up and down shrieking.

We used to play ball like that Helen thought. Then a brutal thump hit her shoulder. A football had hit her from the opposite direction. A man with thick curly hair and a kind wrinkled face came over to collect it.

"Sorry about that. Are you all right, young lady?"

Helen nodded but felt the sting of tears in her eyes. She saw at the table, her mother sitting next to Aunt Bernice. Big dull safe Aunt

Bernice. Grandma lay in the back of the car asleep. Helen sat down next to Aunt Bernice. But immediately Rose Corinne stood up, "Let's go Bernice – for a walk. Helen's here."

She didn't even ask me what I've been doing, Helen thought. She never asks me anything.

"Just the two of us?"

"I'm tired of waiting for Dana."

"Don't forget I'm meeting Eddie." Somehow being with Eddie didn't seem as dangerous to Bernice right then as being with her sister. But she stood up, picked up her handbag. Her sister smiled.

"What about me?" Helen said. "Maybe I have some things to do."

Corky came over and stroked Helen's cheek, "Thanks sweetheart. We won't be gone long. Just keep an eye on Grandma."

"I may have to report a crime."

Rose Corinne and Lily Bernice paid no attention to this startling announcement.

"Get Eddie to take turns with you."

"How can I? He isn't here."

"Did you see him?"

"No."

"I don't mind waiting for Eddie," Bernice said hastily.

"No, no let's go." Once again Corky touched her daughter's cheek. "You're hot sweetheart. It wouldn't hurt you to rest a bit."

The two sisters began to walk away. The sensitive teenage girl watched them.

"I didn't see Eddie anywhere." she called after them. "And I walked right by the place where we were supposed to meet. It wasn't a pleasant experience, believe me."

"He'll show up."

"What if he doesn't?"

It was an unanswerable question and her mother didn't bother to try.

Helen watched them walk away and thought, they don't care. They don't care what happens to me.

As soon as they were out of earshot, Corky asked Bernice, "Why did Sam call you up anyway? It's bothering you isn't it? What'd he stir things up for after all this time?"

Bernice didn't feel like telling her sister the first calls had come from her. As she walked along, she thought, I could go back. There were four or five tables I didn't check. He could be waiting there, arms folded, getting angrier and angrier, swearing he'd never see me again, never. And thinking that, she walked faster.

THIRTY-ONE

Mother hasn't even asked what happened to me. About the pervert. Should I tell her? Does she even care about me? She'll think I made it up. Maybe I did. But Grandma would believe me. Helen looked over at the old woman spread across the back seat. She got up walked over and touched Jessie. She wasn't dead anyway. She looks so old Helen thought, sometimes I can't tell, but I guess I love her, because she always listened to me.

Helen went back to sit at the table. The feeling of love for Grandma stayed inside her for awhile. Grandma had scratched her back when she was sick, had taught her to play the piano, given her money secretly, saying: Go buy yourself a treat, some candy, an ice cream. Grandma was supposed to be there forever and now Helen knew she wouldn't be, couldn't be, not forever. Because there were rules.

Oh yes I am tired. It's good to lie and rest here in the car. The other folk are running all over the place in this heat. Oh my this little bed does feel mighty good.

What's the point of walking around a table? Foolishness. Going round in a circle.

The merry-go-round. I'd like to ride that one more time. Amsden, when I met you I was burdened something awful by my life. Remember when you took me on the merry-go-round – first time: in my life? You were the sanest man I'd ever met. The kindest. Yes you were, Amsden. but fearful quiet. I used to like to stir you up. Do you need stirring up now? Is heaven the way folks want it to be—awful quiet? Is it too quiet?

That's what worries me. What I liked best about Florida – beside the scent of oranges, was that there was always something not quite battened down there – hurricanes and killing frosts, and the people running around were pretty wild too. Did we take Violet there? I can't remember. She grew up different than the other girls somehow.

What were we do, Amsden, when our daughter turned wild? Was it something in us? Did you think that? Did you think, like mother, like daughter. You never said. You never said much of anything.

Sometimes I look for our lost lamb, Amsden. The thought of her comes up now that you're gone. I wonder what would Violet look like now? What would we talk about? The girls talk about her. Why didn't she call us, Amsden, why didn't she come see us? Did she think we'd turn her away? Did we? I can't remember exactly what happened – days, weeks, months, then the years went by. Did we erase her from our minds and doing that erase her from our lives? Is she erased, Amsden?

NO, Violet shouted, loud as she could but of course Jessie couldn't hear her.

Helen was writing in her diary. I hate rules. And I hate God now for making them so people have to die. She looked up a little nervous. Was God listening?

YES VIOLET SHOUTED, LOUD AS SHE COULD BUT OF COURSE HELEN COULDN'T HEAR HER.

THIRTY-TWO

Dana was walking on the path beside the road when he saw Mike Boyle sitting with a woman. Dana stopped to say hello. The woman looked familiar.

Mike smiled, "Haven't seen you in a while, Dana."

"I've been out of town."

"Last time I saw you was your sister Jenny's funeral. She was a sweet woman."

"Yes," Dana didn't want to talk about his sister. Her early death made him angry. But he sat down beside Mike and his friend, because he'd gone to school with him. He liked him. And Mike knew Dana's cousin Tom. So after some chitchat about the old days in the neighborhood, Dana asked about his cousin's friends.

"They want to use my car, Mike"

"Oh the bully boys are up to their games since the war ended. They wanted to rent my truck too but I said no way. I told 'em, no way. Stay out of trouble's my motto.

"Mine too, Mike, but they've got a hold on my old dad."

"How is he, your father?"

"Dying maybe. He's in the hospital." Dana rose, "I'll know tomorrow. Well see you Tom, and you too, Mrs. ... Sorry I don't know your name," he said to Mrs. Blunt, whose mood had been darkening all through their conversation.

"Greta,"

"Nice name," Dana smiled.

Greta said in a determined voice. "My last name's Blunt. I live next door to you."

"Mrs. Blunt. How are you? Sorry I didn't recognize you, I've been away."

At once Greta's mood lifted and the new mantra which had stuttered to a halt commenced again – a person, a person like everybody else.

"Six years I think since I seen you, Dana," Mike said. Were you drafted?"

"No. Flat feet, too old, two kids. How about you?"

"Too old and a bad heart."

Greta looked at him then. "You didn't tell me that Mike."

When the two sisters set off on their walk together, it was Bernice who insisted they go off the path. She wanted to walk on the grass; she even suggested that they take off their shoes. Rose Corinne couldn't imagine her actually doing such a thing. Bernice seems permanently skewered into dignity, she thought, like a light bulb screwed into a light socket. Dignity, dignity, the light was always coming on. So Rose Corinne demurred, claiming the grass was littered with sharp objects and besides they were too old to do such a thing, Bernice said nothing more, just marched away, expecting Rose to follow. Which Corky did. As usual, she thought, even as a kid, Bernice had to be the leader with me tagging along, sometimes whining because she walked at such a pace so far ahead of me. Rose Corinne was taking extra steps to keep up.

She decides everything so autocratically and much too fast. I have to think about things, have to mull them over in my mind, before I can decide something. I even dream about them at night, and here is Bernice making up her mind just like that. This is the way things will be and you will do that. Right now. Hurry up.

As a child, Rose Corinne had yielded. She'd washed the pots when Lily Bernice cooked, closed the doors that Lily Bernice left open. But later, as she grew up, Rose discovered it was more fun to make up her own mind, to dither away until only she could make the decision. Especially when she discovered that those delicious boyfriends would let her dither, indeed behaved as though that made her more feminine in their eyes.

And so Rose Corinne went her own way into adulthood mostly without Lily Bernice.

As she trudged along, trying to keep up with her sister's martial strides, Rose Corinne thought how over the years something had happened to Bernice. She's moved from determined to downright unpleasant at times, she thought, just too bossy by half. It's got so the only people that really want to be around Bernice are people who want their minds made up for them. Her girlfriends are all those lonely autocratic types just like her. They plan excursions or discuss movies like monarchs from separate nations.

Rose Corinne had few girlfriends. She was too busy keeping the home fires going. But on that hot Sunday in July, with all its reminders of childhood Rose Corinne found herself acquiescing to whatever Bernice suggested.

"Let's walk along the slope of the hill," Bernice said, "We'll get a view of the lake that way."

"All right."

"Then let's walk above the boat concession and see how many boats are out."

"All right."

"Then we'll walk way over to the corner where they keep those moth-eaten animals. Do they still have that moth-eaten zoo?"

"I'm not sure, Bernice." By then, Rose was puffing a little. She wasn't much of a walker, she was the first to admit that. Up and down the stairs that was her exercise.

"We'll find out. We'll walk over and take a look. See everything we can today."

"All right."

"But we must walk quickly. Let's go over the hill above the amusement park."

"O.K."

"Can you walk a little faster, Rose?"

"I'll try."

"Remember I have to be back for that canoe ride with Eddie. We're meeting at 5:15."

"5:30. I thought you said 5:30."

"Excellent. That gives us plenty of time."

"Does it?"

"Rose, can you walk a little faster?"

"I'm walking as fast as I can." Rose Corinne was trying to stay sweet. I'm giving it my best shot. What harm will it do to go along with her today? Bernice won't always have somebody to boss around. Not after we go to Denver. If we go. What's Dana up to turning down that job? Well yes, I did say I wanted to stay, hinted he could go back alone, but it was an idea, a suggestion, that's all. He had no business moving on it so fast; he ought to know I like to think things through. Scaredycat, scaredycat. I feel like calling him that.

Oh yes, Corky wanted to slap Dana that's what she wanted to do, paddle him hard. It didn't help that she also wanted him so much. Months and months without him and then he comes back and doesn't touch me. That's cruel, she thought. Is that how Bernice feels all the time? Why is she stirring Sam up? He was happy to see the end of their affair, I can bet on that. It went on so long, and was going nowhere, he wasn't leaving his wife, and now Bernice wants to start it all up again. It's her starting it up.

You can bet on that. Well don't expect any help, Bernice. Not from me.

Bernice was forging ahead; they were heading down toward the lake weaving in and out of families on the grass.

Dana's afraid of going back, that's what it is. In case he falls into the arms of that Miss Wonderful again. Rose was panting. It was much, much too hot for her to be walking so fast. Bernice never seems to sweat.

Rose stopped. "You go ahead, Bernice."

Bernice halted a few feet ahead of her. "Look there's that woman again,"

Rose Corinne looked down and saw walking below them on the path by the lake, the woman with the clipped black hair. Head down, she was trudging along, still holding her black clutch purse. She was wearing a green strapless halter and white shorts.

"She's changed her clothes." Rose Corinne marveled as she came to stand beside Lily Bernice. They both stared at the apparition below.

"She does look like Violet." Bernice was startled. "That is extraordinary."

"I must admit I don't remember so much about her now. I didn't see her those last years. Sometimes I can hardly remember what she looked like."

"Oh I can," Bernice said grimly. "I remember all right. I was the one that identified the body don't forget. That was a sight, I can tell you."

"Her voice." Corky said hastily wanting to shirt this painful subject, not wanting to get into the subject after all. Why oh why had she mentioned it? "Her voice, I remember was that it was flat, but deep. She had a deep voice didn't she?"

"I don't remember her voice that well." Bernice said, "but I do remember her face. Though when I saw it last she was pretty badly beaten. She was beaten up, Rose, beaten to a pulp almost. Somebody didn't like her. It was awful."

Bernice went on staring down at the path where the woman had disappeared.

"How awful." Corky said, "You never told us that, Bernice. I thought you said she drowned." But she thought, It's past, it's done, why does she bring it up like this? It's she that brings it up; nobody else. Rose Corinne had already forgotten she'd asked the first questions.

"She was laid out on a slab and I walked in and I said, 'It's my sister I was the last one of us to see her alive, that's why they called me.' She had my name in her wallet. My name and address." By then, Bernice wanted to stop talking about it too, but somehow the words were forcing their way up through her; her voice had deepened, grown darker. "She looked dreadful. I'll never forget how dreadful she looked."

"It's too hot a day to go into all that, Bernice." Corky said. She started down the hill toward the small zoo. The animals will be hot and smelly today, the place full of people. From smelly bathrooms to a smelly zoo – why are we doing this? Corky thought. Now that she thought of it, it might not be the last time for all this. Dana had said they weren't going. I've spent weeks cleaning house, thinking about packing and then suddenly he decides, oh I'm not going, we're not going. And we planned to sort Mother out this weekend. To talk to Bernice about it. Am I supposed to not talk about it now?

Oh he is a hateful man.

That woman – his landlady. If I'm with him there won't be any time or energy to meet her. She probably can't cook anyway. Probably he was lonely and she was right on top of him, making herself available, that's how it had happened. I can take care of her all right. But Corky felt anger and hurt swell up inside her again.

They were down in the zoo by then, walking up and down the corridors between the animal cages, glancing at its moribund inhabitants. The animals looked hot and smelled hot, they lay on the ground dozing or were hiding in their cages. It's only us that are too stupid to do the same thing. Corky stopped. "Do we have to do this?"

Bernice was determined." They've improved the place."

"No, they haven't."

The zoo smell was a rutting smell – like sex and garbage, along with sweaty fur. "How much will it cost you to take the train to Denver? It would be cheaper to drive. Do you plan on taking Father's car?"

"I don't know, Bernice. I don't know anything yet. I have to talk to Dana."

"The train is expensive."

And then it hit Corky for the first time. Money. Dana didn't have enough money to go back, to take them all back. How could she have been so stupid? And all the time she had more than enough to pay for their trip. She felt a little flush of shame.

Because the zoo was on a slope above the merry-go-round, they could hear 'The good old summertime' played over and over, the sound like a giant playing an oboe; a sound that coiled up, was a lure, a reminder that people were there to amuse themselves – in the good old golden summertime.

"Violet stayed with me a few days before she died," Bernice said suddenly."

"In Minneapolis? And she never called Mother? Never called me?"

"Father knew she was in town. Time to go back, Rose."

"Father? Did he see her?" "Not that I know. There was no time."

Now Corky was interested. Though she panted as she rushed along, she kept up with Bernice who was striding along. "You say she drowned. Where?"

"Never mind."

"Was it the river? Did you see her body?"

Bernice paused. The lie was widening, like a crack appearing in an ice field.

"I told you I did."

"Did she jump in the river? Who beat her up? It's horrible, a horrible thought."

For the second time that day, Corky's imagination jumped to the plight of another, this time the fate of her mysterious bad seed younger sister.

THIRTY-THREE

Eddie ran his hands up Carol's narrow bony spine. She had a tight little body, full of sharp bones and sudden curves.

"Are you going away?" Carol managed to look both pretty and demure, twiddling with a blade of grass. They'd spread a blanket from the car under the half-shade of a lilac bush and were lying side by side – Carol was wearing the friendly red and white playsuit.

"What?"

"To Texas. Helen told me you were going to Texas."

Eddie let go of Carol and rolled over on his back, shielding his eyes from the sun. A surge of annoyance filled him. Blabbermouth Skip. Why'd he tell her anything?

"Maybe."

"Eddie, are you serious?" Carol turned over and looked at him.

"About going to Texas?

"About last night. About us."

"Last night was great." He put his arm around her, pulled her over and gave her a kiss. She kissed back, a moist little smack, then looked around to see if anyone was looking, but there were few people close by, let alone curious ones. They were in the corner of the park with small playing fields, several tennis courts, and no trees.

"Sure I'm serious."

"Am I your girlfriend now?"

Eddie paused. Then sat up. That seemed a definite role, one chock full of responsibility. A girlfriend meant he was a boyfriend and he didn't know if he felt that responsible.

"I like you for sure."

"Are we going steady?"

"Going steady?"

He had to think that one over. Going Steady. He saw it written out in big letters – a place where you were held accountable. Like Bethany Baptist Bible School. And maybe for longer than two weeks.

Eddie looked around. It was hot out in the open. The grass was burnt looking, short and dry. Across the expanse of small baseball diamonds and football playing fields, a few resolute children pursued balls, but there were no adult teams playing by then, they'd retired to enjoy soft drinks, build up courage for the next round of food, drink beer if they'd smuggled some in, while they waited for night to roll in and fireworks to begin.

"Are you saying we aren't?" Carol was sitting up too by then, her voice and face were pouty yet she still looked adorable.

"I didn't say anything at all."

"Oh I know, I know," Carol stared away into the dry distance. Her voice was tragic. "I'm nothing to you now."

Eddie wished he'd brought his fishing rod. He needed fishing. Fishing took away all those mixed feelings that bubbled up when left untended. He'd been fishing the last three weekends.

"I didn't say that."

"You're going to. Oh Eddie, you're going away. Leaving me behind. I knew it would happen."

How did she know so much, so soon? He only knew he liked being with her, that he liked doing it with her. That was important information as far as he was concerned. But it was important he go off by himself too. Like a fish, swimming through cool water, alone, no other fish, only the water and his own skills of survival.

He looked at his watch. It was close to four thirty. He could forget about Aunt Bernice and stick it out here and talk and stuff or he could – yeah he'd better go.

He stood up. "Can we talk about it later, Carol? I've got to go."

"Are you going to dump me here?" Carol stood up too. "That's rude."

"I told you I was with my family. I told you my mother said no friends. I told you I'd have to come and find you."

"I hope I'm more than a friend."

"I have to take my aunt for a canoe ride."

Carol grabbed his hand, pulled him closer. "Oh Eddie. I love you." She put her head against his chest. "I want to go with you to Texas. Let's elope."

When Rose Corinne and Lily Bernice went their separate ways, Corky found an empty stretch of grass and sat down on it to think. She took out of her pocket the piece of the newspaper she'd carried around with her for days. A paper she'd read and reread, how the millionaire financier, James Newell, had died at his home nearly two weeks ago.

She remembered him talking away as usual, telling her -never you mind how I got to be this rich. I am rich. I got myself out of the south, out of the black despair, got myself educated enough to get me some good jobs, had some lucky breaks – never you mind how I made my money. I know one thing for damn sure if they find out I'm three fourths black they'll do their damndest to take it away from me – on principle they'll string me up financially, they'll cut me down to size, the size they think I ought to be and you know something, Missy Rose, I'll go out fighting and I'll go out fast. I won't stick around to be humiliated. I'll use this and he'd showed her the pistol.

She hadn't believed James, she'd thought he was showing off.

Now that Fourth of July, Corky sitting there safe on her meek little stretch of ordinary grass in Minnewana Park, read once again about the millionaire financier leaving all his money to the university, millions of dollars except for some large bequests to family and friends, felt her heart beating faster again, because one of those bequests was to her, and she didn't even know yet how much; the lawyer had said maybe fifteen thousand dollars maybe less; the insurance companies are fighting, some of this, he'd said, leaning forward on his big expensive mahogany desk.

The lawyer, Mr. Marcus Amberson, was a large fleshy man with horn-rimmed glasses and a serious look who said to her, don't you worry, even if they won't pay policies because of the nature of the death, and here he'd paused and looked significantly at her, then sat back in the big leather chair and waited for her to speak but she didn't because Corky didn't know what to say. She knew this lawyer was curious just exactly what was the nature of her relationship with the millionaire financier who killed himself, no next to kin except a couple of children. Corky herself was interested in the bequests and who they went to because she hoped it was to his black family that he'd all but abandoned so she waited and finally the lawyer, whose name was Marcus Amberson, leaned forward again and said, don't you worry, most of the money was his own, safe in stocks and fund and numbered saving s accounts so you'll get yourself a nice chunk of change from that happy fellow, and it seemed such an offhand, such a sloppy casual way of speaking of a dead man, coming from an all-important pillar of the community dignity that she had decided he was being too familiar and so sat up straighter, had gathered in her white handbag and pushed her new white shoes together, both of which she'd bought for this very occasions, though she'd hardly had the money to do it, and so had borrowed the money from Jessie temporarily which Jessie had been very willing to do but would soon forget, and she did forget and fussed for days about her missing money. They let her carry around a twenty dollar bill just to convince her she still had money, and heaven help you if that twenty dollar bill became two fives and a ten, or vanished entirely.

Of course Corky couldn't tell her mother or anyone why she needed new white shoes and a new white handbag, though Helen had noticed and immediately told her mother that white shoes made her feet look big, and several other items of interest to those like Mrs. Rydarksy, who followed the latest styles (Helen having looked through the Rydarksy wardrobe during one of her babysitting occasions).

"When will I know?" Corky had asked after she pulled herself together and was able to speak in a steady no nonsense voice that she knew she was good at.

Marcus Amberson (call me Mark) said "A week maybe. I can't give you money then but I can tell you in a week."

"And when can you give me some of the money?"

"We'll hope in a month or so, if nothing unusual crops up. But I can give you five thousand dollars next week as an advance." He'd sat back again and waited like some kind of psychiatrist for her to gush away about her life and what she knew of James Newell and Corky wasn't saying anything, she knew better than to tell anybody the tale, especially somebody like this, not particularly friendly or unfriendly but bone idle curious. She could tell that much about him.

"Thank you very much, Mr. Amberson," she'd said and stood up which caught the lawyer by surprise and he stood up too.

"Pleasure to meet you, Mrs. McFadden."

Did her eyes deceive her or was the emphasis on the Mrs? And his hand stretched out carry with it a bit too much warmth? Maybe it was only her imagination, but Corky was careful to take: his hand oh so lightly and she wished she'd worn her white glovers – she'd taken them off when she came in because it was so hot, but now she made a great business of tugging them on again like a real lady would.

"Well then, I'll come to your office on Monday, if that's convenient."

"I'll make some time," Mr. Amberson said genially leading her out of his office. "About 2 p.m. Monday then."

He'd made: a great business of instructing his secretary to let her in and Corky, flushed with a giddy little feeling of important thought to herself, I bet if I suggested lunch he'd go for it – a wicked thought but she was needing that – it was two days before Dana came home -but on the phone he told her how tired he was, how he needed a rest.

Melissa Strange, gypsy queen knew what to do. Pow right in the kisser of the philandering prince. She'd be on stage wearing gold coins across her forehead as proof of her gypsy powers over the dark forces.

Why is philander spelled with a 'p' It's very annoying.

Helen was sitting at the table writing in her diary. She looked up and saw Norbett bicycling up the road. There weren't many cars moving around by then, everyone had settled in to wait for the fireworks. She got up, came over to the side walk and looked at him. He wobbled over, and stopped puffing like he'd been running.

"Don't tell my sister I've come over here because she's hopping mad at your brother but I had to tell you to be careful those Williams people are here in the park. I didn't' tell you but they complained to my mom and dad because they thought it was me looking in their window."

"Well it was Norbett. I was there. You dragged me over there."

"I saw them packing up this morning and I heard them talking about the fireworks so they're probably going over for the day just like us and don't let them see you, not close anyway because they may recognize you and Mrs. Williams said if they can catch a better look at the girl they may call the police because she."

"Me?"

"No, Mrs. Williams, she said the girl looked underage and if I was getting some poor little underage girl in trouble, the police should know."

"Well you did Norbett, you did get me into trouble."

"No, I didn't," Norbett almost squeaked. He's kind of cute Helen couldn't help admitting, with his size eleven feet and his long skinny legs and his brush cut and freckles all over his face. "Or I didn't mean to. I didn't mean to have you see them doing that." And Norbett blushed beet red. "I like doing things like that because it reminds me of the commando raids and I knew you were interested in World War II because you told me you were. You were reading a book about it, and that's what commandos do. I think I want to be a marine." Norbett dwindled away into silence.

It sounded plausible and Helen was flattered that Norbett had chosen her over all the other girls he might have dragged to a window to see two elderly people half naked.

THIRTY-FOUR

This is the true story of Jessie's life, the siren voice of the dream soul sang. It is my privilege as her soul, and the destination of the story I will tell her, to bring up what has never come to her mind before, to reveal to her how beautiful all her life has been.

Jessie was snoozing in the back seat of the beautiful blue Ford. Both doors on the grass side were open. Jessie was warm but not too warm and once again drifting in her sleep through the dream world where her soul could speak, a soul now determined to rearrange her life into a beautiful version of early love led inexorably down the path of inexplicable, unassailable, irresistible passion. The soul had a melodious voice, one that was pleasing, but its facts? Jessie had always quarreled with its facts.

It was a beautiful summer that year, Jessie. The town rested in endless fields of green, Deep River like a ship sailing through a sea of emeralds, becalmed in waters so mild, to those who lived there it appeared no storm could penetrate. You and Billy were together every night of the two weeks you boarded with the Blacks. His father Stephen was the town mayor and surveyor and was often away on business. Billy's mother, was very ill, no one saw her except Mrs. Mathews, the serving woman, Billy, Stephen, and Dr. Higgins. The house was hushed and sad. But oh those long, lingering evenings, you and Billy alone in the house, sitting the great mahogany dining table, or side by side in front of the fire. A. slow steady joy grew in you though neither you nor Billy said much in words.

That's enough of that, thought Jessie in mid dream; she stirred and groaned. The soul's dream story was more like a nightmare to her.

Jessie, you two sat in silence, there came into you a warmth of contentment, of surprise that you were opening up to a man you barely knew. Oh Jessie truly that was fate. Destiny. You were in a house filled with the anguish of a coming death, yet life and love urged themselves upon you both; you were young with so much life yet to be lived, so much love still to be expressed. And even as old as you are now, Jessie, haven't you still love that needs to be expressed?

No, gol darn it. Jessie struggled to wake up. Beyond her, the sensitive teenage girl assigned to keep watch over her, closed her diary and rose from the family picnic table. She went and sat under a nearby tree, leaned back, yawned, closed her eyes.

Oh sweet Jessie, remember how you saw Billy's soul one night? You were sitting in the dining room together talking, in darkness save for one lamp, while outside crickets sang and in the sky hung a moon a few days short of full. You looked over and saw Billy's eyes on your face, and that new warmth filled your body; when he stood up and came over and reached down to take your hand, you gave it to him with a smile. He pulled you to your feet and kissed you, then said, You're beautiful, and you felt the chord of destiny between you. You felt completely free. In all your life you'd never felt so free.

Jessie moaned out loud. Nonsense, you're talking nonsense.

Was seeing someone' s soul ever enough? Enough to make up for pain and humiliation and the real losses that follow? Such questions may be asked but the soul rarely answers them in the way expected or desired. In fact, the soul may not even be interested in dialogue with intelligence. It only wants to tell your life story a new way.

No, no, You stop that. Jessie stumbled down the hill. That man knew darn well I was pregnant. He was saying goodbye forever; he had no intention of marrying me.

Even with Jessie awake and moving, the story wouldn't stop. Because the soul never argues or gives up once started, just unrolls the new story, or retells an old one with more interesting parts written in. Two weeks later, you knew. You went to Dr. Higgins and told him exactly what had happened. That Billy Black was gone, perhaps forever. When you returned three days later there was a thick packet on the table. The doctor's windows were open; it was warm and outside, children played ball on the open field beside the surgery.

Their voices were a happy sound. Dr. Higgins, his face and body stiff, thrust some money toward you.

"Mr. Black has been very generous. He's arranged for you to go to Minneapolis, and then on to Denver where there's a sanatorium. The town will learn you've contracted tuberculosis and that he's taken responsibility because you boarded in his house. We've already talked to Mrs. Pringle. Tomorrow is your last day of teaching."

The quickening smell of spring grass rushed in the window. Higgins patted the packet of money and pushed it further toward you. "Here – tickets for the train, a hotel reservation, price of a room at the sanatorium where the procedure can be done are all in here. You understand I can't do it for you."

You sat and stared at the doctor. He meant an abortion. Outside the voices of children sparkled. It was nearly evening.

"Well, what do you have to say?" His face was stern. "You may wish to tell your parents or you may not. That is up to you. You do understand?"

Jessie, you do remember that when Mrs. Pringle, the school trustee, called you out of the classroom toward the end of the two weeks and asked if the rumors were true, and saw your surprise, you tried to convince her of your innocence. You reminded her that the Black's house was a sick room and said perhaps it had been inappropriate to house you there since Mrs. Black was dying of tuberculosis. Her eyes widened, she looked afraid. "You're right." she managed to stutter, "How could we have been so lax?"

You had revealed the family's deception to the town, helped destroy Mr. Black's reputation as mayor. Mrs. Blacks' illness had been kept a secret from the town. TB patients were forced to go to sanatoriums then, but Mr. Black had used his influence to keep his wife at home. Now he would be forced him to send his wife into care.

Jessie's eyes smacked open. That's enough of that. She sat up. I've got to get moving. She wriggled herself out of the back seat of-the car, staggered to her feet. The soul voice ground on. but, half asleep she began to walk away from the car. Looking back, she saw the young girl asleep against a nearby tree. Everybody else was gone. Well I won't wake: her, Jessie thought, she's more trouble than she's worth.

I'll set about doing what I intended to do today. And away she went, walking down the hill, not even bothering to find the shade. Her mouth was dry but she was used to that.

The soul voice ground on. You moved to another family household, and when he said goodbye Billy whispered that he was leaving home too. Going east; he said to try his luck in New York, but you knew he was fleeing his mother's illness, escaping her death in a sanatorium, his loss of you. A double loss for so young a man.

"Well I didn't." Jessie said crankily out loud. "And thinking about it still makes me angry. So I won't think about it. Not if it makes me angry. That's too dangerous when you're as old as me. I might die angry." On the path, two middle-aged ladies in peddle-pushers and hairnets were carrying cold drinks and swerved to avoid her.

Jessie was marching faster now, almost tumbling over rough patches of ground. Drat these shoes of mine she said, forgetting she was wearing bedroom slippers, these are no good for rough ground. She was cross because the story wouldn't stop and so she did. She sat down on a bench by the lake, and said, now stop it, all that is dead and gone, along with the baby and I did my best for her, the little girl, even gave her a name.

"Take the money," the doctor said. Do you remember that his face was sad? He did care about you, please remember that. "You're young. You have a whole life ahead of you. Don't burden yourself with an unwanted child." He talked on and on, trying to convince you, but you thought him unkind.

Well he was, Jessie thought crossly, I was glad to get out of that town, to have enough money to leave. Jessie came to the path by the lake, took a few more steps, stopped, waited. The story had finally ended. Good, she thought, because Amsden's all I care about now, he knew all about it, and he loved me anyway, and he never tried to talk me out of anything I ever wanted to do. I loved him most of all.

She waited for the soul to challenge her but it was silent. She walked along the path toward the merry-go-round, the big golden, glittering turning wheel, with its brass rings and swan boats, prancing wild-eyed horse on rising and falling poles; its circle of gleaming mirrors and musical throat blaring – In the Good Old Summertime.

THIRTY-FIVE

Corky set off walking around the lake alone. Amazed at herself for doing it.

This is so foolish. What's the point? That whole day that was the question she'd been asking herself – Why am I doing this? Nobody cares.

Well I care about walking around the lake, she thought. Still she was soon fed up. It certainly wasn't a leisurely walk, pushing herself through people. My goodness it's crowded and everyone in twos and threes, taking up the pathway, talking among themselves. She felt a wave of homesickness for when she'd had that – a crowd of family or friends around her. My goodness, I haven't walked around the lake alone since I was fifteen and pouting about some hurt feelings. I've always walked around with people.

But it suits me now, she thought firmly, though she felt a little grim marching along in the heat, yes it suits me fine. Everybody passing her was chattering away happily. She had to kick some noisy stupid ducks out of the way too.

Not the geese for she was afraid of geese. But the day was so hot the geese stayed near the shore only looked over at her now and then malevolently. It was the stupid ducks that waddled up demanding to be noticed.

About half way round the lake she stopped to rest. She sat down on a park bench. My it's hot, so hot, the water looks so dirty. She was sweating she felt sweaty. Why had she worn such a warm dress? Other people were in shorts, even in bathing suits, though who would swim in that dirty water? All along the shore, people were lined up holding bags full of bread. This was the duck feeding place and hordes of mallards and their mates scrabbled and quarreled over the bread crusts that the hordes of people dragged out of bags and threw at them.

We used to do that, Corky thought with a sudden wave of nostalgia, though why she should be sorry to see the last of a bag full of stale breads crusts, she didn't know, but it was that kind of day; she couldn't help herself. Everything was a – 'Is this the last time?' question. She felt stalled, held to the bench where she sat while she watched people, watched ducks.

The ducks waddled and swam about in couples and were as eccentric in couples as people. In some pairs the green and black marked male streamed about with a demure and modest female well behind. In others the brown female took the lead while the male submissively followed. Corky's eye was caught by an odd pair – one where the female cruised somewhat apart, near the shore, neatly feeding on whatever she could find and only occasionally checking her mate who kept upending himself in the water in private searches in the middle of an empty stretch of lake. Sometimes he swirled up and down kicking up spray with his wings for no apparent purpose. Corky watched how the little female kept checking on her mate and finally tried to drive him toward the shore where some bread crusts lay unclaimed, but the male didn't seem the least bit interested in bread or anything else practical, only his private display of tricks and games.

That's us, thought Corky, Dana and I. He's off playing games while I try to keep things together. And she watched as the female suddenly abandoned the bread and paddled out to swim round her mate while he dunked and pirouetted. She seemed to be doing nothing practical herself by then, only admiring her mate's ability to stay both playful and afloat.

Hot and suddenly angry, Corky sprang up – Enough of this! She started off again but soon stopped dead in the path, then moved off it so that people behind her could get by. She thought, Why should I go any further? Walk all the way around when it's so hot? She stepped further out onto the narrow beach. She could smell the oily retreat of the water, its out-on-a-binge odor. She thought, I'll turn around and go back this minute. But then she thought, no, I've come this far, and I'll finish it. Because from where she stood she could see way around the lake. It's such a round, round lake, like a slightly askew pancake, she thought. There isn't much beach. On a few wider stretches people layout in bathing suits, but it was sandbox sand not proper beach and most of it was duck littered and ugly.

Then, as she stood there, as so often happened to Corky, her view of the world tilted and she liked it all. The hollow of the park seemed a bowl full of people, everybody moving and busy, the lake and beach like sugar surrounded by ants, and she liked that suddenly, thinking well you couldn't be lonely here if you tried. When she: resumed walking she saw all sorts of people sitting and walking alone – men, women, old people, children. Some of them looked lonely and some didn't, but they were contained by it all – By the crowds, the lake, the trees. The sun was a low hot sizzle in the sky, full of haze and itself. Corky looked up as much as she dared and thought, well you worked hard all day, didn't you sun, time to spread yourself out, to start taking it easy.

The spot where she'd stopped was close to the boundary of Minnewana Park; on the other side of a dry stretch of grass was the highway and there was highway noise, the throttle and hum of cars moving, tires slapping fast going somewhere. She started walking again, and then, right in the middle of the path, she saw a five dollar bill. Stretched out like it needed help. Just lying there. She bent down and picked it up. You couldn't return a five-dollar bill. Not unless someone came running back saying, oh my, oh my, I dropped a five-dollar bill.

So standing there by the path, she waited with the five dollar bill in her hand. Expecting somebody to come by for it. It wasn't an old bill and it wasn't a new bill; she could see it was an in-between five-dollar bill, the kind that are easy to spend. She looked down at it, stretched out in the palm of her hand. Yes it was a five dollar bill. Around her birds in the trees were chirruping and inside her a little bright burst of happiness sprang up. What a lucky thing! That's the most money I've ever found in my whole life she thought. Five dollars and it looks like it's mine because though people are walking by, nobody is coming running back saying, Did you see my five dollars please? Nobody said anything as they walked by either, and so after about five minutes she closed her fist around the five dollars and continued on her way.

It's a sign, Corky thought, it's a sign good luck is coming to me. Telling me I've got to get myself moving and do the right thing and it's going to be all right. She knew instantly and exactly what she was going to do. She had to find Dana and tell him.

She walked faster; she was three-fourths of the way around the lake. She slipped the five dollars into her purse. I won't spend it that's for sure. Not today anyway.

Bernice let herself think about Sam while she waited for Eddie. She was sitting on the bench he had described but she'd gotten there a little early. Not far away a fat man in a wheelchair was watching two young girls push each other into bushes. They were giggling hysterically. Their parents came up the hill and called out to them but the girls giggled still more and chased each other back down the hill,

All that happiness made her sad so she let herself sink into physical recall. She closed her eyes to do that – to remember the feel of Sam in bed beside her, his droopy, fat, warm nearly hairless body next to hers. Sam had filled a bed, taken possession of it. He'd made noises. He'd snored in the night, thrashed covers about, given monumental sighs and grunts whenever he turned heavily, farted. She'd hated it. It had been terrible to spend the night with him and invariably he'd kept her awake. Yet no, knowing she might never again hear such life sounds from another human being in her bed, she remembered them all with pleasure: The weight of Sam when he'd climbed on top of her – he was big, soft, heavy – she'd felt enveloped by his warm wheezing breath when he got excited, when he penetrated her – like a steam engine -She'd liked that too. The actual sex she'd always liked – the thrust pound near hurt of it had glorified her.

Now, just thinking of it for the first time in a long time, created that gnawing inside her that had seemed a voice from another self, lips within that told lewd stories, a mouth into an abyss that was her and not her. Usually Bernice didn't like listening to its muttering, its story telling, those lips never spoke of Bernice Fallsworth, office administrator, owner of fine china and drinker of good sherry. Those lips never remarked on how sensible she was, how patient, how mature. No, those lips said, do it, Bernice, now, with anyone you can get your hands on. She opened her eyes, saw once again the fat man in the wheelchair. The girls had gone and he was wheeling awkwardly but steadily over toward her.

THIRTY-SIX

Helen woke with a headache. When she moved her neck felt stiff. She sat up. How long had she been asleep? Nearby the family that had greeted her were sprawled asleep on their square of blanket, surrounded by a litter of clothes.

She turned around to check on Grandma and was shocked to see the car, all its doors sprung open, was empty. The blanket that had covered Grandma had fallen to the ground.

She jumped up, looked around. Everything looked the same; everyone still dozing, or lazy in the heat. But no sign of Grandma. Not in any direction.

"Grandma," she said loudly, "GRANDMA."

The sleeping family woke, looked curiously at her though they didn't sit up. Helen went over to the empty car and looked carefully through it, as though she might find Jessie hiding behind a seat. She knew it was stupid but it was all she could think to do. Then she backed out and again stood by the car. Feeling furious. How could Grandma keep doing this?

Maybe she's gone to the bathroom, she thought. She seized on the idea. Of course old people went to the bathroom all the time. I'd better check, she thought. Besides it gave her something to do.

Walking closer to the square bunkers she could smell them some distance away. She blanched at the thought and angled over to the neighboring friendly family. "Have you seen an old lady?"

The young woman with very pale white face and ragged brown hair raised her head. "An old lady?"

"My grandma."

"You lost an old lady." The man with the curly hair lying next to the young woman sounded like he was going to laugh; but then turned over and aimed a fat naked brown back at the world.

It isn't funny, Helen thought resentfully and started to walk away. The woman sat up and grabbed the diapers of an escaping toddler.

"Where'd she go?"

"I don't know." The conversation was getting more and more annoying. The man turned around again and smiled from a fat tanned face.

"Try the latrines."

Helen stalked away. Thanks a lot. Big help asking people.

"I hope you find her." The woman called as the baby began to scream against her. Out in the open, the sun was hot on the sensitive teenage girl's head; walking was an effort and the bathroom smell acid and strong. I hate you, Grandma, Helen thought. I hate you a lot. The grass near the latrines was sparse, struggling. The whole rotten day is Grandma's fault. Rotten Grandma. I hate you, Grandma, I hate you. It was a chant, a marching song. It took her right into the public bathrooms.

It was spooky inside. There was a faint murmuring sound, a damp cave water running sound. The latrine walls were concrete bare, the windows high slits which let in only murky underwater greenish light. All along the window ledges lay crumbled flies and spider webs with little bundles in them. The floor was concrete cold, the smell a marrying of human urine and Clorox bleach. There was dirt swept into the comers, hair in the sinks, rubbish in the bins.

"Grandma." The sensitive teenage girl's voice was a hollow sound, not quite an echo more a sound with a hole in it. The water went on running, murmuring – a damp, unfriendly noise. "Grandma are you in here?"

A shuffling noise. Somewhere in the corner. Over there where the half dozen toilets had barricaded themselves behind prim closed doors.

"Grandma is that you?"

Again the faint sounds. Helen walked the length of the stalls to the far corner of the room. She listened again, but this time heard nothing. What if Grandma was dead? She thought. Heart attack – died instantly. She could almost see the words. A lot of famous people died on the toilet. Elizabeth the Great of Russia for one. She could imagine Grandma slipped sideways in one of the stalls, one of those horrible stone dead faces. Eyes bulging. If she opened a door, would a corpse fall out?

She was determined to be careful.

Bending over the sensitive teenage girl began to peer under each door. A ripe swelling of her head aggravated what had been a slight headache. This was the most awful situation she'd ever been in and the toilets smelled even worse close up.

She stood up, went over to look into the small dim mirror in the corner.

Maddened, the beautiful young girl rushed to pound on the hospital door.

Am I going mad, tell me doctor? Sobbing frantically, she sank to her knees (rather like a lovely young sea bird, the doctor thought -he was blond and handsome) Oh please spare me madness, I'm too young, too beautiful. No, she wouldn't say that. The handsome doctor would.

She could hardly see her face in the mirror. Maybe her face was disappearing.

He was a psychiatrist. Psychiatrist is a hard word to spell. I missed it on the test. Helen went back and attacked the doors again. She bent down and peered into another. Empty.

They were all empty.

I saw her in there, she wept piteously, I know I did. Believe me, please believe me. She looked up at him (she'd crawled over in his direction) – the psychiatrist.

There, there, he said soothingly. No that sounds too kind and fatherly. No, how about he kicked her in the side of the head and said, here's your shock therapy.

Crash, the door of a stall opened just as Helen was squatting down to peer under it. She looked up to see a woman, face filled with astonishment, staring at her. She was a big bosomy woman with a coarse red face and mean little eyes. She bulged out of a white short-sleeve bodice and white pants. "You got a problem?" the woman snarled.

She looks like a wrestler, Helen thought as she stood up, wincing when the blood rushed back into her head.

She stepped back. "No." she whispered.

"Then what the hell are you doing?"

"Looking for my grandmother."

The words seemed as feeble as her voice. The woman's face tinged into fury.

"What the hell are you hanging round here for anyway?" She marched forward as Helen stepped back. "Hey – wait a minute. I seen you before." The woman's eyes narrowed further. "You were with some other kid."

Helen backed still further away, flashing a smile that came out feeble too. She realized with horror, she's the woman Norbett was talking about, the one Norbett and I peeping tommed.

We saw her doing It.

Helen turned and fled. Outside the heat of the sun was an awakening blow. She stood for a moment dazed. The sun was real. The moments in the washroom already seemed a green tinged spooky dream.

Meanwhile, Eddie was extracting himself from the arms of a loved one who insisted on gazing intently up at him from close range. Carol was more princess-pale than usual. Her pinched little mouth was turned down. Her nose had turned red. Eddie patted her head the way Grandpa Fallsworth used to pat his when he'd hurt himself.

"You know, we're not ready for ..." he couldn't bring the word out though it trembled on his lips. "We're not even through school."

"You said you weren't going to college."

"I think I might." Eddie said hastily. Suddenly college seemed intriguing, arranged already, a shining future before him, "Go for law or even music."

"A lawyer?" Carol breathed up at him, mesmerized. Her nose was subsiding.

"How long will that take? Eddie, I'll wait for you."

Across the grass swooped a bicycle full tilt, a familiar form standing up on it.

"Is that Norbett?"

"Yes," Carol said cautiously. "I told you he came with me."

"Why?" Eddie demanded fiercely. The bicycle closed in on them.

"I'm not supposed to drive. I've only got a learner's permit."

The bicycle skidded to a stop inches away from them and Norbett dismounted. All his bones protruded in key places: knees, elbows, shoulders. He could hang in a corner of the science lab as the skeleton, thought Eddie sourly.

"Let's go." Norbett said.

"Where?" Carol looked at her brother with apprehension.

"Home."

"We just got here."

"I'm bored."

"Tough." Eddie said, "Who said you should come anyway?"

Norbett ignored him. "Mom and Dad will be home in a few hours."

"I left them a note." Carol said. "I told them you were driving."

"I say we go home now. Give me the keys."

"Wait a minute." Eddie dropped Carol's hand and walked over to Norbett. He removed Norbett's glasses and put them in the pocket of Norbett's shirt.

"You're not setting foot in that car, kid. Forget it."

Norbett shifted sideways and out of Eddie's range.

He looked at his sister. "Want me to talk?"

"About what?" Eddie demanded.

"About certain things I know. Stuff Mom and Dad would like to know about."

"For example?" Eddie took hold of Carol's hand.

"Norbett you weren't..." Carol's voice squeaked, "You weren't prowling around last night?"

"I wasn't sleeping. I never sleep. Give me the keys. I will also tell the parents that you were driving their car around with a learner's permit."

Carol let go of Eddie's hand, walked over to her brother and held out the car keys. Then went back to Eddie and touched his arm. "I'm so sorry, Eddie."

Norbett had acquired a calm almost majestic look. He crossed his thin arms in front of his thin chest. "I want to go home right now, Carol."

Eddie went over to him, grabbed his arm and twisted it behind his back until Norbert bent over with a squeal of pain.

"Give me those keys, Norbett."

"No. I need to go home."

"Later Norbett. After the fireworks."

"No. Now."

Norbert squealed again. Carol hopped up and down with alarm.

"Eddie what are you doing to him?" Her nose was a bright red. "Eddie I don't think you should do that ... if he tells my parents ..."

"He is not going to tell anybody anything, are you, Norbert?" Eddie twisted Norbert's arm just that much more so that he fell on his knees. "Because he doesn't know anything, do you, Norbett? Now the keys."

"In my pocket." Norbett's face was full of pain.

Carol went on hopping up and down. "Stop it, Eddie. I'll get in trouble."

"Get the keys, Carol," ordered Eddie.

Carol fluttered over and reached into her brother's pockets; she averted her eyes from the look of reproach he shot at her as she extracted the keys.

"I guess I do want to see the fireworks," she said as she gave them to Eddie.

"I know that. See you later." Abandoning Norbett's abject body, Eddie waved airily at Carol and walked away. "I'll come back for you when the fireworks start. At the car. I'll drive you home later if you want me to."

He strolled away, moving athletically, adrenaline pumping pleasurably through his body. He heard Norbett muttering behind him.

"I'll fix you guys."

Eddie turned around, "Have you any idea what will happen to you if you try?"

He refused Carol and Norbert a second look. As he passed the tennis courts, several girls smiled and one good-looking one waved. He waved back. He was looking forward to tackling Aunt Bernice next. She'll be waiting for me, he thought. He followed the road as it wound down to the main portion of the park. It was a longer walk than he'd expected. His eye was caught by sun dazzle off a Ford like Grandpa's, but one painted a gleaming metallic silver. The day's too hot for that paint job, he thought. If I drive Grandpa's car to Texas I'll sandblast it and paint it charcoal.

In his pocket he could feel the car keys.

"Do you have a dog?" A boy of about ten materialized from nowhere and began to walk beside him.

"No."

"Why not?" "Do I look like I should have a dog?"

"We have two." The boy was stocky with black hair and slanted, half-closed eyes.

His teeth were white and sharp looking. He was wearing blue jeans with no shirt and his bare chest was covered with sticky goop.

"Great."

"We've got a collie and a spaniel."

"Spaniels are dumb."

"No, they're not." The boy's nasal voice rose in protest.

"I read they have the lowest I.Q. of all dogs."

"What's an IQ?"

"If you have to ask, you've got a low one."

"I don't like you."

"Where I come from we eat dogs."

"No you don't."

"Cook 'em. First we cut them up though."

The boy's mouth fell opened, his half narrow eyes narrowed further, he slowed his walk, "You're kidding me."

"Dog meat is very nutritious."

"You wouldn't eat a collie. They're big."

"I've eaten, personally eaten, a St. Bernard."

"No way." The boy paused by the road while Eddie marched on. They conducted further conversation from an increasing distance. "No way, no way."

"Cooked him over an open fire. I'll invite you and your dogs next time."

"MOM!" The kid ran the other way, toward a group of adults stretched out on blankets under some trees. They looked up as the boy screamed toward them. "MOM!"

THIRTY-SEVEN

Jessie could hear the merry go-round and walked toward its sound. Sometimes she walked on paths, sometimes she didn't. She was so purposeful in her movements, none of the people she passed really noticed her. She was back to talking to her husband Amsden. He might be dead but not to Jessie.

You were the most intellectually cheating man I ever met, Amsden; you were always bragging how faithful you were, but you were usually somewhere else talking to some other woman. Only in Florida did we have good conversations, about death and God and friendship. Otherwise even in Florida you were chatting up some other female. Or fixing her plumbing.

What's it like up there? Are there some good conversations going on? You just save up some talk for me.

Used to drive me crazy the way you sat around like a slug doing nothing, yapping to strangers, and then bam smash crash you were up and doing something like crazy till it was done. Even when you brought in my cup of coffee in the morning. I never knew whether you'd be breathing like a race horse with impatience to get out there and conquer whatever mountain you planned to tackle that day, or whether you'd lie down on the bed beside me, and say in a feeble voice, I ought to do this or that. Those days I knew you wouldn't do nothing.

People thought you were steady as a rock, silent and sure, but I knew you were wandering around inside good old Amsden's body and mind like a Wizard of Oz, figuring out which lever of you to pull. That used to bother me a lot, but now I miss it.

Miss you.

Amsden you were interesting. You were never dull.

When are we going to get together? Seems like I ought to die. I'm old enough. What's keeping me here? I'm losing interest. Not cause the world isn't interesting, it's always been interesting, but because – well I guess I don't know why I'm losing interest, Or why I'm talking to you more and more.

What's happened? Are my roots so shallow I can't go on without you? Coming to this park makes me think of you even more. You proposed to me here on the merry-go-round. Of all the silly places—I was riding a merry-go-round horse and you were standing beside me holding the reins.

There I see it now – the merry-go-round. I intend to ride it this very day. I wouldn't mind dying on that merry-go-round. Think you can arrange it?

THIRTY-EIGHT

Helen had read a book that explained how to visualize people's faces so they got a mental message that you wanted them to come to you. You had to calm yourself down though, she remembered that from the book and that wasn't easy, sitting hot and irritated in the front seat of the Ford. She closed her eyes and tried to visualize Grandma's face but her face wasn't the kind that sprang easily to mind. She could recall the eccentric, crook of her eyebrows and the fact that Grandma had no eyelashes, but otherwise she wasn't doing too well. Still she went on trying, Grandma, Grandma. Come in Grandma. Come back to the car. Come to me, I am in the car. Come to me. Come, Come to me.

It was hot work. Especially since, in actual fact, Grandma was the last person in the world the sensitive teenage girl actually wanted to see. I'm just doing it for Mother, she muttered and opened her eyes, then leaned back against the driver's seat and pretended she was driving away somewhere.

A woman strolled by the car, hands in pockets like a boy. She was wearing white shorts and a green strapless halter. Her hair was a shining black cap, cut close with bangs. She carried a black clutch purse against her side.

She stopped beside the car and leaned inward. Helen could smell her perfume – exotic Dragon Lady type perfume. "You looking for an old lady?"

Helen sat up. "Yes."

"It kind of worried me."

The woman had a hard closed face like a doll, with cheeks that were curved and shiny; her eyebrows were thin and perfect. Her whole face was very still. Her skin was dead white.

Helen moved over to the open door and got out. She was a foot taller than the woman. "Where is she?"

"I knew something was wrong. See somebody like that – old like that – you know something's wrong." The woman's voice was soft but oddly rough edged and flat. "She got any money in that purse of hers?"

"She had a purse?" Helen drew back. Grandma must have taken it from the car, she thought.

"Trotting along like she was going shopping. Is there money in it?"

"I don't know."

"Place like this. It isn't safe." Eyes motionless, eyelids curved, the woman stood paused beside Helen. "Know what I mean?" The doll's unwavering blank stare. "This crummy park's full of creeps, know what I mean?"

The sensitive teenage girl sat back down on the car seat. She thought of the pervert man in the wheelchair. And the woman in the latrines. The woman made an awkward gesture with her left hand. "Hey come on." Her voice, which had been flat and emotionless, tightened, "I'll help you find her."

"Where'd you see her?" Helen stood up again.

"Down by the carny rides. I seen her sitting by herself."

The doll woman strolled away. Helen hesitated, then followed.

The woman's shoes were the harsh color of Mrs. Flatelle's – an aching green. What would they look like in a shoe x-ray machine? Where you saw what was really inside you?

Abruptly the woman stopped.

"You ought to lock that car." She motioned back at the Ford and the girl saw the door was wide open, the blanket still lying on the ground beside it. Flushing she went back and crawled inside to shut the windows, then slam locked the doors. How could she be so stupid? She walked back to her new acquaintance, relieved somebody was there to help her.

"How old is she anyway?" The woman was chewing gum.

"Grandma? I think ..."

"You think?" Her companion stopped in the path, made a face

exaggerated with surprise. "You mean you don't know?" Helen flushed again. "She won't tell her age. Sometimes she lies."

"I figure eighty-six."

"That's what Mom says." They walked past the family on the blanket, both parents were feeding their children with small triangles of sandwiches and homemade cookies. The mother smiled.

"Good luck," she called out.

"You know them?" Helen's companion asked.

"No."

"Nosy parkers huh?"

The woman's glance was intense; her eyes never wavered from Helen's face when she spoke. "You surprised, me knowing about her?"

Helen nodded.

"I seen your whole family before, that's how I knew you. Seen you all together before."

The sensitive teenage girl couldn't think of anything to say. Vaguely apprehensive, she walked slightly behind this stranger who'd taken such complete control of the situation.

"Real nice folks I kept thinking. On an old fashioned family picnic. Real sweet, I thought. Your mother's the one with the flowered dress on."

Helen nodded.

"That your real Dad?"

Helen hesitated. Why was she asking all these questions? She nodded again, reluctantly. "I knew it. Not like some of those bastards. That your Dad's sister?" Helen shook her head. The woman sighed with pleasure. "I thought so. Your mom's sister right? -They got the same butts."

Shocked, Helen edged away from her companion. But inside, some area of her brain calmly agreed. She's right, I noticed that too.

They joined the path circling down toward the lake. Helen slowed. They'd turned in the direction of The Pervert in the Wheelchair. Was he still there beside the path?

"The older kid's your brother."

"Yes."

"Cute."

The exotic scent was heavy, moving with the woman like an extension of her. "You got a boyfriend?" It was a question ominously close to the one asked early that afternoon. And they were approaching the fateful curve in the path downward. Helen's heart started beating hard.

"So you don't like the boys?" The woman looked sideways at her.

Helen stopped in the middle of the path.

"Really, you don't have to go with me. I can find her."

The woman stopped too. She didn't seem surprised. They looked at each other, people walked around them.

"Don't blame you." The woman's face didn't change, her voice remained dead. Several passerby glanced curiously at them. "You about fourteen?"

Helen nodded, almost against her will. Why didn't the woman just go away?

"Your age, I knew a lot of guys." The raspy flat voice darkened. "And you know something? Every goddamned one of them turned out to be a bastard."

The flow of people went on around them; they were two bleak stones fallen into a mountain stream. Then Helen developed a rush of courage. She turned and started walking away, back in the direction they'd come.

"Hey," said the woman.

"I don't want to go that way." She looked back to see the woman staring out at the small island in the middle of the lake -Duck Island.

"When I think of the creeps I've put up with – two guys especially."

Her voice was loud. Two men walking briskly along heard her, and moved in a wide arc to avoid her. "They usually think they're something, but you know something, kid?" She was following Helen, but at a distance. "They aren't." She laughed a sharp mocking sound. "You can bet your sweet ass they aren't."

Embarrassed, Helen sped up. She wanted to get away from this woman, but somehow she couldn't. In a moment, the woman was beside her, she touched the girl's arm, a light butterfly touch.

"What's the matter, kid? Did I say something wrong?"

Helen kept walking. This is a shorter route to the amusement area anyway, she thought. Why was she going that other way? She walked faster and faster but the woman kept alongside her.

"You worried about your Grandma?"

"Kind of."

"We'll find her."

"And I had something bad happen to me going that other way." The sensitive teenage girl hoped the doll woman would ask why, would swell with indignation, would maybe give her some advice, but her acquaintance only shrugged her shoulders.

"O.k. by me, whatever way we go."

They walked along a grassy slope some distance from the Pervert Path, and came upon flowerbeds of mixed red and purple blossoms, remnants of yellow tulips, and stunning orange poppies. Bees rose and fell into flowers with reckless abandon.

The hot sun was a late afternoon rebuke. Fewer people walked around. Instead they lay sprawled out, confiding their bodies to the sun, or were clustered under shade trees asleep. Some ate late picnics on tablecloths laid out on the grass. Children still ran around screaming with delight, but more slept on blankets, thumbs in mouths. And in the distance, the slam and roar of the roller coaster could be heard whenever the persistent loud tubular melody of the merry-go-round fell silent.

They were some distance away when they passed the three lawn chairs of the Miller family. Mr. Miller was asleep. He didn't wake when Mrs. Miller grew restless, when she slowly stood up, nearly falling over as she did so.

"What's the matter, Mother?" her daughter Karin put down her book and rose to go over and hold her steady. "You need to go to the bathroom, don't you?" She looked down at her father and didn't have the heart to wake him, so the two women began to slowly walk toward the public bathrooms. Mrs. Miller lurched dangerously whenever the ground was rough. Nearby, sitting on a blanket, with a little girl reading comics and a little white dog grooming its private parts, two woman watched Mrs. Miller and her daughter limp by. Myrna Henderson got up. She came over to Karin. "Do you need help again? I'm a nurse. I know how difficult walking is for the elderly." Karin smiled with relief. "You're very kind. I wish you lived in our neighborhood."

Meanwhile, Mr. Miller was enjoying a wonderful dream. In it he was listing his wishes to someone important. – I love birds and sunshine, green leaves and calm. I need a long view and someone to love. And I don't want any more worries.

Bernice sat looking down on the lake. No sign of Eddie. She looked at her watch. Fifteen minutes late. She opened up her handbag, took out the flask of sherry and poured some into a cup she'd jammed into the handbag too. She looked around. Nobody was looking.

Bernice took hurried delicious sips of sherry and tried not to think. To keep her mind blank. She didn't want to get angry. At Sam. At Eddie. Only where the heck were they? Why was she sitting here waiting for them? She took a couple more sips.

Why am I waiting for Eddie when Sam might be waiting for me? This idea of canoeing was Eddie's idea. And there were four or five tables I didn't check. Sam could be waiting at one, arms folded, getting angrier and angrier, swearing he'd never see me again. She struggled with this thought. I don't want to see him anyway. It wasn't a good idea. Something bad could happen.

Looking over she saw the fat man in the wheelchair moving closer again. He wanted to park himself right next to her bench.

Good god. Did he want to start a conversation? He didn't look very intelligent.

It was mirrors and brilliant flashing gold, pale painted scenes and patterns of fantastic motion, fancy curlicues and swirls of heated air. The merry-go-round horses all galloped wildly, hair swept into riotous curls. Even the seats were ornate: boats pulled by haughty swans and gilded coaches drawn by elegant rats. But most of all it was the sound -the blaring hollow certitude of In the Good Old Summertime – and the smell – a carny wallop of popcorn, coffee and slightly rancid butter that sketched out this place. Drew walls and ceiling, breathed reality into a shoddy collection of old fashioned rides.

"She was sitting right there." The woman waved a helpless hand at an old green bench. They were standing in the center of the small amusement park watching the merry-go-round twirl past. The green bench was empty and Helen looked toward the merry-go -round again. She felt weighed down by its persistent cheerful throaty sound.

"Sitting right here, I swear it." the woman repeated.

The merry-go-round was half full. Small children were scattered here and there and held tight to the gold bars that speared the horses, horses with haunted eyes and lips drawn back. The children mostly had that look Helen remembered from her own childhood. It wasn't what you expected, not gay nor lighthearted, never quite fun. Three adults perched on stationary horses smiled and pretended to bounce up and down like children but they looked wrong, were too big and graceless. In the center, a young man stood by a lever; he was smoking with an air of boredom, face blank. I wonder what he sees looking through a merry-go-round, Helen thought, Everything must be blurred.

Then Helen saw Grandma, caught sight of that small stubborn expressionless face, the white alert church hat. Jessie was pressed deep into the corner of a swan boat.

"I see her." Helen cried.

"Where?"

"On the merry-go-round." She pointed, waved, but Jessie didn't look out.

The merry-g-round went around. Jessie stared straight ahead. Legs, arms pulled in tight, she was barely visible.

Helen watched Jessie go around again. Then young man, stilled bored, pulled the lever, and the merry-go-round slowed, the music weakened, the horses dwindled. Embarrassed adults jumped down from their steeds, children searched the crowd for familiar faces.

Grandma went by again more slowly. Helen went to stand close to the edge; she wanted to hurry Grandma off.

Slower, slower, the throaty sound deepened, wobbled, then the merry-go-round lurched a little and stopped. From underneath came a huff of warm yeasty air. Helen heard all around her people who called out to family and friends, children talking in high excited voices, the spit and crackle sounds of other carny rides.

You told me to get on and I have. But there's no one to meet me, not you, not anyone. You laughed at magic, Amsden, made fun of me and called me fanciful. But it seems to me that great Pappy in the Sky made a lot of fanciful things, including merry-go-rounds and those cars after the war you were so crazy about. Well, why I ask you, why'd he do that? Maybe He wants a little magic: in our lives too.

You liked the merry-go round. You proposed to me on it, your face so pale. In one of these swan boats; we sat holding hands; I was six months pregnant. You said...you said ...oh I remember all right ...you said you weren't worthy of me.

Mike convinced Greta to go for a walk. At first she walked with her arms folded in front of her. She took short steps and soon felt breathless, but Mike held on to her elbow. They walked beside the road.

"Want to go get a hot dog?" Mike asked.

Quite suddenly, Greta burst into tears. She shook her head. "I got to sit down."

"No you don't. What's the matter, sweetheart?"

"You're so damn nice to me, Mike. You make me think of my brother Jimmy."

He was awful kind to me. Never said a bad word. Why'd he have to die, Mike?" Mike didn't know what to say. Instead he squeezed her hand.

"Come on. We'll get a hot dog. Maybe they got coffee down there, too."

THIRTY-NINE

B ernice stood up. Abruptly. She raised one arm. Turning, she said something to the man beside her and then, with great energy, shoved the wheelchair over on its side. The cripple's hands flailed up in the air. He squealed with surprise. Bernice stuck out one big foot in a white pump, and shoved the chair so hard, it started to slide down the hill.

The mouths of two passerby fell open. On the nearby path the man and a woman stood stunned. Holy Jesus, she's knocked a cripple over.

Bernice stood looking down at the man. She was saying something – not very loudly but her face was angry. She kicked at the chair again, and the pervert gave an indignant shout. He was lying on his side, sprawled, legs kicking a little, hands flailing.

He looks like a beetle on his back, thought Gerda Blunt, the woman in the pair watching all this. Gerda looked around. There was nobody else around. She turned to her friend, Mike. "Should we do something, Mike?"

The man was letting out funny sounds.

"I don't think so," Mike said. He figured the guy had done something out of the ordinary to warrant an attack like that and besides he didn't want to go to the police for anything. "Let's keep walking."

The man in the wheelchair noticed them and shouted Help Help at them. Bernice turned and saw them too. She scowled and they moved away, out of sight.

Bernice saw a boy of about ten years, mouth open, standing under some spruce trees. She scowled again until he waved feebly and vanished down the hill. The man was still kicking with his feet, back and forth, back and forth. One wheelchair wheel was spinning. The man gave funny little squeaks. Swear words mostly.

"You bitch! Put me right. You bitch! Put me right." Bernice gave the tangled mess of wheelchair and cripple another shove and it slid further down hill on the damp grass. The man kicked a little more with his feet, back and forth back and forth, and then he attempted to rise out of the mess. Bernice watched him get to his feet.

He was very fat but he could walk and he could swing his arms okay. He pushed himself toward Bernice. She watched him advance. He stopped. She was a big woman.

"You bitch." His voice went up an octave "BITCH!"

"Bastard." Her voice was way down low and she took a step forward.

At that moment four people ran up the hill toward them.

"I don't put up with that kind of nonsense," Bernice said fiercely and moved away at high speed. She heard the man's squeals of rage as she reached the top of the hill.

"You bitch! Put me right."

I'll pick up Helen and take her down to meet Aunt Bernice, Eddie thought, as in leisurely fashion he strolled back to the family picnic table. He came up behind three women walking in majestic fashion in the same direction. The central figure was a large elderly woman who limped slowly on swollen legs, each of her arms held by a slighter younger companion. As he passed them Eddie saw the elderly woman was Mrs. Miller from next door. One of the younger women had short cropped hair and a tense expression, the other wore her long hair in a single braid.

"Hi Mrs. Miller," Eddie called out as he passed them, but the old woman only looked blankly at him. "Need any help?" he asked the young women.

"Don't think so," said the short-haired one. "Thanks for asking" added the one with the braid and the sweet smile.

That made Eddie feel good for a few minutes but several yards further he came upon a more alarming tableau. Molly Asford was lying spread out on the grass with the twins Edith and Emily sitting like angels at her head, one on each side. The twins bobbed up when they saw him.

"Oh Eddie, we need help -the roller coaster – we were afraid but look what it did to Molly." Molly let out a groan. Eddie went over and knelt beside her. She opened her mouth. Her front teeth were now two jagged stumps.

"I hith ma mouh on the bah," Molly said, "Is thethre blood?" She opened her mouth wider. Eddie leaned closer.

"What happened?" he asked in a horrified voice.

"I juth tol you." Molly said crossly, "Is thethre blood?"

"No, but half your front teeth are gone."

Edith and Emily began wringing their hands, and making little noises of despair. Meanwhile Molly let her head fall to one side. Her eyes closed.

"Oh God," thought Eddie. He sat back on his heels, saw several passerby glaring at him. He leaned forward again, and picked up Molly's hand. He patted it. Molly opened her eyes and looked at him.

"We can't find rna parenths," she said and started to cry. "What will Motha sah?"

"I think you should go to the first aid station." Eddie said.

"Where ith it? I'm tiared ofwahking," she: said in a feeble voice. "I don't think I can wahk anymothre."

Eddie thought fast. Carol's car keys were in his pocket. So was his secret stash pair to the family car. At that moment it seemed safer to use Carol's car. Beside it was closer. "I'll drive you, Molly. Wait here for me."

He stood up. Edith and Emily walked on their knees over to him.

"Oh Eddie, we're so glad you found us."

Helen jumped on the platform; it wobbled underfoot as she treaded through the sleekly painted horses; she could smell their varnish. Grandma's swan boat was stopped on the opposite side and she had the feeling Jessie might be gone when she got there.

She wasn't. Jessie was still staring straight ahead, arms, legs tight together, humped back pressed against the gold paint of the swan boat. She looked up when Helen grabbed her by the arm.

"Who's that?"

"Where have you been?" With the rush of relief came familiar irritation too. Tinged with apprehension – Grandma never did things the way she was supposed to.

Jessie put her hands together. She knew this girl. This girl was an irritation, a know-it-all that knew nothing.

"Leave me be. I've got things to do."

"Like what?"

"I don't have to answer to you."

"To Mother you do."

Jessie's neutral eyes clouded. She stirred, touched her faithful handbag, then crossed one bony knee over the other. Helen saw her soft slippers were filthy on the bottom. "I don't know what I've been doing except riding this merry-go-round." Firmness replaced doubt in her voice. "I'm having a good time."

"Well I'm having a rotten one," Helen said hotly. "I've been chasing you all over the place. Who said you could go off like that?"

Jessie's thin lips pulled inward, her face tightened. She struggled to stand up.

"And who are you to talk to me that way?" She managed to get to her feet, but then rocked unsteadily and grabbed Helen's arm for balance.

"I mean it, Grandma. You were supposed to stay in the car."

Jessie drew in her breath. "My feet are asleep."

They began to walk toward the nearest edge.

"Hey -she hasn't paid."

The young man who'd pulled the lever was coming toward them, weaving through the horses – a solid shape against the flow of dashing curls and galloping hooves.

As he came closer Helen saw he was one of the two boys she'd encountered in front of the First Aid. Station -the taller one. He came up close and she could smell tobacco, saw one hand held against his jeans sported a cigarette. His hair was curly.

"You planning on paying for her?"

Helen leaned against a black horse with red saddle and reins and mean eyes. She didn't have any money. Jessie meanwhile kept moving. Letting go of her granddaughter's hand, she staggered over to the edge of the merry-go-round.

"Kind of dizzy, "she warned. Helen straightened, came over to grab hold of her. "You got any money, Grandma?"

"Money?" Jessie's teeth clicked with the awfulness of the thought. She stiffened, and held tight to her black handbag. "There's not a cent in this purse."

The young man came up to them and stopped. Took a puff of his cigarette. "You're supposed to pay for the ride."

Ignoring him, Jessie and Helen stepped down off the merry-go-round platform, Jessie grunting with effort and holding on to Helen's arm. The young man came to the edge and glared down at them.

"Hey. You two. You hear me? I said you got to pay. That old lady must have had three or four rides." Jessie started walking toward the green bench where the black-haired doll woman sat watching them.

The young man jumped down. "Hey you hear me you old bag?" His voice was truculent. He threw his cigarette down and ground it out with dusty black half boots.

Helen turned around. "She doesn't have any money. Neither do I."

"Tough titty. You can't ride without paying. I could call the cops."

Jessie kept moving. She lurched as though she could fall over any moment. Behind her, Helen saw people were already lined up for the next ride, people impatient to pay, to choose their horse.

"I'll get some money," she said. "Can you wait half an hour?"

"Fat chance." The young man growled, but his face changed. He looked friendlier. He climbed back up on the platform. She followed him, stood next to him. "I promise. I'll get some money from my dad. Just give me a chance."

"You put her up to it or something?"

He was close; she could smell shaving soap. Or was it men's cologne? Was it her imagination or was he smiling slightly?

"I'm sorry for the trouble." Her voice came out meek; she surprised herself with the tone of it. Do I mean this? she thought. His tobacco smells like Daddy's.

"O.k. Come back later. I'll wait for you." His voice deepened and she saw he really was smiling. "Hey, it's o.k. I won't tell anybody. And don't tell your dad you're coming back. Now get off. I've got to crank her up."

An unfamiliar emotion went through her then, a feeling like the last moment at the top of a roller coaster, the one just before you thought -Why am I here?

The young man with the curly hair laid one hand on the saddle of a painted horse, the part where the paint was new and glossy. He stroked it, a smooth sweep of his hand across the horse's ass, then strolled away. She watched him weave his way toward the center, toward the lever that he would pull to begin a ride. She jumped down then, feeling flushed and exhilarated but nearly fell when she landed.

Jessie was sitting on the green park bench. The black-haired woman leaned over to say something to her, but Jessie clutched her purse to her chest, and closed her eyes. It took only a moment for her to drift away, searching out Amsden in order to continue their conversation.

Did you really forgive me for losing my diamond. Amsden? I didn't mean to. The diamond you gave me on the merry-go-round. I lost it the day I came out here with Billy Black. I told you about that day, how he came visiting but I didn't tell you everything that happened. And I pretended I lost the diamond in the house. Remember how we looked all over for it? How I cried? Well I lied Amsden. I lost that diamond here in Minnewana Park – probably out on the island. Yes Billy Black and the baby and I went out to Duck Island that day.

Are you listening? I need you to know all this before I make any moves to get up there. Before I meet you in heaven. And by the way what goes on after death? Whistling in the dark is what we're doing down here -nobody seems to know a thing no matter what the preachers say.

The back ground to Jessie's dream conversations was a lovely vague one, with lots of clouds and waterfalls and distant views. Unfortunately, just then Violet walked into it. She strolled up and took her hand, "Hi Mama. It's me again."

Oh land, thought Jessie. She struggled to wake up. Violet's going to try to talk me into dying again.

FORTY

"Well Mother."

"Well Violet."

"Having a good time?"

"Yes."

"Looking forward to the evening?"

Jessie felt the woman sitting beside her on the bench shift but she didn't open her eyes. Violet was too close to her, too real in the dream.

"Yes. Are you here for the fireworks, Violet?"

"I haven't been in this ratty old park for years."

"Where they found you."

"Don't start that Mother please."

Into the dream came a memory of the night the word had come: Violet dead. Lily Bernice herself had been over to tell them, warning them there'd been nothing anybody could do. Lily's face had been white as paper. Sam her boss had come with her.

"I wanted to look in on you, Mother. You could go out tonight. I could help you. I'd like to help you, Mother."

"That's kind of you, Violet. But I'm fine. I'm going to Denver in a few days. Or so I hear." Jessie was waking up fast.

"I thought you were ready to leave."

"No, not yet."

"Why not?"

"I'm waiting for your father."

"He's busy."

"Doing what?"

"Working out knots with other people."

"I knew it. Just like Florida."

"I'm only here one day. If you go with me, it's got to be tonight."

"I want to see some mountains, Violet."

"Are you so sure the family wants to take you to Denver?"

"I don't care if they do or they don't. I intend to go." And saying that Jessie felt her determination spiking up, filling her mind and heart with purpose. "Didn't see many mountains in my life. Seems a shame to waste the opportunity." Then she: heard Helen calling her and clacked her teeth with annoyance.

"That girl's following me around."

"Rose Corinne's daughter."

"She's a fool."

"Like me?"

"There was nobody such a fool as you, Violet. Now let me be. I've got things to talk to your father about."

Violet didn't leave, so Jessie opened her eyes.

Walking beside the road, Dana reached into his pocket and touched the slip of paper Tom Shannon had given him. He had a job if he wanted it. And what harm would it do to let Tom use the car? If we get home early enough, I can give it to him tonight. Take the bus over to St. Paul in the morning. Dana began walking to the mantra of money. I need money. Money. I. Need. It. Need it for Dad – to see the thing through. Money. I. Need. Money.

Walking faster he thought, it's been this way all my life. At the worst times, I don't have enough money. I can't do what I know I need to do. He hadn't been able to help his mother, or his sister, or even give them much at the end. It was a bitterness that wouldn't leave him.

Dana reached the beautiful blue Ford, then the empty picnic table. No one was there. Everybody gone but where?

He went over to the car. Empty. Tried the doors. All locked. Reached in his pocket. No keys. Then he remembered. He'd put them in the glove compartment.

Damn it. What the heck is going on? Dana thought and sat down at the table.

Nothing to drink. Not even water. The sun was filtered through the trees now. He put his head down on the table and tried to sleep. Somebody will come back, surely to god somebody else has those keys.

Every window in Maddie's house had venetian blinds. He knew he'd remember that – how Maddie lived her whole life behind blinds, blinds that were either pulled down tight against the world or yielded into narrow reluctant bands. That had been a great temptation for him -to withdraw behind slits of yielding with her. To believe the world was just that neat – with slices of sun on polished hardwood floors, cool blank spaces, silence like water, and a scented willing woman in his arms.

How could that be a future that would work? Seen from outside venetian blinds spoke of emptiness. Beyond them the world waited, impatient and full of other people. Yet when he called her that morning to tell her goodbye, her dark hello still penetrated his bones.

"I've thought about it, Maddie."

She'd breathed. Said nothing.

"I'm not coming back. I'm sorry." He'd hung up before she could reply.

Lilly Bernice emerged from the ladies restroom and walked over to the picnic table. Dana lifted his head, blinked, recognized her. He was hot and tired and he didn't like the way she leaned over him.

"Did you see Eddie?" she asked in a cross voice.

"No."

"Where is he?"

"I don't know."

"I don't mind waiting for him, Dana," Bernice sat down beside him and tried out her sweet reasonable voice, "I just wondered where he was."

"Have no idea. I thought you and Corky were walking around together."

"We did."

"Where is she?"

"I haven't a clue. Dana, do you mind if I get something out of the car?"

"It's locked."

"Where are the keys?"

"I wish I knew." Dana put his head down on the table again. He ignored Lily Bernice taking out a pack of cigarettes, removing a cigarette, lighting it, and then blowing out smoke. I'll say no if she asks if I want one, he vowed, but Bernice didn't ask, just sat puffing smoke.

A moment later, Corky came up and sat down between them. When Dana lifted his head she smiled at him.

"I was at the ball park," she said. "Sitting in the bleachers waiting for you to come back. Your cousin Tom thought you were coming back. My he's a difficult man." She looked around. "Where are the kids?"

"Lord knows," Bernice said. She kept her cigarette clenched between her teeth. "I looked all over for Eddie. I thought we were going canoeing. And Rose, I need to get my sun hat out of the car. I think I've had too much sun."

Looking around, Corky noticed for the first time the car doors were shut. "It's too hot for Mother to be shut up like that."

Dana stood up. "Do you have the car keys?"

"Why no. I thought you had them. Where's Mother?"

"Did you bring yours?"

"No. Don't tell me Helen's gone off with Mother and taken the keys?"

"I hope so. If she hasn't we're going to have to break into the car."

"I had some aspirin in the car too," Bernice said, and ground out her cigarette into the grass. Her sister didn't appear to notice.

Something about Corky was different. Both Dana and Bernice, hot and tired as they were, noticed that she seemed buoyant, light hearted. Instead of fussing with them about the keys and the car and the kids, she dredged out of her pocket two bedraggled aspirin for Bernice's headache, and then suggested that she and Dana go look for Helen and Jessie, while Bernice waited by the car. And when they walked away together, she took hold of Dana's hand.

She'd sat in the bleachers and thought more about James. For a moment she couldn't remember his last name. She'd made love to the man and she couldn't remember his last name. Then, James Newell – it sprang out as though gold embossed.

He'd had wallets and a brief case embossed with his name. She'd been impressed with that. Silly school girl. They'd done all the hokey things she'd dreamed about: The Statue of Liberty, the Empire State building. They'd even taken the Staten Island ferry. All on that first time together. Then when they were sitting eating hot dogs and joking in the heat as the Dodgers lost to the Yankees, he'd asked her. The stands had been huge, the crowd immense so that the first time he'd broached the subject of what might come next, the moment had passed easily. She'd diverted him with the game. But he'd persisted. Had suggested a second, third, fourth time, that she should marry him. But she knew what he really wanted was simpler and more basic than that.

But I love Dana her mind had wailed that evening as she'd climbed into the hotel bed with James. It had been a confusing time.

On the last day though, she knew it was the last day. He had too. He'd taken out a gun. A small neat handgun. Black. He'd slid it on the bed between them.

"This is a friend." he said.

"No it's not." She'd never seen a handgun before. "A gun's not a friend."

"My best friend," he said firmly. "Next to you of course."

"I am your friend, James, I want you to believe that."

They'd just come in from dinner. Were sitting in the darkened hotel room, looking out the window at a withdrawing sky. Too late for a movie, too early for bed.

"But this is a good friend too. Go on, pick it up."

But she'd refused staring down at it: Black shape against white counterpane.

"We have conversations, my friend and I. Sometimes I say, well shall I do it today? And sometimes my friend says, o.k. with me, and sometimes it says, no not today."

"Have you ever used it?" she said horrified And frightened too. What was he talking about? Was he angry at her? Enough to do something?

"Never." He said and picked up the gun and returned it to his suitcase on the floor. "Never. But I like asking it."

He came over and sat down on the bed beside her; he smelled of good food and scotch whiskey.

"I'm a colored," he said abruptly. "I thought you ought to know."

She was dumbfounded. Why was he telling her that now?

"I've been passing for years. Three quarters black. You should see my family. I'll go on passing. I've got the job I want. I wanted this – to be somebody educated. And to be unnoticed." He'd looked at her, unsmiling. The room was almost dark. "Would that have mattered?"

Rose Corinne thought hard. She'd leaned back against the

headboard of the bed. Maybe it would have. But in odd ways. She didn't like suffering. Or being conspicuous. She wouldn't have liked the hassle of secrets. But with James, with him, she couldn't say it would have made any difference between them.

"No. Probably not. But I'm marrying somebody else."

"And that's not going to change?"

"No. I've been engaged for a year. I do love him. But I can love more than one man. Is that wrong of me?"

He'd sighed and stood up, went to look out the window. And the moment yawned open, became a huge space, an emptiness like time cracking into event, freezing solid into eternity. She couldn't even cry. It wasn't that kind of moment. But afterwards she remembered it all.

Sitting in the stands waiting for Dana, she wondered about James death. Had he taken out his friend? Had he asked it yes or no? The paper hadn't said. The lawyer wouldn't. But loneliness, despair – they did things to people. And she thought about Dana. About his father dying and Dana's mixed feelings and the fact that his money that he'd worked so hard for was melting so that they couldn't go as a family to Denver and yet – that was what he really wanted. James's money can make it happen, she thought then, but I'll have to tell him everything. So I'll do it my way.

Sitting on the green bench, Jessie's eyes were closed again, because she was still chasing down Amsden. Where are you? Why don't you talk to me? Tell me what you're doing? It was down in Florida I began to wonder about you, Amsden, about all those missing bits and pieces of your life. You had your secrets all right. You came to Deep River when you were full-grown and none of us ever learned much about you.

Then that blasted Violet showed up again. "I thought we could do a trade, Mother. I'll help you and you help me."

"What will help me Violet? I don't think you know me at all, not after all these years."

"Heaven's quite a bit like Iowa, Mother -a lot of green – Isn't any green prettier than Heaven."

"Oh hush up. You always were crossways about things, Violet, even when you were a little girl flouncing around like the Queen of the May. I don't think I even want to know how I can help you."

"You aren't the least bit curious? When I came all the way here to find you?"

"Violet we're pulling you out. You're way way over the top. You're directly interfering," the appalled TWKMTY crew were close by, but Violet wasn't listening to them anymore. She was too busy stirring things up in a world she did understand.

Standing near the merry-go-round, Helen saw Jessie was asleep next to the black haired woman, while all around them was a welter of litter, a sea of smashed popcorn boxes and cigarette packets lay everywhere. There were only a few people on the rides, at the concession stands, the crews were cleaning up. The carney was closing down for the night. In front of her two irritable ducks waddled about underfoot, sorting out popcorn from cardboard.

Ducks must have hardened digestive systems, she thought, and swerved to avoid them on her way over to Jessie. "Grandma" she called out, but Jessie didn't stir. The black haired woman looked up as she approached.

"Gee she's a sweet old lady, your grandma." She didn't smile. had one leg crossed over the other, foot swinging nervously.

Helen touched Jessie's arm, "Come on, Grandma. I've got to find some money to pay for your rides."

The woman turned to Jessie, "I watch her for you. I'm good with old ladies."

Jessie stood up. Her face was white. The black haired woman rose, too.

"She was talking about money being stolen from her purse."

"She gets kind of confused."

"I wouldn't put it past some people. I'd check her purse if I were you."

Helen hesitated. Maybe Grandma did have some money, but how could she look with this woman staying so close? Then, beyond her she saw in the distance a man moving purposefully and rapidly toward them. A duck scrambled to get out of his way. He wore a blue short sleeved shirt and work pants. He came up, put one arm around the black-haired woman's shoulder and squeezed it possessively.

"Could we have a talk?"

Violet whirled. Glared at him. Shook off his hand. "I don't know you."

"Well I know you. I'd know you anywhere. You're: looking good. He smiled a toothy smile at odds with his narrow eyes.

"Goddamn you, get away from me." Again the woman jerked her arm away and he backed up, hands before him.

"O.k., o.k., don't get sore. We know how tough you are." But an undercurrent of mockery lay in his words.

The black haired woman turned her back to him and spoke in a high furious voice straight into Helen's face. "The goddamned bastard."

Then suddenly the merry-go-round started up. In the Good Old Summertime so loud it seemed they all had to listen. The man moved away from the black haired woman and came to stand between her and Helen. She saw he was sweating. Flashes of moisture glistened when he moved, beads of sweat lay on his forehead, along the edges of his coarse black hair, down his fleshy neck. He faced the woman.

"You crazy dame."

"Keep talking, keep talking."

"You ought to know I didn't have anything to do with it. I'm just a messenger."

"I'm talking to my friends." The woman said through bitter teeth.

She turned to Helen. "There's bastard for you" She said this conversationally, not looking at him, and he stirred and moved his arms down, hands on hips. Helen saw the lizard ripple, a dense provoking smell of sweat came out of him as he turned toward her.

"Hello friend," he said but he didn't smile. There was another tattoo on his chest, vivid red and blue scarring.

The world was a glare of falling sun, but a full scouring sun. People moved as though reluctant to invest themselves. The ducks abandoned the popcorn and retreated. Everything, everyone seemed to say, why bother? What's the point?

Then merry-go-round stopped.

"I thought they nailed you once and for all."

"Beat it." Their voices were suddenly loud.

"What do you mean beat it?"

Helen saw the man's fleshy neck darken, the muscles of his forearms tighten. Coarse hands were forced into fists. This is really serious, she thought, frightened for the first time. Deliberately the black haired woman turned her back, the fine strands of her hair wavered like a halo directly under the man's chin.

"I mean Get Lost Jerk."

"My money." Jessie said in a sharp voice." What's happened to my money?" The other three looked at her as she scrabbled through her handbag, old fingers poking into familiar crevices. Abruptly she snapped it shut: and ricocheted up from the bench and away from the others. "The police should know about this."

Jessie's humped back was emphatic. She walked stiffly, short testing steps that soon took her some distance. Helen started after her. When she looked back a few minutes later, the black haired woman and the tattooed man were gone.

FORTY-ONE

"Violet" said Those Who Are There To Help You Through An
Important Transition. "You continue to act way way out of line."

"No, not really," said Violet who had learned how to argue with
authority figures long before she'd reached the other side. Too bad she
didn't finish high school, she could have taken debate.

"You promised me one day. So I used all my allotted energy to
come here and learn. So I'm learning. I see things. I see I can help my
family. I never helped no one much when I was alive. Won't that be
pleasing in the end? I do so want to be pleasing." She said this in the
sickly-sweetest voice she could manage. And she did mean it – sort of.
You can't lie on the other side, she'd learned that much. The lying part
of a human mind vanishes forever – there's only truth, truth, truth –
relentless, bright hot, beyond human comprehension Truth.

"I'm loaning Tom the car for a day or two."

Surprised, Corky turned to look at her husband. "Whatever for?"

They were walking along the road, but not together. Dana was a
full one hundred yards in front of Corky."

"He's paying me."

"I thought you didn't like him."

"I don't. But we can use the money."

"When?"

"Tomorrow."

"I want the car tomorrow."

"So does he."

"I hardly ever ask for it."

"We need the money."

"He's trouble. He's always been trouble. I don't think you should do him any favors. Besides I need the car."

"For what?"

"A funeral. I've got to go to a funeral."

"Someone I know?"

"You never met him."

Instantly Dana was jealous. "Why not?"

"Dana you need to see your Dad tomorrow. You need the car too."

"I can take the: bus."

"Let's not quarrel. I feel bad about your dad. Does Tom know how ill he is?"

"Yes."

"Then why is he asking for our car? What's so important that he needs a car? He's pathetic don't you realize that? You need to honor your father."

"What a stupid thing to say!" shouted Dana. "Honor him! Look what he did to my mother. He did everything he could to make her unhappy. She'd be alive today if he hadn't been such an asshole. And what about my sister? We didn't have a dime to help Jenny. No, it's my dad who's pathetic."

"And what are you?" Corky said in a sharp tight voice. They were wandering through fields, avoiding paths, avoiding people, especially happy children playing tag.

"What about me?" Dana's voice was tight and sharp too.

"He's ill, your dad's very ill. You should forgive him."

"Forgive? You're always telling me what I should do or not do. It's my life. I made my peace with him. I helped Jenny through school. I got Mother away from him. I stayed away. That's kept the anger down. Staying away. Because I hate him. Don't you understand? I swear once or twice I nearly killed him when he was drunk. Smothered him right there in his bed. You don't understand. You had parents who didn't abuse you, who were kind to each other. This hatred won't go away. You don't know what I'm talking about."

"Oh yes I do," Corky said. She stopped dead, let him walk away. "I feel that way about you right now."

He walked rapidly away from her. A solid block of fury rose up like a pipe ramming through him. He wanted to explode with his rage, say everything in his heart. He wanted to be free of the whole mess. Above all he wanted a simple answer.

Dana didn't turn around, but he stopped dead in the middle of an open stretch of grass. There was a simple answer. Protect the family. Take the job. Take Jessie west. Struggle on into the new, taking the most important elements of the old.

And what is the most important? Well that's what the struggle's about isn't it?

Money. I have to find enough money to move the family and to help Dad.

The house? Is it essential?

No.

Is Corky? He turned around. Waited for her to catch up. His face was pale.

"I stopped thinking about you, Corky."

She was just corning up to him and now she recoiled as though he'd slapped her. He walked back to her. "It's as simple as that. When I was out there, working my head off: sending you and the kids money, I was also with her and I didn't think much about you, and that's the truth."

She began to walk on, hands stiff, her whole body stiff, wanting to get away from him. But he followed "I put you and the kids, put everything here in Minneapolis into some kind of compartment and turned the key on it. Walked along with her and dreamed some pretty fancy dreams. I'd go there. I'd do this and that. I'd be somebody different."

Tears were coming down Corky's cheeks, she was crying but he didn't seem to see that. He kept walking faster so now he was beside her. "It'd be different -the future. That's what I thought. I've been the man in the family since I was ten years old, Corky, first for my mother and sister, then for you and the kids. I wanted to be free."

To get away from him she left the road, cut across the grass, not quite knowing where she was going. He kept walking beside her, words erupting out of him, words that had been bottled up for a long time.

"But it was my mind playing tricks. You and the kids weren't in that cupboard locked up at all. You'd come to me. You'd walk into my mind, remind me you were real. I started getting angry. You were the reason I couldn't escape my life, you with your reminders and your fat little butt, your clumsy way of doing dishes ..."

Corky stopped and turned, her face getting red, she was so angry she could spit. But Dana wouldn't stop, couldn't be stopped now that he'd begun.

"I'd remember the way you smell after a hot bath – mostly of kitchen because you scrub yourself that clean. Never exotic, never perfumed. And yet how well I know your body in the dark. I can map it in my mind. Just how many ways I would remember you, and always coming toward me in the Spirit. I felt, feel still, closer to God with you. That other woman ... she couldn't find those ways, would never find them."

The angry words trembling on Corky's lips died, and she was listening, really listening, but tears were still rolling down her cheeks.

Three children on bicycles rode by them, the youngest shouting with exuberance words they couldn't understand. A small spotted dog trotted by going in the other direction, looking worried. A pair of elderly men drove by slowly in an ancient model T. peering out at this man and woman paused by the side of the road. They didn't stay long enough to see Dana walk closer and stroke Corky's cheek with a gentle hand.

"So I never escaped you at all. Never can escape. I love you deeper now than ever before because I know that. But it's probably too late to tell you. I had to find out the hard way didn't I?" She was stalled now, staring up at him. Tears still coming, but then she spoke, her voice low.

"So it came down to sex."

"Yes, it did." Neither noticed the black and white dog walking back in the other direction, still looking worried.

"Man my age – Is there anything else? The mystery of it. God gives it to us."

"God!" his wife stepped back, folded her arms. "I don't know how you have the face to mention the Almighty's name, Dana, after the way you're betrayed me."

"Maybe God lures us into confusion."

Dana began to walk again. Corky dropped her arms. Took a step or two after him.

"That's the devil."

"Aren't they the same?"

Then without really noticing it, they were walking along together, moving slowly toward a nearby bench. They were talking to each other, listening to each other.

"That's sacrilegious."

He was stubborn. "I thought those Bible classes were teaching us that God is everything." Reaching the bench he sat down, she stood before him, reluctant.

"You never went to any Bible classes." "That poor woman was dying out there, alone, without anybody caring about her. A bad husband."

"Don't talk about her. Don't try to make me pity her." She flushed and moved as though to walk away and he reached up and pulled her down to sit beside him.

"You have to. Listen to me – she had nothing – no money except what I paid for the rent, a nice house yes, but no kindness, no love."

"What about me?" Corky was spitting with anger again. "Let's talk about me for a change – night after night alone, wanting you to talk to, to hold."

"You had folks who love you. And you can love others. You have a world here of safety. She didn't have that ... that's all I'm saying. I'm not excusing myself or saying she deserved more than she got. It's just that something opened up in me, some eyes I hadn't opened in a long time and I saw that woman's need. It changed me, Corky. But then I acted on it too definitely. What I mean – the impulse, the seeing was good, but then I found only sex, not that it's only, it's pleasing too, but a commitment, and I wasn't grown up enough to find another way to give what I felt for her, which was compassion."

Corky turned away. Her eyes weren't blazing any more, instead her heart was heavy inside her. Compassion. Oh she knew what he meant all right. But she wasn't going to talk, not any more. She couldn't. This talk was confusing her. She wanted instead the white heat of anger, wanted it so hard she could cry out for it, could stamp her feet and have a tantrum for it. Give me back my righteous anger.

Give me back my urge for revenge. Give it back, oh you heavenly hosts. Let me hate in peace.

"Let's go back to the car, Corky. We need to find those car keys. Let's get moving." But neither of them did. They sat side by side in silence, looking around them at a world of summer fullness. The air was warm and kind, the sun still full.

Around Corky and Dana green grass and trees stretched in every direction. People were streaming down the roadway, scattering themselves across this world, most of them thinking about what to have for supper, or how to get ready for darkness inevitably coming. But they all knew there would be fireworks from the middle of the lake, rising like night promises above them. There had been fireworks every year in that park for a very long time. And so the people in Minnewana believed in those promises, looked forward to the fireworks.

Dana turned to his wife.

"So this is what I'm saying. I was lonely. I was stupid and maybe curious too."

"I don't want to hear all this."

"Forgive me, is what I'm asking."

"Don't talk any more, Dana. My goodness you're so smooth at talking, that new job I guess, or maybe the new woman."

Now Dana felt the hurt. He'd been truthful, he'd opened his heart. It was his old complaint about Corky. She came into her own feelings so quickly, so easily. She didn't give him a chance to find out his. She never let him blossom out to what he felt, what he thought and knew. Always quick quick, hurrying into her words, her interpretation.

"There's ways people grow, Corky," Dana said doggedly sitting still, hands gripping the edges of the bench. He was staring straight ahead. "You fall into it not knowing, doing what you think you have to, and then afterwards you think, I moved. I moved from A to maybe F, here at this time with this person, I'm closer to something, or someone that's ahead of me. That's what happened, Corky, but it's over, my lesson."

Some people chose that moment to walk by – young people, boys and girls, all dressed in shorts and tops, chattering to each other. Boys talking to boys, girls talking to girls, boys talking to girls – all intent, all too busy to glance over at the plain man and woman talking to each other over there on the park bench.

"You got some more lessons planned?" Corky said viciously," maybe another poor little sweetie you're going to feel sorry for? This spiritual search of yours – will the next ones be younger and prettier than me too? Other people call it cheating. Mind if I call it that? Cheating, fooling around? There's worst words aren't there?"

"Cheating's a good enough word," Dana said heavily and stood up, "You ever cheated on me, Corky?"

"Never." But her mouth was dry and she didn't look at him.

"You ever done something made you feel …complicated?"

Corky stopped breathing; her mouth fell open. Into her mind flew all those years ago, flew James Newell and the visit to New York. I'll drop in and see you sometime, he'd said smoothly when he'd put her on the train to come home alone. Some time when you're not too busy to give me some time, I'll stop and say hello. He hadn't paid her ticket home. She'd paid her own way home.

"Maybe."

"Something I don't know about?"

"Maybe."

"Then you understand." She looked at him, all the anger dying, confused.

"Maybe."

"You do. You understand it's complicated. Not one hundred per cent simple."

"No."

"I want you to forgive me."

"No."

"Like I forgave you."

Corky's eyes were big now. Heart beating fast. She stood up.

"How did you know?"

"He came to the house."

"When?"

"Before the wedding. He tried to make me break it off. Said he needed you more than I did."

"What did you say?" Corky's voice was still a whisper, she was that shocked.

"I said he was wrong, that I needed you more. More than anyone and that you'd been mine from the first moment we met and you'd be mine until the day we died. And I meant it. And I still believe it."

"Oh Dana," she felt sick inside, "Why didn't you tell me?"

"Because it didn't matter. It happened. We weren't married. You had to learn about the world, about yourself. I wasn't faithful either, that summer."

"Don't tell me anymore," Corky said, "Nothing more."

"It's over, the past. Forgiven. Now forgive me the present. Let us go on together." He took her hand. "Now for God's sake let's get back to the car and see if the kids have come back with the keys. It's worrying me. I might have to break into your father's car."

Every time Bernice came back to the Twin Cities she thought about Violet. She couldn't help it; her sister had been dead for three years, but it was like she wasn't dead at all. It was o.k. in Duluth because Violet had never come up there, but Minneapolis was full of memories. Now sitting on the bench beside the lake looking out at Duck Island, she thought about how Violet had walked in her sleep. She'd begun fighting with Jessie as a child, it had gone on for years and during one tempestuous spell of warfare, Bernice had been awakened almost every night by Violet's soft definite footsteps descending into the night. Sometimes curious, and a little frightened, Bernice who shared a bedroom with her sister, would get up too and follow Violet. Sometimes she found her in the basement trying to open a narrow· window, or upstairs pushing against the attic trap door. Sometimes the front door would be thrown open, then her mother or father would go outside and draw Violet back from danger. None of them knew then what she was looking for – or escaping from – for when they found her she'd waken at the touch of a hand, look startled, even amazed. Then, quite suddenly, the sleepwalking stopped. As though Violet had found another way out.

Later it was to Bernice Violet always came, One hot summer night she'd come to Bernice's small Minneapolis apartment and asked if she could stay with her sister. She hadn't finished high school and both

Amsden and Jessie were adamant she move back home and do so. But Violet continued indifferent to her parents.

"You're not in trouble?" Bernice asked her as they ate supper in her squeezed little apartment kitchen. Violet had looked at her with almond shaped eyes, black, flat and expressionless.

"Are you kidding? I'm not dumb, Lily."

"I've changed my name." Bernice dished out generous globs of macaroni,

"What's wrong with Lily?"

"It's stupid-calling us flowers."

"So you want me to call you Bernice?" Was that a sly half smile Violet slid toward her? "Maybe I should change my name too."

"Why did you come over here? What's wrong this time?"

Violet shrugged. "All kinds of stuff. Mostly I just got to get away. I'll only stay a couple of weeks. I've got a real job."

"Where?"

"The Hideway."

It was a bar down on Hennepin Avenue. Bernice had never been there.

"Violet, you're under age."

"It's a day job. Hey I want to take it. It'll be fun."

Sitting on the park bench, looking out at Minnewana Lake, Bernice remembered how Violet had never liked going out on the water, never liked swimming or boating. It had been a mystery to her sisters who had both loved taking out a canoe. Bernice thought of Violet's face that long ago morning, how Violet had seemed triumphant, her face gleaming with pleasure. She hadn't understood that either. Violet was a mystery.

If only I'd understood her, maybe I could have reined her in then, before it was too late, she thought. But could anyone have changed Violet? Bernice stared out at Duck Island.

Eddie appeared, strolling along the path, hands in pockets. He stopped. "Hey, Aunt Bernice, ready to go?"

She looked at him groggily, "What do you mean?"

"Out on the lake. Canoeing. Time to go."

Bernice flinched. It wasn't appealing. Why had she said she'd go? She didn't like water anymore. Besides he was late. "You're late."

"Come on, you said you would. You promised."

She looked out over the lake. They'd go too close to Duck Island. No, it didn't look at all appealing. "I don't think I'll go."

"Ah, come on Aunt Bernice, why not?"

"I waited at the place you suggested. An hour I waited."

"I had to help a friend. She was in an accident. I had to take her to the Red Cross Station."

Eddie sat down beside Bernice. "There was some fat guy in there who'd been pushed over in his wheelchair. He was screaming bloody murder about some woman. She tried to push him down the hill. Nearly broke both his legs he said. I guess it happened up there close to the bench where we were supposed to meet. Did you see a fat guy in a wheelchair?" Eddie was chirruping with pleasure.

He really is a dreadful young man, shuddered Bernice. Eddie leaned closer to her. "Tell you what. I'll get the canoe organized and come back here for you."

"No, no, I can l:meet you at the concession, I mean the boats, canoes" My brain isn't working too well, Bernice thought, it must be the sherry.

Eddie leapt up. "Wait here. Twenty minutes. I'll be back."

"All right," she said sullenly. "Where's your sister? I thought she wanted to go."

"Don't know, don't care. Promise you'll wait."

"I promise." Bernice muttered as he loped away. She opened her handbag. She had one cigarette left. The other pack was locked in the car. She closed her bag. I'd better wait, she thought, I might need a smoke later.

Eddie had lied. He did know where Helen was. He'd run into her near the Red Cross Station. She'd lost Grandma a second time, had forced him to loan her two dollars for a merry-go- round ride, while all the time squawking about some pervert bothering her. She's a pain sometimes. What pervert? And then thinking this Eddie stopped dead.

It might have been her – Helen -who'd knocked the guy down the hill. She'd said he was a cripple. A little gust of admiration whirled through Eddie. Not bad for a girl.

His own future was bright. Molly was so grateful for the help he'd given her he'd been invited over to her house while Emily and Edith; were visiting. He'd have to keep that fact quiet. Wouldn't want to make Carol jealous, he thought as he loped around the corner and ran smack into Carol and Norbett.

When Carol saw him her face wrinkled up and she started to jump up and down. Little hysterical nudges rippled over her body. Norbett grabbed hold of her shoulders and looked over at Eddie with a look of – well Eddie could only think of it as sympathy.

"Eddie, How awful how awful awful awful. You took my car. You took some other girls in my car. I saw you. Norbett saw you, Oh you are dumping me, dumping me, dumping me. I know it, I know it."

"Shut up, Carol." Norbett muttered. He looked at Eddie. "We followed you."

"I won't. I won't shut up. He's dumping me. I know it. I know it. He took our car. Our car. Where's our car?"

"Back where you wanted it parked, Carol."

"Who are those girls? Who are they, Eddie. I hate you. I hate them," She was hollering. Fortunately Eddie and Norbett were able to drag her off the path and into the bushes. Norton kept his hand over her mouth. "Shut up," he hissed again.

Eddie shot him a look of gratitude, then shouldering his boyfriend duties, came over and pulled her away from her brother. Or tried to – Norbett yanked her back.

Eddie grabbed her again, Norbert pulled her back. Throughout this tug of war, Carol went on screeching in a high dramatic soprano aria voice. "No, no, no, don't leave me. I want to go with you. I WANT to go WITH you. I want EDDIE MCFADDEN."

Now it was Eddie who tried to smother her mouth.

"EDDIE MCFADDEN. I LOVE you. I gave you EVERYTHING last night."

She was addressing the world, dispensing everything she was to everyone. She looked like she was enjoying herself. They were fully in the bushes by then, but around the corner appeared a woman, a skinny woman dressed in white. She looked alarmed, and stood silently watching them struggling in the bushes.

"EDDIE, Please listen to me, I'll die. I swear I'll die."

"What on earth is going on?" the woman said with a frightened look. She was backing away. Carol saw her and for a moment lowered her eyes and her voice.

"Oh, oh, oh," she sobbed quietly.

"What are you boys doing?"

Mr. Miller woke up. He'd been dreaming of his grandson, had seen his face, full and young and happy looking. He watched Karin settle her mother into her seat, and lay back, content with the good feeling the dream had given him. All around him in the trees he heard the full splashy sound of birds settling in for the night. Are they planning a trip somewhere, or just talking about their neighbors? Mr. Miller chuckled. Soon, he thought with pleasure, soon I'll see the fireworks.

FORTY-TWO

The sun was a hand, spreading itself across the land like a blanket, across life and people, across the word. Light was withdrawing. The greens were darker, drier, the browns blacker, the blues, yellows, reds swallowing themselves.

Helen walked through the carny grounds. It wasn't nice anymore, wasn't fun. Too quiet, and everything looked tired and old. Behind the counters of the concession stands, girls were turned away and at work. The men were closing up rides, locking away supplies, taking down signs.

She approached the merry-go-round. In the late sun it had a dusty indifferent air; long shadows stretched across the horses. She hesitated when she reached it. There was no one near it – no one standing, no one waiting. There was no young man.

She stepped up and felt again the wobble of the platform, its unease. With the gathering in of the light, the horses had turned solemn, yet up close their eyes were still wild. She wove through them, came to the inside edge, stopped. One of the center mirrors was open, was a door, a rectangular slice of black.

Was he inside? The young man? What's his name, she thought, thought too how strange to see mirrors opened up, how merry-go-rounds could be penetrated.

"Hello." my voice sounds hollow, she thought.

She walked in a circle along the edge, looking at the designs etched into the mirrors, the watercolor paintings above. She saw herself, slightly wobbly in the faded mirrors. The merry-go-round was much older, much tawdrier than she'd realized.

She felt a little thrill that she could use that word – tawdry – in the real world.

The gold was too gilt, the mirrors too dim, the painted scenes looked pale and distant. Without its music, the merry-go-round seemed still, like ruins underwater. Only the glossy horses had life, rose up against the air. They and the gold rings dangling overhead seemed designed to incite rides to go on circling.

"What are you doing?"

The young man. He'd come out of the mirrored door, was standing in front of it watching her. He was smoking. She walked the full circle toward him.

"Hi."

"So you came back?" His voice sounds friendly, she thought, but going closer she saw that his face was not.

She walked along the side of the platform – slowly.

The silence is so deep here, she thought.

He watched her, one hand on the edge of the mirror door.

"I'm sorry about not paying."

He took a drag. "Forget it."

"No, I said I'd come back. To pay you."

He strolled over, stepped up on the platform, began to pace the edge toward her. For some reason she felt a little chill of fear.

"I told you to forget it. Your grandma with you?"

"No."

He came up to her, his face looked closed. He was handsome in a tight sullen way, his hair fresh combed into a wet ducktail. He'd changed into a white shirt, open at the neck. His blue jeans were dirty. Stopping a few feet away, he rested against the side of a black horse. Took another drag of cigarette.

"Come here often?"

He's waiting for me to say something, she thought and took a step back.

She searched her mind. Nothing. Nothing came that was right, only things like I'd like to learn about the history of merry-go-rounds, like when they were invented.

She knew already he wasn't interested in that kind of conversation.

And what she did know anything about wasn't appropriate to talk about with a guy like Brent.

"You out with your family?"

"Yes." He looks at least 18. He looks like he's just woken up.

"That's a drag."

"Yeah." It was an accepted conversation, one you were expected to carry forward with various smart remarks about the hideousness of your family but nothing came. Her mind stretched behind her like a deep echoing tunnel, empty for miles and miles.

"This park is dead."

"Yes...I mean yeah."

"So's the carny."

"Yeah."

"You don't talk much do you?"

"Yeah."

"What does that mean? You do or you don't?"

If only his face were friendlier. She stared at him, feeling the miles and miles of empty mind tunnel stretching out into nowhere, nothing there but random collections of stupid facts that interested only her. Then one or two fleeting memories of horror comic scenarios suggested themselves.

"How many murders have there been in this park?"

"What?" He straightened up, frowned.

"Murders."

"What are you – a smart ass?"

"I mean..." It was a lame beginning and she knew right away she couldn't extricate herself. "It's such an old park. I mean have there been any murders here? I like to read about murders...I mean...I read about this woman who got killed in an amusement park." Worse and worse – she ground to a halt. Silence. Nothing else came to mind. Not a shred of information, not even a question about merry-go-rounds.

He still frowned at her. You want to give me the money?"

"Oh sure. How much?"

"Dollar fifty."

She held out the two dollar bills. "You got any change?"

"Nah. The cash box is gone." He looked at her unblinking. He was leaning against the horse, stroking its sleek head. "Hey, tell you what. You want to go for a ride? By yourself?"

"What do you mean?" She stared at him, confused.

"Go around a few times. I'll give you your own private go-around. Pick a horse." She continued to stare at him. "Get on a horse and I'll jack the thing up. That's worth two dollars." He came over and plucked the bills from her hand. "O.K.?"

He climbed down and went over to the open mirror. In a moment there came a humming sound as the machinery came on. He poked his heard around the mirror.

"I won't turn the music on. We're not supposed to do this – but seeing you're so good-looking." His smile was reluctant. "Pick a horse, I said." He waited until she'd gone to stand beside one of the horses, then pulled the lever.

The merry-go-round began to slip, silently, slowly – like the pit of a stomach dropping, like a mouth falling open, like sleep sinking down into a brain that's finally surrendered. Slowly with its silences intact, the merry-go-round slipped forward, rose up and down. She stood, braced, her feet against scuffed planks of the wooden floor of the platform. The merry-go- round moved faster, silently speeding up, but so gradually the sensation was smoothness. There was creaking now from the machinery beneath. The air was a warm wall they were moving through, pushing against, faster, faster.

She stood leaning against a brown horse that was stationary, around her the glossy flanks of others wavered up and down, up and down. Some horses moved, some did not, as though the magic of life was travelling inexplicably from one horse to another, sooner or later to find her. Without music the sensation was closer to flying, to a dream without time. It had been the good old summertime that had made the merry-go-round a giant windpipe, an attempt at song, at fun.

She looked over to see the young man still standing at the lever.

"I'll give you a double ride," he shouted. The only sound then was the wuffing of air, the noise of the machinery –a grinding from beneath her feet – and the creak of horses going up and down.

"Get on a horse," he shouted. She hesitated, thought maybe I'll find Grandma's swan boat, but when she started to walk toward it, she found she didn't want to weave through the moving horses. The young man watched her. She reached up, grabbed a spear slashing the throat of a great white charger, and swung herself up into its saddle.

At once everything changed. Her horse was rising and sinking, rising and sinking, swooping forward then falling back. She was tipped up high, riding a wave. The merry-go-round was moving fast now, atop the horse everything looked dazzling again and, the sound of machinery withdrawn, she could see the gold rings slide past above her, could their clack. She knew she could reach one. She stood up on the stirrups and as she rode under one reached up and slipped it off.

"I have a name!" she called out to the young man."

"What's your name?" he shouted back.

"Helen. What's yours?" But he didn't reply.

They're easy to grab, she thought, slipping the gilded wooden ring over her wrist. You were supposed to get a prize, but the prizes weren't ever anything you wanted. The ride is smooth; I'm glad I got on a horse. I'm a queen riding in regal splendor. Eleanor of Aquitaine, Queen of all I survey. But there isn't much to see.

The concession stands were closed now, men were slipping wooden shutters across their fronts. The gates were shut. She thought, no one can come in now. Then -he's still looking at me.

"What's your name?" she shouted again.

"Brent."

It isn't dark yet. Why are the concession stands closed?

He's come up on the platform. He's right beside me. Reaching up to help me down. "Why does everything close up so early?"

"The speeches at the band stand. We make too much noise."

He's just grabbed my hand. Oh my god. What's he doing? That tension, that frightened thrill in the pit of her stomach. She was afraid of him, of this unknown person.

"Hey, I'm not hurting you. You want to go over and listen to the speeches?"

She looked down at him. He isn't bad looking – just that look on his face.

"No, I hate speeches.'

"Yeah right on. You still in school?"

"Yes."

"What grade?"

"Ninth."

"Oh Christ. How old are you?"

"Sixteen," she lied.

Then the merry-go-round began to wobble, to stutter. It was winding down.

"Oops." Brent said and hurrying back to the edge, stepped down and went to pull the lever back so the whole platform slid to a grudging stop. Without the music it seemed to die with less complaint, was less sinister in its release. Brent stood looking at her. She'd stopped nearly in front of him.

He's looking at me that funny way again.

Reluctantly she climbed down and walked to the edge of the platform. "Thanks. Thanks for the ride."

"Come here." A tightness in his voice. "I'll give you something."

"Why?"

"You got the gold ring didn't you?"

Looking down she saw she'd forgotten the gold-painted wooden ring on her wrist.

"Sorry about that." She pulled it off.

"You get a prize," he said. "Here inside here." He vanished into the mirror door. She didn't move. In a moment he popped his head around the edge of the door. "I said, come here and I'll give you a prize."

"I don't want one."

"You want to see inside? How old it is, all that?"

At once she did. Something to tell Carol, but not just that. To step behind – that was interesting. She walked along the edge, then jumped down. The platform wobbled.

She walked over to the door. It was just her height. Brent had to duck as he came in and out. He took the ring from her, then took her hand, but very gently, and pulled her in through the door.

It's dark inside here.

"It's dark," she started to say but it was too late. Brent pulled her further inside and slammed the door shut.

The thin lady in white took out a small notebook and pencil. "This girl needs help. Give me your names."

"We don't have to." Eddie said.

"This is my sister." Norbett said sternly.

"And I'm a friend," added Eddie The two boys joined ranks, stood side by side, each keeping one hand on a sobbing Carol.

"No you're not, Eddie McFadden, you're not my friend. Not anymore."

Carol was blubbering. "I want to go with you. I want to elope I do I do I DO DO DO."

She was making those odd nudgie jumps again like a small child n the throes of a tantrum, but not very high jumps since a boy on each arm helped hold her down.

The Observer in White stepped forward.

"You need to calm down, young lady," she said sternly. The thin lady in white took out a small notebook and pencil. "This girl needs help. Give me your names."

"We don't have to." Eddie said.

"This is my sister." Norbett said sternly.

"And I'm a friend," added Eddie The two boys joined ranks, stood side by side, each keeping one hand on a sobbing Carol.

"No you're not, Eddie McFadden, you're not my friend. Not anymore." Carol was blubbering. "I wanted to be with you. I wanted to elope. You're CRUEL."

She was making those odd nudgie jumps again like a small child in the throes of a tantrum – not very high jumps since a boy on each arm helped hold her down.

'The Observer in White stepped forward. "You need to calm down, young lady, she said sternly. "You must sit down and calm yourself." There was white all over her body, she was even wearing white gloves.

"Where?" Carol said suddenly in a normal tone of voice, though waspish, "Where can I sit down? There's no place to sit down."

"Do you want to come with me? Do you want to find some place to sit down? What are these boys doing? Why are they unsettling you?"

"I'm her brother." Norbett repeated stoutly.

He's an all right guy, thought Eddie, he's got jam.

"She just got some bad news." he said.

He managed such a calm, mature voice the woman in white winced with surprise. She had a nervous nudging nose like a rabbit; now it wrinkled a little as though she could smell Eddie for the first time.

"Some very bad news." Eddie continued, his voice doleful. "Naturally she's upset. Awful upset. But we're calming her down."

The woman looked stricken with curiosity. What bad news her face neoned, what kind of bad news? A galloping case of let's-pry-into-this afflicted her, but she couldn't quite bring herself to ask.

"In the bushes?" she managed, "You're calming her down in the bushes?"

"She was throwing up," Norbett lied magnificently. "Something awful. Projectile vomiting. She does that when she's upset."

Carol's mouth fell open. The woman in white scuttled backward. Carol looked from one boy to the other. They both looked solemn.

"Well then everything's o.k." the woman muttered and retreated, turning her back only when she'd achieved a respectable distance.

Eddie regarded Norbett with admiration. What a liar. Carol looked at Eddie, then Norbett, saw her defeat in their eyes. She abruptly and dramatically crumpled to the ground. Unfortunately it was wet since hoses had been placed there earlier that day. She gave a little shriek. The two boys looked at each other, shrugged and each one taking an arm, dragged Carol across the wet grass. She struggled to get away but not too hard.

"Let go of me! Norbett, let go. I'm telling Mom. Stop it, Stop it Eddie. I hate you. I hate you!"

"She sure is mad," Eddie said as they reached the crest of the hill.

Norbett was nonchalant. "Ah she's always blowing a hairy about something."

They let go of Carol's arms and flopped down beside her on a dry stretch of grass.

Corky knew who the note was from – the one Helen had found. It had fallen out of her father's papers. She'd been going through his stuff in the trailer in order to throw most of it out. After his death, she'd found a sealed letter with his name on it and out of respect hadn't opened it. But if we're leaving, she'd thought, I best open it. The note inside was from his past – a note so old, so sealed away, he may have forgotten it.

Corky and Dana by then were walking to the car, walking ten feet apart. Corky wasn't sure why the note and a conversation with her father came into her mind.

She'd told Amsden about James, saying she'd loved someone for a little while but it hadn't worked out and Dana was her husband and she knew that everything worked out to the good. They'd been lying in lawn chairs under the striped awning in Florida. Jessie was up a lane somewhere in the trailer court talking with her friends, arranging parties.

Amsden had been taking it easy. It was after his first heart attack, and she and the kids had gone down to visit that Christmas while Dana was away. It had been a long bus ride but she was glad she'd gone. She and her father never had talked much, nor were silences between them as comfortable as those he shared with Bernice. Corky had always felt a little restless around him, afraid he would turn away, would not want her around. He was such a contained man, living so much of his life behind silence, and Corky liked to talk through everything. But that afternoon, in the bright Florida sunshine he'd mentioned how he'd run into some folks who'd grown up in Des Moines where he'd lived before he'd moved to Deep River. Then he said, suddenly, they even knew a girl I knew there, a girl who died young.

And she'd said, "Oh really?" – not interested very much.

Her father had said, "she died so young and pretty. I loved her so."

Corky remembered leaning forward, being interested by then. Such an admission was totally unlike her father.

"I tried to kill myself the night she died, "he said, not looking at her, looking down instead at his old hands, clasped in his lap. "Nearly did too. Shot myself in the chest. But I missed."

Corky was sitting straight up by then. They were sitting in the shade, under the stripped awning her father had rigged so it stretched from the trailer to the fence boundary, creating an outdoor room. The trailer was small with one bed and a narrow blue couch. The MacFaddens slept outside in the outdoor room that at night smelled of oranges from the nearby grove.

Corky had looked across at her father sitting at ease on his lawn chair, not sprawled out like some folks, but upright and neat looking. She saw he was as dry, as contained, as apparently humorless as ever.

"You tried to kill yourself?" she said, and she knew her voice was full of the amazement she felt.

"Twice in my life. Failed both times. Good thing too. My life's been good."

"Twice?"

"She was a beautiful young thing. Like a colt with long brown hair. She had red lips, beautiful brown eyes. The brown filly we used to call her because she had a sister who was blonde. Oh I loved that darling girl to distraction" and his voice lost its dry edge, and for a moment a line of music seemed to trace through words as he said them a thousand times – or thought them.

She listened hard, hungry to know a father aloof from her so many of her years.

"Oh she was beautiful. I used to walk down the street, stand outside her family's garden, hoping I'd catch sight of her. Wrote her notes. Little notes telling her I loved her. Silly young fool I was but she was the first girl I ever loved. And passions in the young run deep."

"How beautiful you are," she'd thought staring at her father, seeing something in him for the first time, a window into the man, the young man he'd been, and never would be again.

"She died so young. Tragic."

"What'd she die of?"

"Tuberculosis," he said, dryly, and got up, the window into him slammed down.

"I'll make us some lemonade. Your mother will be back, wanting something after all that gossiping."

"Does she know?"

Her father looked at her. "No."

"You never told her?"

"No."

"And you don't want me to tell her?"

"No."

"Why not?"

His face didn't change. He walked across to the trailer door.

"When was the other time?"

He turned, looked puzzled. "What other time?"

"That you tried to kill yourself?"

"Oh that," he made a motion with his hand, a brushing away as if not important and she knew that the moment of intimacy was gone. "Nothing important." He started up the homemade stairs into the trailer, then stopped and looked at her.

"That wasn't in Deep River, you understand – the girl. She died somewhere else. I liked her laugh. She had a laugh that was a happy sound." Then he went up the stairs and into the trailer.

Corky was thinking by then that she needed to get that note away from Helen, needed to throw it away without telling anyone what it was or who had written it, because that's what her father would have wanted. She was sitting at their picnic table by then, watching an irritated Dana try to break into her father's car without breaking anything.

"I always bring my keys, she said in a cross voice." I don't know why I didn't bring them today, too worked up I guess." She rubbed her hand along the table and drove a splinter into the side of it.

Dana gave up trying to pry open the driver window with a pen knife and came over and sat down beside her. "Does Eddie have any keys?"

"He might."

"Let's find him. Or Helen in case she took the keys with her – which I doubt."

FORTY-THREE

Helen saw the sun outside was a hot spark lower on the horizon, fire falling into late afternoon. Brent had opened the door, had leaned out to grab his cigarettes but when she came over to look out, he kept himself between her and that outside.

He lit a cigarette.

"Want one?" he said and held one out. Her lips quivered, she shook her head.

"Might stunt your growth?" he laughed in a deep voice but took the sting out of the words by reaching forward to touch the gold heart-shaped locket at her throat.

"Nice. Somebody give it to you?"

She said nothing. It was so quiet outside. The Good Old Summertime had stopped, the roller coaster crackle was gone, the bubbly music from the Ferris-wheel silenced.

"I think I should go."

"Hey I like tall girls. More of them." His hand just brushed her breasts. "How do you like it in here?"

"I can't see much." She looked around but the interior of the merry-go-round was dark and unkempt.

"You're not supposed to."

"My family will be looking for me. And I've got to find my grandmother."

"Yeah." he said in a bored voice and turned his back to stand in the doorway smoking. "Your fucking grandmother."

He's cute but why does he sound angry? Why is he so rude?

She stepped back so he couldn't touch her.

Dressed in red halter and tight short shorts, the beautiful well endowed spy was in Gestapo Headquarters. She'd come to plead for the life of her lover. She would match wits with the Gestapo Chief who used bad language.

Brent threw his cigarette away, turned, and slammed the door shut. Once again they were in darkness, blackness so close it settled like ash on her face.

"Let me feel your breasts." His voice was deep and some distance away. She couldn't see him. Then almost immediately she felt his hands on her shoulders, then her breasts. His hands on her became another kind of darkness.

She jerked away, pulled into the deep darkness of the merry go-round's heart. thought for the first time, Something bad might happen here.

She was surprised.

"You're kind a cute."

Then was against her, breathing hard, kneading her breasts, touching the nipples. She could smell his tobacco, his breath. She felt one hand between her legs, felt a sudden inexplicable sting in her own body as response. Frightened, she pushed him as hard as she could but he grunted, held on, lunged at her again. This time she shoved him hard until he fell backwards, pulling her with them, then he hit a wall. She heard him stumble, and he let go. She felt for the wall, looked for the door knob, but there was only blank wall. Behind her in the dark, he was moving, she could hear him, then felt him yank her shoulders, he tried to turn her around, to return the easy exploration of her, but again she pulled herself away by shoving her hand into his chin and cheek.

"Come here, I ain't gonna hurt you. I just want to have some fun."

But he couldn't find her. She'd moved backward into the darkness again, she was vanished somewhere, like in a nightmare – everything except self had disappeared. She started to cry, but even that sound was swallowed up in the sponge of darkness."

"Hey I wasn't hurting you." His voice was gruff. He stepped back, she heard him stumble against something.

"Let me out of here, I want to go." To her own ears, her voice sounded weak, smothered.

"Hey I'm not going to eat you." Then he laughed. "Or maybe I am."

He was there again, and once again dragging her, found a wall and pushed her against it... She felt the press of something against her legs. He took her hand and thrust it down and she could feel a warm meaty lump between his legs.

"You came back for this didn't you?"

Oh my god, she thought. She had a scream rising in her but the awful thing was she felt inside her a sting, unfamiliar and alarming, a tartness like sour plums.

"Leave me alone," she sniveled. Some other newness was flowering in her too, a shivering spread of terror. She thought, What if I never get out of here? What if something bad happens to me in here?

She shoved at him again, but he yanked her close and squeezed his mouth down on hers. She went limp, helpless, but inside she tried to think.

"Look, let's have a little fun, then I'll let you go. You ever been French kissed?"

Holding her shoulders, he slid his tongue between her lips and let his hand slide down the front of her legs again. The tartness inside her leapt up and terrified she bit down hard on his tongue.

"Ow! What the fuck?" He moved back, into the dark. Now for Helen everything was blackness. a void that still was closing in, and now without sensation, just the brief prickle of his voice, nothing more, with that voice came a sense of her own heart beating with fright, her own breath drawn raggedly, her own betraying body still signaling her to lie down, lie down into darkness, surrender to a tobacco raw voice and rough hands, to the unknown penetration of sulky fury, to the bulge of flesh.

I don't understand, a child's voice wailed inside her. She drew back found the wall, tried not to breathe or make a sound, crept along touching the safety of the wall.

"What the fuck are you doing?"

He was some ways away. She felt for the door, a light switch, anything that would release her from this prison. She bumped into a stack of boxes.

"Get the fuck off that stuff. What are you, some kind of moron?"

She went on stumbling backwards until she was against what seemed to be a pile of wooden crates; she scrambled up on them, then screamed when he suddenly found her, and reaching for her, tried to knock her off the boxes. She scrambled backward, scratching her bare legs, shoulders, staying out of reach. She could hear him panting.

She couldn't see anything but neither could he.

He can't see me, she thought. I have to be quiet. She held her breath. There was a long silence.

A squashed rectangle of light appeared. She stood up. He'd opened the door.

She was standing on a pile of wooden crates.

"Get off that. Jesus you don't listen do you? Bitch."

Jessie walked beside the lake, not the least bit concerned that everybody might be looking for her. She felt fine walking by herself, in fact preferred it. She had her handbag and she knew where she was going. I know this park, she thought. How many times did we come here, Amsden and I and the girls? Every Fourth of July, because the Fourth of July is as much about yourself as it is about the country.

Maybe I won't go to Denver, Jessie thought. It sounds like a lot of work.

Maybe Violet's right.

But then everything seems like a lot of work these days.

She dropped her hand and felt again the sharp scratch on her ring finger. She staggered to a stop and pulled the hand up to look; yes only the claws of the ring gaped back. The diamond had fallen out some time that long ago day. She squinted at the ring up close. Funny how rings look without their burdens. Funny too how it never bothered mer. Did losing it mean something?

Well, Amsden what does it mean? You ought to know now that you're up there. You gave it to me all those years ago on the merry-ground.

Jessie came to the end of the lake where the huddle of sheds and canoes and rowboats promised man would meet water in a safe place. She stood for awhile watching the boats dotting the lake. Funny how I don't feel tired she thought. She looked down, felt again the sharp scratch on her ring finger. She pulled the hand up to look again: yes only the claws of her engagement ring gaped back.

The diamond had fallen out some time that day with Billy. Now she squinted at it up close. Funny how rings look without their burdens. Funny too how it doesn't bother me. Does wearing it again today mean something? Amsden I'm counting on you to tell me – Rings mean something – losing them, finding them. Every ring has a story. Poor thing without its diamond. Are only diamonds forever?

We quarreled out on the lake, Amsden and I -, the last time we took a canoe out on the lake – you didn't like boats all that much. It was summer. You noticed the diamond was gone. You thought it had happened that day. But there was something else bothering you. It seemed like you were accusing her of everything under the sun, so you wouldn't have to tell me what was really wrong. Finally you said.

"I don't believe she died."

"Who?"

"Pansy. You gave her away didn't you? How could she die and I not know what happened."

"You weren't there. You were in Des Moines."

"You didn't kill that baby did you?"

"No."

"You must tell me." His face was white he was so anxious. He'd been working like a demon for weeks and weeks trying to earn the money to buy the store in Minneapolis where you worked as a clerk. "I told you I wanted you to have that baby."

"I know that."

"What about that friend of yours?"

"Billy Black? He's not my friend"

"He's the father. Does he know his baby's dead?"

"No."

"You didn't give that baby to him did you? Did you see him while I was gone?"

"No."

Well it had been a lie, there were a few lies all to do with her life before she'd married Amsden. She turned the questions back on him.

"What's wrong? Something wrong Amsden. Tell me. I'm your wife now."

"Old man Stanton wants to sell both stores to his brother-in-law.

He's trying to squeeze me out. He's setting me up for so much debt I might go to jail."

"Jail?" She'd been horrified – Amsden in jail? –dry, every hair in place Amsden in a place like that – it didn't make sense.

"I bit. Bought stocks with him. Now I'm left wearing the tar and feathers. I put myself up front. Everybody knows I sold them the stocks. He's pulling out leaving me to face the music."

She hadn't known enough to understand, but she saw he was frightened.

"What can we do?"

"Nothing. As far as I can see, I have to ride it out and see what happens."

But he'd been calmer after that, hadn't asked her any more questions.

Jessie saw a blue canoe pull up on shore. A young couple got out and strolled away hand in hand. Nobody was waiting to get in. The canoe sat empty. The young man in the boat hut came down and pulled the canoe in close to the dock, then walked away.

A few minutes later when he turned around he saw Jessie sitting in her canoe, ready to go. He scowled at her, saw how she sat hands in lap, head high, as though she was already floating, already on her way to the island.

Jessie sat in the canoe, hand shading her eyes to look out over the lake. Canoes were scattered like multicolored pencils all over the water, people paddling themselves in and out of togetherness.

I heard them talking about going west, about taking me, not taking me. What a kafuffle. Why don't they ask me? I'll go with my family, course I will. Violet wont' stick around long enough to do anything much with me, she never did in life why would she in death. Though sometimes I wonder if she is dead, the way she hangs around these days.

Greta commenced to stagger a little, like she was too tired to walk– and too fat -any further. Mike kept plodding along.

"I want to go home, Mike."

He grabbed her arm, marched off taking her along with him.

"Can we at least sit down?"

"First we look at the canoes Come on."

When they reached the boat concession they saw an old woman

sitting in a canoe. Greta didn't recognize Jessie and Jessie didn't see her. The young man in the boat concession was complaining to everyone who would listen.

"I've got to get her out of there –all the boats and canoes have to be in by seven o'clock. Now that old lady wants to go to Duck Island. No way she can, not by herself, but she won't get out of that canoe. She says she's waiting for someone. I guess I'm gonna have to call the cops."

FORTY-FOUR

After they found the dry stretch of grass and stretched themselves out three abreast, they started laughing. They thought then how good it was to be spread eagled on a hillside, under a hot sun, laughing together. Carol warmed and was gradually soothed as she laughed. She thought how someone she knew might come by and see her with two young men, one on each side of her. It was worth a lot to be seen as a friend to man. Eddie and Norbett laughed because female hysterics were over and they could go back to doing what they pleased.

Keep it simple, Eddie thought. That was the trouble with school. Always warning you how complicated things are, how organized you have to be. He thought about Molly Ashford. She wasn't that bad looking, just that big happy sappy smile and bossy sometimes. Still, she was mostly all right, while those twins – Edith and Emily –they were more than all right, they were spectacular. Then he remembered – Aunt Bernice – the canoe. He sat up. He didn't feel like being mean to Aunt Bernice anymore, but he'd promised. He stood up.

Carol opened her eyes. "Where are you going Eddie?"

"I have to take my Aunt Bernice canoeing. See you later." And he walked away.

A few moments later Carol sat up, then Norbett, both struck by the same horrible thought: Eddie has the keys to our car.

Bernice trudged along the path. Her whole body felt heavy. Eddie hadn't come back. By then she wasn't sure whether he'd said meet at the boats or at the bench. So she'd have to check. She hoped she wouldn't find him. I just want to go home, she thought. I'll get on that bus to Duluth first thing tomorrow morning.

Sam hadn't come. So why should he? Sam was safe. Moored in a domestic world. Unavailable for contact, unable to see her, unwilling to talk.

So what? she thought angrily. So what? I'll survive. I've always survived.

People brushed by her, tired, happy looking people, some sunburned. Lucky you she thought passing one vibrant young woman with fire engine red cheeks, the sun doesn't bother you. But she was full of anger at them all.

Sam had done all the wrong things about Violet. He hadn't told Bernice until it was too late. He'd called in a panic and said Violet was comatose. What was she supposed to do, revive her? Violet had pushed somebody too far and somebody had pushed back. Always and inevitably Violet pushed everything to a breaking point. So what if I was the last one to be shoved aside? she thought, I don't care anymore.

If only I could forget about her. Erase her from my mind. Flush her out of my system. It was hard when you'd known someone as a child. You had to erase your whole childhood. Bernice couldn't remember much of it anymore – just Violet sleep walking. And their music lessons. Nothing about sleeping together in the same room, the same bed, whispering stories, nothing about comparing clothes, trading lipsticks, the games she and her sisters had played together.

Walking along the path as it curved beside the lake, Bernice clenched her teeth and thought, I don't want to remember any of it – especially that last evening.

When she saw Violet's face she'd gasped.

"What happened?"

"She got beat up."

Bernice had arrived late at night. Shivering. She'd been dragged out of bed, out of sleep. They were at Sam's office.

"But how?"

"How do I know? She's your sister."

"But why did she come to you? Why didn't she call me?"

She'd stood open mouthed before the thing on the desk – Violet's body, her face a bruised red and blue sack of crushed flesh, her sweater and skirt covered with blood. She looked around the office. Nothing had changed. Only she and Sam. They were no longer lovers; she hadn't seen him alone for months.

He was bending over Violet, holding her pulse. Shaking her a little. Trying to keep her alive. "Sam, tell me."

"I called the ambulance."

"Why didn't she call me?"

He straightened, looked over at her. His plump slug white body drooped. Sam was uncharacteristically subdued. "I told her not to. I told her it was bad for you, for us."

"But we're not even seeing each other."

"She didn't know that. It was too late to tell her that. And I told her before to leave you alone. That you'd get somewhere if she left you alone, left your parents alone. She wanted to move in on them."

"But she's my sister."

"She's still a drunk, no good. Listen Bernice, I know a hell of a lot more about these kind of women then you do."

She stared at Violet but had no feeling to touch her. Her body was too gruesome, almost subhuman. Finally she went over. "Violet?"

There was a raw smell about her, blood and vomit all over her.

"Violet hang on. We've called the ambulance."

There was no response, no sound from her.

She turned to Sam, "Is she still breathing?"

He shrugged, a huge, elephant sized shrug that said everything, said: Who knows? He came over. They stood together one last time in his office, sharing the problem of her dying sister.

"Look, I could get into trouble even bringing her in here." He touched her arm. "You realize calling the ambulance is going to involved me?"

She looked at him without quite understanding. Then Violet gave a brief moan – a thin dreadful sound like a crack splitting wood, then came a second hissed slice of breath.

"Violet." She leaned over, touched her sister's bruised cheek. "I'm here, Violet."

"My family, "Sam said, "I don't want my family to get involved. You could say she called you. Then you called me. You could say that."

She looked at him. Yes, her mind reported. I could do that. I still care about the man. I know his family is important to him.

"You want me to lie for you?"

"It's not really a lie. She's your sister. Just tell them you got the first call. Then you called me. That we went together to pick her up. Tell them about her life, what a rough life she had. They'll believe you."

Sam's office was very plain – a big wooden desk, an ordinary swivel desk chair, a small crucifix on the wall. All the pictures were of his family. He didn't have a phone in his office. The overhead light wasn't on only the desk lamp beside Violet's body, a lamp that gave off a burnt smell.

"Or you could say I came down and met you here – to help. And I will help. I'll help in any way I can. I'll pay for her burial. But I don't want my wife and kids involved. Everything would come out. You realize our relationship might come out, all kinds of things about me might come out?"

He'd been almost babbling by then, big know it all Sam.

Of course she'd done it. It had all worked out all right. The police had been kind. They had a long record on Violet by then. She was known to be in constant trouble. She'd been drunk and disorderly a number of times. Using drugs. Whatever. They believed Bernice.

What harm is there in doing it? she'd thought at the time.

It was only later, months, years later that she'd really thought about it at all – after Sam's promotion, after she took the job in Duluth, when the handsome farewell present from Sam came, but signed "from the office" he'd written a thank you note – it was a sterling silver tea set. Yes he knew she liked nice things, but she'd found herself alone in Duluth. He hadn't called, didn't write, refused to answer her letters and phone calls. That's when she'd started to think: What did happen to Violet?

Nobody seemed to know or even care.

Horrid ideas and questions began to arrive in the middle of the night: What if Sam had had an affair with Violet? Had expected her to respect his life as Bernice had done? And what if Violet didn't want to do that, instead decided to make trouble? Could Sam have done something to stop her? He was volatile, Bernice knew that, and she knew enough about policemen to know how angry some of them became. But he'd never touched her in anger.

Face it, you never did anything to make him angry, she admitted to herself. You knew how to handle him – or so you thought. Maybe it really was the other way around, that sneering voice that crept into her thoughts, more and more day and night said, -Sam knew how to handle you and you were too stupid to admit it. Maybe Violet knew more than you, more about men, about the world. What if Sam isn't such a nice guy after all? It was a distinctly nasty voice.

During one midnight session the idea came to her that the body hadn't been Violet's at all. Sam had said it was Violet, said Violet had called him to come get her.

That he'd found her in a back alley. That was Sam – his story. She'd repeated it to the police. But where had the beating taken place? Who did it? What if it weren't Violet who'd died? What if it were someone else dressed in Violet's clothes? How could she know? They didn't make sense, but the thoughts wouldn't go away.

Bernice had rounded the corner, she was approaching the lake. She saw Jessie sitting in a canoe. There was no sign of Eddie. Abruptly she wheeled around and quick marched away, all the way across the park at high speed – to the picnic area. She would try one last time to see if Sam were there, was willing to talk it all out at last. The low smoldering anger in her seemed to have destroyed whatever passion she'd felt for him. So what if he's sitting there, arms folded in anger at me for bothering him? she thought. He's a ghost, And Violet's a ghost. I'm ridding myself of two ghosts.

She approached the picnic area. And she saw him – Sam – sitting on a bench outside the picnic area – Sam was waiting for her. When he saw her he stood up.

Eddie strolled up to the young man running the boat and canoe concession.

"Did she pay? The old lady?"

"No and I want her out of there. Do you know her?"

"She's my grandma."

"Well get her out of there. I called the cops cause I'm not touching her."

"I'll take her out in the canoe. I'll pay." And Eddie handed over the money and strolled as casually as possible over to Jessie's canoe, and climbed in.

They were walking again, Corky and Dana, side by side, not holding hands, following the path down to the lake. Into Corky's mind came another memory of James. He'd been sitting at the table by the window writing in one of his many notebooks. She'd said something and he was caught off guard. And she remembered how sad his face was.

"We don't belong together, James." That's what she'd said.

"You can belong together and not be in love." He had a deep baritone voice, a voice like a sound in a well.

She'd like best of all doing that, lying in bed listening to him talk. He could talk for hours, rattling on about his friends, about the latest book he was reading, about what offended him in the newspapers and in the world. She didn't know what to say, couldn't formulate intelligent responses, but when he stopped and asked if he were boring her, she cried out passionately no, not at all, go on, I'm listening. Curled up in the hotel bed, she thought of herself as in a small boat, the room swimming around them, the city outside a vast unknowable ocean, and they were struggling together to navigate its waters.

How could she know then that later, all these years later, that would be what she remembered the city outside locked into its night, she snuggled into the pillows of an impersonal hotel bed, he talking, talking of the deeds of great men, or reciting bits of poetry, declaiming on the ridiculousness of politics and other people's opinions; the sound of his voice weaving the room and herself into a tapestry of belief.

Long afterwards, guilt at last vanished, she understood that James had led her into the astonishment of connection, of knowing and not knowing another human being in a new way, with vehemence. Had introduced her into the lure of the intellect, into knowing that it could devour everything and everyone when it held a man or woman under its spell. It had been the great adventure of her life. She'd needed no other until this hour.

"I want to go west." Corky announced. Dana looked over at her. "I want to risk everything and do it. Go to Denver."

"Tom Shannon offered me a job."

"I've thought about it. I've got some money saved, enough for the train and to stay out there a few months. I could go out and look for a house, look for work."

Dana stopped dead. She trailed a few steps further down the hill then halted too.

"I could. I worked before we were married. If I went out there and looked for a house, found work while you stay, take that job for awhile, look after Moth…"

"Are you out of your mind?"

"Don't belittle me!" Her voice gusted up, she shifted her body, settled herself on both feet as though rooting herself into the ground. "Just don't do that. Not after all these years of me taking charge, making do while you traveled here and there. I said I have enough money for the fare out, and to find a place to live. If I found a job, if we both had jobs – we could make it."

"You don't have to work!"

"Yes I do!"

They were standing facing each other, this plain faced man, this plain faced woman. Where was the black haired handsome youth the vivid young beauty? But when they saw each other, they saw those two still.

"If you lost your job again, then we'd still be all right. And I want to, Dana, I want to work."

"But go out there by yourself?" Dana's voice was a mixture of doubt and astonishment.

"What an adventure!" Corky's eyes were sparkling now. "It's time I had an adventure or two." Then seeing his eyes darken with jealousy, for he'd always been a jealous man, she came over to him and touched his arm. "Not that kind of adventure, Dana, I don't want that. I want only you, you know that." And she put her arms around him and kissed him sweetly on the lips. He grasped her tightly, tightly, but it was he that drew back first.

"You forgive me?"

"Yes."

He took her hand. "Corky…"

"If it's over." Her voice tightened and she drew her hand away. "If it's really over and you promise…"

"I told her. Today."

"You called her?"

"Yes."

"Is the room still there? Still yours I mean? Maybe I could use it." He shuddered with the horror of that thought – Corky staying in Maddie's house.

"What do you think? I could use that room while I house hunt." But her voice was mischievous and that told Dana more than anything else that the subject was closed, that they would go on together.

And they did because the path had reached the lake. They wandered along it, away from the amusement park, the locked car, and toward the boats, toward Duck Island, barely noticing anything but themselves, as they walked beside Lake Minnewana, holding hands.

FORTY-FIVE

They were all out on the lake now – Jessie and Lily Bernice and Eddie and rose Corinne and Dana. The whole lake was covered with canoes or so it seemed; the sun was waning, the water gleaming. The light had changed, was deepening, darkening, dwindling, yet all about were spots of bright red and green and yellow and orange, colors that were canoes, each with its complement of people. And all these canoes, and their elder cousins the brown rowboats, all seemed to be moving, moving around in every direction; canoes slipping across the blue gray water yet seemed also not to be moving at all, and if they were moving, what they moved toward, or away from wasn't at all clear for the behind and the ahead were the same, every direction on the flat oval circumference of the lake was a looking toward shore, or away from shore, yet that too did not seemed to matter, all that mattered was that there was water, that there was yet summer, that the sun still shone, and there existed canoes to paddle in the evening air.

Helen looked around – yes there were her parents in a red canoe. They were talking, Daddy leaning way out while her mother turned to look behind. Yes Eddie and Aunt Bernice and Jessie were in a yellow canoe near Duck Island, but they were going in circles, round and round.

Can Grandma swim? she wondered, she was so old if they capsized, somebody would have to save her, the thought worried her. She would want Grandma to be saved.

"Can you swim?" she asked the stern paddler behind her.

Yes she was in a canoe too, a blue canoe and with a stranger, yes definitely a stranger, and looking again at Norbett she thought, he isn't really good looking – too skinny, with a tense face, glasses, and that short brush cut the army favored, yet I feel safe with him; he's smart and he'd made decisions fast when he'd rescued her.

"Sure" Norbett said. He was paddling faithfully toward the island.

Her first luck – or was it just luck or because she started praying in that merry-go round?- was that Tom O'Shannon had recognized her He was standing outside when Brent opened the door. When Daddy's cousin saw her his mouth fell open, his face whitened so the freckles stood out, then he flushed,

"What the hell. You're Dana McFadden's kid."

Brent slammed the mirror door shut and darkness enveloped her again, but she rushed to the door and pounded on it.

"Hey let me out." She'd touched back into the safety of people who recognized her. Surely her Daddy's cousin would help her. "Help, Mr. Shannon."

The door was yanked open, and Helen stumbled out into what seemed the brightest of daylights though it was not, was instead the shaded light of early evening. The merry-go-round lay brazen and silent around her. Tom Shannon's face was still flushed, he looked at Helen, then at Brent. They were all standing between the mirrors and the platform.

"What's she doing in there?"

Brent shrugged elaborately.

"Who put you up to this?" Shannon said fiercely to Helen. "To coming over here and snooping around?"

"She wasn't snooping." Brent folded his arms over his chest.

"Oh wasn't she?"

"It's none of your business anyway."

"Oh isn't it? I know this kid." He stepped forward, grabbed Helen's shoulder with a rough hand. "Does your father know you're down here?"

Helen hesitated. It's odd how angry he is, she thought, There's something wrong. "I said does your father know you're here?"

It seemed safer to pretend he did.

"Yes."

"Did he send you? Did he do that? Send you up here to snoop around?"

"No."

It was too late to take back the words. Brent was looking at her too, his face was changing, into his eyes came a look of anger, and something else, something that looked like a tinge of respect – she wasn't just some stupid little moron of a girl – she was a threat – Dana McFadden's girl.

"Skip!"

She looked over and saw Norbett standing on the other side of the low wire fence.

That surrounded the carny. Norbett was perched on his bicycle. Relief shot through her.

"I'm looking for your brother." Norbett called out.

"I know where he is." She called back and walked over to the fence.

"Damn" Tom Shannon said.

"What do you want to do?" asked Brent. Behind her, they were talking faster now, a language of muttering. "Do you want to do something?"

"What do you suggest?" the older man snapped, "You got us into this."

Norbett squinted at her. "You know where Eddie is?"

"Norbett, help me get out of here."

"Try the gate."

Helen went back over and jumped up on the platform. She wove her way through the horses still speared into position. Neither of the men followed her. When she jumped down and half ran, half walked to the gate, Norbett had bicycled over to meet her. He squinted at her.

"How'd you get locked in?"

He was the same old Norbett, casual and unassuming. He jiggled the gate but it was locked. Looking back she saw the merry-go-round still there, soundless, but the two men had vanished. Instead, a caretaker dressed in gray overalls ambled over and without saying anything, unlocked the gate and let her out.

Now, sitting in front of him in the canoe a mysterious happiness filled Helen. The canoe bobbed beneath them and, looking down into the water she could see the wavering brown eyes of underwater grasses spelling out a mysterious unapproachable reality.

beneath them. She looked up again at Grandma in the yellow canoe.

She was still there, sitting hunched in middle of the yellow canoe, looking weary yes, but still gazing out, just like she did in the car, looking out at everything. Eddie and Bernice were shouting something at each other, still going haphazardly in circles and zig zags, but Helen thought it was o.k., everything was o.k. as long as grandma was there.

Then as she looked around again, the whole lake seemed to her to be covered not with canoes but with flowers growing up on a blue earth. The lake itself was an earth container, one held together by people, all the people in it, and then thinking that Helen felt instead of happiness a new and intense loneliness, a separation from everything she saw around her, from her mother and father so close to her, from her brother and aunt busy fighting, from this canoe she was in and the boy paddling it behind her, even from grandma. She felt lifted away, loneliness penetrating everything and especially herself.

Last summer at camp there'd been a place, a little lake that the girls had snuck off to. You'd jump into the icy water and swim out alone into the middle of the lake and float, just float and look up at a remote powerful sky and you were really alone, the water like liquid silence protecting you and then a kind of peace came over you and there with it, a safety, as though you were safe from yourself. Because of there was a force inside you, -building up in secret – you didn't feel safe from yourself – from what you might do.

Because of that force you did all kinds of stupid ugly things like making fights, and talking about people you really liked, nasty things. You didn't find good ways for it to be in you because you needed to be alone and most of the time you weren't. Family hemmed you in, it worked on you the wrong way – nobody understood that.

Yes, said Violet to The Powerful Beings Helping Her Through a Difficult Transition. That's it exactly. That's the first warning. Can I go and speak to her?

No.

I must. It's my only chance to know her, to warn her.

No.

Helen looked over and saw a woman on the shore waving at her. She hesitated then waved back. She couldn't tell who it was.

Violet, you've broken the rules again. You're out of here.

The woman vanished.

They weren't angry were the TPBHHTADT for how could they be? But they knew exactly how a transition period for any officially dead person should go. Hadn't they all been through one?

Violet, you are resisting us because you want to stay inside time forever. You are used to it. You're afraid to move on into truth. You can't imagine timelessness for imagination itself rests in time.

Violet tried not to listen but their voices were inside.

Timelessness and truth are one, Violet. You can't have one without the other.

Oh let me stay until the fireworks, Violet said humbly. I promise I won't say anything – or interfere. Please, please let me stay until the fireworks are over.

Forty-six

Eddie ignored Aunt Bernice's commands and paddled hard toward Duck Island. He'd been smart enough to climb into the stern of the yellow canoe and so assumed control. Why she was so furious he had no idea. He'd already decided not to dump her into the water, just take her around a little then get back to shore. Though when she'd charged up, he'd been engaged in convincing grandma to get out of the canoe. She wouldn't budge, had pretended she didn't hear him, had kept pointing dramatically at Duck Island. The boat concession lout came over and started arguing with them.

"That old lady won't get out."

Four or five canoes, painted different colors, each with its own bold number were already pulled up on the beach. A rowboat was against the wharf, five people were awkwardly crawling over each other to get out.

"Are you with her?" the lout waved an arm at Jessie who remained motionless perched in the middle of the yellow canoe with the number seven painted on it. She was sitting on a stack of life jackets.

Eddie nodded.

"Well get her out of there."

"Get out Grandma."

Jessie stared straight ahead motionless.

"Get her out of there."

Eddie turned to him. "What's your problem kid?"

"I'm not letting an old dame like that take out a canoe."

He breathed noisily, an indignant sound.

"I paid," Grandma said.

"She's been sitting there half an hour."

He was skinny, short and surly looking- shorter than me, Eddie thought.

"You're supposed to get out Grandma."

"Who said?" Jessie looked up at the two boys, like a gopher peering cautiously from a hole at two dogs.

"Me!" said the boat concession operator. "I'm in charge here."

"I paid." Jessie said firmly.

"Are you going to get out?"

The rowboat family struggled up the path, shaking stiff limbs, grumbling good naturedly about being damp; they smiled as they passed Jessie in the canoe, then slowed, glanced curiously; they were listening.

"I paid." Jessie repeated.

"I'm not letting you take that canoe out," the lout said, "Do you think I'm crazy?"

"She says she paid." Eddie said.

"Well she didn't. If you want to pay you can take a rowboat. You can go to Duck Island in a rowboat if you're stupid enough to want to."

The operator turned his head, to glance around at the canoes and boats already out on the lake. I'm in charge here clearly written all over his skinny body.

Eddie didn't want to pay, shelling out for his sister had taken half his hard earned cash. While he was considering this, Aunt Bernice arrived. Right away she'd begun snipping at him. But she'd agreed Jessie should go along because just then Officer Hakkenson had shown up, having been called to do something about an old lady who wouldn't get out of a canoe. Aunt Bernice had greeted him like an old friend and they both agreed with the concession lout that a canoe was too dangerous for an old lady, but Jessie didn't move She sat motionless, scrunched together, wretched knees pulled up like a child playing hide and seek. She pointed at Duck Island.

"I want to go there."

"Mother get out."

"I paid."

"No she didn't." the lout said, but he looked nervously at Officer Hakkenson.

"He says you didn't pay, Mother."

"I paid."

"Where's you get money." asked Bernice scornfully.

Jessie patted her purse, "Here. Right here."

"You paid for the time you've hogged it." The lout pushed back his cap.

"She can sit down," Eddie said, "if she's tired. It's a free country."

"Not in my canoe she can't. Get her out of there."

Officer Hakkenson, removed his cap, assumed his Christ-like pose, "Now folks, let's sort this thing out."

"I don't want to go to Duck Island." Bernice said firmly.

"I do." Jessie said.

"Get her out."

"Now folks."

The family was still halted just up the path; the father, a short balding man moved slightly toward them, one hand stretched out as though to offer some words of wisdom. He had a good natured face, but a bewildered expression. The boat concession lout glanced over at him, at all the family watching them. So did Officer Hakkenson.

"Move on folks."

They moved on.

"Look," said the boat lout, "she didn't pay me. I swear to God she didn't pay me. Now if you want to take Grandma out in a canoe, fine take her. I couldn't let an old lady like that go alone could I? If there are two more going, I guess it's okay." His voice was filled with self righteousness. "See that she puts on a jacket." He walked away, shifted his baseball cap back and forth before letting it settle in.

"Fine. Lily Bernice, you're going aren't you?" Officer Hakkenson looked with some doubt at Eddie, then back at Bernice. "Fine out on the lake, wish I could join you."

Bernice moved over to chat with Officer Hakkenson while he leaned over and held the canoe for Eddie, who reluctantly climbed in.

"You'll put a jacket on your Grandma, won't you son?"

"Yes." Eddie held his head down because an explosion of anger had burst in him then and its ferocity surprised him. Officer Hakkenson, or Hank as he again suggested Bernice call him, turned to help her into bow of the canoe.

The lout watched from a distance. So did the family, collectively nodding their heads with relief, oh it's all right, They've sorted everything out. They walked away.

Then off they went, Eddie and Bernice paddling like pros, Jessie content in the belly of the canoe, while Officer 'Hank' Hakkenson watching them with some tenderness from the shore. But once safely out of ear shot, == Bernice announced she had no intention of going to Duck Island, but wanted to go down the lake, all the way to the far shore if fact. So Eddie, full of righteous anger, forced his paddle hard and steered toward the island, instead, while she naturally resisted, working hard to point the canoe toward the far shore.

The only thing over there is the Red Cross Station, the police hut, and the picnic grounds, thought Eddie and Duck Island is a heck of a lot closer and where Grandma wants to go.

Soon they were going round and round in increasingly vicious circles.

"You think you know what you're doing don't you?" Bernice said in an ugly voice.

"I do."

"Do what?" she snarled, splatting her paddle into the water.

"Know what I'm doing."

"And just what is that?" her voice full of sharp clacks.

"I'm sleeping with girls."

She stopped paddling, turned around, "You are, are you?"

"Just color me normal."

"What does that mean?"

"I like it." He too stopped paddling.

"Does the girl?"

"She likes me."

"Oh really?"

"Trust me."

"And what do you know about girls?"

They were two war ships moving along side each other, guns blazing; sooner or later one or the other would close in, would prepare to board. A spirited defence was the only possibility.

"What do you think I know?"

"Not much."

"Neither do the girls." He laughed. That infuriated Bernice.

"How old are you?"

"Eighteen."

"That's not old enough."

"For what?"

"For what you're doing."

She was still turned looking at him, her mouth wrinkled with disapproval.

Actually her mouth wasn't bad, wasn't ugly or old, Eddie surprised himself by noticing that Aunt Bernice's face was still young and smooth.

"What am I doing?"

"Never mind."

"You brought it up."

"You're a very rude young man."

"Ever thought that you're rude?"

She looked surprised. Eddie was surprised to see how surprised she was. The thought had obviously never occurred to her. He pressed upon the advantage.

"Ever thought you don't know everything?"

"Of course I don't."

"Ever thought you might be wrong about Grandma? Thought she's a real person, with real feelings?" Eddie started paddling again, harder. The canoe moved faster now, he was aiming it straight at Duck Island.

"She's my mother." Anger flushed her cheeks, she turned and began paddling, deep heavy strokes that parted the water. She thought, I can do this, I haven't forgotten how to paddle a canoe.

"You push her around. Treat her like dirt," shouted Eddie, feeling a renewed surge of anger, feeling the strength of her pull toward the far shore.

"I do not!" Emphatic words matched the deep strokes of the paddle.

They'd turned, were moving toward the far shore, the police hut, the picnic area.

"We're going to the island." Eddie said noticing this change in direction, and taking up his paddle, again directed a turn back toward the island.

"No, we're not."

"That's where Grandma wants to go." Eddie was paddling vigorously.

"Too bad." And Bernice dug her paddle deeper, pulled with greater force.

"I paid." said Jessie. She sat in the middle holding on to the sides of the canoe, bony hips resting on the life jackets, not wearing one because she'd refused to put one on, but gazing around, enjoying herself. She didn't seem to notice they were going round and round in big awkward circles. A hodgepodge of picnickers in varying degrees of undress were watching them with amusement from the shore as they went round and round in big clumsy loops. What were those people doing out there? And was it safe with an old lady like that? They watched Bernice stand up, turn around, and knock Eddie's paddle out of his hands. Watched Eddie lean way over to try to reach the paddle as it drifted away and fall in. The canoe wobbled dangerously, a few on the shore gasped. They watched him finally come up to the surface and swim over to the paddle, collect it, bring it back to the canoe. Most of those on shore didn't notice that two other canoes, one red and one blue, both filled with two dismayed people paddling desperately toward him, people who were all thinking – oh no, he's got our car keys.

Eddie swam back to the yellow canoe with number seven on the side and tried to climb back in but the canoe shook violently, and Bernice paddled away from him.

"I hate men," burst out of her, "I really do!" But she looked with guilt at her young nephew swimming first toward his paddle which kept getting away from him and then toward the yellow canoe which also kept getting away from him. It wasn't his fault; he didn't know about the years of smoothness, of not saying how she really felt. It wasn't his fault that liquor unlocked doors to feeling just at moments when she thought she'd drunk enough to lock them up. Most of all he didn't know about her meeting with Sam.

The table had been secluded, surrounded by thick bushes. It was a table for a big family, could seat four on each side, but somehow

Sam filled his half. He'd slid into place and folded his hands in front of him on the table.

"Well," he said, "You wanted to see me."

Then he fell silent. Bernice pulled out her handbag sitting open beside her and took out her package of camels. She had two left.

"You want one?"

He waved his hand dismissively.

"I've quit. Doctor's orders."

"You've been ill?"

"Nah. But he says my chest ain't so hot. I decided I can live without 'em.

"You decided that about me too didn't you?"

Bernice's voice picked up a trembling at the end of this sentence.

He stared at her, hands still folded. "Matter of fact I did."

"Why?"

"It was too complicated – you being up there. In Duluth."

"It was your idea. I thought you were going to follow."

"I changed my mind."

His voice was cold. Bernice felt a deep pain in her belly, a fit of knowledge was overwhelming her, destroying even her sense of what might have been, what had been and was no more that had kept her going for the last six months.

"How in the hell was I going to get up there?"

"You bastard." She stared at him.

"Look," he said. He unfolded his hands, put them on his lap and leaned forward. "I'm not leaving Marie. I made up my mind to that. And it was over between us. It was. You had trouble seeing it, but it was. It was a lot of work going over there, propping you up when you got the sulks about something, I've got a hell of a job now. I'm station sergeant. I got responsibility." He leaned back. He could see the look of disdain on Bernice's face. "Jeez, he said "You're one ugly broad sometimes."

The stab went into her heart, the wound of feeling the words created like none other she'd felt. "Ugly," he'd said the word. "Ugly."

Her eyes filled with tears, which he saw but his eyes didn't relent. She whispered. "Sam" from trembling lips, but she didn't move otherwise.

"You won't take no for an answer. I told you not to call and you've called three or four times. Now you're calling me at home. I'm sick of it, Bernice; and if you keep it up I'll find a way to make it tough for you, I swear I will." His voice was low and mean.

"You're threatening me?" Even to her own ears, Bernice sounded surprised.

"You bet your life I am. I'll beat the shit out of you, for one thing."

A little shock went through her. It was so far removed from the Sam she'd known, from the life she'd known, her head jerked back as though he'd really struck her.

"Like you beat up Violet?"

"I didn't touch that broad."

"Somebody beat her to death."

"Maybe."

"What do you mean by that?"

"You saw her that night. She wasn't breathing. She was dead. But you're the one that identified her. Was that your sister? Maybe it was somebody else."

It was some kind of sick game, a game she didn't want to play.

"I thought so. Yes…well her face was so bad. I thought it was her."

"Well there's usually something a birthmark, something."

"It was her."

"So don't come around bothering me. That's the sort of thing that happens to women that don't want to keep quiet."

Sam was round faced, round headed, balding, wearing glasses, an ordinary looking man, but his solid body was tough, strong and his eyes were narrow and a sharp blue. She remembered his body on top of her, grinding its way into her, like a warrior demolishing his enemy and she'd liked it. She'd wanted his strength, his certainty.

"I loved you Sam," she managed to say with a restored voice, but tinged with martyrdom.

He rose, slammed his hand on the table. Forget it. I have. It's over. Got it? It's over. Get that into your head or you'll be sorry. Now I've got to go."

Then he was gone. Bernice sat at the table, her whole front aching as though she'd been struck physically. She'd been grateful for the seclusion, for the silence, A small family had come bearing picnic baskets and babies, had stood waiting hoping she'd leave. Finally the middle aged woman with dark stringy hair falling into her face, said a little sharply. "Do you mind if we join you?"

"No, no I'm leaving," Bernice had said and walked away. She'd walked across the park to the lake, but in a daze.

Jessie held tight to the sides of the canoe. She'd never been in a canoe before. They'd taken out row boats, they'd taken row boats in the sloughs and rivers beside her parents' house, at the school lots of times, even tipped them over a few times.

Laughing. Usually the boys came up and helped the girls back in.

She watched Eddie swimming. Odd that boy, why is he swimming in his clothes?

Amsden, remember those big old wooden rowboats? They were so rotten and full of splintered wood -, that day I came here with the baby, with Billy Black, a sliver went into my foot, and Billy Black took it out. He held my foot and pulled it so neatly it didn't hurt and he didn't let go of my foot but held it, then he'd leaned over and kissed it and said you have the most beautiful feet, Jessie, the most beautiful feet I ever seen on any woman. Oh I tingled with the shame and wonder of it, oh that Billy Black and his words and his love. Just for that day Amsden, that day here before he went to war. You asked me about the bandage on my foot. And when I told you, you scolded me for taking my shoes off. It was more than my shoes, Amsden, I took off more than my shoes that day.

Jessie hadn't cared or while they still struggled through circles and zig-zags as Eddie and Bernice had fought for power in the yellow canoe. She did notice when Eddie was winning, when they drew closer to the island closer closer, drab little Duck Island with its scrub trees and raw grass. The yellow canoe bobbed and jiggled and went in two directions, but slowly, slowly; it had just about reached Duck Island when Bernice stood up and knocked Eddie's paddle into the water. She noticed too when Bernice began paddling them away from the island. Drat that Bernice, Jessie thought, and she stood up, took two steps toward her daughter. Bernice. Everybody watching on shore gasped while Rose Corinne and Dana and Helen and Norbett all rushing over to try to rescue Eddie who could swim but was chasing his canoe paddle as it floated away from him, all the time endangering two sets of car keys,-saw that Jessie was in danger. They all shrieked with horror, shouting, Sit down Mother, Grandma, so that Bernice turned around and saw her mother closing in on her.

Forty-Seven

"I want to go there." Jessie pointed imperiously from the center of the canoe, a canoe that was wobbling. Bernice had stopped paddling.

"What for?" her voice was suspicious.

"I want to go there. To the island."

"Duck Island? Why?"

"There." Jessie's long wrinkled finger looked like a talon poking the air.

"No." Bernice said abruptly. She began paddling again.

"Yes." Jessie said, and took another step forward. The canoe swayed dangerously.

"No." Bernice said and dug her paddle in. deeper.

Jessie turned to look for her family. Her face was pale in the softening light. In the red canoe, Corky caught her breath. She urged Dana to paddle harder toward but when they encountered Eddie, thrashing in the water, on their way, Dana couldn't resist stopping beside him. "Do you have a set of keys to the car?"

Face dripping with water, Eddie blinked with surprise. He treaded water, clumsily since he still had his shoes on. He reached under water and felt the outside of his right pants pocket "Yes."

"Give them to me."

Corky shifted uneasily. "Dana, don't you think it's a bit dangerous to try to…"

Dana didn't look at her. "Eddie, we're locked out of the car. Loan your keys to me. I'll give them back to you when we find the other pair."

Eddie dug them up, handed them up, all the time treading water. "Can you give me a hand into your canoe, Dad?"

"You go back there and get your grandma off that island. Meet us at the car."

Eddie stared after them as they paddled past him, turning around he saw that Jessie, Bernice, and the yellow canoe had disappeared from view.

Helen looked down at the water. The color of the lake was green black – deep water. Still some distance away, the island was a hunched blot of dark land.

."Can your Grandma swim? Norbett asked.

"I don't know."

"They're going around to the back of the island."

What if they capsized? Into Helen's mind flashed a picture of Grandma struggling in the water, drowning. Sinking like a stone, or float, like the witches are supposed to do, another voice from that other part of her brain remarked, the part they sometimes made her want to burst out laughing – or crying.

At camp they'd practiced falling out of canoes and getting back into them. You grabbed the thwarts and heaved yourself in. But you were wearing a bathing suit.

They watched Bernice paddling from the bow, Grandma still standing behind her.

"They're going around the back of the island." Norbett said. "Let's follow them."

"Star Island." Again the talon slashed the air. Straight ahead, my mateys, it seemed to command.

"It wouldn't hurt to land her there," Bernice thought, for a few minutes. Just to calm her down.

Bernice turned around. Her face was lopsided.

"Mother if you sit down, I'll go over to Duck Island."

Jessie took two cautious steps back and jerkily sat down. The canoe wobbled in protest again, then calmed.

It wasn't Duck Island then, it was Star Island. Because someone found a piece of star on it. Fallen from heaven, at least that's what folks said. My Billy and I laughed about that, didn't we? We laughed a lot in those days. The park was young, like we were. Young trees, no buildings nothing like those noisy place, people eating all the time. Everything was easier then, more generous, bigger silences and smaller pathways. And none of those little rocks hurting your feet.

"I have a mind to see the island" Jessie said crossly.

"You're not supposed to," Bernice snapped. She turned around to glare at Jessie.

"But that's what you said you wanted. So get out."

"I can't get out here." Jessie stood up. The canoe rocked.

Bernice stepped out into the water; helped a complaining Jessie out up onto the muddy beach. She got back into the canoe, sat hands in lap, stared glumly across at her mother staggering up the beach.

"This is nuts." Bernice said.

From the shore Jessie waved an imperious hand.

"You go on."

"Where?"

"Leave me be. I've got some thinking to do."

"I'm not leaving you." Bernice said stoutly.

"Go away I said. Come back in an hour."

For some reason, Bernice's mind went blank. She stared at Jessie. Her plan had been to look at the island for five minutes, then get both of them back to shore as soon as possible. She watched absently as Jessie disappeared into the scrub brush. There was a long silence. Flies began to land on Bernice. She swatted at them. No sign of the hunchback of hunchback island, she thought.

"Bernice erupted. "That's it. That's it. That takes the cake. That is the most selfish woman I have ever known." Come back here," she roared. GET BACK IN THIS CANOE!"

No sound.

She stood up, the canoe career wildly while she recaptured her paddle, she stumped back and sat down in the stern.

"Let her be. That's what she wants." She paddled away, muttering to herself, "I have a mind to leave her there." The canoe was leaping forward, leaving the island behind. Without Jessie. Bernice slowed. Looking back she couldn't' see her elderly mother. She started to try to turn the canoe around. At that moment, Eddie tried swam up and tried to climb back in.

Jessie took a few steps. Cautious steps up off the beach.

This park isn't steady in my mind anymore. We used to come out here. Star Island. Billy Black and I. When he came up to see me, we came here. That was before these blasted ducks and geese. Rocks not smack in your way. The water clean and with a voice in the fountains, a voice like thrushes singing. Yes the park was different.

No it wasn't the park so much that was different but me, it was me like a thrush singing, me with bigger silences and no rocks in the pathway. Living my life.

Oh it's all over now.

Poor Lily Bernice making herself miserable. Doesn't she understand, nothing's in the way nothing stops; it's only us that stops.

Well well look at this island. Not so different. He hid in those bushes, Billy Black – right over there – waiting for me. I laughed so hard. He wasn't too bright was Billy, but loving.

It hunched up, that odd little island, a scruffle of trees at one end, a small sigh of sand that looked like a beach for children until you came up and saw it was mud, on the other. The island rose to modest hillock covered with scratch brush in the center. Grass wouldn't grow but funny little scrubby plants did. There were fluffy down splodges of duck here and there, and plenty of bird shit. One tree was slightly grander than the others, a fir tree pressing its dark green arms out like a cry for help. Help, help, get me out of this belittling environment, this rotten downhill world. Underneath it, something had died, and there were scattered bones. Small bones, nothing impressive. Just death sinking into the ground as it had a habit of doing. But the island didn't smell of death, it smelled of ripeness, of bursting open and spreading itself, as though the island itself was growing, hatching out into a new skin. There wasn't a duck in sight that evening. And across the lake on the big island, men put the finishing touches on the fireworks display, two men, proud of their skill, of their knowledge of fireworks, certain this display would be the best ever.

"Norbett."

"What?"

Helen turned around and looked at him. "Norbett do you know anything about sex?" They stared at each other. She wanted to tell him about the merry-go-round, how it had felt to be touched by a stranger, she wanted to tell someone so it would seem real.

Norbett had acquired a haunted look however.

Yes." His voice squeaked.

"What?"

Norbett paused, appeared to think something over I did it once."

"Really?" she was impressed. "What's it like?"

Norbett squirmed and the whole canoe shivered. But he stared straight at her,

"It's hard to explain. But I liked it."

Jessie was getting tired with all the walking. She sat down on the ground, on the hillock right in the center of the island and wondered if she'd be able to get up again.

This island smells of rot. And wet weeds. Or something else too. There's a whiff of something dramatic.

Jessie sighed and settled herself. The air was warm and the ground too. The center of the island was in the sun all day.

Nothing damp and dark about Star Island. It's full of light.

There's none of them yours, Amsden, the girls. Have they told you yet? They were all Billy Black's –or I think so anyway.

I figure they must have told you by now. The girls don't know, never will. Why should they? Only Violet – she knew.

I was never sure about Bernice. She's so know it all, and good with money – if any of them are yours it'd be Bernice.

Well what do you expect Amsden?. You were always too busy. Making money, spending money, gambling it away.

Billy was impulsive and free. We laughed a lot. He'd go off on an adventure and I'd miss him and have you. Then off you'd go on some business or other and I'd miss you and have him. It was a wonderful life for a woman.

Yes I know – the Holy Trinity wouldn't approve.

Violet found out. I told her in a weak moment when we were celebrating her arrival home. You wouldn't' see her, Remember? That hurt her more than you know.

Helen and Norbett started toward the back of Duck Island where they'd seen Bernice and Grandma go. They skirted around the yellow canoe where a struggle between Aunt Bernice and Eddie had reached a World War II grimness, a batten down the hatches and prepare to attack at dawn grimness. Eddie was trying without success, to get back into the canoe. Bernice, relentless in resistance, dipped her canoe paddle in and out, in and out, in order to get away from him, but also moving rapidly away from the island. All around them the lake was covered with canoes and row boats turning toward shore. The sunlight lingered brightest over the water, and none moved very fast. On the shore beside the concession stand, people stood awaiting the return of their loved ones. One rowboat, a dark green one, however, separated from the huddle of its fellow's canoe, and steadily closed in on Eddie and Bernice.

"Go back." Eddie shouted. "We've got to go back to get Grandma."

Ignoring him, Bernice went on paddling hard, as he edged his way back holding on to the canoe side, he grew so close to her at the stern, he managed to reach up to yank the paddle away from her, but she pulled it away and whacked at him lightly. Edging toward the center again, he lifted one knee over the side and almost fell in, which made the canoe rock wildly. Bernice stood up and whacked his backside with the paddle, but in doing so, threw the canoe so out of balance, it flipped on its side. Eddie went deep underwater, while Bernice splashed down a few feet away. The canoe bobbed away.

Bernice swam toward shore.

A blue canoe with two young women in it zipped toward Eddie who treaded water and waited for it. The two young women in it paddled steadily and with a certain satisfactory precision over toward Eddie and the monster aunt who had made her escape. Eddie treaded water, saw it was Carol and Molly Ashford. Molly was paddling in the stern, Carol, tidy in her little red and white costume, in the bow.

"Eddie!" Carol called. The canoe approached. "Eddie." Carol was very close to Eddie now, though she was dry and he was wet. "Eddie, you told Molly you were going over to visit her cousins didn't you?"

Eddie looked quickly at Molly whose face tightened with guilt, then back at Carol. She was staring fixedly at him.

"Do you think I could get into the middle of your canoe?"

"I am not eloping with you ever."

"What are you talking about?"

Molly held her paddle suspended over the water. She was staring at him too.

"Where are my keys, the keys to my car?"

"In my pocket. I forgot to give them to you?"

"I know that. Give them to me now."

"O.K." He felt around in the pocket of his pants, produced the key chain with two keys and a leather tag on it., and held it out to her. She took them.

"Do you think I can try getting into your canoe?"

"No."

"Just try."

"Sure," Molly said but then glanced at Carol.

"No. No, it isn't safe, Molly." Carol's voice went up into a high arched satisfied sound; she smiled sweetly at Eddie. "Sorry about that Eddie, hope I see you on shore."

They paddled neatly precisely away leaving Eddie treading water.

Molly was horrified. "Carol, what did you do that for?"

"I hate all men." Carol said. "back to shore." She waved an imperious hand.

Watching this, Norbett said, "Your brother's crazy, "Why didn't he get into their canoe?"

"So's your sister. She probably wouldn't let him"

They rested easy, paddles on laps, Norbett in the stern, Helen in the bow. It felt so natural, so comfortable, so safe.

"We could help him."

"We should find my grandma."

They began paddling again, going round the island to the beach at the back, pleased with their errand of mercy.

Meanwhile, some distance away, rescue had arrived for Eddie in the shape of a violet canoe, the only violet canoe on the lake. He swam toward it. strongly, resolutely, without deviation, straight toward that violet canoe. He came up alongside, bobbed up to peer into the warm brown eyes of Emily and Edith Brown.

"Where are you swimming to?" Eddie, or was it Emily giggled.

Eddie dog-paddled. "You." He said and mockingly waved his arms around. "Help, help!" he hollered in a silly voice.

The girls laughed. Eddie, taking no chances, deftly heaved himself over the side, and lay like a stranded fish in the bottom of Edith and Emily's violet canoe.

"Hi," he said, face down and dripping water.

The girls giggled again and picked up their paddles. Eddie lay listening to those light wind-chime voices, then turned and stared at Emily's (or was it Edith's?) thin delicious legs and curved thighs, in the stern. Later he sat up and stared discreetly at the rounded slightly muscular bottom of whichever one was sitting in the bow.

"What's your name again?" sighed the bow paddler, not daring to look round.

"Edward McFadden. I'm eighteen."

The girls giggled together like musical chimes and Eddie lay back again to stare up at the blue gray sky. The sun close to the horizon and the air seemed fated to become particles of blue black deepening and darkening into true black. That promise seemed present at last, making fireworks possible.

"I like canoeing,' he announced. "Girls, I'm your captive, I hope you're taking me someplace I want to go." Then he assumed a phony deep voice. "Torture me as you will. But don't put me ashore."

"Oh look at the sky." one of the paddlers of the violet canoe said, and stopped paddling. Her twin stopped too. "There's going to be a sunset." she replied.

FORTY-EIGHT

Dana got in the car and started up the motor.

"Get in," he said to Corky. "We'll go get me some cigarettes."

"Cigarettes?"

"Maybe we'll just start driving."

"Where? What about Mother? She's out in the middle of the lake."

Corky was alarmed. She thought, has he lost his mind? We were out in a canoe, right out on the water, and Dana suddenly turns back to shore, doesn't even go to the concession hut, just beaches our canoe and walks away.

"Get in the car, Corky."

"We'll lose our parking place. We can't leave the others Dana. What's wrong?"

"You don't want me to smoke because you don't like the mess. Well I'll clean up my own mess. Look in the glove compartment. Are our keys there?"

Corky got in the car. He still wasn't making much sense. They sat with the motor running while she pawed through the maps and pencils and odd scraps of paper and found the keys. She pulled them out, held them up to show him and shoved them into her purse. Dana turned the ignition off, rolled down the windows, leaned over and rolled down hers, his face touched her bare arm. He paused to look up at her. He smells good, she thought, but said, "This car's as hot as a baker's oven" and opened her door and leaned out away from him.

"Tomorrow morning, you and I are getting up, Rose Corinne, and we're going to drive to Denver."

"Denver? Tomorrow morning? I've got to go to a funeral and you're visiting your dad.

"Well Wednesday then. The car's running okay. You get your money out of the bank, Corky."

"The money I saved?" she said in a small sweet voice.

"Every nickel of it. We'll leave whatever's left from my pay check for the kids and to help my dad."

"Dana are you crazy?" Her voice was cross but her heart was beating faster.

"You and me, Corky. We're going out there and we'll stay in some goddamned motel- just you and me – and I'll take that job and you can house hunt and those kids can damn well take care of your mother and themselves and to hell with Bernice."

"But Dana…"

"I'm going to make love to you in that damn motel and there's going to be no old ladies or kids or phones ringing, nothing, just you and me."

She was pleased, was excited, then she remembered. "I haven't packed. The house will have to be cleaned."

Dana shifted restlessly, straightened, held on to the steering wheel, looked out the windshield. People were walking up and down the road, strolling in clusters of two or three or four, faces soothed, calm. Evening faces. The sky was bleeding into rose and gold streaks, the sun bronzing the horizon.

"Well go to the funeral. Say goodbye to whoever he is. I'll take care of what's left of Dad. Then we're leaving. And you forget about packing or cleaning the house. If Bernice wants to help, fine, but we're not going to beg her. Those kids can look after things. Eddie's old enough to take responsibility."

Already Corky's mind was working faster and faster, organizing it, thinking through just what had to be done. To leave in three days. Well that was an adventure.

"Maybe Bernice could come up for the weekends."

"You damn well bet she could. You just ask her to come up. Tell her she can drink up all the booze."

"She doesn't drink all that much."

"I know a drinker when I see one. I'm an expert on lushes and she's moving in that direction. That's okay she can keep an eye on Eddie."

"Dana, you know they will fight."

"Let 'em go to it. They like each other."

"No they don't."

"Yes they do. They're both extremists."

"What about the car? You were going to loan it to your cousin Tom."

"I'll call him up and tell him to go to hell. Then I'll call Sean Duggan and find out what my father owes him. Maybe he doesn't owe anything. Those Irish bastards are always calling in the cards. Saying you owe them. Back six generations now, everybody owing for the father before him. They told my dad he owed for his dad. I'm breaking it off. I'll ask them what I owe, if anything, and paying it off it I must and to hell with them. To hell with all the Irish Icabod Cranes."

"Icabod Cranes? What's that?"

"Never mind. You just be ready to go Wednesday morning."

"There's something wrong. What'd Tom say to you, Dana? It's made you mad hasn't it?"

"According to that crew I owe them. Me! Well to hell with that. I'm taking the job in Denver. I broke with the woman. You forgave me. Now I'm breaking everything off with my family too. After Dad goes – that's it. We're starting out new – you and me and whoever else wants to tag along."

Corky was feeling more and more alarm. He was talking so fast, acting like there was no family left.

"Helen still has school, you know that. And my mother – you said yourself she needs care. Dana we can't just dump everything…"

"First we get a house. We won't move them until we find someplace to live. Then we'll see about building one."

"Building?"

Corky leaned over and kissed him on the mouth and he kissed back but not so he was particularly interested and she knew he was thinking out all the things that had to be done to leave by Wednesday, but she knew too that the very dry peckness of that kiss was a promise of their future. Just the two of them somewhere, that lay ahead – the two of them, kids grown, mother gone, their family scattering yet held together by love. She wondered where Jessie was, hoped Helen was keeping an eye on her, Eddie rescuing her. thought -should they have some supper before they settled down in the dark? – for Corky believed that everyone would be back s it when it grew dark, when the fireworks began.

The sun had dipped below the horizon, And once gone out came shadows, those first remarks by that other world, the one they didn't know, but knew them.

Maybe I'll tell her, Dana thought, still staring out the windshield, maybe when we're on the road. He'd seen Tom Shannon, he and a young man talking to Sean Duggan. They were up to something and he didn't want to know about it. It's better to get out fast, he thought, before I'm tempted back into their kind of trouble. Nobody knows me in Denver and I like it that way.

"Want a cold drink?" Corky asked. "Or some coffee? There's a little left."

"Coffee."

"Give me the keys.'

He pulled the keys from the ignition and gave them to her. She got out, opened the trunk, put the keys down inside and shifted the boxes, found the thermos and two cups, slammed down the trunk. With the car keys still inside. Almost at once she knew what she'd done.

"Oh no."

"What?" Corky came around to the driver's side. "I locked the keys in the trunk."

"What?"

"I accidentally locked the keys in the trunk."

"Where's the other set?"

"Don't you have them?"

"No."

"Didn't I give them to you?"

"No. You put them in your purse. Where's your purse?"

"In the trunk. I thought we'd sit at the table and drink this coffee and I didn't want to be bothered with…Her mouth opened up. She looked like she was about to cry.

"What the he…" Dana got out, went around the back, stared with disbelief at the smooth car backside.

"I don't believe this."

"I'm sorry," Corky's face was rueful. She stood holding the thermos and cups. "How are we going to get home? Any ideas?"

Dana was tired. His voice was a rasp. H was actually furious but didn't want to show it. Not with Corky newly forgiving.

"I usually carry keys in my pocket. This dress doesn't have any. Pockets I mean." Corky said fretfully. She walked over to the table and deposited the thermos and cups. "What a stupid thing to do."

Yes." Dana was tight-lipped. "I'd call it stupid." He tugged at the trunk, examined the lock. "Well the sooner we do something the better. While it's still light."

"But what can we do? The tools are in there."

"We'll break the lock." But they looked at each other with the horror of the thought. Amsden's beautiful blue Ford – ravished?

Just then Officer Hakkenson came along. He saw Dana standing beside the beautiful blue Ford, saw Corky sitting mournful at the picnic table a hundred feet away. Hank Hakkenson was driving slowly along in his unmarked police car; so when he stopped in the middle of the road and leaned across the front seat, his shirt wet with sweat and his hat on the seat beside him, he stopped traffic too.

"Problem Mr. McFadden?"

Dana gritted his teeth, attempted a smile. "Locked out."

"See that. Let's give you a hand."

"Appreciate it."

Officer Hank Hakkenson double parked his car, and ignoring the stiff looks that greeted him as other cars drove around it, got out, hitched up his pants and came over. He handled a big ring of keys, slipping them through his fingers until he found one that felt right. "That ought to do it."

He slipped the key in the lock but it wouldn't turn. He pulled out another, it wouldn't work, but the third one did. "That ought to do it."

Dana opened the trunk, extracted his key ring and Corky's purse, and closed the trunk again. "Thanks, Mr. ..."

"Hakkenson. Call me Hank. Thought that would do it."

"Can we give you some coffee?" Corky called out from the table.

"No thanks."

Corky came over. "Thanks so much, Harold."

Hank (Harold) Hakkenson shifted uneasily. He touched Corky's shoulder.

"Rose, could I speak to you for a moment?"

He caught Dana's eye, "Just a word or two about Mrs. Fallsworth."

Helen had forgotten to give her mother his message that morning so Corky was caught by surprise. He walked her toward the table. Dana was left standing by the car.

"Have to tell you in private something, Rose Corinne."

"What is it, Harold? What's wrong?" her face changed, "Oh my god. One of the children? Or my mother."

"No. But didn't know it you wanted your husband to know."

"My husband knows everything about me."

"Somebody's mentioned you in a suicide note."

Jessie lay on the ground.

Jessie lay in the bushes. Naked.

The earth beneath her felt good. The air and the earth were warm; there were fringes of sunlight amongst the scrub brush. There's nothing in or on the earth I fear, she thought. Her eyes were closed.

As a child on the farm in Iowa, she'd lain just this way. You couldn't be afraid when the land held you, when you were a child on a farm, you knew the land owned you, not the other way around.

How did I come so far, she thought, so far, and alone, belonging and not belonging to anything.

Then she felt a little funny. What am I doing here? Not a stitch on. Where'd I drop my clothes? And who's coming for me?

She dozed off thinking that and woke a few minutes later when the trickle of an ant across her thigh told her she was lying on the ground. Naked as a jay bird.

What am I doing here?

And then she thought, Because I want to choose my place. Want my death to sink into the ground, life going on around me, I want to die in a place known to me.

Was death a place? she sighed. I'll pray to God, to the father.

Will you listen to your daughter, Father? You've got a son. Do you want a daughter? Let me find my place. Let my death sink me into this ground, my blood be holy too.

She dozed off again. And woke again. To the trickle of another ant, or perhaps it was a spider walking across her nakedness. She lay for a minute and was rested and sat up. Well he isn't listening. As usual. I'm still here. Still waiting.

She had prayed before to die and nothing had happened. And where was Violet? All that talk of being there to help me. Where is she?

She looked down at herself, at her old body, humble, ugly, the house of an old woman, worn out. Did God the Father love that body? In the old Testament the kings only loved young women, saw only their bodies as beautiful. Is this old body loveable?

She lay back down. The earth felt safer than the sky.

The best thing about being old is being a child again. Those last years in Florida, Amsden, that's when it began for us because we were children again, and best friends like those we had as children.

But you took my mother's money, Amsden. Said you used it in your businesses.

My mother wanted that money to go to her granddaughters. With that money they could have had an education, all of 'em. But that didn't seem to be important to you. Or if it was you thought about it too late, With some money I could have gone to see those places I heard about. Well we lived well enough. But then you took it all, put it to work you used to say. Only it was my mother's money, not my father's. Not yours. And I knew Amsden, knew all those years together, your secret, that you gambled most of the money away on your 'business trips.' You won't have to tell me about that when I see you.

Violet didn't hear her mother. Violet was far away, watching everything from a distance. And what was that distance? Space, time, other dimensions? – Violet didn't know, but what she saw, what she felt was beautiful, was holy and truthful; and anger departed from her, pulling away like scotch tape; the empty space within her filled with a slow seep of new emotion one she'd felt only as a small child. -Violet struggled to name it, then did – Joyfulness. Yes, a small glowing spark of joyfulness now rested within her.

FORTY-NINE

Norbett and Helen had nearly reached Duck Island when they both happened to look over at the same time and see Bernice being hauled into a rowboat by a heavy set man and woman. Helen squinted over at them.

"Norbett."

"What"

"Look at those people helping Aunt Bernice."

"That's your aunt?"

They both stared with horror. It was the couple they'd peeping tommed. who were pulling Bernice, disgruntled and dripping, into the bottom of their boat; she sagged there, wet and ungainly while the middle aged couple rowed energetically toward shore.

The canoe took a great leap backward. Helen looked around to see Norbett paddling frantically away from the island.

"What are you doing?"

"We can't go where they can see us. They know me."

"Who are they?"

"Our neighbors. If they recognize me I'm dead meat.""

"She already saw me."

Norbett stopped paddling.

"In the ladies room. I think she recognized me."

They paddled round and round in neat backward loops until they saw the rowboat pulled up on shore. Other boats and canoes were headed in too. All around them the light was dimming, the water gleaming, a gun metal sheen touched with the last of the golden sun rays, the park was giving way to evening, and to its darkening mood. But Norbett and Helen aimed for Duck Island.

On the shore Aunt Bernice was talking to the Cardstons.

"Thank you for helping me."

The woman was squat with narrow black eyes. She was wearing white pants and shirt. "Who is that rude boy?"

"Rude?"

"Hasty." Amended her husband. He was stout with a determined face. Bernice recognized him from years before, as an acquaintance of Sam's. She'd never liked him.

"Very rude." His wife said emphatically.

"Couldn't help it. Some girl took the keys to his car." said the husband, staring at their passenger.

"My nephew." Bernice began to edge away.

"Oh…" Their faces shone with curiosity.

"Lover's quarrel." Bernice said with satisfaction. "You know how those go."

They nodded with a slow acceptance of her sophistication, but you could see written on their faces the thought, don't go hoity-toity on us, thank you very much.

"Some girls are so bold," said the woman.

"Very bold" agreed the man.

"We had some girl peering in our window the other night."

"Very bold" the man repeated, "girls like that." He sounded wistful.

"I had a sister like that." Bernice said firmly. She took a step forward. Her hair was still dripping. They took a step back.

Behind them the boy manager of the boat concession slammed down the front of his kiosk. Two men standing in the darkened area behind the counter were talking emphatically at him.

"Really?"

"Went wild."

"Oh I see." The woman's mouth turned down.

"Slept with every man she could find. Right into the sack." Bernice spoke with relish. She looked at the woman, then the man. Their eyes were goggling. They'd picked up a very bold fish, their faces seemed to say, a very bold fish indeed.

"She left home at seventeen."

"We'd best find a place to sit," the woman said hastily, glancing at her husband. He was still staring fixedly at Bernice. "For the fireworks." She began to walk away; her husband followed. For such a large man he was delicate in motion. Meek and mild and a little tooty-fruity – the wicked voice inside Bernice muttered.

"Going to watch the fireworks?" she managed finally to call after them.

"What we came for," the husband said, "Mustn't miss 'em." He'd placed both hands around his belly as he walked. Bernice stood on the path for a moment, looked out at the lake, then up at the hillsides.

All around everything was winding down, simplifying, people were gathering not scattering any more. They placed themselves on blankets, on the ground, quieted children. The light was that gray kindness that settles in on summer nights, like a gentle snowstorm – light scattered into particles and the particles scattering in to smaller particles so that nothing sharp existed any more, not even darkness, there was only dissolution, preparation, beauty.

"There's no fireworks." Bernice said boldly and hurried to catch up with the Cardstons. A fire of argumentation had entered her. She wanted to rile these people ahead of her, to provoke them, to make them glower and rage. The liquor she'd drunk earlier was still burning in her head, anything and everything made sense with the energy of anger, nothing made sense without it. She wanted another drink, and decided she might indulge herself but when she looked around for a place to sit she saw none.

"No fireworks?" Mrs. Cardston turned around to look at her while Mr. Cardston plowed on "Of course there's fireworks. It's the Fourth of July."

"Is it?" Bernice came up behind her. "Are you sure of that?"

"Oh come on dear." Mrs. Cardston pursed her lips and her narrow eyes gleamed black, like a small sharp rodent. Her hair was a mousy brown, but she bulged all over.

Like a fat rat, thought Bernice as Mr. and Mrs. Cardston walked rapidly away from her again.

"I heard there were no fireworks this year. Economy move," she shouted after them and took a quick neat nip of the gin in the small bottle inside her purse.

What a delicious sharp surge of nastiness she felt then. Oh thank you, God, she thought, for nastiness, and liquor and derelict sisters who sleep with men. Oh thank you that everything isn't neat and sure and little mean eyes of rodents. The chaos inside is the same chaos outside and I won't be afraid.

Violet was shocked out of her new-found joy. Her sister was praying for her, but the bad her! She sought Those Who Were There To Help Her Through A Difficult Transition and started to tell them, but they already knew and were regarding her like proud parents at an elementary school graduation.

Hank Hakkenson liked talking to women like Bernice. Big riled-up women; crabby. He liked watching them sooth down, the way they settled into plumages, into contented cooing. They reminded him of hens on the farm, chased around, irate. As a child he'd been afraid of them until he saw you could quiet them down. You told them – –now you settle down right now – and if they didn't behave you upended them. Grabbed them by the feet and held them upside down until they were back on the nest.

Women needed nests just like chickens.

He watched Bernice out of a corner of his eye, watched her stumble up and plump herself, still dampish all over, at the picnic table. He was still talking to Rose Corinne, but he could see she wasn't comfortable him knowing anything, and he himself didn't see how much gossip he should pass on. Hank Hakkenson loved gossip. He didn't pass it on too much, because of his job, but he loved collecting it, loved going home to his bachelor apartment and thinking how peculiar and just plain nuts half the human race was. He saw them all in his police work. That's why he liked big firm women like Bernice who squawked around and really needed very little to make them happy. He wished Sam had been kinder to her. But Sam wasn't a kind man. Nor honest.

"Rose, the note said if he hadn't' met you he would have given up, but you made it possible for him to go on another twenty years. Did he leave you anything in his will?"

"Thanks so much for telling me, Harold, but let it be." Corky stole a glance over at Dana who was running his hand along the side of the precious blue Ford. his baby now. Hallelujah, make a joyful noise. That car was a joyful noise.

"The suicide note said you weren't afraid of what you saw, and didn't turn away. Said he always remembered you, Rose."

Hakkenson's face was twitching with curiosity, little quivers around his eyes and nose. Corky flushed and put one hand on Officer Hakkenson's shoulder.

"I'd just as soon nobody knew about this, Harold, but thank you."

"Said goodness burns in the memory like a slow fire."

"Harold, please." Corky was edging away, her face tight.

"It was a long note. I was the first one on the scene."

They stared at each other. Officer Hakkenson looked away first.

"Rose, to tell you the truth, the note didn't make a lot of sense. That your sister over there? I recall her. Name's Bernice, Lily Bernice."

"Yes." Corky turned her back and walked away, toward Dana, but Officer Hakkenson hitched up his pants, and strolled over to the other end of the picnic table.

Bernice glowered up at him.

"Lily Bernice, we've met, I do believe."

"You probably gave me a ticket," Bernice snarled. "That's the way you spend your time isn't it? You and Sam."

Hank leaned down and smiled warmly right into her flushed and angry face.

"Lily's a pretty name."

You bastard, she almost said that out loud, thought why don't you go catch the child molesters and the murderers? I know about cops now, believe me I know.

"Bernice is a fine name too. Which do you prefer?"

Shut up, Bernice was thinking at him, but she blinked. Twice.

"Lily's the kind of name says you ought to play the harp."

Bernice blinked again. She wondered if she'd heard him right.

"Do you play a musical instrument?"

"No," snapped Bernice. Why didn't the fool go away?

Hank Hakkenson smiled and strolled away but inside he was pleased. What an angry woman. What a bitch! Into his mind flashed a vision of calming her down, smoothing those ruffed up hen feathers.

"Bye now," he turned and smiled and waved at Lily.

Bernice glared and turned her back. But she felt calmer somehow. She watched Corky and Dana unpack what was left of the food. It was seven thirty. Time to eat, just time, before dark and the fireworks. They'd eat and stretch out on blankets.

Dana reached out and touched Bernice's handbag. "You got any left?"

"In the car." Bernice rose, went over, plucked her extra pack from underneath the driver's seat where she'd hidden them so Corky wouldn't confiscate them. She gave one to Dana, who lit it.

"Why are you smoking again?" Corky sat down beside him.

"I like smoking." Dana said. "I don't want to stop. Not just because somebody tells me to stop."

"Somebody that loves you."

"The whole time I was out in Denver I smoked my brains out."

"Does she smoke?"

Dana hesitated, "I thought we weren't going to talk about that anymore."

The air was humming with a groaning life burden smell – all jumbled together, grass and spore, dead plants, live plants, ducks, dogshit, popcorn, candy floss, sweat and gasoline, cigarette and cigar smoke, coffee, coke. What a mixture! Thick and sure, lingering, coming in from the lake, rising over the shoreline, visiting the trees, the picnic tables. No way of escaping, not now, with the evening breeze rising.

"Maybe we should go home, Pack up and go home. It's going to be a long evening." Corky sighed. The evening stretched before her, so much work gathering everyone into family again. Feeding them, making them rest together on the hillside.

A family has to be together for the fireworks. she thought, but the young don't know that and the old forget. Suddenly she was conscience-stricken. She'd forgotten all about Jessie.

"Where's mother?"

Probably drowned." Bernice said. Dana's head snapped back with surprise.

Eddie sat up. Grandma? He'd forgotten her. She was still out on the island.

"Hey girls."

Edith and Emily were manoeuvring the canoe into shore. The dark-haired, angry looking lout was waiting to yank them in. They were the next to last canoe on the lake.

Darkness was swooping in from the far corners of the world; magnifying the shores, darkening the water. There came with it a stillness that had weight, that could be felt by everyone on the paths, on the hillsides, even in the bushes.

"Girls, stop."

But it was too late. They were pulled in. Edith and Emily climbed out, turned around to look at him. He stood up and walked forward as though to get out, then ignoring the lout's hand extended to help him as he had the twins, Eddie flopped back down in the stern, grabbed up the paddle and pushed the canoe away from the dock.

"What the hell do you think you're doing?" the lout said. He lurched forward to catch hold of the rope, but the canoe was moving away and he pulled back.

"We're closed," he bellowed. "You can't go out again."

"Somebody's been left on the island."

"Fuck that."

"My grandma."

The boy's eyes narrowed, his face was angry and flushed.

"The little island? That old lady's out there?"

"Yeah."

The lout's eyes narrowed. "Wait. I'll go out there with you."

Eddie kept paddling.

Mike and Greta Blunt were back in front of Mike's truck, sitting on hard stools, drinking water, and watching the policeman question those people over there by the latrines.

"Wonder what they did," Greta said. "He's sure giving them a hard time."

She'd cheered up somehow but Mike was edgy. He'd run out of coffee.

"Glad you brought me, Mike. I ain't been to this park – it must be fifteen years.

"They ought to keep a couple of the refreshment stands open at night."

There was fresh boiling coffee on the breeze.

FIFTY

Do you begrudge his knowledge of me, Amsden? That some of the children were yours and some had his blood in them? But didn't he give that blood over there in France? When I knew he'd died, that sad wrongheaded glorious death of war, I was glad, he'd known me, that somebody had loved him. Those secret years together he shared only half of it – the creating half-you had the rest, the bills and the laundry, the day to day. But then he gave his life didn't he? Spewed his blood in the mud of France. Didn't it all work out all right?

Violet knew. Knew it all. Violet was a little sneak, a listener behind doors. She liked to go through letters, was always finding out secrets. Billy didn't pay enough heed. He kissed her once, and laughed and said she was the spitting image of him as a child and she looked at me – well then the cat was out of the bag.

And the money you took, my mother's money – when Violet found out about that she tore into me. Told me I was spineless.

Men spend too much time chasing money, that's the truth, money and glory.

Jessie didn't notice the sun was going. The air was still warm, almost stopped. Only her feet lay outside the bushes. There's nothing as good as this she thought touching the warm earth. She liked the smell of the island, of its dirt and grass and bird shit heated after a long day of sun. On the farm of her childhood, lying on the earth, she had pretended ... well what was it I pretended then, stretched out on the earth?

They'd penetrated the bushes, were sitting near the canoe which floated in the water. They'd tied it to a sawed off little mutt of a tree. The dusky air was still warm.

"Norbett, let's do it." Helen felt full of confidence. What a wonderful feeling. Was it the island or the insertion of evening? Or was it Norbett staring dramatically across at her. They'd sat down cross-legged like Indians facing each other, faces flushed.

"You mean it?" An ecstatic look flashed over Norbett's face. Then concern. "Are you kidding?"

"I've never been more serious in my life."

"Here? Now?"

"Now," she said pushing into her voice all the courage and adventure she could manage. She couldn't help noticing how much bird shit lay on the ground.

"Aren't you afraid?"

"Of what?" she said, dramatically.

"Well... you know."

"What?"

"I don't know," He looked away, "of getting pregnant?" He rushed the last word, swallowing hard. He had one of those Adam's apples you could see riding up and down his throat like an elevator.

"Oh I won't get pregnant."

Norbett leaned forward, lay her gently on her back, then climbed on top of her. "Why not?"

She stared calmly up at him. "Because I won't."

"What do you mean?" He was breathing into her face.

"I don't intend to have children until I'm at least thirty."

Norbett stared at her, then climbed off, slowly, like unpeeling a reluctant Band-Aid.

"Listen Skip," his Adam's apple swooped. "I don't think it's a good idea."

"I won't get pregnant," she said stoutly, "I've made up my mind."

Norbett stood up, hitched his pants. "Come on, let's walk around. Look for your Grandma. That's why we came, though I bet your brother already took her off."

The man in a rowboat zoomed across the water. The shores of the lake were blurred. To Eddie in the canoe they appeared to be moving, rushing toward him. Instead it was the rowboat fitted with an inboard motor that headed him off.

"Get the hell back to shore." The man with the bandage on his head said. The lout, sitting in the bow, smirked at him.

"I have to get my grandma."

"Nobody's allowed out here after dark. We'll get her."

"You don't know what she looks like."

"You think there's a mob of old ladies out there? The goddamned fireworks start in half an hour. Beat it."

He waited ugly eyed, until Eddie turned his canoe around and paddled back to shore. The rowboat followed, and once there, the lout jumped out and pulled the canoe up. Edith and Emily were waiting. They smiled streaky blonde hair smiles and fluttered their hands in the air.

The McFaddens and Bernice spread out blankets, nibbled on sandwiches. Corky fretted because Eddie, Helen and Jessie hadn't come back yet; she wanted to send out a search party or go herself, but Dana said wait, they'll get here. Bernice said nothing. Her clothes were almost dry. Nobody had even noticed how wet she'd been. Funny how nobody notices, she thought, like I'm invisible. But she didn't feel like talking and lay down on the green and red plaid blanket Corky had spread out for her and closed her eyes. She thought about Sam. Well, so what, she thought, so what? It's over, so what?

He'd wished her away. But she could do that too. You could wish people into being ghosts. Isn't that what ghosts were? People wished into it. No room for them anymore. Squeezed out of space needed by others.

There hadn't been space in any of their lives for Violet. She'd worn them out. Maybe Sam was the one that squeezed Violet past the point of believing in living anymore. He had a way of doing that, of turning you off like a radio. Maybe that was all Sam had done. Told Violet to stay away from her sisters, her parents, then said stay the hell away from me too.

I'll never know for sure, she thought. Maybe I don't want to know. Because we meant something to each other. Loved each other. How many times does that happen?

She wanted it left alone. Besides Sam didn't have the passion in him to kill.

Or did he?

I have to stop thinking about it.

What if Violet caused trouble? What if he got angry?

She dozed off, lying on the green and red quilt, as the light dissolved around her, as the murmur of people's voices became pinpricks in the air.

Helen and Norbett wandered around the island. There wasn't much to see. Helen thought how funny it was that she felt closer to Norbett then anyone else she knew. How could that happen so fast? She wanted to talk to him. She didn't feel like talking to her diary anymore, or to her family, but to Norbett.

"Why do we have to go away? I think it's hateful. I hate them all, the whole family. They're all so complicated, they make everything complicated. And it's so far away – Denver."

"I might go to college in Colorado." Norbett said.

Her mouth shut in surprise. "What?"

"I like skiing. But I want to be a dentist. There might not be a school out there."

They were close to the shore facing the other, larger island. Norbett halted.

"Stand back." He said hoarsely and waved her away. She retreated. He dropped to the ground and began to crawl toward the water on his elbows, combat style.

"Well it's done. Over and done, and we were in the end, happy, Yes we were, Amsden. We were friends. You had more time for nonsense when you were old, and I was mostly nonsense by then. Still am." Jessie sat up. Thought, about Violet, surprised still that she had seen her, and then not seen her. Surprised too to find herself alone in some prickly bushes. The light was dimming. Though the heat lingered, and she wasn't cold, she knew she was naked. Time to go home, she thought, enough of this lollygagging around. She felt around until she found her bundle of clothes. But her body felt stiff, and she put them under her head and decided to rest a few more minutes. Surely someone would come to take her somewhere. She-hoped it wouldn't be Violet.

Tom Shannon strolled up, hands in pockets. Dana took his hat off his face and looked up from the Canadian blanket he'd stretched out on. He didn't get up.

"Tom."

"Dana, I came to find out about the car."

"Oh." Dana waited a long minute, then sat up. He put his hands around his knees and clasped them; the posture revealed his thin ankles, gave him an air of vulnerability. "Well that's a problem, Tom."

"Is it?" Tom sat down at the picnic table a few feet away. Corky who was sitting across from him, shifted uneasily, but he nodded pleasantly toward her.

"Rose."

"Hello Tom."

"No car is it?" Tom leaned forward, hands clasped on one knee.

"I should have checked with my wife. She needs it tomorrow."

Tom turned and looked at her again. Corky met his eyes.

"A funeral," she said.

"Your dad is it? I should be going to it too."

"A friend. I don't know about my dad. He's bad, very bad."

"So I hear."|

"We're going to Denver."

"Are you?" Tom's voice was cool.

"The whole family."

"Is that so."

"I've got a job waiting for me out there."

"Maybe you should talk to Duggan."

"We won't have the time."

Dana sat calmly, hands clasped. Tom looked at him. Corky folded her hands on the table. There was a long silence, the silence of generations, past, present, and future.

"Nor the inclination I'm thinking."

"I didn't say that."

"Where will you be in Denver?"

"Haven't got an address yet."

Dana rose, came over to the table and sat down next to Corky. He put an around her. Tom kept his bent posture, but turned to watch Dana move around behind him.

"You've got to excuse us, Tom, we've got to collect our kids. We're staying for the fireworks."

"Saw your daughter."

"Oh?"

Dana was neutral, eyes calm, body quiet.

"She's kind of a nosy kid."

"Where is she?" Corky started to rise, but Dana kept his hand firmly on her forearm and she subsided.

"Not that I've noticed." Dana said.

"People should keep their noses out of other people's business."

"I agree with you there, Tom."

Now Dana rose, walked over to his car.

"Well, nice talking to you Tom. I'll let you know about my dad. In case I don't see you for awhile -Good luck and all that." He opened the trunk and leaned in to fuss with the boxes inside. Reluctantly Tom Shannon stood up and without another word strolled away.

They were standing well back in some brush trees. A speedboat was heading out from Minnewana Island, site of the fireworks display straight toward the smaller island.

"Let's get back to the canoe." Helen said.

"What about your Grandma?"

"She might be dead. I didn't know what to do."

While stomping through the brush, Helen had shoved aside a bush and almost stepped on a pair of bare feet. They looked like Grandma's but she was wearing slippers.

They retreated to the canoe and paddled along the shoreline until they were opposite to the landing parties. "Hey, look at that," Norbett climbed out of the canoe into the water. A long aged fir tree hung out over the lake, its branches combing the water.

"What?" Helen sitting in the canoe leaned forward.

"Down there, underwater, something white in the tree roots."

Helen bent leaned precariously over to peer into the lake. Just under the tree the water was deeper. A sudden drop from wading depth to chest high water. Something was caught in the tree roots. Something long and white.

"What if that's a body." Norbett said.

"Ugh, Norbett, what a gruesome thought."

He turned to look at her, an owlish expression on this face. She was glad he wore glasses too. They were both tall and skinny and wore glasses. Like a race apart.

"It is gruesome, Skip. Are you sure you saw those feet?"

Somehow she didn't mind him calling her Skip.

"Yes. Sticking out of the bushes."

"Do you think it was your grandma?" he asked in a doctor voice.

She didn't answer because she didn't know. And she didn't want to think about it because once in the canoe, she felt like they were Indians silent, paddling without noise as the enemy approached. When they saw the second boat, the speedboat, depart from the larger island toward theirs, they saw a second tough looking man in it, and knowing already, the man from the boat concession with his helper was prowling through the bushes looking they had plenty of enemies. But how could they leave Grandma behind.

If it had been her because when they went back to look, the feet were gone.

"Do you think she's dead – your grandma?"

"Maybe. She's pretty old and decrepit."

But now she hated the thought, she didn't want Grandma to be naked and dead on this ugly little island. As though bound by a silver cord they both bent down and examined the long blur of white nestled in the tree. Nothing identified it as a body, no head, no arms, no legs.

Norbett leaned even further, the canoe rocked a little, then they heard a crashing sound behind them and both turned. The man with the tattooed arms was standing on the little shit-covered knoll that was the center of the island.

"What the hell are you two doing?"

"Nothing."

"Making out are you? This here's a bird sanctuary."

"What does that mean?" Norbett said in an innocent stupid voice.

"Birds." The man with the tattoo's fists were on his hips, scowling he walked closer. "You ever heard of birds?"

Just then from behind him, appeared the man with the bandage on his head followed by the concession lout.

"Well, if it isn't the big man himself." Said the man with the bandage on his head. The man with the tattoo's turned around to face him. They were the same big brute shape though the man with the bandage was taller. The lout wavered behind him.

"I can take care of his." Bandage said.

"Oh yeah we know how you take care of things." Tattoo moved up to stare him in the face, the lout wavered further back "Get off the island."

"Make us" Bandage said.

"Jimmy told me something I don't want to believe. Maybe you better tell me. Where's my sister? I hear you've been hitting on her pretty hard. So asshole where is she?"

"How the hell do I know?"

"That's not what Jimmy said."

Bandage turned around to look at the lout but he'd vanished.

"You kids beat it," Tattoo bellowed at Norbett and Helen. And they did. Paddling with a haste that was more instinctual than well thought out, so they were well away from the island. Behind them the two men squared off.

"You fucker. You did something to her. Where the fuck is she?" You fucker. Where is she? Where? Where's my sister? Tattoo shouted as he pounded away mostly at Bandage's face who tried to give back blow for blow. Helen turned to look at Norbett and at the exact same moment they both stopped paddling and turned to watch.

The men were exchanging blow after blow, Punching each other as hard as they could in a grim mindless dance. Neither man noticed the blurred white shape that emerged from the bushes. It was Norbett and Helen from their safe distance that saw her.

"Holy Moses" Norbett croaked with surprise. "I think that's your grandma."

"It is. Grandma!" Helen shouted. Jessie didn't look over but the lout lurking in the bushes did. He waved at them to come along the side of the island away from the two men beside themselves with rage. Tattoo managed to knock Bandage down and then kicked at his chest and head, but Bandage jumped up again.

The spectral form wandered toward the two men who noticed for the first time. They stopped in mid-blow. Fortunately Jessie was at least half dressed.

"That is your grandma isn't it?"

"Yes." Embarrassed. Helen was bending down to retrieve her paddle before it floated away.

"She's carrying most of her clothes."

"I know."

From their safe distance the two in the canoe watched Jessie walk around the clearing where the men still stood panting, both stung into immobility, mouths open. Jessie lurched up to them. She looked a thousand years old, looked weak and contrite yet incredible strong, a body that was more packaging around bone than flesh. If bone is a hymn, a chant, a resolution to go on living, she was singing to everyone.

By then it was evening, the lake gleamed with that silky reproof of distant water, of depths, the kind of promises no one wants kept. The air that time of night seemed to swell, everything magnified and pressing in. People had quieted down, slipped in toward each other; families multiplied and those alone found comfort sitting near strangers. The wind sighed up carrying summer smells. There seemed nothing bad in those moments, nothing stretched out looking for trouble, no evil bursting forth. Though as always there was much evil loose in the world, there was good too, and it had gathered there. There in that safe place to be, this park, Fourth of July, some time ago, yet not that long, not really. This place of comfort and family, Promise and memory.

What made it so fine? The heated air? The long day of sun? Was it the life promises of trees and grass, the recollections of flowers and animals? Perhaps it was people gathered together because they wanted to be. Tired questions, of disbelief and fear, answers weren't necessary.

Only fireworks. Fireworks had to be there. They were why people came, why they waited. The night scarred with light. So people could go home with dazzle in their minds, with urgency and thrill in their hearts, with belief in all that was larger than themselves. There had to be fireworks.

While Bandage Man leaned over to catch his breath, Tattoo looked at his watch, He walked around in a circle shouting at Eddie and Helen. "We're shooting them off in twenty minutes. Everybody get the hell off this island NOW."

They parted at the shore.

"Should we tell somebody?" asked Helen.

"Why not?" Norbett shrugged his shoulders.

Leaving Grandma slumped over asleep in the canoe (there was no one around to collect it or her); they went to the telephone booth beside the boat concession and Helen called the police because Norbett said his voice squeaked when he was nervous and they wouldn't believe him but she sounded grown up.

"I want to report something bad," she said.

"What?" came the little policeman voice at the other end.

"Two men are beating each other up on Duck Island."

"Where's that?"

"In the middle of Duck Island."

"And I said where's that?" the cross little policeman voice repeated impatiently.

"IN the middle of the park."

"What park?"

"Minnewana."

"Oh that Duck Island."

"Yes."

"What were you doing out there?"

That stopped her; she looked at Norbett who shrugged his shoulders.

"I said, what were you doing out there?" Some devil got into her. "Looking for a body."

"Sure."

"There's a body out there. We saw a pair of naked feet sticking out of the bushes" "That's a bird sanctuary, Duck Island."

"We know that."

"Whose we?"

"Never mind."

"Look kid..."

"While we were out there these two men came and started fighting and one was screaming where was his sister and that's all we want to tell you."

She slammed down the phone.

"You didn't give your name." Norbett said.

"I didn't want to. He was a pretty stupid person."

"Are you going to tell your mom and dad?"

"Probably."

"Why?"

"Don't' you think I should?"

"I never tell mine anything interesting."

They stared at each other. Then Helen walked back to the canoe. She helped Grandma get out. She walked Jessie slowly up the: hill, up to the car, and the table and the family, up to the safety. In a few minutes Norbett walked past them. He said nothing, was headed in a different direction. Then he turned around and in the gloom, for it was nearly dark by then, quite close to full night, suddenly asked:

"Did you get my note?"

"What note?"

She wasn't really listening, concentrating on holding on to Grandma who limped and lurched on her poor old feet in their flimsy knit slippers. They were wet too.

"Carol was going over there so I told her to give it to you."

The words penetrated, she stopped. Jessie grumbling staggered against her. Helen held tight to her hand, with the other felt in her pocket. It was empty. The note was gone.

"What did it say?" she called after him.

"Oh never mind."

"What did it say, Norbett?"

"I'll tell you some time."

"Norbett..."

But he walked away.

FIFTY-ONE

They waited on the hillside, the family. Sitting silent, motionless, together. Around them others waited too, patchworks of possessions all across the hillside and the lakeshore, the sounds of people filling up the darkness like a cup.

Intent on private games, children still ran about calling out to each other; they alone seemed unwilling to acknowledge the deepening of the well. The adults, silent, only occasionally stirred, only rarely murmured a few words, now and then some called out a warning to a child – stay close you hear? Cigarettes wavered in the dark like fireflies, the air was sweet with the scent of tobacco and crushed grass. Here and there lingered heady whiffs of beer, of coffee.

All around and within the people grew a sense of waiting, of awareness, of knowing they were paused all together on a hillside, on a lakeshore. Even the trees seemed caught in it, waiting with that curious listening look of plants at night, life grown larger, more distinctive even as it blurred. Then an evening wind began like a whisper far away, stirring, forming, weaving like fate through the trees, scattering their leaves into protesting ripples.

Bernice sat smoking, half on the plaid blanket, half on bare ground. Her legs were stretched straight out in front of her like a small child. Beside her, Jessie lay against Corky, groaning whenever she shifted bony hips against the hard ground. Corky had one arm around her, but talked in a low voice to Dana beside her on the grass.

"Look at that woman over there – she's half dressed. Oh that child – Dana do you think he's lost?"

Dana listened and nodded, knees pulled up in that way that revealed his ankles, thin and vulnerable Corky leaned over to her mother,

"Are you warm enough, Mother?" and half asleep, Jessie grumbled. "My feet are cold."

Dana picked up one of her feet in the wool slippers and kneaded it, then the other, slowly, not really looking at the little knitted bundles. Corky tucked in the jackets they had brought out from the car around her and whispered to him. "I wonder if we should have stayed, she's so frail."

"She's all right," he replied, smiling, still absently rubbing Jessie's feet as he looked around. On the other side of him, Helen leaned sleepily against his shoulder, feeling the stir of his muscle, happy to be close to him, to hear his voice deep and sure again. Behind them, Eddie stood with Norbett and Carol, drinking clandestine beers, their hands cupped against thighs, muttering comments followed by deep laughter. At least Eddie and Norbett were laughing.

Nearby Mr. Miller lay sleep in his chair, beside him Mrs. Miller was asleep too. Their daughter Karin had moved over to the blankets spread out by Gloria and Myrna and was talking to them, plans were afoot. Little Danielle held the little dog Butch, she was wide-awake and looking up at the sky, but the dog, eyes open listened to the wind talking through the leaves. Butch knew not everything the wind said was nice.

At last, the night was truly come; the stars were many but faraway pinpricks, like the dust of promises, nothing more, and the wind continued warm and mysterious to grow stronger. Then, between one moment and another came a sudden tearing of the black sky. And with the first flower of light, a sigh went up from the people waiting on that hillside, on that shore; it was a sigh of recognition. They remembered. Remembered their past, all its promises.

The fireworks rose up from the big island, its earth a darker blot against the satin black of lake. From that heavy heart, one by one, fireworks flowered, scattered fell. One by one sparks met themselves in the lake, light melted into black ribbons of water. The first fireworks were welcomed counted named, but as the display went on breaking, scattering, vanishing – a constancy of bursting sound and scents, of burning colors of the rainbow, the people forgot to count, forgot to name. It seemed that in every family, in every person, no matter how knotted, individual, different, happy or unhappy, through everyone moved the deeper knowledge, a current that collected them; they felt themselves carried up, scattered with fire, their hearts opening with each burst of jubilation, they were one with the fireworks, and one with each other. The distant popping sounds, the violent rush of light, the drifting smell of sulfur, these now were collected into their hearts.

A pause came. Helen looked down and saw for the first time that it was dark, a darkness that came up close. She shivered: looking down one remembered how cold, how dangerous night could be. She moved numb feet, shifted position, put her head on her daddy's shoulder. Bernice leaned forward so that Dana could light her cigarette; she spoke to him in a low amused voice, words that Helen couldn't hear. Corky reached over to cover Jessie more certainly, and the old woman scattered words that Helen couldn't understand either, but it didn't seem to matter. She was safe with family.

Corky murmured to Jessie as she patted her lightly, then stretched one hand out to squeeze Helen's: Her daughter squeezed back.

The family waited in companionable silence. Helen cold feel the moist tickle of individual blades of grass beneath her palm lifting that hand she breathed for moment the hopeful scent of the grassy world. She could hear Carol laughing and she didn't mind. Norbett was back there too, somewhere in the darkness.

"Look they've started again!" Corky cried out like a child and once more they stared up at a night sky where great skeins of colored fire, and stars, and mystery unfurled.

Mr. Miller wasn't asleep in his lawn chair next to Mrs. Miller. He was up in the fireworks. His body down below was empty. He was free.

"Bobby, Bobby." The voice was familiar but he couldn't see through all the colored sky. "Bobby, this way." This is what's it's like to be a bird, he thought with joy, and flew in the direction of the voice.

Later that night, driving home, they were silent -the family. Dana turned the wheel of darkness. It was late, nearly midnight and they were almost home. Jessie in the front seat, leaned against Bernice, but then stirred, and grumbled and jiggled herself upright. "Did I hear a sermon?"

"Yes," Three voices chirruped immediately and almost together."

Midnight. Corky and Dana walked hand in hand through the summer darkness. They walked home along 35th Street, but they understood for the first time that home was now themselves. When they came to the edge of the Miller yard they stopped. They could smell roses; they leaned forward and kissed, drawing in the scent.

In the Miller house, lights were on. Karin was on the telephone, making arrangements. She was crying, but upstairs her mother enjoyed the sleep of the near dead.

Across the street Myrna was already asleep, her little daughter in the trundle bed beside hers. Opposite, Greta Blunt sat on her front porch sipping whiskey. I'm going to get myself a little dog to keep me company she thought. She eyed the sacks of bottles around her. First thing in the morning, I'll throw that trash out.

In the cot upstairs in the Fallsworth house, Helen was between day dream and dreaming. She saw herself as a woman wearing white, standing in this Greek temple sort of place. She had long flowing hair and bare feet and she was chanting messages to a bunch of men (most of them very good looking) and for once everyone was listening. Really, they were all dumbfounded, their mouths were open because what she said was so important. Ariadne is a good name, she thought and reached under the cot for her diary.

Jessie lay in bed and said her prayers, Dear Lord, guide me to where you are. Also to where you want me to go. But, Dear Lord, I'd sure like to see some mountains.

Eddie was slipping out of the house through the porch window. He was wearing white pants and a white shirt that almost glowed in the dark. He drifted through the fine edges of the dark street surefooted. Carol had said she wanted to make it up to him and he had a pretty good idea how she was going to do that. He'd learned girls got jealous. You had to be careful what you said, you had to touch them and tell them they looked nice. And you let them apologize. At the rate he was going he'd know everything he needed to know about women in a couple of weeks.

Bernice was writing a letter, sitting under the sharp hot light of indoors, a paper pinned to the table before her. She was writing to the newspaper, informing them how there were all kinds of peculiar people in the parks these days and somebody should do something about it. As she scrawled each black stroke on the pristine white of the paper, the thought occurred to her that she should send a copy to that smart-ass policeman.

What was his name? Hakkenson. Yes she'd do that. And maybe just maybe she'd suggest that there was a deep level of corruption in the police department. She couldn't name names she'd say, but she'd like to report what she knew. She sat back smiling. She'd hand deliver the letters. A day or two more in the Twin Cities wouldn't hurt.

I like coming here, Violet thought, walking down the front steps and along the cracked front sideways, she looked up and down the dark streets knowing they were all there in their houses, knowing too that her family were safe in their personal real worlds.

Can I come again? she asked The Helpers. I'd like to see them all again?

No.

Why not?

Violet. You came to find love and joy, and you found it, you understand now that pain and loss are part of love. You're ready to move on.

Drat, thought Violet, and moved on.

FIFTY-TWO

" For what reason did you talk to him. For what reason?" Jessie used to question the girls over and over. She didn't like them talking to strange men. Then why wouldn't she know about the bastard down the street? No imagination, Bernice thought still brooding over her mother, sitting upstairs in the bedroom that once had been hers only she wouldn't have been allowed a picture of a black bear at the bottom of her bed. No, she and Rose and baby Violet had shared this room with flowered wall paper, a pattern her mother had chosen, their room never quite their own in the way this room was her niece's. They hadn't been allowed to put things up on the walls, or plaster things all over their beds. They had three drawers each and that was that.

Her mother would come in to hear their prayers, and Violet would be asleep, Bernice rattled through hers, but Rose would go on and on; Bernice had hated lying in the dark listening to her sister meander through her entire day, thanking for this and sorrying about that.

In winter dark and cold, their mother would hurry them along, reluctant to sit and listen to the wind outside, or to their father calling from down stairs needing something and so finally Jessie had stopped coming up. Then they could go to bed together and talk, giggle, say their prayers silently. Bernice had said them well into her twenties and then slowly, imperceptibly they'd slid away from her because how could you pray to God while you made love to a man that wasn't your husband? It was better to forget and settle for grace over meals and cups of tea at family gatherings. Should I try to say them today? she wondered. Should I pray for Dana's father? It was a long time since Bernice had been to a funeral. Only "Now I Lay Me Down To Sleep' came into her mind.

"It's a beautiful day," Corky said to Mrs. Blunt who emerged out her back door, and into the sunlight. She stood blinking dazed against that light. She was dressed in a long sagging beige skirt and a coral colored blouse, all stained and wrinkled. Mrs. Blunt bent over and shakily picked up a rusted garden tool that lay in her path.

"Yes," said Greta Blunt. "It is." And then surprisingly she looked up and into Corky's eyes and smiled a big tremulous I think I trust you smile. "Yes the whole world's beautiful isn't it? Everything in it."

Corky was taken aback. "Yes," she managed.

"God's world." Mrs. Blunt said and then flushed and turned away. She bent down to put the rusted tool back beside the door only this time she leaned it against the wall. "Everything's God's," she looked briefly shyly into Corky's eyes again. "Especially the birds, I love them, don't you?"

Again Corky didn't know what to say. "Yes. Yes I do."

Greta Blunt smiled again and tucking her hands into the sleeves of her blouse, she wandered gently back inside her house. Corky stood for a moment in the middle of the driveway where she'd been walking when she came upon poor Mrs. Blunt. Only she didn't somehow want to call her that any more. She went back inside her kitchen but her heart had lifted. Yes it was a beautiful day, even if she was going to a funeral.

Bernice came in and stood beside the sink. She looked out at Mrs. Blunt's back yard. "What a mess. I'd call the city."

"Leave her alone, Bernice, she's a sad creature. Leave her alone."

"She ought to be made to clean that garden up. After I move in maybe I could do something about it. I know Some people down at city hall. I'll talk to them."

"Please Bernice, leave her alone."

Rose Corrine turned and there were tears in her eyes. Bernice backed off and instead looked around the kitchen. "Anything need doing? Need any help in here?"

"Not really."

"Good morning young lady." Bernice turned to greet her niece

"She's across Nicollet, Mom."

"Oh for goodness sakes, why didn't you stop her?"

"You know where she's going." Bernice said. "She's going to church."

"It's Wednesday." Helen said.

"Wait until Eddie comes, you can get her in the car." Corky pushed her daughter toward the back door. "And tell your father we're ready to leave."

The blue Ford rampaged up the driveway, then slowed to a careful roll as Eddie stopped just past the kitchen window. He didn't get out. Corky and Helen went out and told him they had to find Grandma. Helen climbed in beside him. He backed down the drive way before Dana even had a chance to come out from the back of the garage where he was sitting listening to the radio. When he did emerge he scowled after the car.

"What's the kid doing?"

"I told him to get Mother," said Corky. She touched his shoulder. "More Coffee?"

He moved away from her. "O.K. I can't believe my dad is dead." Inside the house, pouring out coffee, Corky answered the phone when it rang.

"Rose Corinne is that you? Tom, Tom Shannon."

"I heard about your father-in-law. I'm sorry. Is the old man there, your boyo?"

"He's not here right now, Tom." Corky lied. "He's running an errand."

"Is he coming over to St. Paul?"

"Don't know. But I'll tell him you called." Corky hung up. Dana didn't need his bad edged cousin today, not today.

Madness, madness, madness, Dana thought. Everything. He was wandering around the empty garage, he couldn't accept it, the radio was playing some kind of cornball tune and he turned it off:-accordion music the kind his dad liked and he thought, he can't be dead with me about to see him one last time, and he couldn't believe it after all these years of wishing his dad was dead. Now he was dead. The poor old drunken fool of a man, a big kid, a kid that never grew up, that should never have married, never have had kids, his dad couldn't face life as it was, only as he wanted it to be – easy, or maybe not that. God knows he didn't have it easy in the war over there, as soon as the job went on too long, or the hours grew heavy and there wasn't enough time to play, well he'd go on a binge, he'd just disappear and nobody could find him sometimes he went over to a buddy's and sometimes he'd hole up in a hotel room and he'd just drink himself out of the world, he'd drink somewhere else, he never came home drunk, not after I grew old enough to stop him at the door.

All this Dana was thinking as he walked round and round the garage until he looked up when Eddie and Helen and Jessie drove up.

Then they were all in the car. Then they were on their way. The world swam around them and there was a sun beyond and above them, though they were too snarled up, too engaged and disengaged, too saddened to notice what a world it was, full of splashes of color and sound and sights both natural and unnatural—billboards, store signs, old men walking along in shambly clothes; and fat women in house dresses, and little dogs wetting on the wrong parts of the sidewalks; kids running faster faster to get away from other kids. It was full of life that day was the city, full of sun and heat and knowledge and stupidities, trees, grass, flowers, cement, dust and dry dog doo. It was full of bliss and anguish and lust and love, full of big and small, wide and lean. Full of energy spreading itself out and talking a lot, Talk talk talk, radios were blaring; it was afternoon in central Minneapolis, never a noisy city, but some days it spread its wings a little and today was one of those days -everybody back to work, to shopping, to visiting.

They were going to a funeral. They were in that car, the beautiful sanctimonious, untouched by real life blue car of Amsden's. His last decision, his last choice. They were packed in, six of them, squeezed tight against each other, thigh against thigh, shoulder touching shoulder, Dana was driving, and Bernice sat next to him, Jessie at the window so she could breathe fresh air, Helen in the middle of the back, riding the hump, Eddie behind his father, and Corky behind her mother. They had all taken their places in the world's smallest room, that private place of families where everything becomes clear. And they were as separate as sea anemone, locked in land creatures with solid shells and hidden hearts. Dana was pushing away thoughts about Marianne and welcoming thoughts about his father. Bernice was stuffing down fury against Sam, peevish with her family and her life, but somehow reckoning on Hank Hakkenson. Jessie was worrying away at Amsden and thinking about her money, how she had lost it somewhere. Better yet it may have been stolen. Helen was thinking about Carol, about Norbett, wondering what would happen, and who the note belonged to and if anything exciting ever happened in Denver. Corky was still angry at Dana, but loving him too, thinking how could she get out of going to Denver and thinking too of James Newell, how long ago and far away that escapade seemed now and what a surprise that such good luck came from it, only she hoped it would be good luck, because what would Dana think and how could she be angry at him when she'd had her own secrets? Eddie was juggling how to handle Carol and yet have some freedom to look around, and also feeling guilty because he'd signed the air force papers and nobody knew and he didn't know if he'd tell them. And so they were all stories sitting untold, physically close and yet their hearts and minds separated from each other as profoundly as human beings could be

Outside the long heartwarming realities of Nicollet Avenue swam by, houses, isolated or huddled together, back yards bright with grass and flowers, over clogged lots full of used appliances and derelict cars, small stores with coca cola signs, cigarette advertisements painted on the sides of buildings, stop signs, people walking into comer ice-cream stores, people walking out of drug stores; it was midday, everybody out and about, there weren't many churches on Nicollet avenue, it was life at its most particular.

All around them cars were ruffing along full of hot sticky crowded people just like them. Did they have as many stories? As many secrets? Were they sharing them? Helen didn't know, couldn't know. She had her own stories —of the hospital, of the fright she'd felt there, of being sick in the night and seeing only the gleam of the floor, hearing only the sound of white shoes squeaking. Here on the road, the sound was that of the engine, a comfortable plebian noise that she liked, without sharps, only dulls in that sound, and oh the hot air, syrup thick with moisture, Minneapolis in summer was like a weight all around your body, and usually the sun was not this direct, but today, oh today it was a hot beautiful July day and all of them were quiet, not talking, not even Bernice, nor Dana, Eddie Helen or Jessie. They were all in a silence as thick as weighted as the air.

On 35th Street, next door to 21W, a little girl ran down Mr. Miller's garden to chase away a black rabbit eating his carrots, a rabbit that was very surprised to learn humans could move that fast" while upstairs the little girl's mother stripped sheets from a bed and helped Mrs. Miller to the bathroom.

Mr. Miller watching from the opaque side was amazed at how well organized death was. He would see his grandson lost in the war. "Let's go," he said to those who were there to Help Him Adjust. "Everything's going okay down there without me."